BEFORE DOROTHY

Hazel Gaynor is an award-winning, *New York Times*, *USA Today*, *Irish Times* and internationally bestselling author known for her deeply moving historical novels which explore the defining events of the 20th century. A debut author recipient of the 2015 RNA Historical Novel of the Year award, her work has since been shortlisted for the 2019 HWA Gold Crown Award, the 2020 RNA Awards, and the Irish Book Awards in 2017, 2020 and 2023. *The Bird in the Bamboo Cage* was a national bestseller in the USA and her most recent novel, *The Last Lifeboat*, was a *Times* historical novel of the month and a 2024 Audie winner for Best Fiction Narrator. Her co-written historical novels with Heather Webb have all been published to critical acclaim. Her work has been translated into twenty languages and published in twenty-seven territories to date. She lives in Ireland with her family.

To keep up to date with Hazel and her books, please visit hazelgaynor.com and connect with her on social media:

 hazelgaynorbooks
 @HazelGaynor
 @HazelGaynor

Also by Hazel Gaynor

The Girl Who Came Home
A Memory of Violets
The Girl from the Savoy
The Cottingley Secret
The Lighthouse Keeper's Daughter
The Bird in the Bamboo Cage
The Last Lifeboat

Co-Written with Heather Webb

Last Christmas in Paris
Meet Me in Monaco
Three Words for Goodbye
Christmas With the Queen

BEFORE DOROTHY

HAZEL GAYNOR

HarperCollins*Publishers*

HarperCollins*Publishers* Ltd
1 London Bridge Street,
London SE1 9GF

www.harpercollins.co.uk

HarperCollins*Publishers*
Macken House, 39/40 Mayor Street Upper
Dublin 1, D01 C9W8, Ireland

Published by HarperCollins*Publishers* 2025

1

Copyright © Hazel Gaynor 2025

Hazel Gaynor asserts the moral right to be identified as the author of this work

A catalogue record for this book is available from the British Library

ISBN: 978-0-00-851871-4 (HB)
ISBN: 978-0-00-851872-1 (TPB)

This novel is entirely a work of fiction.
The names, characters and incidents portrayed in it are
the work of the author's imagination. Any resemblance to
actual persons, living or dead, events or localities is
entirely coincidental.

Set in Sabon LT Std by HarperCollins*Publishers* India

Printed and bound in the UK using 100%
Renewable Electricity at CPI Group (UK) Ltd

All rights reserved. No part of this publication may be reproduced,
stored in a retrieval system, or transmitted, in any form or by any means,
electronic, mechanical, photocopying, recording or otherwise,
without the prior written permission of the publishers.

Without limiting the author's and publisher's exclusive rights, any unauthorised
use of this publication to train generative artificial intelligence (AI) technologies
is expressly prohibited. HarperCollins also exercise their rights under Article
4(3) of the Digital Single Market Directive 2019/790 and expressly reserve this
publication from the text and data mining exception.

This book contains FSC™ certified paper and other controlled
sources to ensure responsible forest management.

For more information visit: www.harpercollins.co.uk/green

*This one's for you, Fran and Joe!
With love. x*

'Now I could tell my story.
It was different
from the story told about me.'
        – from *Mother Ireland*, by Eavan Boland

'I believe any man must see beauty in mile upon mile of level land where the wheat, waist high, sways to the slightest breeze and is turning a golden yellow under a flaming July sun. To me it is breathtaking, the most beautiful scene in all the world.'
        – from *Farming the Dust Bowl*,
        by Lawrence Svobida

List Of Contents

PROLOGUE	1
PART ONE Chicago, 1932 & 1922–1924	3
PART TWO Kansas, 1924–1929	95
PART THREE Chicago and Kansas, 1932	187
PART FOUR Kansas, 1932	293
PART FIVE Kansas, 1932	357
EPILOGUE Many years later . . .	375

Prologue

Extract from *Wonderful –
A Life on the Prairie* by Emily Gale

*T*he first time I saw the prairie was like waking from a dream, suddenly and vibrantly aware of my surroundings in a way I'd never been before. Every colour was brighter, every sound clearer, every flowering thing more beautiful and mesmerising and fragrant. I gazed upon the shimmering mirage of emeralds and golds, and couldn't believe such a place existed, or that I would now call that place home. It was Heaven, if you believe in such a thing. A fairytale, if you don't.

Back in the city, I had marvelled at the great showmen and carnival hucksters with their clever tricks and impossible illusions, but those first months on the prairie taught me that nature is the only true magician. Spend a moment watching the hypnotic beauty of a single stalk of golden wheat nodding in the gentle morning breeze, or feel the thrill of the first green shoots pushing up through the dirt, then tell me there isn't magic here, that you are not bewitched by its beauty, as I was. Some thought we were *fools to try and build a new life here. Others thought we were brave. Perhaps we were a little of both.*

Even with the storm that whirled in my heart, heavy with the knowledge of what I'd left behind, I felt the thrill of arriving somewhere extraordinary. Here was a place I could call home, a life to be fully lived, a story waiting to be written among the furrows of our newly ploughed earth. I dug myself in; planted my hopes and dreams and love into the rich Kansas soil and waited for them to flourish beneath the generous sun and benevolent rains.

I had yet to learn that the prairie would not be so easily tamed; that our story here wouldn't be shaped by the colour of our dreams, but by the struggles we would endure and the courage we would find to keep going . . .

Part One

Chicago, 1932 & 1922–1924

'A heart is not judged by how much you love, but by how much you are loved by others.'
— *The Wizard of Oz*

I

February, 1932

The city was a colourless palette of grey as Emily Gale arrived at her sister's South Shore row house. Even the familiar brownstone building that had once carried shades of copper and gold in its brickwork was now dulled. She paused at the foot of the steps and drew in a long, anxious breath. The frigid air caught the back of her throat and made her cough.

Courage, Em. Courage.

Henry's parting words were a distant echo, muffled by the miles she'd travelled from Kansas, and further diminished by the city's towering skyscrapers. She had never felt so out of place, so uncertain, so entirely alone. There was no sweet meadowlark's song to cheer her, no comforting rush of rippling, ripened wheat, no trace of the purpose and renewal usually carried by the first hopeful day of spring on the prairie. This was a place of sorrow and uncertainty.

A wave of grief and guilt consumed her.

Courage.

She took a moment to compose herself, stiffening her shoulders before she walked up the steps and lifted the heavy iron knocker, letting it fall, just once, against the imposing ebony door. The sound carried the sombre tone of a church bell at a funeral mass. Appropriate, in the circumstances.

A moment passed.

Silence.

Perhaps there'd been a misunderstanding, an alternative arrangement made. Guilt chided her for hoping it might be so. The child was her responsibility now. Hers, and Henry's. How she wished he was beside her, ready to offer his calm encouragement and steady reassurance. 'If I come with you, there'll be nobody here to welcome you home,' he'd said. 'I'll make cornbread. Sweep the porch.' His attempt to lighten the mood was appreciated, but the usual crinkle at his eyes had been absent. What would home mean for them now?

A stiff breeze swirled, capturing early blossom in tiny whirling cyclones at the edge of the steps, tugging at Emily's cloche as she caught her reflection in the bevelled glass panels of the door. She practised a reassuring smile, befitting a kindly aunt, but all she could manage was a grimace. Her words also failed her. She'd carefully rehearsed what she would say to the child, repeating the sentences over and over in her mind, but now that she was here, everything felt wrong. There was nothing she could ever say to make this better.

She tried to relax, desperately searching in the glass for the confident young woman who'd stood here countless times before, arms full of flowers to bring a smile to her sister's face, or laden down with newly discovered novels to press enthusiastically into her hands. 'You'll love this one, Annie! It's all moody moors, and destructive passion!' She'd believed anything was possible back then – a world at peace after years of war, exciting new opportunities to be grasped by those brave enough to take a chance – but the woman looking back at her now carried no blooms or books or bold ambitions, only the trace of life's cruel lessons etched into her pinched expression and tangled among the first silver hairs at her temples. They said the prairie aged folk prematurely. She was proof of it.

She lifted the knocker again. Let it fall, again.

Despite the spring day, winter still laced the Chicago air. Steely clouds smothered the sun, leaving a cold flat light as the sharp bite of the wind off Lake Michigan sent a shiver through Emily's bones. The lining of her black mourning coat had been sacrificed for a shirt for Henry last fall, the remaining garment no match for the drop in temperature between Kansas and Illinois. A day's journey by railroad – and yet the place Emily had left, and the place she had arrived to, were so entirely different that she might have travelled for a hundred years. She shivered again, the wintry day not the only cause of her rattling bones. She had good reason to be anxious.

She knocked twice more in quick succession, the dull *thud thud* matching the heave of her heart.

Finally, a figure approached on the other side of the glass.

Emily swallowed a swell of nerves. She smoothed the creases from her coat sleeves, pushed back her shoulders and pinched her cheeks to summon some colour there, but her fidgeting and fussing stopped abruptly as the door opened and a woman – a maid? – stepped forward.

'Mrs Gale, is it?' The woman's face was milk pale. Her eyes carried the unmistakeable ruby hue of grief.

'Emily Gale, yes,' Emily replied. 'Annie's sister.' She hesitated a moment. 'I'm sorry. We haven't met. And you are?'

'Cora McNulty. The housekeeper.' The woman dabbed at her eyes with a lace handkerchief. 'I'm so sorry for your loss, Mrs Gale. *Ar dheis Dé go raibh a hanam.*'

The burst of Irish language caught Emily by surprise. Her reply to the offered condolences came naturally, but not easily. '*Go raibh maith agat.*'

She hadn't heard anyone speak *as Gaeilge* for so many years that to hear it now summoned an overwhelming ache for her sister, for her family, for Ireland. The place she'd first called home.

Cora offered a thin smile as she reached for Emily's small travelling case. 'Now, would you ever come on inside, Mrs Gale. That wind would slice you in two, so it would. You must be tired after your journey.'

Emily was glad to get out of the cold, but a chill lingered on her skin as she stepped into the wood-panelled entrance hall and time seemed to stand still. It was all so hauntingly familiar: the fleur-de-lys ceiling rose, the glittering chandelier, the soft light from the Tiffany wall sconces. Annie's fur coat on the stand, John's hat and cane beside it. But it was the trace of perfume in the air that took her breath away, the seductive scent of tobacco and jasmine, as if Annie had just that moment breezed past in that effortless liquid way of hers. Not walking, but floating. Emily could see her so clearly, spritzing a cloud of scent into the air before twirling around beneath it so that it settled on every part of her. '*It's called Habanita, by Molinard. All the flappers use it. Isn't it delicious?*' Her exaggerated French accent had made Emily laugh. There had been so much laughter back then. So much fun. So much love.

Emily stiffened as a haunting melody punctuated the silence.

A child's voice.

A reminder of the reason she was here.

'How is she?' she asked.

Cora shook her head. 'Terrible quiet. Hardly said a word since, God love her. And the dreams keeping her awake at night.'

'Dreams?'

'Nightmares, really. The poor thing gets in such a state.' Cora crossed herself in the Catholic way as a distant look fell across her face.

The singing came again, a little louder this time, beckoning Emily toward a room on the right of the entrance hall.

She remembered her niece only in thin fragments and wispy memories: a bawling newborn, pink as a prairie rose in her crib; the barely-there sensation of the infant in her arms; the sweet nutty scent as she'd whispered goodbye; the way the child had looked at her, as if she already knew how their story would end.

'Does she know why I'm here?' Emily asked. 'Or where she's going?'

'I've tried to explain as best I could, but who knows what's going through her mind? It's so much for the wee creatúr to take in.' Cora dabbed at her eyes with a handkerchief. Emily recognised the delicate Connemara lace. 'Here, let me take your coat,' Cora continued, 'then I'll take you to her.'

'I'll keep it on, if you don't mind.'

'Of course. That wind gets into your bones when it blows from the east. I've a fire lit inside. You'll soon warm up.'

Emily's reluctance to remove her coat was nothing to do with the weather, but from a sense of shame at the tired black dress beneath it. Being back among such opulence made her feel more like a farmer's wife than the prairie ever had, suddenly conscious of her dry, wind-reddened skin, and the seam of Kansas dirt embedded beneath her cracked fingernails.

'Come along, so. She's just this way.'

Heart in her mouth, Emily followed Cora to the dayroom where a fire crackled in the grate and a gold carriage clock ticked and whirred on the mantel. The cushion fabrics and wallpaper were still in the Art Deco style Annie had so admired and which Emily had helped her choose. Her gaze flickered quickly across the room, taking in everything that was so familiar before settling on a chair beside a sash window and the one thing that wasn't.

Dorothy.

Her back was turned to the room but a slight falter in her singing indicated that she sensed she was no longer alone. In an admirable act of defiance she continued her song as she swung her stockinged legs, pendulum-like, beneath the chair, her feet not yet able to reach the floor. She looked so small. So dreadfully alone.

Emily stood as stiff as the porcelain figurines in the glass cabinet beside her and watched, numbly, as Cora walked to the girl, crouched down next to her, and spoke softly for a moment.

The child nodded and turned slowly on the chair until her eyes met Emily's.

For a moment, Emily could hardly breathe. The little girl looking back at her was so remarkably like Annie: soft curls in all the colours of a New England fall, emerald-green eyes full of sorrow, heart-shaped face, rosy apples in her cheeks. Smart red shoes with gleaming silver buckles offered a defiant burst of colour amid the permeating air of grief. They reminded Emily of a favourite pair of red shoes she'd once owned. It was hard to believe that she'd ever worn anything so pretty.

Cora coughed lightly to catch Emily's attention, tilting her head toward the girl, encouraging Emily to do something; say something.

Emily put her purse on the settee and stepped forward, approaching the child as if she were a skittish colt, or some other nervous creature. Animals, Emily knew. Seven-year-old girls, she did not.

Following Cora's example, Emily crouched down beside the child.

'Hello, Dorothy.' Should she shake her hand? Touch her arm? A hug felt too intimate, too presumptuous. 'I'm your Auntie Emily, your mother's sister.'

'Hello.' The child's voice was barely a whisper.

For someone so slight, the child's impact was immense. Emily faltered as a wave of emotion washed over her. 'You can call me Auntie Em if you like. Or Aunt Em. Whichever you prefer.' The crack in her voice betrayed her uncertainty. 'You're going to come and live with me and your uncle Henry, on a farm in Kansas. We have a cow and horses, hens and pigs, and the sweetest little chicks.' Her heart lurched as she glanced at the toy lion in the child's hands. She'd kept it, all these years. 'Your lion can come too, if you'd like. What's his name?'

'Lion.'

'Of course.'

Dorothy turned back to face the window and continued her song.

'They say there's bread and work for all.
And the sun shines always there
But I'll not forget old Ireland,
Were it twenty times as fair.'

It was a lament Emily recognised, a mournful tune her mammy used to sing whenever she was missing Ireland. *'Do you remember, girls?'* she would say. *'The apples in Connemara? Do you remember?'*

Emily closed her eyes and listened to Dorothy's song, summoning courage from the gentle memories it stirred: a perfect coil of apple peel on the old oak table, the damp smell of the turf fire as she and her sisters had watched, transfixed, while their mammy worked the paring knife, the peel expanding in shades of russet and green until Emily was sure it would break. But still the knife turned until, finally, the single coil dropped onto the table and they all clapped. But even more mesmerising was the way the peel formed the shape of the apple when Emily placed it in the palm of her hand, as if it held the memory of the fruit it had come from.

'You'll remember this, girls,' her mammy had said as she'd sliced the apple into thin circles and shown the three sisters the shape of apple blossom formed by the imprint of the pips in the centre of each slice. 'The same way the apple remembers the blossom it grew from, and the way the peel remembers the shape of the fruit it was attached to, you'll always remember this little cottage in Connemara on the edge of Ireland, and that the three of ye ate slices of apple while the autumn sun turned Annie's hair to flames, and Nell got a fit of the giggles when your da took to snoring, and Emily was after playing the fiddle like a banshee.'

Emily remembered it all: the heather-bruised hills reflected in Lough Inagh, the whispered secrets of swaying rushes along the shoreline, mackerel clouds drifting in shoals above, the peeping cry of a kestrel carried on the breeze. Such simple treasures, such happy memories, conjured by nothing more than an apple.

That was all it had taken to anchor her to a time and place where she'd felt loved and safe.

She opened her eyes. 'Cora, would you have an apple handy?'

'An apple?'

'Yes. There's something I'd like to show Dorothy.'

2

There was no chance of sleep that night.

Emily lay in the dark, wrestling with her thoughts and tormented by memories. She missed the distant howls of coyotes and wolves, the soothing snort and snuffle of animals nearby, the warm press of Henry's body against hers. The sharp noises of the city beyond the window kept her awake, while the sudden cracks and creaks inside the house set her nerves on edge. But it was the cries from Dorothy's room, as the child woke from a bad dream, that Emily found the most disturbing.

She lay stiffly beneath the bedsheets, hobbled by indecision as she heard Cora go to the child. Should she go and help, or leave Cora to it? How would she and Henry ever console the child if the nightmares continued in Kansas? Her mind was a muddle of questions for which she didn't have any answers.

The jarring awkwardness of her earlier attempts to interact with the child taunted her through the small hours. Their conversations had been stilted and forced, Emily's manner overly-friendly one minute and too serious the next, every painful pause emphasising the emotional distance between them. Even the apple peel trick had failed to impress. Cora, watching from a distance, had encouraged Emily not to give up.

'It's no surprise she can't see any wonder in the world, Mrs Gale. She's lost everything. She'll come around, in time.'

The words had fixed on Emily like a compass point to guide her. That was her responsibility now: to restore a sense of wonder to Dorothy's shattered world. The prospect was terrifying. What wonder was there left for the child among the rubble of such an awful tragedy?

It still seemed impossible that a telegram had arrived a week ago bearing the devastating news that Annie and John had drowned in a boating accident on Lake Michigan. Emily was sewing flour-sack dresses at the time. She'd been saving the sacks – printed with blue-and-white gingham – the pattern a favourite among the girls. Now, the blue-and-white checks would forever remind her of the single word that had fallen from her lips as the telegram dropped into her lap: 'Dorothy.'

*

With no bodies recovered from the lake, there'd been no wake, no caskets, no burial, no graveside farewell. Emily and Henry had missed the memorial mass due to bad weather.

'A few friends and business acquaintances attended,' Cora had said. 'Dorothy's teacher and schoolfriends. And a man who sat at the back and left straight after the service.'

Everything Emily had learned about death, every part of the mourning process that was meant to bring comfort, had been denied her, but it was Annie's lingering presence in the house that made it so hard for Emily to believe that she was gone. How was it possible when she'd seen the imprint of Annie's lipstick on the rim of a water glass beside the bed, the furrows of her fingertips in a jar of Arden's Eight Hour Cream, her bookmark poised for her to return to the story, an appointment diary full of approaching anniversaries and arrangements? Annie was everywhere, and yet nowhere, leaving Emily suspended in an emotional no man's land, unable to mourn her sister properly, unable to find the tears that Cora couldn't keep at bay.

As Cora padded back to her room and a hush descended over the house again, Emily lay in the dark, willing herself to sleep so that she might get some relief from the boulder of grief and guilt that had rolled over her heart.

*

The morning brought no release. After a few fitful hours' sleep, Emily washed and dressed and began to make her way downstairs. As she passed Dorothy's bedroom, she noticed that the door was slightly ajar.

She paused, and peered inside.

The child was fast asleep, russet hair spilling in rumpled waves over her pillow, one arm wrapped around her toy lion, one leg dangling out of the covers. Emily stepped quietly into the room, lifted Dorothy's leg back into bed, and straightened the comforter. She stood for a moment, watching her, waiting for a surge of maternal affection for this sweet little girl who'd lost her mother and father, but all she felt was sorrow. For them all.

Downstairs, she absent-mindedly prodded her fork at a mound of scrambled eggs.

'Not hungry?' Cora asked.

Emily shook her head and put down her fork. 'Not especially. I'm sorry. You went to so much trouble.' She sipped her coffee, glad of the bitter liquid's warmth.

Cora assured her that a couple of scrambled eggs and a round of toast was no trouble at all. 'You should try and eat something all the same. Keep your strength up. You're ever so pale.' She offered the toast rack, and a sympathetic smile. 'They say we've to eat more wheat. Wheat with every meal, to help the farmers. But I don't need to tell you that. Is there as much surplus as they say?'

Emily nodded. 'Millions more acres were ploughed up last year, and there's more and more folk arriving on the trains every week, fooled into thinking they can turn wheat into gold. We're growing more grain than anyone knows what to do with, and surplus grain means prices are at a record low. Breaks our hearts to see all that hard work left to rot by the grain elevators at the station.'

She took a triangle of toast, but what she saw on her plate was last year's mouldering grain and the look of despair on Henry's face as he recorded the plunging prices in his ledger. The toast turned to dust in her mouth. She put it down and reached for her coffee again.

'Which part of Ireland are you from, Cora?' she asked, eager to change the subject. 'It's nice to hear the accent again.'

'Donegal. Ballyliffin. Can't get much further north before falling into the Atlantic. Do you know it?'

'I don't, but I hear Donegal is very beautiful. You must miss it.'

'I've lived in Chicago eighteen years and still feel as Irish as the day I stepped off the boat. I even made a St Brigid's cross yesterday.' Cora pulled the distinctive woven cross from her pinafore pocket. 'Couldn't let the first day of spring pass without it.'

Emily offered a tired smile. The familiar shape of the St Brigid's cross reminded her of happy moments with Annie and Nell as they made the traditional crosses every year to mark the arrival of *Imbolc* and to bring good fortune for the new season. A memory came to her then of her father weaving dolls of straw to bring good weather for the harvest. The Irish traditions were embedded in her like a seam of iron in rock.

'I was only five when we left Ireland,' she said. 'But my parents insisted we continue to speak the language and learn the traditional songs and stories. I feel more Irish than American.'

Cora nodded. 'Ireland will always be home, no matter where I lay my head at night. Now, will ye have more coffee. Or would you prefer a decent cup of Irish tea? I've some in the caddy. A gift from a friend who went to visit her family in Galway last month.'

Emily smiled. 'Coffee is fine. I'll need it to stay awake.'

'Couldn't sleep?'

Emily shook her head. 'Not really.' She paused before broaching the subject of Dorothy's dreams. 'I heard Dorothy cry out in the night once or twice. Does she have the nightmares often?'

'On and off since she was very small. Used to walk in her sleep too, but she doesn't do that as often now.'

'As often?' An image of the child wandering across the prairie in the middle of the night flashed across Emily's mind. 'How often?'

'Hardly ever. I expect it's the shock has brought it all on again. I'm sure it'll pass soon enough.'

'What does she dream about?'

'Nobody knows. The black wind, she calls it. She can't remember anything about it the next morning, thanks be to God, although it's terrible real to her at the time. Such a curious child. Black wind one minute. Flying monkeys the next. I can't keep up with her! Shelves full of books and a head full of stories, that one.'

'She likes books?'

'Oh yes! Dorothy is a real little bookworm!'

Emily was glad to hear it. 'I'll have to take her to the town library. They don't have a huge selection, but I'm sure she'll find something she likes.'

'She'll enjoy that. Annie read to her every night. Irish legends and myths, stories of the Little People, *Tír na nÓg*, *Fionn Mac Cumhaill*. And, of course, *Gráinne Ní Mhálle*, the pirate queen. That's Dorothy's favourite.'

'It was my favourite, too.'

'Well now. There you go. You have something in common already.'

'Perhaps.' It was a glimmer of hope, although Emily knew that stories of pirate queens and mythical lands wouldn't keep Dorothy entertained forever.

'And you'll be glad of the extra pair of hands on the farm, no doubt,' Cora added as she reached for the marmalade. 'Must be hard going with just the two of ye. My old da always said farming folk are family folk.'

Emily stalled. It was an impossible statement to respond to without elaborating on the absence of children, and nobody ever wanted the detail. 'We didn't . . .'

'Don't mind me, Mrs Gale. I talk too much. It's none of my business.'

'It's fine. I just . . .'

Cora waved her hand in the air, embarrassed and eager to move on. 'No need to explain.'

For a rare moment, Emily wanted to explain, but Cora had already moved on.

'Dorothy needs time to grieve, and to get to know you.' She placed a reassuring hand on Emily's arm. 'It's not going to be easy, Mrs Gale, and there'll be plenty of bumps along the way I shouldn't wonder, but you'll figure it out, the two of ye. You're her mother's sister, after all. Family's family.'

Their conversation was interrupted by Dorothy calling for Cora.

'Should I go?' Emily asked, standing up.

Cora was already at the door. 'Finish your breakfast. Try to have a bit of something, at least. You'll be no good to anyone if you're half famished.'

Emily refilled her cup from the brass and copper coffee pot decorated with Egyptian figurines, a style that had been so desirable during the Tut-mania craze of the early twenties. She remembered Annie's excited plans to see Luxor's tombs and temples like Lady Evelyn Herbert, or to fly across the Atlantic like the aviators whose daring exploits she followed avidly in the news. Emily could see her so clearly, head tipped back in laughter, charming everyone in the room during a dinner party. What would she say if she could see her once more? What would she change if they could have their time over?

Cora returned shortly and started to tidy the breakfast things. 'What time is your appointment?'

Emily glanced at the clock on the sideboard. 'Ten.' She was dreading the formality of the attorneys' office, but it was a necessary part of the process. 'We've to be there for ten.'

'Plenty of time, so. Dorothy just needs her coat and hat, and mittens. And a clean handkerchief in case she gets one of her nosebleeds.'

'Nosebleeds!'

'Nothing to worry about. Common enough in children her age. She knows what to do. And best make sure she's used the loo before you go. Nothing worse than being caught short.'

Emily felt lightheaded as she stood up. 'There's a lot, isn't there. To remember.'

Cora paused for a moment. 'I suppose there is. But it'll all become second nature to you before you know it. Maternal instinct is a wonderful thing.'

The words crouched in Emily's heart, afraid to be considered too closely. Any maternal instinct she'd ever felt had been carefully folded and packed away, like an unsold department store dress no longer in fashion. She'd put her focus into the farm instead, raising her crops and animals, nurturing the land, turning all her unused love loose to roam the prairie. She wondered now if she could ever get it back, capture it and corral it and train it, like a wild mustang.

She made her way upstairs and knocked lightly on Dorothy's bedroom door.

'Dorothy? It's Auntie Em.' She felt like a fraud every time she said the words. What sort of an aunt was she? A stranger. An interloper. 'Can I come in?' She pushed the door open a crack to find Dorothy sitting cross-legged on the floor, surrounded by her toy animals and teddy bears.

Emily joined her, sitting beside the circle of toys. 'Are they having a tea party?' She kept her voice bright and breezy, friendly and encouraging. Everything a performance. 'They look like they're having a lovely time.'

'They're at a funeral.'

The words landed on Emily like knives. 'Oh dear. That's very sad.'

Dorothy pointed to a stuffed monkey beneath the bedstead. 'Monkey is dead and the other toys will never see him again, just like I'll never see Mommy and Daddy again, and it's not fair.'

The words were so blunt and raw that Emily didn't know what to say. A knot of emotion stuck in her throat as she reached for Dorothy's hand.

'I'm so sorry, Dorothy. It isn't fair at all. I miss your mother, too. Ever so much. And I miss my mother.'

'Granny Frances?' Dorothy's eyes met Emily's as she seemed to respond to the idea that she wasn't the only one to have such a devastating thing happen to her.

'Yes. Granny Frances. She was my mommy – mammy, as I used to call her.'

'Can you remember what she looked like?'

Emily nodded. 'I remember everything about her – the sound of her voice, the scent of her hand cream, the way her nose crinkled when she was about to sneeze. And you'll remember everything about your mommy, too. I'll make sure of it.'

'You don't look like Mommy.'

'You don't think so?'

Dorothy shook her head.

'People always said we had the same smile.'

'But you never smile.'

Emily faltered. The child had an unsettling ability to notice her failings and insecurities. 'Well, I guess I don't have much to smile about at the moment.'

Dorothy's eyes filled with tears. 'I can't remember what colour her eyes were. And I can't remember her birthday.'

Emily pulled Dorothy gently to her feet. 'Her birthday is February fourteenth. St Valentine's Day. Her eyes are – were – as green as emeralds. And when she smiled, they sparkled like jewels.' It was many years since she'd last looked into Annie's eyes. She could still feel the hurt they'd carried as she'd stepped into the car the last time she'd visited them in Kansas. 'Your eyes are the same colour as hers.'

This pleased Dorothy. 'The exact same?'

'Almost. Except one of her eyes had the smallest fleck of brown in it, like a nut she was keeping there for the winter. That's why my father – your grandpa Joseph – nicknamed her Squirrel.'

This brought the first hint of a smile to Dorothy's lips. 'Squirrel?'

'Funny, isn't it! And my nickname was Emmie. Our older sister, Nell, was just Nell, because that's already short for Eleanor.'

Dear Nell. How she'd wept when Emily had telephoned her with the terrible news. California had always felt impossibly distant, but it now seemed further away than ever. Nell wished she could do more to help, but with five children of her own and a sick husband to look after, she already had more than enough on her plate. Besides, it was Emily and Henry who'd been named as Dorothy's guardians, much to both sisters' surprise. 'Perhaps John wanted her to be with his cousin,' Nell had suggested. 'Retain the Gale family connection. And despite all your disagreements, I know Annie still loved you the most.' Emily had promised Nell she would write with an update as soon as she returned to Kansas with Dorothy.

'Do you have a nickname?' she asked as Dorothy began to tidy up her toys.

Dorothy nodded. 'Dot. It was Mommy's special name for me.'

Of course. Emily remembered that now. '*I'll call her Dorothy. Dot, for short.*' 'Would you like me to call you Dot sometimes?'

Dorothy shook her head.

'Oh. That's a pity. Why not?'

Dorothy turned as she picked Lion up from the floor. 'Because you're not my mommy.'

And there it was, the brutal, unchangeable fact, laid bare.

The room seemed to spin as Emily stood up too quickly. She took a moment to compose herself before telling Dorothy to be downstairs in five minutes, with a handkerchief in case she got a nosebleed.

Emily's heart raced as she walked along the landing to her room where she lay on the bed and stared at the ceiling: mind whirling, heart lurching, all her courage leaching from her. How would she ever endure this? How would she ever fill the gap left by Annie?

She couldn't.

The fact was that she would never be enough, *could* never be enough for this heartbroken little girl. Dorothy had nothing, and she now needed her Aunt Em to be everything.

3

Dorothy's inclination to rush ahead made Emily anxious as they made their way to Keogh & Sons, Attorneys. She insisted the child hold her hand, even though Dorothy said she wasn't a baby and didn't need to hold hands anymore. They walked at a different pace, their arms swinging awkwardly out of time, unable to find a rhythm to their step until Emily eventually gave in.

'Very well. You can walk beside me, but no running ahead. Or skipping.'

Dorothy folded her arms defiantly across her chest. 'Walking is boring.'

Emily couldn't argue with that. She'd been a restless child herself, always rushing ahead of her sisters, eager to be the first one there, wherever 'there' was.

'You can run as far as you like on the prairie,' she offered, spotting a chance to cajole the child. 'You can run and skip for miles there and never see a single motorcar.'

'What does the prairie look like?' Dorothy asked.

Finally, Emily was on familiar territory. 'Everything's much bigger there for a start – the sky soars for miles above, the sun hangs like an enormous shimmering ball of gold, and we have hailstones big as apples. And when the wheat dances just before the harvest, oh my, it makes your heart soar.'

She sounded like the railroad salesmen pushing their promises of prosperity on the so-called suitcase farmers – city folk whose ill-advised and inexperienced endeavours at prairie farming inevitably came to nothing apart from fewer dollars in the bank and more abandoned claims turned to dust. And yet the prairie had once been the way Emily described it to Dorothy. When she'd first arrived, she'd never seen a place more beautiful.

Now, millions of acres across the Great Plains had been deeply scarred by the new farm machinery, and baked hard by the suffocating heat of last summer and months without rain. Reports of a towering cloud of dust that had rolled across Amarillo last month had folk saying the earth was on the move. But for all the prairie's changes and challenges, Emily still longed to be back there. Chicago was claustrophobic. Even the sky felt hemmed in, trapped between the skyscrapers that seemed to sway when she looked up at them. She'd once loved the bustle and chaos of the city. Now, it choked her.

'Does the prairie have shops?' Dorothy asked as they walked on, passing the stores that had survived the crash and the Depression.

'Of course! In the towns, at least. But the farm gives us most things we need. The windmill draws water from the well, the hens provide eggs, and the cows provide milk and cream, which we swap for coffee and sugar. Anything we can't grow or provide for ourselves we buy at the general store.'

'What's a general store? Is it like a department store? Like Marshall Field's?'

Emily came to a sudden stop, the name Marshall Field's stirring a vivid memory of rushing to work with Annie, both of them laughing as they chanted the store's motto, 'Give the lady what she wants!' and earning the sharp end of their supervisor's tongue when they were late again. As Field's girls they'd thought they had the world at their feet, but war had cruelly turned their world upside down.

'A general store is like a very small department store, I suppose,' Emily replied. 'It has all the essentials like oatmeal and calico, ribbons for dresses, tobacco for the men.' As she described it, Emily wondered what Dorothy would make of their humble prairie home. Kansas was a world away from Chicago's skyscrapers and the instant convenience of department stores.

'What if the general store doesn't have the things you need?' Dorothy asked.

Her endless questions were exhausting. Emily's head ached and her patience was wearing thin.

'Then we do without.'

Her words were well-timed as they passed a long line of men waiting for their share of the city's benevolence at the soup kitchens and ten-cent flophouses. Struggle and loss was etched on their faces. If Emily felt changed by the seven years since she'd left Chicago, the city was almost unrecognisable after the Depression that had followed the stock market crash of '29. A vibrant place that had once sold the promise of a better life to ambitious men now saw those same sorry souls selling nickel apples on street corners. Emily bought two from a pale-faced man and wished him better times ahead, all too aware that he would need to sell an orchard full of apples to get back on his feet.

She gave an apple to Dorothy in the hope that the process of eating it would at least keep the child quiet for a few minutes.

As they turned the final block, Dorothy ran ahead to chase a piece of paper being blown down the street. Emily's cries to slow down were either unheard, or ignored. When Dorothy caught the paper beneath her shoe, she stooped to pick it up.

'Look, Auntie Em! The circus is in town!'

'Let me see.' Emily studied the pamphlet's bold declarations of *Incredible Wonders!* and *Astonishing Marvels!* and the promise of *Lions!* and *Tigers!* and *Bears!* and *Other Exotic and Wild Animals!* She turned it over to read the announcements on the reverse, her mind tumbling back through the years as she did so.

Dorothy tugged on her coat sleeve. 'Can we go? *Please!*'

Emily looked at Dorothy's eager face and saw herself as a young girl again, Annie and Nell beside her, eyes wide in amazement as the red velvet curtain was pulled back and they stepped inside Ringling's circus tent for the first time. They'd never known such excitement, never seen a more thrilling spectacle than the brightly painted wagons, and signs promoting the mysterious sideshow attractions. She could almost smell the wet grass and paraffin, the musty scent of the animals, the sugar-sweet aroma of cotton candy floating through the crowds. She could almost hear the gasps and cheers and thunderous applause. Every year, they'd returned to see the crystal gazers and the beautiful bareback riders tumbling and turning as the horses galloped around the ring, the lion tamers in their scarlet jackets cracking their whips, Mademoiselle Beaudelaire on the high wire, the Aerial Lorraines soaring on their trapeze overhead, defying gravity. Every year was more mesmerising, the grand finale more thrilling than the last. *Introducing Leonardo Stregone as The Amazing Aerialist! See him Ascend to Impossible Heights!* She could see Annie's face illuminated by the electric lights, the sense of wonder in her eyes. She could still remember the prickle of danger in the air as the snare drum began to roll and the finale act began and the gathered crowd fell silent.

'Auntie Em? *Please!*'

Emily stirred as Dorothy tugged at her sleeve, and looked again at the leaflet in her hand. A sense of relief washed over her as she noticed the date.

'I'm afraid this is several months old, Dorothy. Look. It's from last year.'

Dorothy was bitterly disappointed. 'I wish we could have gone. Mommy loved the circus.'

'She did. Very much.'

Too much.

Emily reached for Dorothy's hand. This time, the child took it without complaint. 'I'm sorry, Dorothy. There'll be other chances to see the circus, I'm sure. Plenty of travelling carnivals pass through Kansas. And we have the county fair to look forward to. There's always plenty to see there. Now, come along, or we'll be late for our appointment.'

She folded the pamphlet and pushed it into her coat pocket, mindful of the dozens of circus tickets and posters Annie had diligently kept over the years, carefully packed away with her precious hourglass. Not just a treasured collection of memories, but a collection of memories within which her greatest secret was held.

And Emily was now the reluctant custodian of it all.

*

Keogh & Sons' office was in a high-rise overlooking the Soldier Field stadium. Dorothy was fascinated to be up so high, especially as a distant rain shower had left a double rainbow arcing over the city, but Emily kept well away from the windows.

'It's terrifying up here,' she said as she took off her hat and gloves. 'Aren't you afraid it'll fall over?'

Mr Keogh Sr assured Emily the building was made from concrete and steel and was perfectly safe. 'Not a fan of the skyscrapers, Mrs Gale?'

'Not a fan of heights,' she said. 'I'm definitely not in Kansas anymore, that's for sure. The tallest thing there is the windmill on our farm, and that's not much higher than a house.' She gladly took the seat on the opposite side of the room, beside Mr Keogh Sr's desk.

'How is she doing?' he asked.

They quietly observed Dorothy for a moment as she launched into an intense conversation with her toy lion.

'I'm not entirely sure,' Emily replied. 'One minute she seems remarkably unaffected, the next she becomes quiet and withdrawn. She talks to her toys a lot. Dorothy has a very vivid imagination.'

'What seven-year-old doesn't?'

'You have children?'

'Five of the dreadful things! Which, I might add, is four too many.' His mouth curved into a smile. 'Of course, I love them all dearly.' He moved a pile of paperwork from a filing tray onto his desk. 'Now, let's get down to business, shall we. I don't want to keep you any longer than necessary.'

It was an uncomfortable process, chilling in its formality. The legal statutes and lengthy forms cared nothing for the devastating tragedy that summoned them from their filing cabinets. Sign here, initial there, every scratch of the pen searing the permanence of events onto Emily's heart like a branding iron.

Finally, the last form was stamped and the transfer of ownership was complete, as if Dorothy was nothing more than a horse being traded at the county fair.

'That's everything, Mrs Gale. You and Henry are now Dorothy's legal guardians.'

'And you're certain nobody else was named in the will?' Emily asked.

'Nobody else. It's actually much easier this way. A cleaner cut, if you like. It isn't unusual for everything to be directed toward one family member, especially when there is a connection on both sides, as is the case with you and Annie.'

'Yes, we quite surprised everyone by marrying a pair of cousins. Although you'd never know John and Henry were related. I've never met two men less alike, in looks or personality.'

At this, Mr Keogh Sr offered a small smile. 'And yet you and Annie are so alike. In every way.'

'Not every way, Mr Keogh. We had our differences.' Emily sighed as she pushed the last form across the desk. 'It seems too easy, doesn't it?' she said quietly. 'Too clinical for something that will bring such enormous change to Dorothy's life.'

'That is what the legal system is for, Mrs Gale. We hope we never need to use it, but are immensely glad of its clarity when we do.'

'I presume there'll be a sizeable trust fund for Dorothy when she comes of age?' It offered Emily some comfort, at least, to know that the child's financial future would be secure, even if her present was as turbulent as a winter storm.

Mr Keogh Sr straightened his necktie and cleared his throat. 'Ah, yes. I was coming to that. Unfortunately, things aren't quite as you might have hoped.'

'Oh?'

He leaned forward, his voice low as he spoke. 'It has come to light that your brother-in-law's business affairs were rather . . . troubled.'

'Troubled?'

'He was in serious financial difficulty.'

Emily's jaw tensed. 'How serious?'

'As serious as it gets, I'm afraid. There is no delicate way to say this, Mrs Gale, but John was essentially bankrupt. Loans taken at exorbitant interest rates, poor investments made – the list goes on. We've uncovered a rather grim paper trail of final demands and arrears. While he successfully rode out the initial tremors of the financial crash, the aftershocks appear to have caught up with him. He'd evidently kept the severity of the situation from your sister.'

An awful thought occurred to Emily that the boating accident might not have been an accident after all. She'd heard stories of desperate men taking the most drastic action to end their financial struggles after the crash, unable to face the shame of bankruptcy or poverty. Yet, while she'd never especially liked John, he would surely never hurt Annie or Dorothy?

'I hope you don't mind my saying this,' Mr Keogh continued, 'but I can assure you that there is no suggestion of foul-play.'

Emily looked up, a flush of guilt spreading across her chest as he'd appeared to read her thoughts. 'Gosh. No. Of course not.'

'The rogue wave that struck the boating party was a complete anomaly. A freak of nature. Nobody could have predicted it, or planned for it. It was a tragic accident. Nothing else.'

Emily reached for a glass of water and pushed the thought from her mind, relieved to have some certainty on the matter.

'Take a moment, Mrs Gale. I'm sure this has all come as a huge shock.'

The financial revelations were, indeed, a shock, but not entirely surprising. John had always pushed things to the edge with his investments and business dealings. He was a man of risk and reward. A man who thrived on the thrill of the chase. John Gale was the exact opposite of Henry. One a man of capitalism and industry, one a man of community and nature. For sisters who'd seen eye to eye on almost everything since they were little girls, and had even married men who were cousins, their husbands could not have been more different. But it wasn't John and Henry who'd caused them to drift apart. The blame for that lay elsewhere.

'What does it mean in practical terms?' Emily asked as she glanced over at Dorothy, who was still happily lost in her imaginary world of rainbows and lions.

'I'm afraid it means that the house and all assets will be liquidated to pay John's debtors. There is, in effect, nothing left. No inheritance. No trust fund.'

Emily nodded and drew in a long breath.

'I'm so sorry to share such difficult news with you, Mrs Gale. It is never easy when a loved one passes away. To leave a complicated financial situation, such as that left by your brother-in-law, only makes matters all the worse.'

'I can take some things from the house though? Small, sentimental things? For Dorothy.'

Mr Keogh Sr steepled his hands and leaned across the desk. 'Whatever isn't there to be itemised will never be missed.'

'Thank you. It won't be much. Just a few trinkets and mementos.'

'Of course.' He paused for a moment before opening a file on his desk. 'There is one other small matter, Mrs Gale.' He pulled a slim envelope from a file and pushed it across the desk. 'Your sister left a letter, to be given to Dorothy on her sixteenth birthday, in the event of her death before such time.'

Emily looked at the envelope, almost afraid to touch it. *Dorothy – Sixteen* was written on the front in Annie's neat handwriting.

'She added it to her file shortly after Dorothy's birth,' Mr Keogh Sr continued.

'Did she say what it was about?'

He shook his head. 'She just left instructions for it to be given to you, as Dorothy's guardian, in the event of her death. It's not uncommon, actually. It never ceases to amaze me how organised people are. All eventualities covered. No stone left unturned.'

Emily reached for the envelope and slipped it inside her purse. It felt like a living thing, the words inside beating against the paper like wings, desperate to be freed. She felt suddenly hot, hemmed in, anxious about being so high up.

'Is that everything?' she said.

'That's everything, Mrs Gale. Thank you for your patience. I know it can't have been easy.'

Emily hurriedly gathered up her gloves and hat, and told Dorothy to put on her coat. 'Come along, Dorothy. We're all done here.'

'Are we going to Kansas now?' the child asked, as if going to Kansas was as simple as going to the grocery store.

'Not yet, dear. We've a few more things to organise first. And there's somewhere I want to show you.'

Emily thanked Mr. Keogh Sr again and was glad to take the elevator down to the reassuring solidity of the ground floor.

While she hadn't planned to take Dorothy across the city, she needed fresh air and had a sudden longing to return to the place on the shores of Lake Michigan where she'd first stood as a little girl newly arrived in Chicago. If she went back to the start, perhaps she would find that eager little girl again, and the vibrant young woman she'd become.

When they arrived, Emily guided Dorothy to the shoreline, offering words of caution and direction as they picked their way over the seaweed-slick rocks.

'This is where we came when we first arrived in Chicago,' Emily said. 'My mother and father, your Auntie Nell, your mother, and me. Back then we called it Rocky Shore. It was known as Rocky Ledge Beach for a while until it was given its new name, Rainbow Beach, after the war. I liked to come here and pretend that Lake Michigan was the Atlantic Ocean, and that if I looked hard enough, I'd be able to see Ireland.'

'Did you?'

Emily smiled. 'No, dear. It's too far away. But when I closed my eyes and listened to the water, I imagined I was back on the shores of Lough Inagh, where we lived before we came to America.'

'Mommy used to tell me stories about Ireland. She said we would go there one day, but that won't happen now, will it.'

Emily was about to say that she would take her, but stopped. She shouldn't make promises she couldn't keep.

'Perhaps not. But I'll tell you the stories, and teach you the songs. I'll even show you how to play the fiddle if you like.'

At this, Dorothy brightened.

Emily drew in a deep breath. She felt fortified by the fresh, brackish air; strengthened by the sound of the water as it lapped at the shore. When she closed her eyes, she was a little girl again, standing with her sisters on the shores of Lough Inagh, their hands linked together like the chain that held the iron cooking pot over the turf fire: Nell, Annie, Emily, in descending order of size. Emily was the youngest – an Irish twin to Annie, each born at the bookends of the same year – but she wasn't the youngest child in the family. That honour belonged to sweet baby Joseph, God rest him.

She remembered the tips of her ears burning with cold beneath her bonnet, the last curl of turf smoke rising from the cottage chimney as they'd said goodbye to their home. She remembered the moody, roiling Atlantic; the sting of salt spray on her cheeks; a damp woollen shawl draped around her shoulders – the smell of turf still entwined between the fibres; a turnip-faced man with a *bodhrán* kicking up a hoolie belowdecks; and the reassuring tug of the piece of Connemara marble in her pinafore pocket as their immigration cards were stamped and she'd walked toward a new life, her hand in Annie's, the promise of a place called America taking root in her heart.

She opened her eyes. 'Come along,' she said, turning to Dorothy. 'Let's find some pebbles and build a cairn. See how tall we can make it.'

While Dorothy searched for the perfect pebbles to build their tower, Emily studied her reflection in the water, searching beyond her dull complexion and tired eyes and the silver hairs at her temples that aged her beyond her years. She knew she was still in there somewhere – Emily Margaret Kelly – dressed in all the colours of the rainbow, a sense of wonder in her eyes, the distant murmur of adventure ringing in her ears.

'Where are you, dear Emily?' she whispered to the water. 'Wherever did you go?'

4

Ten years earlier

Chicago, November, 1922

The sidewalk was a carpet of colour, tempting Emily to kick through the crisp fall leaves as she and Annie made their way to 159 Kildare Street, a brownstone boarding house they would now call home.

'Rent is due Thursdays. The front door is locked at eleven sharp every night. Garbage is collected Mondays, if you're lucky.' The landlady, a Mrs Feeney, spoke with a thick northside Dublin accent and a cigarette that clung bravely to her bottom lip. Emily watched the cigarette bounce up and down, spilling ash over the linoleum floor as instructions and rules tumbled with it. 'Bathroom's across the hall. The rats are free. Any questions, ask one of the other tenants. And no visitors. Get your kicks elsewhere, ladies. This is a boarding house, not a knocking shop.' She slammed the door behind her as she left.

'Let's hope we don't see *her* too often,' Annie said as she took off her hat and walked to the window of the damp and draughty room. 'Dear Lord, it really is awful.'

Emily looked at the patches of damp on the walls, the cracked pane of glass in the window, the bare bulb suspended from a dubious-looking wire on the ceiling. 'We've seen worse – just.' She pushed the cigarette ash beneath the threadbare rug with the toe of her shoe and joined Annie at the window. 'But, as Mammy would say, God rest her, it's ours now, even the rats.'

Annie smiled at the memory as she crossed herself. 'God rest her.'

'And God rest Daddy. And baby Joseph.'

The pain of losing their parents was still raw, despite the second anniversary that had just passed. Their infant brother was always remembered in their prayers, his fleeting existence marked by the little grave beside their Connemara cottage and the love he had returned to their hearts.

Emily wrapped her arm around Annie's waist and held her close, seeking reassurance in her presence, just as she had as a little girl, cowering beneath the blankets during a thunderstorm. 'Welcome to our new home. I hope we'll be very happy here.'

'*I* hope we don't get murdered here.'

Emily laughed. 'It's not that bad.'

'It's terrible, Em, but I guess we'll make the best of it.' Annie turned to Emily and grabbed her hands. 'We must plan our first soiree, darling!' She spoke in a faux high society accent. 'A string quartet beside the wonky table, perhaps. Canapés on the broken fire stairs.'

Emily matched Annie's voice. 'And we'll simply *have* to move the moth-eaten chair to make room for the cocktail trolley.' She put her hands on her hips and let out a long sigh as she took it all in. 'It just needs a bit of love and—'

'Knocking down?'

'I was going to say, care.' Emily took off her coat and pushed up the sleeves of her sweater. 'Coffee? Or would madam prefer a soda to toast her new abode?'

'Madam would love a stiff gin, but coffee will have to do I suppose. *Strong* coffee.'

Emily rummaged in one of the boxes they'd hauled up the three flights of stairs. 'Do you remember which box we put the cups in?'

It was a familiar scene. Emily had lost count of the different towns and cities they'd called home since they'd arrived in America. She only had paper-thin memories of those early places – the damp chill of a sagging mattress, the piercing wail of a baby's cry, the scratch and scrabble of rats in the boards – but no matter how dire a place was, she'd always felt loved and safe. Through all the departures and arrivals that had punctuated two decades of her life in America, the one reassuring constant was family. Now, like a stick whittled down from a great spreading branch, it was just her and Annie. First, Nell, the oldest of the three sisters, had moved to California with her rancher husband, Bill Hugson, then their dear father had succumbed to the deadly influenza epidemic after the war, and their brokenhearted mother, having lost all sense of purpose without him, had slipped away in her sleep only a month later.

'Do you remember Da's map of America?' Emily said as she opened another box. 'And the stories we made up about the places we found?' She could still remember the powdery feel of the paper beneath her fingertips as she'd traced imaginary journeys across state lines, sounding out the curious names: San Diego, Los Angeles, Pasadena. That map had felt as magical to her as any fairytale.

Annie smiled. 'We always tried to guess where we might go next.'

'And we were always wrong!'

A draughty tenement in Boston had been home for the first two years, the three sisters squashed into a lumpy bed, Emily sandwiched between Annie and Nell like a rasher of bacon in a sandwich. They'd spent a miserable winter in Pennsylvania, breezed through a hopeful spring in Ohio, and wilted beneath the heat of an Indiana summer. Eventually, the Union Pacific railroad had delivered Joe and Frances Kelly, and their three young daughters, to Chicago, Illinois, where home became a scruffy boarding house in the Irish community on the South Shore. 'It's a start,' their mother had said when they'd looked at the dismal room. 'And a start is all anyone needs. And what's more, it's ours. Even the rats.'

The words had imprinted themselves on Emily. She missed her mother's pragmatism and guidance. Frances Kelly was a woman forged from the Connemara earth, as solid and unyielding as the weathered stones of the Burren. Emily felt adrift without her, like a ship with a broken anchor, blown here and there by the fickle tides of life.

'Oh, Annie. Look. It's Mam's Bible.' Emily turned to the front page, and took out the pamphlet her mother had kept there. She carefully unfolded it and read the large text on the front. 'THE STATE OF KANSAS AND IRISH IMMIGRATION by Reverend Thomas Ambrose Butler.' The Irish priest had worked as a missionary on the Kansas prairies in the last century. His words had captured their mother's heart.

Emily turned to the most well-thumbed page and read the words aloud. 'Hesitate not, if you have health and strength, and money enough to bring you out; come to the great free country, where you may soon grow rich and independent *as a farmer*, with yellow corn waving upon the breasts of the prairies, and cattle grazing upon the hills . . .' The words were so familiar. She'd lost count of how many times she'd heard her mother read them to her father over the years. 'It sounds wonderful, doesn't it. All that clean air and big skies. No wonder she was charmed by the idea of settling there.'

'Poor Mammy. I wish she'd seen it,' Annie said. She kicked off her shoes and sank into a threadbare armchair until she was almost encased in it, the cushions having lost their spring long ago.

'I think she did, in a way.' Emily returned the pamphlet to the Bible and the Bible to the box. 'She read that pamphlet so many times, I'm sure she could touch the wheat and feel the rain.' She turned to the view of the city's endless grey buildings beyond the grubby window. 'We should go there one day. See if the Reverend Thomas Ambrose Butler was right.'

'To Kansas?'

'Yes, Annie! To Kansas.'

'I'll stick to the city, thank you very much. A life of cherry-pie homesteading isn't for me. And I'd also like to stay somewhere for more than five minutes before thinking about moving again. You're as bad as Da.'

'I wonder how Nell's getting on,' Emily said as she tried one more box for the coffee cups. 'California seems so far away. I wish she'd married a nice man from Chicago instead of falling for a cowboy.'

Annie laughed. 'Don't let her hear you calling Bill Hugson that! Size of that ranch he owns, he's no hired cowboy. Our big sister landed on her feet. No doubt she's getting on just fine.'

'We should write to her anyway. Send our new address. I hate to think of us losing touch.'

Emily missed her sister's gentle wisdom. Nell was the smartest of the three, always clever beyond her years and with the sweetest disposition. Annie was a hopeless romantic with a big heart, while Emily had always been considered the brave one, standing up to bullies who called them names, catching the spiders that crept into their beds, and climbing the tallest trees. She didn't always feel brave, but had learned that it was a sure way to please her family and entertain them, because what she craved most of all was their love and affection. With that, she felt strong enough, brave enough and powerful enough to face anything.

Annie reached for Emily's hand. 'We'll be all right, Em. We'll muddle through together, like we always do.'

Emily gave up looking for the coffee cups. 'To hell with coffee! Let's unpack the gramophone. And I'm sure there's half a bottle of hooch in here somewhere.'

They set up the gramophone and put on a Benny Goodman record. Emily laughed as Annie attempted the new Charleston dance, swivelling her feet and circling her hands with her palms facing out.

'You look like you're having a seizure, Annie! You're doing it all wrong!' While Emily's natural curls weren't suited to the sleek hairstyles worn by Louise Brooks and Clara Bow and the flappers she and Annie admired, the one thing she managed to emulate was the new dance. 'Try it this way. Click your heels together, then step to the front with one foot. Click your heels, step behind with the other foot, click your heels, step in front, click, step behind.' She added the hand movements, but Annie still couldn't get it.

'It's a silly dance anyway,' Annie declared as she gave up and started to hang her dresses in the wardrobe of the tiny bedroom they would share.

'You can't buy the silver shoes until you've mastered it,' Emily teased as she joined her sister, the two of them jostling for hanging space. 'They're much too pretty to waste on feet that can't even dance properly.'

They'd both admired the silver dance shoes in Marshall Field's window since Annie had added them to the Thanksgiving display a week ago. She'd promised to treat herself if they were still there on Christmas Eve. Emily had already asked for them to be put by on approval so she could buy them for Annie as a Christmas gift.

When she'd unpacked her clothes, Emily took up her father's fiddle and bow. She loved the feel of it in her hands, the sensation of the smooth wood resting against her cheek, the familiar scent of rosin to keep the strings supple, a trace of her father's tobacco. She played their favourite ballads and reels, the simple melodies infusing the sparse room with warmth and happy memories as Annie took a miniature hourglass from a box lined with tissue paper and set it carefully down on the dressing table. She turned the glass, watching silently as the sand slipped through while Emily's bow danced across the fiddle and time turned its face to the past, and the night of Annie's sixteenth birthday.

They were at Ringling's circus. All around them, the crowd gasped in amazement as *The Amazing Aerialist* performed his daring act, filling his balloon with gas before ascending to a terrifying height from where he performed a trapeze act, suspended beneath the basket, high above their heads. Leonardo Stregone, the scrappy Italian-American boy who'd started his life as a circus performer by bravely climbing to the top of the human pyramid formed by his brothers and uncles, had matured into an enigmatic and powerful showman, and Annie was enchanted.

Later that night, when they returned home, she showed Emily and Nell a miniature hourglass Leonardo had given to her when they'd snatched a moment alone while the others were absorbed by another act and their mother hadn't noticed her absence. *'He said it's to count the hours until he returns. He says he'll marry me one day!'*

Nell laughed and said that's what all the boys say. Emily was too shocked by Annie's behaviour to say anything at all.

She remembered it still, so vividly. Something about Annie had changed that night, as if she'd been given some great power that she didn't know how to control.

Emily put the fiddle down and reached for her sister's hand. 'You still think about him, don't you, Annie.'

'Every day.' Annie turned the glass again. 'Every minute. Every hour.'

For several years, he'd returned to Chicago with the circus as promised, the passionate liaison between them intensifying each time until war summoned him back to Italy. Annie hadn't heard from him since, but she refused to believe he was dead; refused to let go entirely.

'You only get one true love of your life, Em. When you find yours, hold tight and never let him go.'

Emily smiled. 'I've already found the love of my life, and I'm not letting you go anywhere, Annie Kelly! You're stuck with me. For better or worse, 'til . . .'

They looked at each other, happy to leave the remaining words unspoken as the present and the past trickled hypnotically through the hourglass, carrying them toward a future where nothing was certain but everything was thrillingly possible.

5

December, 1922

'Rise and shine, Em. It's a beautiful morning.'

Emily stirred from a dream. She was standing in a field of golden wheat, the sun on her face, wispy angel clouds in a perfect blue sky, a simple farmhouse in the distance, laughter carried on the air. She was warm and happy there. She didn't want to wake up.

Annie tugged on her toe. 'Come on, Sleeping Beauty. Time to earn a living.'

'What time is it?' she asked, as she opened one eye.

'Time you weren't in bed.' Annie pulled the covers off in one quick move. 'Kyteler will turn us into toads if we're late again.'

The chill of the room made Emily scream. 'Annie Kelly! You're the worst roommate ever!' She yanked the blanket back and pulled it around her shoulders. 'And her name is Miss Kielty. You'll be calling her Kyteler to her face if you're not careful.'

'I doubt she knows Alice Kyteler was accused of being a witch.'

Annie hunched herself into an old crone. 'Anyway, Kielty *is* a witch. She makes everyone's lives a misery.' She mimicked their supervisor's voice as she wagged a threatening finger at Emily. 'You're on your last warning, Emily Kelly. Just because you're a pretty little thing doesn't mean you can get away with tardiness. No wages for you this week.'

Emily laughed. 'You do that far too well.'

'I know. Maybe *I'm* a witch, too!' She pulled another hideous crone face, making Emily laugh. 'Now, get up. Coffee's on.'

Emily reluctantly reached for her slippers. It was like putting her feet into blocks of ice. The boarding house was even worse than it had appeared on first impressions. The radiator didn't work, the tap dripped, the mattress was thin and lumpy, and the other tenants were a dangerous concoction of bootleggers and molls. Annie said she wouldn't be surprised to find Al Capone himself on the stairwell, it was that kind of place. Emily reminded her that it was the only kind of place they could afford on the wages of two shopgirls.

She shivered as she washed quickly with the tepid water Annie had left in the bowl, then pulled last night's pins from her hair, teasing out the curls with her fingers before dressing in her Marshall Field's uniform – black calf-length dress, black stockings, black shoes. Not for the first time she wished she was putting on the American Red Cross uniform she'd proudly worn as a volunteer during the war and the influenza epidemic, but that was all in the past. Life had returned to something like normality, and for most women, that also meant returning to their usual roles: wives, mothers, shop assistants, domestic help.

Emily stared at her reflection in the mirror and sighed. Who cared about selling expensive silk lingerie to wealthy ladies who looked down their perfectly powdered noses at you? Field's paid well enough, and there were worse places to spend your day than beneath the famous Tiffany glass ceiling, but Emily was bored by it all. The pull of something else – something more – was ever present. She spent most of her time at work daydreaming about a life where she and Annie were glamorous silent movie stars, or explorers travelling the world together like they'd always imagined, or brave aviators like Harriet Quimby and Bessie Coleman. There had to be more to life than selling chemises and corsets.

'Coffee's going cold!' Annie called from the little cubbyhole that passed as a kitchen. 'And find me a pair of stockings, will you? I've a runner in mine.'

Emily wasn't entirely surprised by how easily Annie had slotted back into her role on the shop floor after the war. She'd set her heart on working as a Field's girl from the moment their mother had first taken them to admire the windows dressed for the holidays. Shopgirls were a step up from the domestic service roles where most Irish girls found work. Field's girls were held in even higher regard, and Annie had made the best of it, impressing customers and management with her cheerful disposition and natural charm. She'd recently been promoted to window trimmer, using her imagination and artistic flair to create the impressive seasonal displays that drew crowds to the store in the thousands.

The beat of a swing record on the gramophone brought a smile to Emily's face. She swayed her hips in time to the music as she rouged her cheeks, pencilled an arch in her eyebrows and lightly kohled her eyes.

'Finally!' Annie studied her sister as she emerged from the bedroom. 'You've done your hair differently. And is that a new lipstick?'

'New to me.'

'Emily Kelly! Buy your own damn lipstick!'

Emily planted a crimson kiss on her sister's cheek. 'And why would I do that when I can borrow yours?'

She grabbed her hat, coat and gloves and fled from the room, racing down the three flights of stairs, Annie clattering behind, their giddy shrieks earning a sharp *shush!* from Mrs Feeney who was nursing another hangover after a night in a speakeasy.

'Mother of God! Would you two ever keep the noise down. It's like living in a feckin' circus.'

Her comment only made them laugh even more as they rushed down the remaining steps and emerged into a beautiful winter morning of golden sunlight and clear blue skies.

'I wonder if Mr Gale will stop by again today,' Emily said, looping her arm through Annie's as they hurried to the L train. She liked to tease Annie about the wealthy businessman who'd taken a shine to her in recent months. 'He'll surely invite you out to dinner soon. There can't be many more silk ties and pocket squares left for him to buy!'

Annie dug an elbow into Emily's ribs. 'John Gale is a gentleman. He knows how to treat a lady, which is more than can be said for some.'

Emily laughed. 'You're a lady now, are you? I see!'

The biting wind swirled between the great steel and glass skyscrapers as they hurried on. Emily was reminded of her mother telling her Chicago had Ireland in its foundations. 'When those great iron girders sing on windy days, remember they're singing the songs of the Irish labourers who rebuilt all this from the ashes of the Great Fire.' Emily could hear it now, the hum of the broadside ballads, the thump of a *bodhrán* beating out the rhythm of a reel. The wind stirred a wildness in her, her skin fizzing like the electric lightbulbs that lit up the theatres at night. She felt restless, as if she was meant to be somewhere, but had forgotten where, or when.

Annie grabbed Emily's hand. 'Let's go out tonight, Em, find a speakeasy and dance until we can't feel our toes!'

'Sounds lovely, but rent's due tomorrow and it isn't pay day until Friday.'

'I'm sure somebody will buy us a drink. Some young buck sitting on a railroad inheritance, or a wealthy widower.'

'I thought we were independent women, making our own way in the world.'

'We are. And one night isn't going to change that.' Annie stopped walking and looked at Emily, her face unusually serious. 'Don't you ever get tired of scraping nickels and dimes together to make rent? Mammy and Daddy worked hard all their lives, struggling to make ends meet, and what good did it do? They died as poor as the day they were born. They wanted more for us, Em. They wanted *everything* for us.' She took a breath. 'Let's have a bit of fun. See where the wind blows us. You can wear those red shoes you got in the thrift store.'

Emily brightened a little. The ruby-red Mary Janes were almost brand new and had quickly become a favourite. 'Fine. But I'm not letting a desperate old widower buy me drinks all night.'

They arrived at Marshall Field's just as the Great Clock struck the hour.

'See you at five,' Annie said as they hurried inside and headed in opposite directions. 'And don't forget—'

'Give the lady what she wants!' they chimed, together, and Emily wondered what it was that *she* wanted, because she knew it wasn't this.

*

The day passed slowly behind the familiar pantomime of a rictus smile offered to well-heeled ladies with too much money and a debt of manners. As the hands of the Great Clock inched towards five, Emily wearily packaged up another parcel of Parisian silk lingerie. But what she saw in her hands was calico and cotton, and what she felt as someone brushed past was the flutter of her skirt stirred by a gentle breeze.

The customer was in a rush. She tutted as Emily struggled with the slippery silk bow.

'Could you hurry. I have another appointment to get to.'

'I'm sorry, madam. It won't take a minute.'

'It has already taken three minutes, and you're still not finished.'

Emily bit back a terse response, and started again. Finally, she was done. The customer didn't even thank her as she took the package and hurried from the store.

As she clocked out and took her coat from the cloakroom, Emily stood for a moment, watching the steady stream of perfectly made-up girls as they left the building. Tomorrow, they would all clock back in, and do it all again. And the next day, and the next. She felt as if she was drowning beneath the drab monotony of it all. There had to be something better she could do, something more meaningful, something that mattered.

'No home to go to, Miss Kelly? And that skirt looks as if it hasn't seen an iron in weeks.'

Miss Kielty. Dressed in her black uniform and with her elongated chin, she really did resemble a witch.

'Yes, Miss Kyte— Miss Kielty. I'll see to it this evening.'

'Make sure that you do. There are plenty more girls out there who dream of wearing the Field's uniform. You're easily replaced, Miss Kelly.' She clicked her fingers together. 'Just like that, I could make you disappear.'

Emily walked downstairs, wishing she *could* disappear.

For now, dancing with Annie would have to be distraction enough. For a few hours she could forget about paying rent and lining the window frames with newspaper to keep out the draughts. She would suspend her restless thoughts and ignore her turbulent heart and step into a world of jazz and bootleg gin, where seductive men charmed impressionable women, and tomorrow none of it would matter because it was all an illusion –

the flirty conversations, the forced grin, the dull fog of it all. It was make-believe; a fairytale for grown-ups.

Annie was waiting outside. 'There you are.'

'Yes. Here I am.' Emily let out a long sigh.

'Oh dear. Bad day?'

'Same as every other day.'

'There are worse jobs, Emily.'

'Like what?'

'You could be cleaning somebody's toilets, for a start.' Annie grabbed her hand. 'I'm afraid there's been a change of plan for tonight. John called in earlier. He's invited me to dinner. Do you mind?'

If anything, Emily was relieved. 'Not at all. That's exciting.'

'It is. I suppose.'

It was always the same with Annie. Whenever someone showed any real interest, she hesitated, afraid to get too serious in case the man she really wished she was with reappeared like the perfect prestige at the end of a magic act. But no matter how painful it was to accept, the reality remained that her beloved aerialist, Leonardo Stregone, was as lost to Annie as it was possible for a person to be, and the only illusion left was for Annie to try and forget him.

'What will you wear for dinner with Mr Gale?' Emily asked.

'I have no idea. You can help me choose. And please call him John. Mr Gale sounds so serious.'

'Old?'

'Don't be mean. He's very charming.'

'The worst ones always are.'

Annie ignored her. 'He's invited us both to his New Year's Eve party. And before you protest, I already accepted. You never know who you might meet there. John knows most of Chicago society!' She looped her arm through Emily's and hurried them both to the train. 'I think things are finally looking up for us, Em. I have a feeling the New Year is going to be a good one.'

'You say that every year.'

'I know. And one year, I'll have to be right.'

Emily smiled, unable to resist her sister's optimism. She tilted her head affectionately toward Annie's. 'What will I ever do without you, Annie Kelly?'

'Oh, I don't know. Live a colourless life of despair and misery, no doubt! Come on. I'll treat you to a hotdog.'

6

Chicago, January 1923

The new year blew in on Arctic winds that brought the first heavy snows of the winter and left Emily with a bad cold that saw her stuck to the bed for a week. Annie did her best to be sympathetic, but she was too busy being courted by John Gale to be at Emily's beck and call. Emily didn't mind. She was happy to be left alone.

She groaned at the burst of daylight as Annie flung open the drapes and flopped onto the bed beside her. She was still wearing last night's dress and the silver shoes Emily had surprised her with for Christmas and which she'd barely taken off since.

'You made it home last night, then?'

'Of course. John respects me that way. I told you, he's a gentleman.' Annie pressed her hand to Emily's forehead. 'Temperature's almost back to normal.' She peered at Emily's face. 'You still look like hell, but much better than you did a few days ago. You should get out for some air today. Blow the cobwebs away.'

'Do I have to?'

'Yes. We're having a dinner party next week.'

'We are?'

'Not *us*! Me and John. He's celebrating a business deal.'

Emily felt a little foolish. Of course it was Annie and John's dinner party. It had been Annie and John everything since their first dinner date. John had enchanted Annie with his generosity and flattery and old-fashioned courtship. Older than Annie by ten years, and a widower, having lost his wife to the influenza, John Gale had inherited his father's railroad fortunes, and was now a successful businessman in his own right.

'And Henry's coming,' Annie added. 'So you have to make an effort.'

Emily groaned. 'You're not *still* trying to fix me up with John's cousin?'

Annie smiled. 'Trust me. he's lovely. I'll even let you wear my new perfume.' She lifted a beautiful glass bottle from the dressing table. A Christmas gift from John. She spritzed a cloud of perfume into the air and twirled around beneath it. 'It's called *Habanita*, by Molinard. All the flappers use it. Isn't it delicious!' Her exaggerated French accent made Emily laugh. 'Wear this and dear sweet Henry won't be able to resist you!'

*

The following week, Emily arrived at John Gale's impressive South Shore row house and took a moment to check her reflection in the bevelled glass panels of the ebony door. The wind tugged at her red velvet cloche as she rehearsed a confident smile. She looked pretty, all traces of her sickness finally lifted. Her eyes were bright, her cheeks attractively flushed with the cold, but her heart wasn't really in it. She would stay long enough to be polite and then make her excuses to leave.

She lifted the heavy iron knocker and rapped twice. She was about to add one more knock, for luck, when the door was opened by the housekeeper, an overbearing Polish woman called Marta, whom Annie had told her about, and was a little afraid of.

Emily stepped inside. She took a moment to admire the décor as Marta took her hat and coat: the fleur-de-lys ceiling rose, the glittering chandelier, the soft light cast from Tiffany glass wall sconces. The best of everything. It was even grander than Annie had described.

'Well, don't you look absolutely divine!' Annie floated down the long entrance hall and kissed Emily on the cheek. She'd arrived earlier to get everything ready. 'The green dress was the perfect choice. Emerald to enchant! Dear Henry will be smitten!'

'Is he here?' Emily had partly hoped he wouldn't be. She was oddly nervous about meeting him after all Annie's talk.

'Arrived early, and sporting a new moustache. He looks ever so handsome!'

'Here. For you.' Emily handed Annie a posy of Christmas roses. She was a little embarrassed by their simplicity compared to the extravagant floral displays in John's home.

'They're so pretty! Thank you.' Annie asked Marta to put them in a vase and told her that Emily was the last of the guests.

Emily found it amusing to see Annie acting like the lady of the house but she did it very well.

She followed Annie to an elegant dining room which was already full of smartly attired guests who all seemed to know one another. The hum of conversation and laughter filled the room, but it was toward a tall man, standing beside the fireplace, that Emily's eyes were drawn. She could feel his gaze follow her as Annie led her through the awkward process of introductions and small talk with John's self-important business colleagues and their dull wives, until they eventually made their way to the far end of the room.

'And this is John's cousin, Henry,' Annie said brightly. 'Henry, this is my sister, Emily. Now, if you'll excuse me, I need to check on progress in the kitchen.'

Henry shook Emily's hand. 'It's very nice to meet you, finally. Your sister has told me all about you. You were certainly missed at John's New Year's party. I hope you're feeling better.'

'I am, thank you. I heard it was quite the night.'

He smiled. 'John's parties always are. These business dinners, on the other hand, can be quite an ordeal. I'm always relieved when they're over.'

Emily felt her shoulders relax, glad to know she wasn't the only one silently dreading it. 'Do you know everyone here?'

'Thankfully not.' He lowered his voice as he leaned closer to Emily's ear. 'Business this and politics that and let's all congratulate one another on being *enormously* successful. Between you and me, I find it all a bit dull.'

Emily was surprised. She'd assumed Henry was a businessman, like John.

'I'd much rather be getting my hands dirty,' Henry continued. 'Building something real. This is all just make-believe.'

Emily's heart quickened. She already felt drawn to his playful humour, the crinkle of his eyes, the curve of his smile.

'You look very pretty, by the way,' he added as both their glasses were refilled with champagne. 'The green suits you.'

'Thank you.' For a moment, she didn't know what to say. She couldn't remember the last time someone had complimented her so nicely; so naturally. 'I like your moustache,' she said eventually. 'Very Valentino.'

He narrowed his eyes and smouldered dramatically. 'You're very kind, but I think we both know it's really more Chaplin than Valentino.' He twirled an imaginary cane in his hand and waddled his feet.

Emily laughed. 'You're right. Definitely more Chaplin!'

Henry held her gaze for a moment and raised his glass to hers as they were called to take their seats at the table. 'Here's to surviving the night, Miss Emily. Good luck.'

'Amen to that. We could always escape after the fish course? Make a run for it.'

His eyes sparkled. 'Too obvious. Meet you beneath the table after dessert. We'll crawl our way out. They'll be too drunk to notice by then.'

*

Dinner was an impressive performance of consommés and souffles and rich dishes with fussy names that Emily didn't have an appetite for. She was too restless to eat, picking her way around each perfectly presented plate as her eyes searched for Henry's across the table. The conversation oscillated between business and politics, all of which Emily found tiresome. She was glad of the distraction Henry offered while John held court and Annie played house.

Much younger than his cousin, Henry Gale didn't share John's bombastic extravagance. It was his quiet assurance and refreshing honesty that drew Emily to him, and despite her plan to leave at the first opportunity, she found that she was happy to stay, eager to find out more about this intriguing man.

John refilled Henry's wineglass as the conversation turned to the expansion of the railroads and the thousands of folk turning their hand to farming the Great Plains.

'My cousin here plans to work the land. Turn wheat into gold, or some such fairytale,' John scoffed. 'I keep telling him to invest in industry. Shares are soaring and the economy's booming. You're a banking man, Henry. You must see the gains being made on the commodity markets. Steel, coal, manufacturing. That's where the future lies, not in wheat and corn.'

'I'm a bank *clerk*, John. I process paperwork. Stamp forms for loans and debts. It pays a decent wage, but it haunts my soul.' Henry turned to the rest of the table. 'As you'll all be aware, my cousin doesn't have a soul, which is why a life of hard commerce suits him perfectly. I'm quite sure that if you tapped his chest there would be an echo where his heart should be.'

Everyone laughed at that.

John explained how his and Henry's fathers – estranged brothers – had followed very different paths. 'My father made his fortune on the railroads. Henry's father followed his heart toward a farming life in the Texas panhandle. I'll let you draw your own conclusions as to whose father made the wiser choice.'

Henry talked fondly of his parents, expressing his admiration for their resilience and determination, and the years of hard work it had taken to build their farm from nothing.

A man seated beside Henry was interested.

'What are your plans, Henry? Pick up a free claim, or take your chances on one of the old ranch plots they're selling off for forty-five dollars apiece. Seems to me they're mostly selling a lot of hot air.'

Henry nodded. 'That's exactly what they're selling. First you see the brochures from the developers, then you see the developers locked up for fraud. I have no intention of joining the No Man's Land nesters, or the sodbusters in their Dalhart dugouts. I'm saving up to buy my own plot on the Great Plains – Kansas or Oklahoma – although at this rate there won't be any land left by the time I can afford it. I have plans to farm in a more modern way. Invest in combustion engine machinery.'

'Sounds impressive.'

'Farming has progressed a long way since the hand ploughs and horse-drawn ploughs of my parents' generation. The new machines do most of the heavy work in a fraction of the time. More efficient farming means more crops sown and higher yields come the harvest. Seems like good business sense to me, and if there's a more beautiful place to call home, then I'd like to see it. Those enormous endless skies, the swaying oceans of wheat . . . It's enough to reduce a man to tears.'

Emily listened attentively. Henry was so animated when he talked about the prairie and his plans to build a life there. There was something intoxicating about his determination, a power in the way he spoke about the beauty of the place and the pull of an honest day's work. It reminded her of her mother's dream of seeing Kansas one day.

'I believe it's a very hard life, Henry,' Annie offered.

'It isn't for the faint-hearted, that's for sure. Nobody farms for an easy life. My father always said it was an addiction, a love affair between a man and his claim.'

'Or a *woman* and her claim,' Emily added. 'We mustn't forget the farmers' wives.'

Henry smiled. 'Quite right. I've never met a successful farmer who didn't have a strong woman beside him.'

His gaze lingered on Emily's a moment more than was necessary.

'You wouldn't really leave the city, would you, Henry?' Annie asked. 'Give it all up and start over?'

'I would, Annie. In a heartbeat. When the time is right.' He glanced at Emily again as he took a sip from his glass. 'Farming is a life that chooses the person, rather than the other way around. Once you feel the pull, it's hard to ignore.'

'Oh, I'd find it perfectly easy to ignore,' Annie said, laughing. 'Our parents left behind a life of living off the land to search for something better. We would never go back to that way of living, would we, Emily?'

'I think it's an admirable life,' Emily said, meeting Henry's gaze. 'A life of risk and reward. Not unlike your business investments, John. But with more dirt.'

At this, everyone laughed, and the conversation moved on, but

Emily's attention lingered on the man across the table, and her thoughts strayed to the big skies and fields of golden wheat he had described as if reading from her mother's pamphlet.

She enjoyed the evening so much that she was sorry when the last of the dishes were cleared, the last of the wine was drunk, and the guests began to make their way home.

Henry helped her into her coat as they stepped outside.

'Well, that was surprisingly enjoyable,' he said. 'Thanks to you.' He reached for her hand. 'Could I take you out for a proper meal one evening? Something simple to eat and easy to pronounce. Spaghetti and meatballs? A diner milkshake and fries? Or pizza, if you prefer?'

Emily's heart danced. 'I'd like that.'

'Which one?'

'Everything.'

His eyes crinkled as he smiled. 'Everything sounds good to me.'

She felt the prickle of fate as they held each other's gaze. It was as intoxicating and thrilling as any circus sideshow. Henry Gale was the difference, the change, the adventure she'd been looking for. She felt the same sensation she'd sensed in Annie all those years ago when Leonardo had given her the hourglass on her sixteenth birthday, and she'd first felt the great and powerful sensation of being in love. It was crazy to feel so certain when she'd only just met him, but there was no point in denying what she felt in her heart. With Henry, she would chase her wildest dreams; follow the road she was meant to take.

'We all need a dream,' her mother had once said when Emily had asked her why she'd kept the pamphlet about the prairie all those years. 'We all need something magical to guide us, something bigger to hope for, a reason to believe that the impossible might just become possible after all.'

'Golden fields of wheat as far as the eye can see, herds of wild horses, a creek to bathe in on a warm spring day . . .'

7

Chicago, 1932

Kansas was calling her home.

She closed her eyes and imagined the sun on her face as she listened to the melodic rustle of wind through the crops, like an incantation as the song of the prairie grew louder, summoning her to return. She longed to feel the earth beneath her feet, the grain running through her fingers, the cool water from the creek, the touch of Henry's tender embrace.

She stirred from her thoughts as Cora knocked lightly on the bedroom door and peered inside. 'There you are. I thought a tot of whiskey might help you sleep.'

Cora's warm smile was a balm, the whiskey even more so. Emily gladly accepted them both.

'I'm sorting through the last of Annie's things.' She looked at everything strewn across the bed. 'Although I seem to be making more mess than progress.'

There was so much of everything – clothes, tableware and glassware, enough books to build a small library, carefully curated scrapbooks about female explorers and aviators, artwork, photographs, paperwork, furs, trinkets and ornaments, jewellery fit for a queen – on it went, room after room. It made Emily uncomfortable to see the excess when so many had so little.

'Never an easy job,' Cora said. 'Impossible really. Let me help. We'll get through it a lot faster together.'

Emily was glad of Cora's company and pragmatism as they placed items into the boxes for the liquidators. Most things meant nothing to Emily – extravagant gifts from John which, she now knew, he couldn't afford. She wanted nothing of John Gale's false riches and grand gestures, but she did keep a ring of Annie's that Dorothy especially liked, a cluster of emeralds, set into an intricate Art Deco surround. The child deserved to keep something of value at least. But it was the smaller, personal items of Annie's that stirred Emily's emotions and memories: a lace handkerchief their grandmother had made, Annie's communion prayer book, an Irish penny, a collection of buttons from their mother's sewing basket, an age-spotted bundle of letters postmarked Eire, a tiny man made of metal.

Emily gasped as she lifted the tin man out of an old snuffbox and turned him over in her hands. 'Hello! I'd forgotten all about you.'

Cora turned to see who Emily was talking to. 'He's a dotey little thing! Is that an axe he's holding?'

'Yes. He's a woodcutter. Our father made us one each as a Christmas gift from scraps of metal. We called them Chip, Stick, and Twig. The names were Nell's idea. We used to have such fun together, making up little games and stories about them. I lost mine a long time ago.'

'Your father worked in the steel factory? That's a tough life.'

'He used to joke that he'd worked there so long he would rust if you left him out in the rain.'

As Cora studied the tin man, Emily's thoughts turned to her

father. Joseph Kelly had the biggest heart she'd ever known. He'd been the steady harmony to their mother's restless song, the gentle calm that followed her storms, the reassuring hand at all of their backs. Tears pricked her eyes as she recalled the last time she'd seen him. 'Years of factory fumes and smoke damaged his lungs, leaving him vulnerable to infection. He died during the influenza epidemic. My mother went soon after. They'd never spent a day apart. She died of a broken heart.'

Cora offered her condolences. 'I'm so sorry for your losses. I try to believe in God, Mrs Gale, but I struggle to understand Him sometimes. How He lets one person live, and another die.' She fussed with a handkerchief in her hands. 'Annie talked about you often. She used to tell me how you'd been the best of friends. She never told me why you drifted apart, but I know it tormented her.'

Emily busied herself with the contents of a jewellery box, evading the question Cora had hinted at but hadn't dared ask.

'Families are complicated,' she offered eventually. 'Sisters, especially so. Would you like to keep something of Annie's? You seem to have been very close to her.'

Cora was very touched. 'That's very kind of you. Annie was different to other women I've worked for. She was kind, and gracious. She even let me borrow a dress once or twice, for a special occasion.'

At this, Emily smiled. 'We used to swap clothes all the time, but Lord forbid I so much as looked at her favourite shoes! Those were strictly off-limits.'

Cora stood up and reached into the wardrobe. 'You mean these?' She pulled a pair of silver shoes from a box. 'The silver dance shoes?'

Emily stared at Annie's shoes as if she was bewitched by them. They were as good as new, bar a few scuffs on the heels. They seemed to encapsulate everything good about the post-war years when she and Annie had started to make their way in the world, dancing in Chicago's jazz clubs and gin joints, wondering what the future held for them both. The silver shoes conjured so many memories and emotions that Emily was almost afraid to look at them.

'She slept in them the first night she got them,' she said. 'Declared she was never going to take them off. When I woke up, all I could see was a pair of silver shoes sticking out of the bedcovers.'

Cora smiled at the image. 'You should take them with you.'

Emily shook her head. 'I don't have much call for silver dancing shoes on the prairie. Henry would think I'd lost my mind.' Emily glanced at the collection of items she'd already put aside to take to Kansas. 'Besides, I'm not sure there's room to take anything else.'

'There's always room, Mrs Gale. Dorothy might like them one day, when she's older.' Cora placed the shoes into a box marked *Kansas*. 'We make room, don't we. Find space for the things we treasure.'

Emily's stomach lurched as she thought about the space she and Henry would need to make for Dorothy in their humble prairie home, and in their lives and hearts.

While Cora folded John's suits and shirts, Emily looked through Annie's collection of circus memorabilia, stored in a Marshall Field's hatbox beneath the bed, along with the hourglass, carefully wrapped in tissue paper. Emily recalled how they would sit and watch the sand trickle from one end to the other. She did the same now, turning the wooden casing, but among the sand that fell from one end to the other, she also saw secrets and regrets. If only she could go back, make things different, force the sand to run in the opposite direction. But time was not forgiving or sympathetic, and regret was the heavy cost Emily must now pay.

'That's a beauty,' Cora said as she saw the hourglass in Emily's hands. 'You're unearthing all sorts of treasures.'

'It was a gift from a circus performer Annie fell in love with. He gave this to her so that she could count the hours until he came back.'

'Oh, how romantic! Did he? Come back?'

Emily nodded. 'Every summer.' She recalled her mother's disapproval and Nell's quiet envy. She remembered the exotic scent of hair pomade and cigarette smoke Annie carried with her when she returned from their secret liaisons. 'He came back every year, until the war. We heard he'd gone to Italy to join the army.'

It was as if another life was held within that old hatbox; a trace of whispers and secrets and dangerous things carried among the musty leaflets. She replaced the lid, put the hatbox on the dressing table to take to Kansas, and looked around the almost empty room.

'A whole life packed away. It's as if Annie never existed.'

Cora placed her hand on Emily's arm. 'She existed, Mrs Gale. Even without a single thing left, your sister will live on, in your heart, and in Dorothy.'

Finally, they took down the heavy velvet drapes from the windows. The material would be donated to the Women's Benevolent League to sew into dresses and skirts for those who had no closet to fill with clothes of their own.

'Will you stay on here?' Emily asked. 'I presume the new owners will need a housekeeper.'

Cora shook her head. 'It wouldn't be the same. I'll find a new position somewhere, although there's not the same call for housekeepers now, what with everyone going through hard times, and domestic staff being cut back.'

'You could always come to Kansas with us? We live a simple life, but we're comfortable – most of the time.' Emily hadn't planned to offer the invitation, but it occurred to her that it might not be the worst idea. She'd enjoyed Cora's company. She was a touchstone back to her Irish roots, and someone Dorothy knew and trusted. It would be good for her to retain something familiar. Suddenly, Emily couldn't bear to leave Cora behind. 'You'd be more than welcome.'

Cora shook her head. 'You're very kind to offer, but I'm a city girl now. Don't think I'd last long on the prairie.'

'Then promise you'll visit sometime. Head to Liberal and ask for Mrs Miller at the general store. She'll point you in our direction.'

'I'll do my best. Let's see where the wind blows me. Now, I'll fix us a bit of supper and leave you to finish up in here. Can I get you anything else? Another whiskey?'

'No, thank you. This has gone straight to my head.'

Emily took a moment alone in the room, her fingertips walking through memories as they brushed against the bed where Annie had laboured through a storm, and the window seat where she had first held her infant niece. She remembered it so clearly: the fragile feather-like feel of her, the almond-sweet scent of her, the soft nuzzle at her neck when she'd held her to her shoulder. She'd loved her so much she could hardly bear to let her go as she'd placed her in Annie's arms.

She turned then to the collection of things she'd put aside and opened the shoe box. The silver shoes sparkled when she lifted them toward the light, as if they were alive.

'*Oh, Em! You got them for me! You're the best sister in the world!*'

She had tried to be. She really had.

As she returned the shoes to the box, she noticed the corner of an envelope beneath the bottom layer of tissue paper. She pulled the paper back and lifted out a bundle of envelopes, tied together with a ribbon. She recognised Annie's handwriting on the front of each envelope. *Dorothy – 1*st *birthday. Dorothy – 2*nd *birthday*, and so on. There were seven envelopes in total. One for each birthday Annie had celebrated with her daughter. The envelopes were still sealed.

Seeing them reminded Emily of the letter the attorney had given her, for Dorothy's sixteenth birthday. Again, she wondered – dreaded – what it might contain. Were all the letters to be given to Dorothy on her sixteenth birthday and, if so, what secrets might they reveal? The remaining birthdays stretched ahead like a held breath. Nine birthdays, and nine letters, which were Emily's responsibility now.

*

Stomach full of knots, she went to wish Dorothy goodnight, watching her silently for a moment through a crack in the doorframe. She looked so small and alone in the middle of her bed as she packed a small suitcase with a few favourite books and agonising over which toys to take and which to leave behind.

Emily still couldn't quite comprehend that the child was coming to live with them. Not just for a week, or a short holiday, but until she was old enough to have a home and start a family of her own. The months and years ahead seemed to spool at Emily's feet like a thousand unravelled cotton reels. How would they ever untangle their very separate lives and thread this new family together?

She stepped into the bedroom and showed Dorothy the tin woodcutter. 'I thought you might like this. He belonged to your mother.'

Dorothy took the little man and turned him over in her hands. 'What is it?'

'He's a tin man. His name is Twig. Your grandfather made one for each of his daughters when he worked at the steel mills. You can keep him if you like.'

Dorothy smiled at the little man as she put him on her nightstand beside her lion. 'Hello, Twig. I'm Dorothy. And this is Lion. We're going to live in a place called Kansas. It's very far away, but you mustn't be afraid.'

As Dorothy spoke, Emily pictured herself, Annie, and Nell in a frosty boarding house room on Christmas morning, their eyes alight with wonder as they admired the little tin men their father had made for each of them, and suddenly her heart surged with affection for the child. Finally, she felt a connection, a bond forged by the tin woodman.

'Why can't I take all my toys to Kansas?' Dorothy asked as she closed her suitcase and fastened the buckles.

'Well, we don't have room for them all for a start. There are rather a lot.' The child had clearly been spoiled. 'And I thought you might like to give some to a children's orphanage, for the boys and girls who don't have toys to play with.'

'What's an orphanage?'

'It's where children go to be looked after when they don't have a mommy or daddy to look after them. They're called orphans, and they live at the orphanage.'

Dorothy thought about this for a moment. 'Am I an orphan?'

The word pierced Emily's heart. It was so bleak, so lonely.

'You're what's known as a niece. *My* niece. And Uncle Henry's. A very special niece.'

'Where do nieces go to be looked after? Do they go to Kansas?'

Emily's hands stalled for a moment as she pulled up the bedcovers and tucked Dorothy in tight beneath them. 'Yes, dear. That's right. They go to Kansas.' She took a moment to swallow a knot of emotion in her throat. 'Time to get some rest now. We've a long journey tomorrow.' She placed the back of her hand against the child's cheek, as she'd seen Cora do, then walked from the room and switched off the light. 'Goodnight, Dorothy.'

As she had every night since she'd arrived, Emily waited a moment, a pause in the dark before she pulled the door behind her, except that night a small voice punctured the silence.

'Goodnight, Auntie Em.'

The drought of tears finally broke that night as Emily wept for the little girl who would grow up without her mother's tender touch and reassurance. She wept, also, for her own parents, and for the dear sister she'd lost, and for the impossible task that had been asked of her and Henry.

She lay in the dark and thought about the life they'd planned together before Dorothy was even a whisper on the wind, when everything was still a dream and anything was possible.

8

Chicago, 1923

By the time the last daffodil had unfurled its cheerful yellow trumpet, and the last of the cherry blossom had been scattered like confetti among the city's streets and park benches, Annie and John were married. The hourglass that had once turned as a measure of Annie's love for another man was packed away as she began a new life with her husband and time turned in a different direction, and ever faster, it seemed.

Emily worried that it was all too rushed but she soon learned that saying so wasn't going to make any difference. Nell sent a long letter to offer Annie her congratulations along with an apology for missing the wedding because of another baby due any day. *I hope you love him madly, dearest,* she'd written. *I had no idea how hard marriage was. Men cleverly hide their worst habits until they get a ring on your finger. No doubt John will snore like an elephant and leave his underwear on the floor and expel wind at surprising volume, but try to enjoy the marital obligations nevertheless. If it helps, sing 'Molly Malone' in your head. It's usually all over before I reach the final verse. I wish you both all the best and many happy years together. I will try to visit as soon as I can, or perhaps you could come to California. The children would love to meet you, and the weather is better here for a start. I miss you, and sweet Emmie. Send my love to her.*

John made no secret of the fact that he was keen to produce an heir to his business empire, and that he wasn't prepared to risk anyone else staking a claim to Annie's affections. It was clear that he adored her, although his way of expressing it was as cold and calculating as one of his business negotiations. Even his wedding speech had felt like an opportunity to brag. 'A smart businessman always knows when to close the deal. Marrying Annie is my best investment yet.'

For her part, Annie was easily seduced by John's charismatic charm and the comfortable life he could offer her. She insisted she loved him, but Emily had seen Annie in love, and this was not the same. What Emily saw between Annie and John was merely a consolation prize to the bigger gift that had eluded her.

But despite her reservations about Annie's true affections, and her lingering distrust of John's ruthless approach to business, Emily put on her brightest smile and offered Annie nothing but her unwavering support. She longed for her sister to be happy, and reassured herself that the love Annie had found with Leonardo would come with John, in time.

'How are things at work?' Annie asked as they met for their favourite lunch of Mrs Hering's chicken pot pie in Field's Walnut Room restaurant. 'Miss Kielty still as awful as ever?'

'Nothing ever changes at Field's, Annie. You know that. You could ask me the same question in ten years and I would give you the same answer.' Emily reached for Annie's hand across the table. 'I miss you, though. You were the only thing that made it half bearable.'

John considered shop work too demeaning for his wife and had insisted Annie leave her role. She'd said she was tired of dressing windows anyway, but Emily knew she wasn't.

Annie offered a sad smile. 'I miss you, too. You weren't the tidiest roommate, but at least you didn't snore! How's the new girl?'

'Hardly ever see her, apart from the feathers and sequins she leaves around the place. It's no fun since you left. It's quiet.'

Apart from missing Annie at work, Emily's domestic arrangements had also been altered by Annie's marriage. She now shared the Kildare Street boarding house room with Kate Westbury, a young showgirl recently arrived from Galway. Emily didn't see her much, their schedules rarely intersecting since Emily was usually asleep while Kate was at work, and vice versa. The arrangement suited them both.

'The offer still stands,' Annie added. 'You're more than welcome to stay with John and me until you get a better offer.' She paused for a moment. 'How is dear Henry? Still making his plans to roll out west and chase the herd?'

Emily chose to ignore Annie's sarcasm, letting her attention settle instead on the squeeze of her heart at the mention of Henry's name.

'Henry is a delight, and yes, he is still planning to become a farmer. Thank you for the offer, but I'll stick things out at Kildare Street for now. Kate's a nice girl – and besides, what would Mrs Feeney do without me to shout at?' Secretly, she couldn't think of anything worse than playing gooseberry to Annie and John in their honeymoon period. She imagined John Gale was as loud and self-congratulatory in the bedroom as he was in the boardroom. 'How is married life anyway?' she asked. 'Exhausted already?'

Annie blushed and took a sip of water. 'There's no need to be quite so crass. It's not all about *that*. I'm not a brood mare.'

'What *is* it about, then? What do you do all day?'

'Oh, lots. There's always something to organise. A charitable luncheon to write invitations for, or a business event to attend. I'm redecorating at the moment – the first Mrs Gale had dubious taste – so I'm drowning in curtain fabrics and wallpaper samples.'

Emily couldn't suppress a burst of laughter.

'What's so funny?' Annie looked at her, half-smiling, half-offended.

'It's just so strange to hear you talking about curtains and luncheons. I'm sorry. I didn't mean to laugh.'

Emily's laughter concealed her discomfort. Her conversations with Annie were increasingly forced and awkward, as if they were both reaching for something that had fallen beyond their grasp. It broke her heart to feel the strain of something that had always been so natural. She hated how much things were changing between them. Annie was mostly oblivious, distracted by the demands of her new life, but Emily missed the secrets and closeness they'd shared as little girls, the easy companionship and friendship they'd shared as independent young women navigating a new world. She missed the Annie she knew and loved, grieved for her and the wild adventures they'd once planned together. With their parents dead and buried, Nell happily married in California and Annie now Mrs John Gale, Emily felt abandoned and alone.

Despite the surprising joy of Henry in her life, it was hard to let go of the close family bonds that had been her safe haven for so long. Even the excitement and adventure she desperately craved felt suddenly terrifying when confronted with it becoming a reality. A childish part of her wanted to cling stubbornly to the familiar and safe, and yet the thrill of something new and unknown still called to her.

'I could come over if you like,' she said as she let go of Annie's hand. 'Help you choose the fabric.'

'Would you? Really?'

'Of course! Why wouldn't I?'

'I thought you weren't interested in such things.'

'I'm not, Annie. But I *am* interested in you. If I have to look at fabric swatches to spend time with my sister, then that's what I'll do.'

Annie smiled. 'Thank you. I really don't deserve you.'

Emily knocked her feet against Annie's beneath the table. 'No. You don't.' She finished her last delicious mouthful of chicken pie and leaned back in her chair. 'By the way, I see the circus is coming back next month. I saw the posters being pasted up earlier.' She was being deliberately provocative. Testing. Challenging. 'Shall we go? For old times' sake?'

Annie stalled and fussed with her napkin. 'Aren't we a little old for the circus? You and Henry go. You can tell me all about it after.' She picked up the menu. 'Now, the important question is, do we have room for dessert?'

More deflection and distraction. Annie never had room for dessert.

*

The seasons passed and fall painted the city's trees in shades of rust and flame. Emily loved the rich jewelled tones of the season, the way the trees of the city's parks glowed amber and garnet and ruby beneath a generous golden sun. But the turning of the seasons also reinforced the widening void between Emily and Annie, the bright colours of the decaying leaves an echo of their diminishing closeness. Emily had only seen her sister a handful of times since the wedding, their lives spinning in opposite directions, like markers on a weathervane – east and west, north and south.

But Annie's marriage wasn't entirely to blame. Emily's time and thoughts were consumed by Henry. Even when she was at work, or alone in the boarding house, just the thought of him sent her stomach tumbling. She'd always thought the phrase *weak at the knees* was for silly girls who didn't know their own minds, and yet a simple glance or touch from Henry had her melting. Yet there was nothing of weakness about her feelings for him. It was the strength of it, the power and certainty, that scared and excited her beyond measure.

'Did you and Annie have a nice time today?' Henry asked when they met that evening to celebrate Emily's birthday. He'd booked their favourite table in their favourite Italian restaurant. The soft candlelight and busy hum of the diners cocooned them in a warm glow.

'She cancelled again. Isn't feeling well. A head cold, or something. She left a message for me at work.'

Henry reached for her hand. 'I'm sorry, Em. I know it upsets you not to see Annie as often. Why not drop by tomorrow? Surprise her. She's your sister, after all. You shouldn't have to wait for a formal invitation.'

As always, Henry was a rock of good sense. 'You're right. I'll take her some books and flowers to cheer her up.'

He reached for her hand. 'How about we forget about all that and celebrate you instead?'

She smiled and leaned across the table to kiss him. 'Celebrate away, Henry Gale. A girl has to feel special once a year!'

He studied her for a long moment as a playful smile curved at his lips. 'I'd like to make you feel special every day. Emily, I . . .' He paused as their plates of spaghetti arrived. 'Let's eat,' he said, the moment lost. 'And then I'm taking you dancing.'

It was a bitterly cold evening. The chill seeped through Emily's thickest coat and settled against her skin as they left the restaurant and passed the gin joints and backstreet jazz clubs Annie had once dragged her into. The raw hopeful energy of the post-war years still pulsed in the notes of the musicians' instruments, but Emily kept walking when Henry offered to take her inside.

'Not this one,' she said. 'Let's walk a bit further. Find somewhere a bit quieter.'

Chicago was a city of bootleggers and mobsters, showmen and businessmen, a place where capitalists and industrialists like John Gale thrived, spurred on by soaring commodity prices and greedy stock market traders. She felt a calling in a different direction. She wanted to listen to a different tune, dance to a different song. When Nell had written recently, Emily had read the pages over and over, mesmerised by her sister's descriptions of cattle drives and rattlesnakes, cotton fields and creek beds full of gold. More and more, she felt pulled toward a similar life. The question was, did she have the courage to go and find it.

'We still seem to be walking rather than dancing,' Henry teased as they passed more places.

Emily turned to him. 'I'm sorry. I don't feel in the mood for dancing tonight.'

Henry stopped to buy roast chestnuts and a newspaper from the street vendors. The headline carried the grim detail of another murder.

'Don't you ever get tired of it all?' Emily said as they walked on. 'All the traffic and noise. The gangsters and violence.'

Henry laughed. 'I've been tired of it for years. I've made the most of it, but nothing feels real to me here – bonds and loans and speculation on the stock market. It's all so intangible. I want to get my hands dirty. I want to work the land and feel the pull of the earth as I turn the plough.'

Emily loved to hear Henry talk about his love of the land. It reminded her of her mother, always looking for the beauty in the world, despite the ugliness she'd known. She'd taught her daughters to wonder and observe, to care for a single blade of grass the same way they would care for an entire field, to treat a beetle the same way they would treat a mighty cart horse.

'Did I ever tell you my mammy dreamed of settling in Kansas?' she said as they walked. 'She kept a pamphlet about it inside her Bible. Brought it with her all the way from Ireland. I used to listen to her reading it to my father.'

'Why didn't you go?'

'My father secured a good job in the steel factories. Mammy found work as a seamstress, and then as a dressmaker for Marshall Field's. Then war came, and then the influenza . . .' Emily took a breath. 'They ran out of time. Isn't that the saddest thing.'

Henry came to an abrupt stop and turned to face her.

'Let's not run out of time, Em. I want to wake up to a sunrise reaching across fields of golden corn as far as you can see. I want to bring in the harvest and live in a home built with my own hands. I want to struggle and thrive and breathe fresh clean air. I want to swim naked in a creek whenever the mood takes me!'

Passion burned in his eyes as he spoke. Emily was scorched by it.

'That's a beautiful dream you have, Henry Gale.'

A smile skirted his lips as he reached for her hands. 'But it's no fun having a dream of your own. It could become *our* dream, Emily. Our reality. Yours and mine.'

Her heart quickened as she sensed what was coming.

Henry dropped to one knee and took her hands in his.

'Emily Margaret Kelly, would you do me the greatest honour of my life? I don't have a ring, but I can't bear to spend another day without you. Will you marry me? Come to Kansas with me?' A hopeful smile lit up his face. 'Swim naked in the creek with me sometimes?'

Emily started to laugh, and then Henry laughed, and for a minute they were both helpless with laughter, tears streaming down their cheeks as the freezing Chicago wind whirled around them and Emily's heart soared.

She pulled him to his feet, placed her hands on his cheeks, and kissed him.

'Is that a yes?' he said.

'Yes, Henry Gale! *Yes*! I'll marry you and go to Kansas with you.' She kissed him again as she looked into his eyes. 'I'd go anywhere with you.'

With Henry, she knew she could weather any storm. Whatever happened, and wherever life took them, they would share it together, for better or worse. She loved him, truly and wildly, this sweet, funny man whose name echoed the wind.

*

They were married at the city hall a week later, an early dusting of snow for confetti, two strangers as their witnesses. Emily wore a dress in cream chiffon and a garland of orange blossoms in her hair. Henry looked handsome in a tan suit and brogues. It was perfect. Emily loved the spontaneity and secrecy. Loved the simple intimacy of the occasion. Annie would have insisted on turning it into a great production, and she doubted Nell would have been able to make the long journey, so she'd decided to tell her sisters after the event. Emily knew Annie would be terribly hurt, but hoped that her happiness for them both, not to mention gaining Henry as a dear brother-in-law, would outweigh any damage to her feelings.

They spent their wedding night in the fanciest hotel they could afford. Emily wasn't shy with Henry. He was so gentle and sure that she quickly responded to his touch, allowing herself to be swept away on wave after wave of desire until she wasn't sure where Henry stopped and she began. As night gave way to the lavender light of dawn, she lost herself to him again.

She woke to a golden path of light that shone through a gap in the drapes and caressed their entangled limbs. It was unfathomable to her that she could wake like this every day now.

'Can we stay here forever,' she whispered. 'Just you and me.'

Henry stirred and planted kisses on her cheeks. 'My dear sweet Emily, I'm afraid I could never afford it. This place is five bucks a night.'

She threw a pillow at him, and loved him even more.

9

Chicago, October 1923

Annie sat in stunned silence, face pale, hands shaking.

'I don't understand, Emily. Why wouldn't you tell me you were getting married? I'm your sister!' The ruby roses Emily had brought as a peace offering hung their heads in shame. Annie was deeply hurt, and even more upset than Emily had anticipated. 'And why the sudden rush to move to Kansas? You and Henry have the whole world at your feet here.'

'We don't want the whole world, Annie. We just want our own piece of it.'

'But you've both got good prospects here. *Real* prospects, not those of a silly pipe dream. Do you have any idea what you're getting yourself into? How hard it will be?'

Emily tried to stay calm, despite Annie's heightened emotions. 'This isn't a silly pipe dream, Annie. It's more real to me than anything I've ever done.'

Annie laughed bitterly. 'It's an illusion, Emily. You're blinded by love and the false promises of prosperity made by fraudulent businessmen. "Come to the Great Plains where all your dreams will come true."' She threw her hands in the air. 'Dreams aren't always about rainbows and happy endings. They can be dark and dangerous. They can lead you astray, tempt you down the wrong road.'

'What do you mean?'

Annie huffed out an exasperated breath. 'It doesn't matter. John will give Henry a position in his business if it's more money you need. You'll want for nothing and never have to work again.'

'But I want to work, Annie. We both do. Thanks to John's investment advice, Henry has enough saved in the bank to buy a plot of land and some machinery to start us off.'

'This is all Henry's doing, isn't it. He has you completely under his spell.'

'There's no spell, Annie. No trickery or influence. I love him. I love him with all my heart, and want to build a life with him. Henry has plans and ambitions and money, yes. But this is my dream too, Annie. You know how bored and restless I've been here, how I've felt there was some bigger adventure calling me.'

'Yes, and I remember a time when I was part of that adventure. You and me against the world. What happened to that?'

'You married John Gale. That's what happened. You're the one who changed everything, Annie, not me.'

Emily's words cut through the tension in the room. For a moment, neither of them spoke.

'Yes, Emily. I did marry John. And you married Henry, although forgive me if I don't remember your anniversary.' Her words were raw, her tone cutting.

It was difficult to see Annie so emotional – hysterical almost. It wasn't like her.

'Kansas isn't so far away,' Emily offered, reaching for something positive. 'Not even a day on the railroad. You can visit whenever you like. I'll make peach cobbler.'

'Emily Kelly, a homesteader! Listen at you, playing house like a romantic fool. Anyway, it isn't that simple.'

'Why not?'

Annie's eyes filled with tears. 'It just isn't.' She threw her hands in the air. 'It's all totally impractical, Emily. You don't know the first thing about farming. What if the crops fail, or a prairie fire rips through, or a tornado tears your home apart? What if it all goes wrong? What if you hate it?'

'But what if it all goes right, Annie? What if I love it? What if this is what I was meant to be doing all along?'

'Now you're just being obstinate.' Annie loosened the button at the neck of her blouse. 'You've never even been to the prairie, let alone Kansas. How can you go rushing off to live somewhere you've never even seen?'

'Isn't that exactly what Mammy and Daddy did when they left Ireland? They took a leap, Annie. Took a chance. What if? Where next? Remember?' She looked at the table set so perfectly for the Temperance League luncheon Annie was hosting that afternoon. 'Life can't always be carefully considered and meticulously planned.' She couldn't hide her excitement as she grabbed Annie's hands. 'This is the adventure I've always wanted, Annie. I want to build something from nothing. Do something real. And with Henry beside me, we can do anything. I know we can.' She took a long breath. 'Do you remember the stories you used to make up when we were little? Your *Wonderful Adventures*.' Annie's made-up tales of magical lands and mythical creatures had seen them through fevers and thunderstorms, tiresome train journeys and long summer days. 'I could almost touch those imaginary places; feel everything you described as if I was there. It's the same when I think about Kansas. I feel like I already know it. Like I've known it all my life. I wish you could be excited for us.'

'And I wish you'd never met Henry Gale! I wish I'd never introduced you to him.'

Emily stood up. 'That's a terrible thing to say. You don't mean it.'

'I *do* mean it! Every word.' Annie's face hardened. Emily had never seen her so furious. She crossed her arms and stared at Emily defiantly. 'When will you leave?'

'Henry wants to go as soon as possible, to look for the perfect plot of land and start to build our home.' She reached for her sister's hands, trying one last time to find the smallest seed of understanding. 'Remember what you said to me, what you told me to do when I found my true love?'

'To hold onto him.'

Emily nodded. 'I found him, Annie. I'm going to hold on to him.'

Annie stood up and walked to the window with a heavy sigh. 'You really mean it, don't you.'

Emily nodded.

'And there's nothing I can do to change your mind?'

'Nothing.'

Annie took a deep breath and turned to face Emily. 'Not even if I told you I am pregnant?'

*

The news of Annie's pregnancy hit Emily hard. She was happy for Annie, but she was also afraid that it threatened to interrupt her and Henry's plans when everything had been so perfect.

She was unusually quiet when Henry met her after work the next evening.

'Em? What is it? Not having second thoughts, are you?'

'No. Not at all. It's just . . . Annie's expecting.'

'But that's great news. Isn't it?'

'It is, I guess. But she's not herself, Henry. She seems really upset about it. Frightened, even. She keeps talking about Mammy losing baby Joseph, and women who die in childbirth.'

A look of realisation crossed Henry's face. 'She wants you to stay, doesn't she? Until the baby comes.'

Emily nodded. 'She practically begged.'

He let out a long breath. 'Then you should stay. I can go ahead to Kansas. Find the perfect plot of land and build you a home.'

Emily's heart sank. She felt pulled in two directions – duty to Annie one way, devotion to Henry the other. 'But we planned to build our home together, Henry. Start our new life together.'

'And we will, when you follow on. What difference will a few months make when we are planning a whole lifetime together?' He offered a sorry smile as he brushed an eyelash from her cheek. 'You'll only regret it if you don't stay. She's your sister, Emily. Family's family, after all.'

She knew it made sense. She wasn't afraid of hard work, or getting her hands dirty, but what did she know of building a timber home? Annie's baby was due in the spring. It wasn't long, but it felt wrong to be apart from Henry when their plans had been made together.

He pulled her into his arms. 'In the end, when we're old and grey and sitting on the porch watching the sunset, I doubt we'll even remember the first few months. If you leave Annie when she needs you the most, she might never forgive you – or you yourself.'

Emily snuggled into the crook of his arm. 'I can't wait to grow old and grey with you.'

'Then stay with Annie. Meet our niece or nephew. Kansas will wait for you.'

'And you? Will you wait for me?'

He kissed the top of her head. 'I've been waiting for you my whole life.'

*

Henry left in early December, before the first heavy snowfalls.

Emily moved in with Annie and John, packing up her few belongings once more. Staying in her sister's guest bedroom was far from the start to married life she'd imagined, but as Henry had said before he'd departed, 'A few nights apart in exchange for a lifetime together? I'd say that's a pretty good deal!'

The thought of the years stretching ahead of them sustained her as she lay in bed, imagining the prairie wind whistling beyond the window and the bright song of her fiddle and bow filling their new home with music. She pictured them bringing in the harvest, their grain a river of gold as it slipped through her fingers.

She felt the first breaths of a new life bloom within her just as surely as a new life bloomed within Annie.

Precious beginnings.

Seeds of hope taking root in the earth.

10

Chicago, January 1924

They marked off each day on a desk diary, like prisoners counting down their sentences: Emily waiting to be freed of her promise to Annie, Annie waiting to be freed of the physical demands of her pregnancy.

By the turn of the year, as winter held the city in its icy grip, the end was in sight. But as Emily left for work, rushing because she was late as usual, she slipped on a patch of black ice and fell awkwardly down the front steps. The pain was so sharp and intense it took her breath away. She felt dizzy and nauseous, her vision blurring as a heavily pregnant Annie appeared at the top of the steps, about to rush to Emily's assistance.

'No, Annie! Ice.' She managed to get the words out before a blackness descended and she passed out.

'Six weeks' rest,' was the doctor's prognosis when she came round on Annie's chaise. 'Ligament damage to your ankle. You need to keep your foot elevated as much as possible. Time and rest are what you need now. And salt for those steps. You're lucky it was you who took the tumble, and not your sister.'

Annie's face was as pale as Emily's. 'It doesn't bear thinking about, Doctor.'

Time dragged ever more slowly.

The following week, Henry wrote to say he'd secured the plot and was gathering timber for the house. Emily read his note to Annie. *'It's a real beauty, Em. Plenty of water from an underground spring, and fertile prairie as far as you can see. I'm helping out on a farm just outside Liberal, a town close to the Oklahoma state line. Beyond that, Texas and the settler towns of Dalhart and Amarillo. I'm being paid in lumber and have a good stack already to build our home when the weather improves. The snowstorms here are like nothing I've ever seen! I miss you. I hope all is going well with Annie.'* Emily's heart ached as much as her ankle. She longed to be with Henry. Every day that she wasn't left her feeling increasingly resentful toward Annie.

'It sounds like an awful lot of hard work,' Annie said.

Emily smiled. 'Henry will be in his element. It's what he's always wanted – hard physical work.'

'Yes, but it isn't what *you've* always wanted, is it?' Annie closed the book she was half reading. 'I'm sorry, but I still think you're making a huge mistake, Emily. You hate the cold. You'll be miserable in the winters.' Her face softened a little as she reached for Emily's hand. 'Write to Henry. Tell him you've changed your mind, before it's too late. He'll understand.'

'But I haven't changed my mind, Annie. As soon as your baby arrives, I'm going to Kansas.'

They'd reached a fork in the road, pulled in different directions. Emily wondered if they would ever travel the same path again.

A dull cramp in her stomach and a throbbing ache in her ankle sent her to bed early with a hot water bottle.

*

Emily woke just after midnight. Excruciating cramps in her stomach took her breath away as she felt a rush of warmth between her legs. She turned on the lamp and pulled back the bedsheets. Her cries brought Annie rushing to her.

It was all over by the time the doctor arrived.

There was nothing she could have done, he said. One of life's unfathomable mysteries. Nature's way. There would be others, he said.

'Did you know?' Annie asked as she sat with Emily.

Emily shook her head. 'Not for definite. I'd missed a couple of periods but thought I was just late. There were no other indications. Nothing at all.'

How could she not have known? Women talked about instinct and signs all the time. A feeling, a hunch, in tune with their bodies. She'd been oblivious. Now, she was numb.

The bedsheets were washed, the mattress scrubbed and turned, sweet tea administered for the shock. Within an hour, every physical trace of the child Emily hadn't known she was carrying had been erased. And yet it lingered in the aftershocks that came in deep waves as she curled her knees to her chest and held herself tight.

When she eventually slept, she dreamed of a little girl carried aloft on Henry's shoulders, both of them laughing as he walked through a field of corn bathed in gold.

She woke at first light and lay perfectly still. She felt lifeless. Colourless. Empty. She was the still air at the centre of a cyclone, destructive winds whirling around her. She was neither a mother nor childless, forever suspended in some twilight place.

Another month passed.

Emily's ankle healed, the cramps stopped, but the crack in her heart remained.

11

Chicago, February 1924

'Emily! It's happening.' Annie's face was ashen, washed of all colour by fear and the dim afternoon light as a storm raged outside.

Emily grabbed her hands. 'Are you sure?'

'My waters broke. The pains are coming every five minutes. I've been counting.' Her eyes were wide with panic.

Emily settled Annie in her bed before telephoning the doctor, but the lines were down. John was out of town on business and Marta was visiting her sick mother in Vermont and wasn't expected back for a few days.

'Is the doctor on his way?' Annie asked when Emily returned with towels.

'Yes. He'll be here as soon as he can,' Emily lied. She sat on Annie's bed and held her hand. 'Try to stay calm, Annie. We could be in for a long night.'

'Thank you for being here with me. I know it hasn't been easy to be away from Henry.'

But it was more than being away from Henry. It had been agony, these past weeks, to watch Annie in the full bloom of pregnancy. A cruel reminder of what might have been. Emily had tried not to blame Annie for her miscarriage, but the simple fact was that if she'd gone with Henry to Kansas as planned, she wouldn't have slipped on the ice and fallen. She could still be carrying their child.

Another contraction rendered Annie speechless.

Everything Emily remembered during her time as an American Red Cross volunteer kicked in as Annie laboured through the early evening and long into the night. As well as her basic training in routine tasks, Emily had helped with whatever was needed, and on several occasions that had meant assisting with a birth. But delivering a baby alone was an entirely different scenario.

Annie was exhausted and frightened. 'Where is the doctor, Em? He should surely be here by now?'

Emily assured her he was on the way and prayed for the baby to come quickly and easily as the wind echoed Annie's moans and she begged for chloroform to ease the pain. But Emily had nothing to help her, other than her reassurance and a hand for her to grip until her fingertips turned white.

Finally, Annie was ready to push, but despite her efforts, the child wouldn't come. Emily had seen this before. If the baby got into distress, it could be very dangerous.

'One last big effort, Annie. I know you're tired but I need you to bear down. Hard. One last strong push and your baby will be here.'

It was torture to see her sister in such pain, but Emily knew the baby had to come, now.

'That's it! I can see the head. Push now, Annie.'

Annie let out a great bellow as the infant began to emerge, but Emily could see what Annie couldn't. The child was blue, the cord wrapped around its neck.

87

'Stop, Annie! Don't push. Pant. Blow out the candles like I showed you.'

Annie exhaled in short puffs. 'What is it? What's wrong?'

Emily got to work, remembering the breach babies she'd seen delivered, and how to gently turn the infant to loosen the cord before the mother pushed again. She knew it was painful, but she also knew the danger the child was in. Annie screamed in pain as Emily inserted her hands and gripped the child as firmly as she dared, rotating it ninety degrees until the cord loosened.

'Now, Annie! Push again. Almost there.'

Annie roared one last time and it was done. The infant slipped onto the bedsheets in a rush of blood and fluid, and Emily got to work, clearing the airways and tying off the pulsing cord. She only relaxed when the child let out its first mewling cry.

'A girl,' Emily said, emotion choking her words. 'A beautiful little girl.'

A perfectly healthy baby girl. A little on the small side, but she would catch up. They always did.

All the noise and drama of the birth was replaced with an all-consuming hush as Emily cut the cord, wiped the infant down and swaddled her in a blanket. She'd always loved watching this moment, when the nurse placed the child in its mother's arms, but she delayed and lingered now, fussing with the swaddling longer than necessary as she carried the child to the window, to see her better.

She was as light as a feather, and yet the feel of her in Emily's arms, the almond-sweet scent of her, was so immense she had to sit down.

The child opened her eyes. They looked at each other, searching for something – someone – familiar.

'Hello,' she whispered. 'I'm your Auntie Em.'

'Is everything all right?' Annie asked.

'She's perfect.' Reluctantly, Emily walked to the bed and placed the child in Annie's arms. 'Congratulations, Annie. She's beautiful.'

The ache of letting go, the emptiness in her own arms, was unbearable.

Annie looked so peaceful as she gazed adoringly at the child. 'Hello, little one. *A leanbh. A hiníon.*'

Emily felt a pang of sorrow as Annie repeated the familiar Irish words of affection their mammy had spoken so often. My child. Daughter.

'I'm your mother,' Annie continued. 'I've been waiting to meet you for a very long time.'

'What will you call her?' Emily asked.

'Dorothy,' Annie said, without missing a beat. 'I'll call her Dorothy. Dot, for short.'

'It suits her. Why Dorothy? Is it a Gale family name?'

Annie smiled. 'It was her grandmother's name.'

Emily stepped from the room, taking a moment alone in the kitchen. She wished she could leave, wished she could open the door and run away to Kansas to be with Henry. She made coffee and toast and carried it back upstairs for Annie. But as she approached the bedroom, she paused on the landing, listening a moment at the door as Annie cooed to the child and spoke to her in a low whisper.

'You have my eyes, and your granny's nose, and I just know you have your father's brave heart and adventurous spirit. He would love you so much, little *Dorotea*. Maybe you'll meet him one day and he'll show you his tricks. Maybe we can be together after all.'

Emily froze. Her heart thumped in her chest. Her mind raced, chasing conversations and moments back through the previous weeks and months. *Oh, Annie. What have you done? Whatever have you done?*

She rattled the tea tray and stepped on a squeaky board, loudly announcing her presence before she breezed into the bedroom and put the tray on the nightstand beside Annie.

'Thought you might like a bit of something,' she said. She gently pulled back the blankets to admire Dorothy again. 'She looks like you, Annie. I don't see much of John in her, though. Perhaps she'll take after her father in other ways.'

Annie didn't take her eyes off Dorothy's for a moment as she brushed the infant's cheek lightly with the tip of her finger. 'Yes. She will. I'm sure she will.'

*

Emily kept herself busy over the following week, finding excuses to run errands, to get more diapers and other essentials, looking for any excuse to leave the house to escape from the infant's furious cries.

It was such an infuriating, plaintive sound.

So beautiful.

So heartbreaking.

Annie was an emotional see-saw. Full of love and joy one minute, inconsolably sobbing the next. Emily heard her during the night, crying while she tended to the baby. Marta said it was normal for new mothers to feel bewildered, and not to give it a moment's thought.

Emily made coffee, baked cookies, set the fire, changed the bed linen. Annie was so exhausted she hardly noticed Emily was there. When John returned to admire his daughter, he hardly noticed Emily either. But Emily observed and heard everything. Every kiss, every declaration of love, every perfect family moment. Annie was playing a dangerous game and Emily didn't want to be part of it any longer.

'I was thinking I would make my way to Kansas,' she said as she watched Annie struggle to change Dorothy's diaper. 'Join Henry.'

'So soon? I thought you would like to stay a while. Get to know Dorothy.'

'I would, of course, but now that John's back I thought you'd like some time together. As a family.'

Finally done with the diaper, Annie lifted Dorothy to her breast to feed her.

'I suppose I can't keep you here forever. Lock you up against your will!' She laughed, but there was nothing of humour in her voice or mannerisms.

'Are you sure? I must admit, I can't wait to see Henry.'

Annie nodded, but she wouldn't meet Emily's eyes. 'We'll muddle through. Marta will help until I replace her with someone younger and less prickly. I've heard of a young Irish woman looking for a position. John has agreed to interview her.'

She looked so sad and alone that Emily's resolve almost broke. 'I could stay a few more days, I guess.'

Annie shook her head. 'Absolutely not. I've delayed you long enough. You'll only resent me if you stay.' She reached into the drawer of the nightstand and pulled out a leatherbound journal. 'I got you a farewell gift. It's not much but I thought you might like to write it in, keep a record of your life on the prairie.'

Emily was touched. 'That's so kind, Annie. I will. Thank you.'

There was so much more Emily wanted to say, but she couldn't find the words.

Thankfully, Dorothy broke the silence with a sneeze that made them both smile.

'I don't want you to leave, Emily, but I know I can't make you stay, either. And so, we have reached a crossroads.'

'I have to follow my heart, Annie. I know I'm doing the right thing, even if it scares me a little.'

Finally, Annie looked at Emily. 'You're right. We must all follow our hearts, even when it scares us, because the most frightening thing of all is to not do the thing we are meant to.' Annie turned her gaze to Dorothy, asleep in her arms. 'And even the wrong thing can become the most perfect thing of all.'

That was when Emily noticed that Annie's precious hourglass had been returned to the dressing table, but rather than the measure of devotion it had once symbolised, it seemed to her now like a dangerous thing, harbouring a dark secret within its grains of sand.

*

She left quietly the next morning after John had gone to work and while Annie was still sleeping. Before she left, she lifted Dorothy from her crib and held her one last time, marvelling at her miniature fingers and toes, her perfect ears, her precious little face.

'Goodbye, Dorothy. We might not see each other very often, but I hope we will always be friends.' She placed a toy lion at the foot of her crib. 'And when I'm not here, this little lion will be your friend in my place.'

She tied a ruby-red ribbon to the crib, remembering the old Irish superstition of protecting newborn babies from being stolen by the fairies.

The house was still and quiet as she crept downstairs, like a breath drawn in and held.

She left a note for Annie, propped against a vase of spring flowers – daffodils and tulips in as many colours of the rainbow as she could find. She refused to give in to the murky shadows that seemed to tinge the edge of everything now. A new life was waiting for her. A life full of colour and opportunity. And nothing was going to spoil it.

As she boarded the train, she locked Annie's secret away, concealed it in the deepest part of her heart, where it would never, could never, be found, no matter how many miles from Chicago she travelled or how many years passed. Nobody could ever find out. Not John. Not Henry. Least of all, Dorothy.

The whistle blew. The locomotive lurched forward.
Finally, she was on her way.
To Henry.
To Kansas.
Home.

PART TWO

Kansas, 1924–1929

'True courage is in facing danger when you are afraid...'
 – L. Frank Baum, *The Wonderful Wizard of Oz*

Extract from *Wonderful – A Life on the Prairie* by Emily Gale

*I*felt so small and insignificant when I first saw the prairie, humbled by its vastness. I became a child again at my mother's knee, wide-eyed and innocent, with everything to learn. Mammy used to say that nothing could compare to the view of Lough Inagh on a bright autumn day; that no church in the land could make a person feel closer to God. As I watched my first sunset on the prairie, I felt the same way. This place is a religion all of its own, and my pilgrimage had been worthwhile.

Like the first seeds of wheat sown in the autumn, I dug myself into the earth, planted myself here and resolved to flourish and grow. And I did, for a while. We all did.

You might not believe there was such vibrant beauty here once, that the desolate desert of dust you see now once danced in all the colours of the rainbow and hummed to the sound of prosperity and ambition, but that is the Kansas I remember – a *place of dreamers and dreams, a life built by women and men who harvested hope with every turn of the plough. That's the story I want to tell – of the dreamers and their dreams.*

We didn't know we were destroying the land we loved; that we would soon be harvesting our despair . . .

12

Colour welcomed her to Kansas; a symphony of cheerful reds, lush yellows and mellow oranges, vivid emeralds and softer greens, shades of blue, indigo and violet. Everything was so vibrant, so rich and alive. It was more beautiful than Emily could ever have imagined.

She felt alert, awake to her surroundings in a way she'd never been before, as if she'd just woken from a dream. Every colour was brighter, every sound clearer, every flower more beautiful and fragrant. She gazed upon the shimmering mirage of emeralds and golds, and couldn't believe such a place existed, or that she would now call that place home.

'It's Heaven, Henry!'

'If you believe in such a thing.'

'A fairytale, then!'

She sat up in the seat of the Model T Ford that Henry had borrowed from a man he knew who owned the general store in Liberal. She wanted to drink in all that was new and exciting. In time, she would tell Henry what had happened in the months they'd been apart, but now was not for dwelling on things left behind. Now was for the giddy thrill of arrival.

'What's that over there?' she asked, pointing to a bird that resembled a cross between a grouse and a hen.

'That's a boomer.'

'A boomer!'

'A prairie chicken. Named for the noise it makes. Delicious. Tastes a little like beef. I prefer wild turkey though. And it's just coming into sage grouse season – you'll hear their funny popping noise – and wait until you see their courtship dance! And those jackrabbits there, see, by the roadside? Tasty as heck in a stew, cooked slow.'

'Is everything here a meal?'

'Pretty much! Except the wolves and the coyotes. *We* are their meal.'

'Henry! Don't joke.' Her eyes searched his, a smile on her lips, laughter in her cheeks. She felt so light and free after the heavy burden of responsibility she'd carried in Chicago. Here, she felt buoyed by Henry's infectious enthusiasm, his delight at seeing her again, his carefree obliviousness to all that had happened while they'd been apart. 'I missed you,' she said.

'I missed you, too. Couldn't sleep for thinking about you, and now here you are, looking like a dream.'

She'd made a last-minute decision to swap the practical beige two-piece outfit she'd picked out the night before for a soft rose-coloured sweater dress and her favourite ruby-red Mary Janes. A burst of colour and confidence to begin her new life.

'Although it might not be the best outfit for hauling water and skinning rabbits,' Henry teased. 'We need to get you some proper clothes, Mrs Gale! Get my farm girl some dungarees and some chewing tabacca!'

Their laughter filled the air as the Model T bumped over potholes and juddered over cattle guards. Emily asked question after question, like an inquisitive child eager to learn, as Henry gave her the names for the native flora she didn't know: green buffalo grass and blue grass, the blue-grey sagebrush, purple verbena and the delicate prairie violet, fields speckled with yellow tickseed, groundsel and cinquefoil. He spoke fondly of the folk he'd met and the friends he'd made. He told her about the jobs he'd completed and those yet to tackle. He asked about their niece. Emily kept the details brief.

'Annie still think we're making a terrible mistake?'

'Of course.'

'And you?'

Emily turned in her seat. 'Pull over, Henry.'

'What? Why? Are you serious?'

'Pull over.'

He pulled the car to a stop and looked at her, his face unusually serious. 'Emily, what is it?'

'I want you to promise me that you will never ask me that again. I don't care what Annie thinks. I know what *I* think. I know that you are the best thing that ever happened to me, Henry Gale, and that we are going to build a wonderful life here. Together.'

His concern made way for a grin. 'I promise never to ask again. I'm sorry.'

'And now you can kiss me.'

He leaned toward her and took her face in his hands. 'Oh, that I can do easily. That I can definitely do for the rest of my life.'

They were entirely alone, watched only by the birds that darted among the crops and the 'hoppers that chirped in the long grass. They clambered into the back seat, laughing like high school lovers as they searched for each other with passion and urgency and the prairie wind danced in gentle waves against Emily's skin.

*

The motorcar rumbled on for mile after mile, the wheels turning steadily as they passed lush, fertile land, flat and unending, like a thousand starched bedsheets laid end to end.

'Folk say there is more of nothing here than something,' Henry said.

'I can see why,' Emily said. 'It's so flat. So endless.'

It really was. The view just kept going until the land met the sky some unfathomable distance away. Emily turned her head this way and that as she took in the vastness of the landscape, and the promise of a new beginning that had prickled at the back of her neck all the way from Chicago became a stronger, more visceral sensation. She willed the wheels to turn faster as her pulse quickened in anticipation of her first sighting of the home Henry had built for them.

He reached for her hand. 'I hope you like the place.'

She pulled his hand to her lips and smothered it with kisses. 'I'll love it. I'd live in a woodshed, as long as you were there with me.'

He laughed. 'Let's hope it doesn't come to that.'

Eventually, she saw it. A sloped roof in the distance. A chimney. A white picket fence. A pretty timber house surrounded by a swaying ocean of winter wheat.

Henry turned through a gateway, drove along a rutted track marked out by fence posts, and pulled the motorcar to a stop.

'Last stop, miss. Gale Farm. The end of the line.'

She placed a hand to her chest as she took in the pretty timber home, the steps up to the porch, the swing seat, the flower boxes at the windows.

'Oh, Henry! It's beautiful.'

She stepped from the motorcar and placed one foot on the ground, then the other, swivelling the toes of her ruby shoes back and forth as if to root herself into the earth beneath.

Their earth.

She felt for the piece of Connemara marble in her pocket,

remembering how her Granny Mary had pressed it into her hands the morning she'd left Ireland. *'A piece of home for when you're far away. Keep it safe, a grá, and it will keep you safe in return.'* She tipped her head back and took a long deep breath, filling her lungs with the sweet meadow-scented air. No hint of motor fumes or suffocating smoke spewing from factory chimneys. This air was pure and clean. She felt restored by it.

Henry joined her, his arm around her waist as they admired their new home together.

'It's perfect,' she said as her eyes searched his, a smile on her lips.

Months of working outdoors and hard physical labour had left their mark in the weathered tan on Henry's face and the new muscles in his arms. He seemed taller too, like the sunflowers the state was known for. He studied her face a moment before he scooped her into his arms, walked up the porch steps, shouldered open the screen door, and carried her over the threshold, just as he'd promised he would.

'Welcome home, Mrs Gale. There's no place like it.'

She laughed as he put her gently down.

She turned a full circle to take it all in, then walked from one side of the house to the other, opening doors and drawers, running her fingertips over the table and bedspread, lifting things up and putting them down again. There was a good-sized kitchen, a laundry room and larder, a living room with a fireplace and rocking chairs either side of the chimney breast, a bedroom with an iron bedstead and a primrose-yellow bedspread. He'd thought of everything. There was even a bowl of apples on the table.

Apples.

She smiled to herself.

'Where ever did you find everything?' she asked, a bemused smile on her face. 'I didn't have you down as a homemaker!'

'Mrs Miller at the general store helped with the finishing

touches. She said I couldn't possibly let you arrive to an unmade bed. You'll meet her soon. She and Hank have been a great help.'

'Where's the washroom?' she asked, realising she hadn't seen a bathtub or a toilet.

Henry laughed. 'We've a copper bath, and an outhouse. We're prairie folk now, Em. Back to basics.'

Of course. It was going to take some getting used to.

'And there's one more room. The most important room in the house.' He lifted a rug to reveal a hatch, which he pulled open. A ladder led down into a dark space beneath. 'The cyclone cellar. This is where we'll shelter when a tornado comes through. And it will. Sure as eggs is eggs.'

Emily nodded. 'I know.'

Henry had told her what to expect. He hadn't shied away from the threat from tornadoes and snakes and scorpions, the wolves and coyotes, the hard work, the unpredictability.

'Go ahead,' he said. 'Take a look.'

She climbed down the ladder into the dark space. It was just high enough to stand upright, and wide enough for a couple of people to hunker down. She couldn't imagine being cooped up down there while a storm raged above.

Henry peered through the hatch. 'So, what did I miss in Chicago, apart from baby Dorothy arriving in the middle of a storm?'

Emily stalled. She was so happy. Too happy to bring any sadness to this hopeful new world.

'Oh, not much. Annie being overly dramatic. John being full of himself. The wind biting chunks out of your skin. The usual.'

Henry laughed. 'Seems like I had a lucky escape!'

Emily pushed aside the ache of her loss and the nagging dread of Annie's secret. She would hide those dark thoughts in the cyclone cellar where Henry would never find them.

'You used extra strong nails, right?' she said as she climbed back up. 'Good timber?'

'The best and strongest.'

She walked to the window then and looked outside. Behind the house, a short distance along a dirt path, was a well, and a windmill that brought the water up from the old riverbed below. She'd lived close to water most of her life, so it felt strange to be so far away from any lake or ocean. There was nothing but land and sky as far as she could see. Not one other home. Not one other soul. They were entirely alone, with only each other and endless acres of fertile prairie for company.

'It's like we're the last people on earth, Henry.'

He placed his hand on the small of her back as he joined her at the window. 'It'll take a bit of getting used to after the city, but I already feel at home here. You will too, in time.'

But he'd misunderstood. The sense of isolation was unfamiliar and daunting, but it was thrilling. It made her feel alive. 'I already feel at home,' she whispered. 'I already know this is where I was meant to be.' She turned to him. 'It really is perfect, Henry.'

He smiled as he kissed her nose. 'It isn't perfect yet, but it's a start. And it's all ours. Every last inch.'

Emily heard the echo of her mother's words. It was her only regret – that her mammy would never see this perfect place Henry had built for them, would never know that every word she'd read in the pamphlet was true. Emily closed her eyes and made a silent promise to honour her mother's dream of coming here, to stitch her parents' memory into the samplers she would embroider and hang on the walls of this sweet little prairie home.

'There's something I'd like to do, Henry,' she said. 'A tradition, to bless this place and bring us good luck.'

She fetched her father's fiddle from the car and brought it inside. She closed her eyes and played the songs from the old land, songs of remembrance and longing, a piece of her past to root her to the present as she felt the warm embrace of her family surround her once again.

Emily lay awake that night, listening to the silence, her eyes searching the dark unfamiliar corners of her new home, settling herself within its impenetrable blackness, making peace with the howls of coyotes and buffalo wolves in the distance.

Too alert and excited to sleep, her mind wandered the vast landscape beyond their front door, so full of promise of the life they could make here. She made a pact with the prairie that night: They would treat it well, if it would be generous in return.

Eventually, her body pressed against Henry's, she slept.

She was safe and loved here.

She was home.

13

Over the first few weeks on the prairie, Emily felt the distance between Kansas and Chicago expand, her former life blurring and fading as new chores and responsibilities, and her love for Henry, absorbed her energy and thoughts. She felt the distance grow between her and Annie, too. She'd telephoned from the store to let Annie know she had arrived safely, and to ask how baby Dorothy was doing, but the conversation was strained, interrupted by a crossed line and eventually cut short by Dorothy's furious hungry howls in the background. 'I'm sorry, Em. It isn't a good time.' Frustrated by Annie's lack of interest, Emily had written a long letter to Nell instead, telling her all about her new prairie home.

Dearest Nell,
I wanted to let you know that Annie had a lovely little girl – Dorothy. She is the image of her, and they are both doing well. And I am now (at last) with my dear Henry in Kansas. I wish you could meet him. You would love him

so. Promise you'll visit soon. It has been too long since I last saw you.

Henry has built us the most perfect little home and our land stretches for miles. How we will ever turn it all to wheat and corn I don't know, but I am excited by the prospect, if more than a little terrified.

Please send words of encouragement and advice. How long was it before you felt settled, or that you had any idea what you were doing? Everything is so different here. So new and strange. It feels like learning to write with my other hand . . .

There was much to learn, but Henry was a patient teacher and Emily was an eager pupil. During the day she worked hard at the many physical tasks: feeding the animals and cleaning out the barn, collecting eggs, sweeping the floors, cooking meals, fetching water, cleaning and oiling saddles and tools, and anything else that was needed. At night, she swapped her beloved novels of Woolf, Wharton, and Fitzgerald for titles like *Soil Culture Manual, How to Get Rich on the Plains,* and *Yearbook of Agriculture,* which she borrowed from the town library. She remembered Nell's early letters from California, and how she'd talked about there always being so much to do on the ranch that she often fell into bed at night with her boots still on, she was so exhausted. She'd presumed her sister was being dramatic – she'd always been considered too pretty to get her hands dirty – but Emily understood that physical exhaustion now, understood Nell's life now. She had more in common with Nell than Annie, and often found her thoughts and letters travelling in the direction of California, rather than Chicago.

'You'll make a great farmer's wife,' Henry said as he found her poring over pages on crop management and irrigation and cotton weevils.

'I'll make a great *farmer*,' she corrected. 'I'm not here to just bake pies and darn your socks, Henry Gale!'

'I wouldn't dare to suggest it!'

'I'm serious, Henry. I want to learn everything. Do my share of farm work. Ride the tractor and turn the plough.'

Henry crossed the room and kissed her cheek. 'I know how much you want to make this work, Em. Truth is, I only married you for your stubborn determination and the way you scowl when you don't get your own way. How could a man resist?'

She laughed and tossed the book at him.

'But the first thing to learn is what's safe around here, and what isn't,' Henry continued, becoming serious. 'It's no use knowing how to plough a hundred acres if you get yourself bitten by a rattler.'

Emily listened carefully as Henry taught her how to identify the rattlers and copperheads, cottonmouths and scorpions, black widow and brown recluse spiders. It felt as if everything on the prairie wanted to kill her or hurt her.

'Is there anything *not* venomous or deadly?' she asked.

'Plenty! Prairie dogs and antelope, and wild mustang thundering by. The prairie is like any living thing, Em. If you respect it and treat it well, it will be good to you in return. I believe that with every fibre of my being.'

She believed it, too. Her mother had instilled a deep love of nature in all her children. Emily could feel her at her shoulder, guiding and encouraging her, urging her on.

As if the prairie had listened to their conversation, it delivered a gift that evening – a pair of antelope, grazing just beyond the picket fence as dusk fell. Emily and Henry watched from the porch.

'They're a symbol of new beginnings,' Henry whispered. 'A sign to trust your instincts.'

Only when a distant howl pierced the silence did the animals twitch and startle before bounding away into the long grass.

Emily was determined to harness her instincts, to learn what was safe and what was a threat. She would make a success of things, prove that she was as capable as any fourth-generation farm woman, like Laurie Miller at the general store who seemed to know everyone in Liberal, and everyone who'd come before. And although she would never admit it to Henry, Emily was also determined to prove to Annie that she had been wrong to doubt them. That, perhaps, was her greatest motivation of all. The words, 'I'll show you, Annie Gale,' were always on the edge of her lips as she struggled through some other, unfamiliar task.

New farmers and homesteaders were a source of great interest among the Liberal locals, and Henry, with his machines, caused more interest than most. He'd bought the best he could afford with his savings – an International 22-36 tractor, a Case combine, a twelve-foot Grand Detour one-way plough – and invited the other farmers to take a look and have a go. They were all astonished by the speed and efficiency with which the machines could do the hard, physically demanding work.

'It's a technological miracle. In three hours, I can plant and harvest an acre,' Henry explained. 'A job that would take several men, a race of horses, and three days to complete. And the combine cuts *and* threshes in one pass!'

But not everyone was impressed. The older farmers eyed the new machines with suspicion. For those like Ike West, an old-timer who'd always worked the prairie by hand, the new farming techniques raised eyebrows and suspicion. Ike lurked at the barn door, reluctant to even step inside.

'Prairie ain't s'posed to be farmed this way,' he said as Henry showed the men the steel blades that would slice through the ancient prairie and buffalo grass. 'Tear up all the grass and y'all got nothin' holding down the earth.'

Those who'd worked the old cowboy ranches echoed Ike's

concerns. Others, like Hank Miller, shared Henry's belief that there was great prosperity in the new ploughs and combustion machinery.

'We have to move with the times, Ike. Take advantage of progress. If you don't, someone else will. Our hesitation will only become some Last Chancer's gain.'

But Ike wouldn't budge. 'Prairie ain't s'posed to be farmed this way,' he repeated. 'Gives me a bad feelin'.'

'Be careful not to offend the men, Henry,' Emily cautioned when they'd all gone. 'Ike West was here long before us. Maybe you should listen to his concerns.'

Henry disagreed. 'Old-timers like Ike West are stuck in their ways. He'll come around, in time. He's afraid of change, is all. Afraid of doing things differently. And besides, I'm not inclined to listen to him, of all people. The West family aren't well liked. Ike's nieces are meddlesome busybodies. Wilhelmina West, especially. That woman causes nothing but trouble.'

'I'll be sure to keep away from her, then.'

'Glad to hear it!' Henry helped Emily as she climbed up into the seat of the tractor. 'We're sitting on a gold mine, Em. Wheat might not be selling at wartime prices of two dollars a bushel, but with the amount we can sow and harvest with these machines, we'll soon be burning dollar bills for fuel!'

His exuberance was infectious, his confidence a fever that burned like a prairie fire in his eyes.

Emily ran her hands over the tractor's steering wheel. 'You'd better show me how to work this thing then.' She insisted on learning how to operate the farm machinery, just as she'd insisted on learning how to drive the motorcar.

'It's powerful,' Henry cautioned. 'Different from being behind the wheel of the Model T.'

'Just show me, will you? I'm not made of fairy dust!'

It took a while to get used to. She made a disastrous first

attempt at ploughing a straight furrow, but within a couple of days she'd mastered it.

'What's next?' she said as she jumped down from the combine and brushed dust and dirt from her hands.

Henry shook his head and smiled. 'You're some woman, Emily Gale. You'll make a wonderful mother for our daughters to look up to someday.'

Emily stiffened, the sudden talk of children catching her by surprise. She laughed to conceal her disquiet.

'Mother! Daughters! Where did that come from?'

He reached for her hands. 'I've been thinking. Wondering if I'll be a good father and imagining how nice it'll be to have little ones running about the place one day. Two of each. Plenty of extra hands to help out on the farm when they're old enough.'

The memory of Emily's loss surfaced as the guilt of keeping the truth from Henry sat like a boulder in her stomach. She hadn't told him about her lost pregnancy because she'd wanted to preserve the happy optimism of their new start, but as the days had settled into weeks, she hadn't found the right time, or words. Now, it seemed impossible to tell him.

She laughed lightly to hide her discomfort. 'Well, if we are to be blessed with children, I hope they might give us a little time to get settled first. See out our first harvest without anyone else to worry about. There's no hurry. Is there?'

Henry wrapped her in his arms. 'I suppose not. I just want to make the most of our life together, Em. Not waste a single second.'

'Then let's enjoy every moment without thinking too far ahead. Life happens how and when it is meant to, not how and when we want it to. Nature will do its thing.'

'Just like the land.'

She offered a smile. 'Exactly. We have to trust it. All of it. Follow our instincts.'

That afternoon, as she drove into town, she thought again of the truth she'd kept from Henry, and the note she'd left behind in Chicago the morning she'd slipped away.

Dearest Annie,
I'll be on my way to Kansas by the time you read this. You looked so peaceful that I didn't want to wake you.
I know you think I'm making a mistake, but I know where my heart lies and I have to follow its pull. Henry is my future – my north star – and although it doesn't make sense and I can't fully explain it, I know that Kansas is where I belong.
I'll think of you and Dorothy often and hope you can visit when we are settled.
Don't be a stranger, Annie. My home is your home. Always. If you ever need me, you can find me at Gale Farm, Liberal, Kansas. My door, and my heart, will always be open to you.
Tabhair aire duit féin, a chroí.
Emily xx

As the Model T juddered over the uneven road to Liberal, Emily wished she could confide in Henry, to share the heavy burden of Annie's secret. Like the weeds that grew in her vegetable garden, secrets thrived if ignored, wrapping themselves around everything within reach. They had to be pulled up by the root, before they took hold. John was Henry's cousin, after all, even if Henry didn't especially care for the man. But Annie was her sister, and she hated the thought of betraying her.

She drove on, weighing the pros and cons like sacks of grain on the scales.

If she shared Annie's secret with Henry, perhaps she would feel absolved from keeping a greater truth from him. Of course, if

John ever found out that another man was Dorothy's father, the consequences would be awful. But if Henry discovered there'd been a child that Emily hadn't told him about, it would break his heart. And if there was one person Emily couldn't bear to hurt, it was Henry.

Annie's infidelity was the easier secret to share.

14

While the farmers were curious about Henry's machinery, their wives were just as curious about Emily. Some eyed her warily as she went about her chores in town. Others were more welcoming.

'How you folks goin' up there?' Mrs Miller asked as Emily paid for a yard of fabric to make curtains. 'Finding your feet?'

Laurie Miller, the town's schoolmistress, and wife of the general store's owner, Hank, was well-known in Liberal, and well-liked. With her children raised and years of farming experience behind her, she was also well-respected. Emily was eager to make a good impression.

'We are starting to find our feet, thank you. There's a lot to learn, but we're a good team.'

'Well, that's more important than anything else. A decent bit of rain and some good summer sun and you'll be well on your way.' Mrs Miller wrapped the fabric and added a measure of ribbon trim, for good luck. 'Say, why don't you join us ladies Thursday night, for our supper and singing club.'

'That's very kind, but I'm not much of a singer.'

'None of us are, dear, but it gets us away from the men and their damned baseball.' Mrs Miller thought for a moment. 'Do you play the piano?'

'No, but I do play the fiddle.'

'Even better! We'll see you both at seven.'

'Both? Me *and* Henry?'

'Lord no! We don't want men passing their opinions when they're not wanted. It's the one time of the week we get rid of them! Just you and your fiddle. Nobody else.'

Emily thanked her again. 'We'll see you at seven.'

She was grateful for the invitation. The Millers were held in high regard in the town. To have Mrs Miller's support and friendship was worth ten times that of folk like Ike West casting aspersions and suspicions, and his spinster nieces who looked down their noses at everyone. Emily knew the assumptions they'd made about her – a pretty young thing blown in from the city, hands like porcelain that had never seen a hard day's work, come to play farm with her husband.

Henry had told her about the suitcase farmers, trying to hit a crop, and how the real farmers hated the way they breezed in from the city, rented a tractor and a plot of ground, ploughed it up and planted winter wheat before heading back to their comfortable city lives, returning only at harvest time to reap their rewards. Emily was desperate to show those awful West sisters, and others in the community, that she and Henry were serious. She wanted to be accepted here. She wanted, more than anything, to belong.

*

That Thursday evening, while the men debated Babe Ruth's latest performance in the World Series and the merits, or otherwise, of internal combustion machinery, the wives gathered for their weekly supper and singing club, where everyone shared food and complained about their men, and singing was very much an afterthought.

The women were a friendly group, but while Emily appreciated the invitation, she felt like an outsider, conscious that she didn't have much to contribute when it came to trusted family recipes or knowledge passed down from generations of prairie folk. Nor when it came to complaining about Henry.

'Newlyweds never complain,' Laurie said. 'Give it time, honey! You'll soon be fending him off when he comes at you looking for an early-morning ride!'

The other women howled with laughter.

'Not much to be done about it when they're full of corn whiskey, mind,' May Lucas added. 'Fallin' on you like a lead weight, huffin' and puffin'. It's the only time I'm glad to hear him snoring. Means it's all over.'

The women laughed again.

Emily felt the flush of colour in her cheeks. This wasn't the conversation she'd expected.

'Don't mind us, Emily,' Laurie said as she placed a reassuring hand on Emily's arm. 'We're only having a bit of fun. Lord knows, if we didn't laugh, we'd cry. You enjoy your Henry while you can. He's a fine thing. He'll have you in the family way soon enough, no doubt.'

'Oh, we're not in any rush.'

'Nobody ever is, dear.'

Emily politely nodded and smiled as the others shared stories of the latest clever or silly thing their children had done, but she found the conversation a little tiring. What she really wanted to talk about was her vegetable garden, the best time to sow and harvest beets and onions and cabbages, how to pluck a chicken, how to cook a rabbit. She had so many questions, but she would have to bide her time, gain their trust.

Glad of a break in the conversation while pies were sliced and iced tea was poured, Emily drifted toward a younger woman, around her age. Ingrid Anderssen, and her husband Eric, were Dutch immigrants who'd settled on their claim a year ago, 'lungers' who'd travelled west in search of clean air for their young son, Pieter.

'Pieter was born with a hole in his heart,' Ingrid explained. 'He struggled beneath the choking fumes in Manhattan. The doctor advised us to leave, for his health.'

Emily watched the child as he chased after Mrs Miller's dog. 'It seems to have worked. I'm exhausted just watching him!'

Ingrid called Pieter over and introduced him to Emily. He clung to his mother's skirts, as if he could sense Emily's awkwardness. She never knew what to say to children, and they never seemed to warm to her in return.

'You're a long way from Ireland,' Ingrid remarked as Pieter clambered onto her lap. 'Do you miss it?'

'I was only very small when we left. I feel it more than I remember it, if that makes sense. My parents always encouraged us to speak the language and learn the stories and songs. I miss those moments and memories. Before she died, my mother asked me to promise to keep Ireland alive, in my heart.'

'Your mother was wise,' Ingrid said. 'We must never forget our first home. Even when we leave to go in search of another, we must never forget the places that have shaped us.' She helped Pieter eat his slice of pie. 'I hope Pieter will learn about our home in the Netherlands. That he will learn our stories and sing our songs.'

Emily detected a trace of sadness in Ingrid's eyes. She recognised that faraway look, the shared experience of every immigrant, half of their heart in the place they now called home, half in the place they had left behind.

'I'm sure he will,' Emily said. 'And he'll be very proud of his heritage.'

As the evening progressed, Emily began to feel more at ease among the women, relaxing into their friendship and conversation. She'd forgotten how much she missed female company – the shopgirls at Field's department store, and Annie and Nell. She was surprised at how open the farm women were around her, that her addition to their group didn't seem to inhibit their conversation at all. They gossiped and reminisced as if Emily had always shared their confidences.

'You heard Mary Myers finally got found out?' May said as the jug of iced tea was passed around. 'Turns out her sister cracked and told her husband about Mary's secret lover. And what did her husband do? Only spilled it to Myers's face when they got into an argument at Walker's pig sale. Myers nearly killed the man when he found him. Never tell a man anything, I say. No good ever comes of a secret shared. I barely even told my Zeb I was expectin' until I was pushin' those babies out.'

The others laughed, but May's words settled on Emily like a cautionary tale.

As the evening drew to a close, Laurie encouraged Emily to give them a burst of something on the fiddle. 'We'd like to hear you play, wouldn't we, ladies?'

The instrument was a familiar companion, nestled against Emily's shoulder. It still carried the scent of her father: turf smoke and tobacco, the oil he rubbed into the wood to keep it supple, the pine scent of the tablet of glassy orange rosin he used to treat the strings and bow. She recalled his gentle encouragement when she'd first learned how to play. 'Don't drag the bow across the strings. Dance it across. It should be a caress, Emmie. Like a feather brushing against your skin.'

She played an old favourite of her father's, a jig that soon had everyone tapping their feet. She was a little shy to play for the women, but she closed her eyes and let memory and instinct take over, the rhythm and notes of her past easily returning to her, and with it, her mother and father returned too, and Annie and Nell, and a wide-eyed little girl called Emily Kelly who'd sat at her father's knee, spellbound as the bow had danced across the strings while her mother sang.

'Who taught you to play?' Laurie asked, as Emily finished to a warm round of applause and encouragement to play another.

'My father. We moved around a lot when we first arrived in America. It was always the first thing he unpacked when we reached somewhere new. Said it was his last piece of Ireland. That, wherever he was, he felt at home with the fiddle in his hands.'

'Will you play another tune?' Ingrid asked as Laurie poured everyone a last glass of corn whiskey for the road. 'Pieter seems to be enjoying it.'

Emily picked up the fiddle and placed it to her chin. Almost as if the bow chose the melody for her, she found herself playing a lament, a mournful tune her mam used to sing whenever she was missing Ireland. *They say there's bread and work for all, and the sun shines always there, But I'll not forget old Ireland, were it twenty times as fair,'* and as the melody filled the air, she knew that she could never betray Annie. Whatever secrets she carried she would keep to herself. There was no need to tell Henry anything. 'Best left alone,' May had said. 'All marriages have their secrets. It's when folk start poking and prying at them that the trouble begins.'

*

The evening was still warm when Emily and Henry returned home, the sun low in the sky as they sat together on the porch swing seat. Emily stretched her legs over Henry's as he rubbed the aches from her feet. They were happy, busy, enchanted with each other and the life they were creating. She couldn't understand why the other wives grumbled about their marital duties. She loved being with Henry that way. Besides, marriage wasn't just about physical intimacy. Henry's unexpected little habits touched her heart: the wildflower he left on the windowsill for her every day, the wooden press he'd made so that she could keep the flowers to cheer her in the winter months. Marriage was a waltz, a rise and fall, and they were enjoying the harmony of the song they were dancing to.

Later, when Henry had turned in for the night, Emily picked up the journal Annie had given to her as a parting gift. She'd written in it most days. Sometimes a few quick lines. Sometimes whole pages poured out of her. The journal was quickly becoming part memoir and part confessional, a place to acknowledge her triumphs and joys, her failings and disappointments and fears. But there were some things she kept even from the pages of her journal, afraid to add permanency to them with ink and paper.

She turned to the front page and read the inscription Annie had written inside.

To my dear Emily,

Mammy used to say there is no place like your own home. I hope you will always be happy in yours.

She wondered how Annie was adjusting to life as a new mother, and how little Dorothy was doing. She wondered how Nell was managing with another child to add to her brood. Emily was aunt to six nieces and nephews now, but there was something special about Dorothy.

She wondered how long it would be until she saw her again, and if the child would remember her, or feel the connection she'd sensed as they'd looked at each other in the quiet morning light before Emily crept away.

Most of all, she wondered if Dorothy would carry the wonder of the circus in her heart? Would she feel drawn to the magic and mystery that had once enchanted her mother and led her to the man who had forever stolen her heart.

Extract from *Wonderful – A Life on the Prairie* by Emily Gale

Henry was drawn to the earth, to the rich soil that would nourish our crops, but it was the immense prairie skies that captured my heart. Chicago skies had always made me feel dizzy, the rushing clouds giving the illusion that the skyscrapers swayed. Here, the first thing I did each morning was step outside and look up.

Magic!

Who needs a city art gallery when the sky paints such masterpieces!

No day was ever the same. No hour was ever the same. I watched the ever-shifting palette of colours and moods, of wild storms and flat calm, of sunrises and sunsets in such stunning colours it took my breath away. And when the sky darkened from inky blue to perfect black, and one twinkling star appeared after another until an ocean of stars danced above, there was no place on earth I would rather be . . .

15

Time turned to the reassuring tune of the prairie. The steady click of the windmill's sails, the squeak of the rusted iron weathervane on the barn roof, the satisfying flap and flutter of bedsheets drying on the line, the creak of the hand pump as Emily drew water for cooking and washing and bathing. She enjoyed the physical challenge. She didn't mind the ache in her muscles when she fell into bed at night, glad to feel the effort of another hard day's work. It was a different tiredness from that she'd felt after a day on her feet at Field's. That had been a nagging weariness. This was satisfying exhaustion. She was beginning to understand the prairie, beginning to fit in and to belong.

The air smelled ever sweeter as the late-spring meadows put on their Sunday best and the first crops of wheat and corn began to grow. Henry tended the green shoots like a proud father. Emily was equally in thrall, measuring the height of the stalks each week and recording their growth on a chart. She lovingly cared for the vegetable patch she'd planted beside the house and was surprised at how thrilled she was by the first green shoots of onions and beets, salad greens and potatoes. They planted an orchard of cherry, plum, peach, and apple trees, following government advice to farmers to add trees on their claims as they would return moisture to the air through evaporation.

'In three to five years we'll have our first crop of fruit,' Henry said as he pressed the freshly dug soil around the base of the young trees.

'Five years! I wish everything didn't take so long.'

Henry laughed at Emily's impatience. 'Farming is like marriage, Em. A long-term commitment. But imagine it – the best apple pie you ever tasted. Made with our very own apples.' He pulled her into his side. 'I wonder what we'll be doing five years from now. How much the farm will have grown in that time – and us. Maybe there'll be little hands to help pick these apples.' He looked at her with hope in his eyes. 'Nothing doing yet?'

Emily tensed a little, as she always did when he brought up the subject of children. 'Not yet.' She pictured a perfect coil of apple peel and heard the cries of delight around the old oak table. 'I wish Mam could see all this. She would have loved it so much.'

Henry placed an arm around her shoulder. 'You should write to Annie. Invite her to come and see what we've done with the place. Invite Nell, too. It's about time I met your big sister. Heck, invite everyone!'

He was so proud of what they'd achieved, eager to show it off to anyone who cared to come and look. But Kansas was so far from California, and while Chicago wasn't as long a journey, Emily made excuses on Annie's behalf, claiming it would be difficult to travel with a small baby.

'Maybe when we have everything more established,' she said. 'I want Annie to arrive to golden fields of wheat as far as she can see.'

'You want to prove that she was wrong to doubt us, you mean.'

Emily smiled, acknowledging the truth. Henry knew her too well. 'Perhaps.'

'Write to her, Em. Annie won't mind if things aren't perfect, and I know you're dying to see Dorothy again. I'd certainly like to meet my niece before she's all grown up and married!'

Emily did want to see Dorothy, but something made her hesitate. She was almost afraid to see Annie again: afraid to acknowledge the tension that had simmered between them, and what she knew Annie was hiding from John. As long as Annie was in Chicago, it wasn't Emily's problem. She could pull the curtain over it, pretend it wasn't real. If Annie visited, she would have to confront it.

She picked up her gardening tools and started to walk back to the barn. 'I'll invite Annie. In time. There's no rush.'

*

By the time the gentle promise of spring had given way to the wild-rose-perfumed air of June and the heavy heat of high summer that followed, Emily could hardly remember life before the prairie. She threw herself fully into her new life, taking pleasure from the hand-to-mouth simplicity of it all. Sunshine, rain, fertile land, seed. Her sun-kissed skin and weathered cheeks were evidence of her hard work in the fields, and the callouses on her fingers were well on their way. Laurie Miller admired them like a proud mother and said she would have the hands of a real farm woman by the fall. But it was inside, within the walls of their humble little home, that Emily found herself increasingly happy.

Henry had built them a good solid house, but Emily made it a home. She was surprised by how much she enjoyed the domestic aspects of prairie life, even though she enjoyed being with Henry in the fields. She could hear Annie laughing at the pride she took in lifting a perfect pie from the stove, the care she took choosing fabric and ribbon at the general store, her patience in hemming curtains for the windows and pasting a pretty paper to the kitchen walls. She'd chosen a pattern of wildflowers so that she could have flowers in the house all the year round.

Henry appreciated her hard work. He noticed the little touches she added and the care she took.

'You're a natural,' he said as he helped her to ladle jam into jars. 'You never told me you were a talented cook.'

'I didn't know I was.'

She'd learned the skills by osmosis, from years of watching her granny and mammy mend and darn, stitch and sew, cook and bake. She had a light touch with pastry, knowing that the trick was to work quickly and not to let her hands get the mix too warm or to overwork it. She instinctively knew how to crimp a pie, how to salt a ham, how to sterilise jars in the stove, how to make a pickling liquor for beets and onions, how to preserve lemons and how to check for the telltale crinkle of perfectly set jam. Soon the larder shelves were well-stocked for the winter. Her industriousness was an antidote to the challenges the colder months would bring. With tornado season having passed without any major event, it was the threat of winter snowstorms that loomed. The well-stocked larder offered assurance for the barren months ahead.

For now, the greatest threat came from prairie fires. It took nothing more than a spark from a lightning bolt to set the tinder-dry grass alight. Emily had seen how easily the land could burn and how quickly the flames raced across the prairie, fuelled by grasses and tumbleweed. Prairie folk like the Millers and Ike West still talked about the terrible fire that had ravaged the Wisconsin logging town of Peshtigo some fifty years back. Henry ploughed a firebreak around the house and Emily learned to use wet gunny sacks to beat back any small fires that jumped the break.

'They won't be much help for your scarecrows, though,' Henry teased. 'They won't stand a chance if a fire rips through.'

The scarecrows were a regular sight across the Great Plains, standing tall among the ripening crops. Emily had enjoyed stuffing Henry's old shirts with straw to make them. She'd given one plenty of extra stuffing and christened it John.

'Don't joke, Henry. The thought of fire terrifies me.'

'We need the fires, though. It's how the prairie keeps itself alive, dying and regenerating to become healthier and stronger. As long as we're prepared, we can have both: a healthy prairie and a farm that's protected.'

Henry was right, but Emily knew that it wasn't an equal relationship. Nature was far cleverer than them. It could easily outsmart them.

*

Every Thursday, Emily and Henry drove into Liberal and went their separate ways: Henry to the saloon to talk business with the farmers, Emily to the Supper and Not Much Singing Club, as she called it. The farm women were an odd group of unlikely friends, thrown together by fate and circumstance, but they complemented one another well. They prayed for one another at church, watched one another's kids, fixed one another's hair, swapped clothes and worries over jugs of peach tea and thick slices of cherry pie. Despite living many acres apart, they came together as a community in the same fond way Emily remembered among the Irish community in Chicago. These women reassured her when doubt crept in. They encouraged and inspired her, and entertained her. Like her, they struggled and succeeded as the months passed and the seasons turned along with the great spades of the farmers' ploughs. Like her, they worried and hoped in equal measure. The prairie women were a force when they came together. She imagined she would rely on them a lot over the months and years ahead.

Warm summer nights also meant whist drives and other card games and dances in town on Fridays and Saturdays. Festoons of electric lights illuminated the streets and bootleg hooch flowed as the band struck up a tune and the men and women shook off the working week, losing themselves to the intoxicating *whump* of the double bass and the exuberant trill of trumpets. Emily loved those sticky summer nights when she and Henry danced a prairie jitterbug beneath a ripe strawberry moon and the smell of the just-harvested winter wheat infused the air.

Prairie folk were thriving. They had money in the bank and enough wheat to feed the nation. Prices were holding steady at around a dollar a bushel, and the new machinery meant more acres could be quickly ploughed up, and more seed planted to bring even greater yields the following year. As Henry stepped on her feet they laughed and stumbled into other couples, and in those heady, carefree moments she forgot about the secrets she carried, and her heart was light and hopeful.

The issue of motherhood didn't preoccupy Emily as it did the other women in town, and Henry hadn't mentioned the subject for a while. They were both too busy to think about anything much apart from the crops and the animals, too exhausted most nights to even think about making love, the eager passion of their first weeks as newlyweds having settled into something more relaxed as they each grew in confidence and familiarity with each other's bodies.

Month after month she bled, meeting the familiar dull ache in her belly and the dark stain on her underwear with quiet relief. She wasn't ready to raise a child. Not here. Not yet. Perhaps ever. She scrubbed at the stains with lye soap against the washboard, the water turning muddy brown as Mother Earth reclaimed what was hers. If she couldn't start, or sustain, another life, or harness the primal urge to become a mother as so many other women seemed to, she would put her love and energy into Henry and the farm.

Life on the prairie was so all-consuming, so vast and immersive that, at times, Emily almost forgot that any other place existed beyond the Great Plains. News of the outside world reached

Liberal in the pages of the *Kansas City Star*, delivered to the general store once a week. Emily read the stories as if reading about another world: female aviators trying to break records the men had set, stocks and shares soaring, Al Capone's latest scandal, politics and government. She felt so removed from those people and events and was glad to have left it all behind.

Until a letter from Annie brought it all rushing back.

Dear Em,
I'm slowly feeling much more like myself. We will come to visit next month when the worst of the summer heat has passed. You won't believe how much Dorothy has grown!

Suddenly, Emily wasn't ready to see Annie at all.

She felt so fiercely protective of everything she and Henry had built, and while she desperately wanted Annie's support, she was also afraid of her response. Would it live up to Emily's descriptions? Would Annie think it all rather basic?

And there was something else.

Emily was afraid of how she would react to seeing Dorothy again. She'd tried to put the child out of her mind – had been too busy, frankly, to think about her often – but the memory of the infant in her arms, and the way the child had looked at her, had never left her. What if Dorothy reminded her of the child she'd lost, and had kept from Henry, and couldn't seem to give him again? And there was also the issue of Dorothy's appearance. What if she looked nothing like John? Would Henry remark on it? And how would she, or Annie, react if he did?

Annie and Dorothy's impending arrival felt like an approaching storm that threatened to upend the perfect little world she and Henry had built, and there was no cellar to shelter in this time.

This storm was one she would have to confront head-on.

16

The heat of the prairie summer was oppressive and relentless. By day, the land shimmered in the heat haze and the afternoons saw thunderheads roll in on huge cottonwool clouds. Emily watched the sky closely, her gaze constantly drawn to its soaring immensity and the ever-shifting story she was learning to read. She recognised the sundogs that foretold of rain, the thick flat clouds that carried a short heavy downpour, others that brought the early summer hailstorms and the hailstones as big as apples that flattened a crop in minutes, ruining a year's work in the time it took to scatter a single sack of seed. She learned how to track a thunderstorm, to check if it was moving away from them, or towards them.

When Henry put a thermometer in the ground, the mercury shot up the scale, reading well over a hundred regularly. Beads of perspiration bubbled up on Emily's skin as she completed her chores, the chirping songs of 'hoppers and frogs a constant background accompaniment as she took shelter on the porch and fanned her face with whatever she could find – a spatula, a newspaper, a phonograph grabbed from the old Victrola – while Henry studied his ledgers, tabulating his expenses and profits for that month. Yields were reaching record highs as more and more acres of good grain were harvested.

'Hank Miller was telling me the elevators in Dalhart are full,' he said as they sat together on the porch at sundown. 'Grain sitting in great towers waiting to be transported. We'll have enough to feed all of Europe again if they keep bringing more folk in to farm. Land developers are offering forty-year loans at 6 per cent interest. Almost anyone can afford the repayments of thirty-five dollars a month on a five-thousand-dollar loan.'

And almost anyone did, it seemed. Like many other towns across the Great Plains, Liberal was heaving as the railroads delivered carriage after carriage of folk eager to grab an opportunity to make money from the land. Prairie farming was producing a new breed of businessmen, and once-empty towns were now thriving communities.

'Laurie was telling me some woman out Haskell County way is boasting of profits reaching some seventy-five thousand dollars,' Emily said. 'Ida Watkins. Have you heard of her? The so-called Wheat Queen of Kansas.'

Henry shrugged. 'Wheat Queen! Silly headlines to sell their newspapers. What next? Prairie Princes. Kansas Kings.'

Emily smiled. 'Henry Gale, Wheat King of Kansas. It has a nice ring to it!' But beyond the joking, there was a more serious concern. 'You don't worry it's all happening too fast, do you?' she asked. 'That we're living in a wheat boom and setting up for a bust, like the California gold prospectors?'

Henry reached for her hand. 'Let's hope not. I reckon we're about at the peak of it now. There can hardly be anyone else left to come here.'

But there was.

The great influx continued all summer. Reports reached them

of millions more acres of ancient prairie grassland being torn up across New Mexico, and from the southern swathe of the Texas panhandle all the way to the unforgiving dugout-littered No Man's Land of Dalhart, on through Kansas and Colorado and up into Nebraska. Emily watched the men and their machines in the fields and remembered Ike West's words. *The prairie ain't s'posed to be farmed this way.*

For her part, Emily continued to educate herself with renewed fervour. She turned to *Campbell's Soil Culture Manual*, the much-revered Bible of dry farming. She read whatever she could find about the Comanche and other Native Americans who'd once inhabited this great land along with their buffalo. She learned about the reservations and allotments and the last buffalo hunt organised by Charlie Goodnight from his ranch in Palo Duro Canyon. She wept as she learned the terrible history of the Lakota people at the Battle of Wounded Knee. She felt that she shared something of their pain in Ireland's history of oppression, and felt a pang of guilt to be on these ancient native lands at all.

As she and Henry walked to the creek together that evening, Emily listened to the cry of the eagles and Cooper's hawks that wheeled above.

'Native Americans believe the great birds of prey represent the spirits of their ancestors,' she said as she looped her arm through Henry's. 'I like that idea.' She tipped her head back to look up. 'They're so magnificent, aren't they. They remind me of the buzzards and kestrels I used to hear in Ireland.'

They walked on, enjoying the golden light of early evening.

'I've been reading about the people who lived here before the white settlers,' Emily continued. 'Does it ever make you feel guilty to know we are on their land? I sometimes worry that we shouldn't be here. That the land doesn't want us here.'

'Crosses my mind now and then,' Henry said, 'but the government aren't going to return the land to them, no matter how folk feel about it. If we don't farm here, it'll only be farmed by some other white folk. Things change, Em. We can't always correct the mistakes of the past, or be responsible for them. We work hard and we're making a good life here. Let's not spoil it by worrying about things in the past that we can't undo.'

Emily knew he was right, but still the thought nagged at the back of her mind that they were now profiting from these past atrocities. She felt for the piece of Connemara marble in her skirt pocket and felt the pull of her ancestors. The Irish knew well what it was like to be chased from your land and your home, stripped of your language and culture.

As the birds wheeled and cried above, she felt them watching her, making sure she was being respectful to this place their ancestors had called home. She asked them to guide her, to show her the way.

That night, she took the pamphlet from her mother's Bible. *'Come to the great free country, where you may soon grow rich and independent as a farmer, with yellow corn waving upon the breasts of the prairies, and cattle grazing upon the hills, and no master over you but the Great Lord of Heaven and Earth.'* She could hear her mother reading the words out loud, her voice carrying through the thin walls. 'Sounds like Heaven, doesn't it, Joe.'

Emily had terrible dreams that night, haunting visions of Native American mothers screaming as they watched their children being slaughtered. She woke to a crack of lightning as a thunderstorm rumbled over the house. As raindrops fell like hammer blows on the roof, she felt the tears of a thousand women fall with them, and resolved to do her best here, to honour their memory, to atone for the past.

17

Annie arrived on a humid late-September afternoon when distant thunder rumbled and the threat of rain hung in the air. Emily had hoped for a calm, clear day, when the light was at its most benevolent and the house looked twice as big, but the prairie paid no heed to visitors or first impressions. She prayed that the storms and rain would at least hold off until she'd shown Annie around.

Emily was pickling cabbage for the winter, preparing salt pork, storing up dried beans, and organising canned vegetables and fruit to see them through, when she heard the motorcar approach. Her hands stilled against the sink. Her heart began to race.

Annie had telephoned the general store the previous week, leaving a message for Emily with details of her arrival. Henry had driven to the train station that morning while Emily paced at the house, unable to rest or settle.

She wiped her hands on her apron, then took it off and bundled it into the copper to be washed. She checked the house one last time. Everything had been scrubbed and swept and polished, everything washed and ironed, odd jobs finished, pictures and embroideries finally hung up on the walls, cushions plumped, bedspreads smoothed, flowers picked and placed in jugs here and there. Whatever Annie might make of it all, Emily's heart swelled with pride when she looked around. It had never looked nicer, despite the gloomy skies.

Voices carried through the open window. Emily held her breath a moment, listening keenly. Annie sounded different, her accent more refined. For a voice she'd known all her life, it was like listening to a stranger.

She walked to the window and watched for a moment – unseen – as Annie took in her surroundings, her hand on her hat to stop it from blowing away in a stiff breeze that had whipped up from nowhere and sent a dust devil whirling in the distance. She heard Henry tell Annie about their winter and summer crops, the fruit orchard and vegetable patch. Neither of them seemed to be in any hurry to bring the child out of the car.

Emily checked her reflection in the mirror one last time, straightened her shoulders, and breezed onto the porch with a smile.

'Annie! You're here! You're really here!' She hurried down the steps, delighted now to see her sister, all thoughts of approval or disapproval lifting from her.

Annie met Emily with a warm embrace, then pulled back to take a good look at her.

'I never would have believed it if I hadn't seen it with my own eyes! Emily Kelly – I mean, *Gale* – a proper farmer's wife!'

'I'm getting there. Not fully fledged yet!'

'Nonsense! Look at you! All sun-browned and windswept, and whatever *that* is you're wearing!'

'They're called dungarees. More practical than a dress.'

'And so alluring! How can you resist her, Henry?'

They all laughed, but Emily felt the sting of Annie's teasing, just as she had when they were children.

They studied each other for a moment, searching for the familiar easy connection they'd once had and the closeness that had eluded them recently. Annie looked like her old self again after losing the weight she'd gained during her pregnancy. She was more striking than ever, like a Tamara de Lempicka painting, in a fashionable drop-waist dress and elegant Mary Janes, all fresh from the racks of Field's new-season ladies' wear collection, no doubt. Emily felt like discarded seconds beside her and wished she'd put on a dress after all.

Annie reached for her hands. 'It's really good to see you, Em. How are you?'

'I'm doing well. We both are. And you? Dorothy, and John?'

'All wonderful.'

Emily peered over Annie's shoulder. 'Should you get her from the car? Is she sleeping?'

Annie hesitated a moment. 'I'm afraid Dorothy isn't here.'

Emily frowned. She presumed Annie was playing a prank and that Henry would appear with their niece at any moment.

'What do you mean, she's not here? Of course she's here!' She laughed lightly as she searched Annie's face for the truth, but all she saw was a sympathetic smile.

'I knew you would be horribly disappointed. The poor thing developed a temperature yesterday morning. I wasn't going to come, but Cora insisted.'

'Cora?'

'The new housekeeper. Replaced the awful Marta. She's Irish, and a godsend. Dorothy loves her.'

'She's really not here?' Emily's heart sank. She'd thought about nothing else all week, and Henry was so looking forward to meeting his niece. 'You're not teasing?'

Annie shook her head. 'I'm sorry, Em. I was so excited for you to see her. I've brought lots of photographs, though. You'll hardly recognise her! I hope I make a decent consolation prize!'

'Of course!' Emily tried to push her disappointment aside as she looped her arm through Annie's. 'Come on. Let me show you around. I can't believe you're really here!'

They danced around each other like a shy couple on a first date – overly polite, too enthusiastic, filling awkward silences with hollow small talk. Emily was glad of Henry's good humour and easy manner. He defused some of the stiffness, adding to the conversation when it threatened to dry up, asking Annie about John and Dorothy while Emily fixed dinner. She kept one ear open, alert to any clues or hints from Annie, but she gave nothing away.

Emily filled everyone's glass from a jug of iced tea and said grace before they started to eat.

'Henry was telling me about the women in town, Em. They sound like a nice bunch.'

'They are. They can be a little unconventional, but they've made me feel very welcome.'

'You'll have to introduce me to them. Let me see who has replaced me since you ran away to Kansas!'

'Nobody could ever replace you, Annie.' Emily took a sip from her glass. She knew Annie was playing with her. Testing her. But she also knew there was some truth to Annie's playful accusations. 'But I'm certainly never short of someone to turn to for help or advice, and I've needed plenty of both.'

'I can imagine. There must be a lot to learn. A bit like becoming a mother, I guess. Although I haven't had a group of helpful women to guide me. My sister ran away to the prairie and abandoned me when I needed her the most.' She laughed.

Emily and Henry laughed along, but it was a hollow joy. Forced.

'I'm sure John is enthralled with her,' Emily said, unable to prevent herself from prodding and poking. 'He must be a very proud father.'

Was there a beat? The slightest pause?

'He is, of course. But you know how useless men are – no offence, Henry – when it comes to children.' Annie let out a long sigh. 'Poor Dorothy. Born to the least maternal woman in America. It has been a matter of trial and error so far, but she's still alive so I suppose I must be doing something right!'

Emily offered a reassuring smile. 'I'm sure you're doing a wonderful job. As for trial and error, I know how you feel. I'm still muddling my way through here.'

Henry reached for Emily's hand. 'Your sister is a marvel, Annie. She's done wonders with the place. It was just bare timber walls when she arrived. All the homely touches are her doing. And it turns out she's quite the cook, too, as well as a more than capable farmhand. This pot roast is delicious, Em.'

Emily was grateful for his sweet cheerleading. She nudged his foot beneath the table to show her appreciation.

'And Henry is the newly crowned wheat king of Kansas,' she said. 'He has made quite the impression with his machinery. He's the envy of the town!'

Henry brushed off the compliment. 'Not the whole town. Some are still suspicious of the machinery, but I guess time and harvest yields will tell.'

'John sends his regards and apologies, by the way,' Annie said. 'He would have come, but business has him practically living at the office. I hardly see him. I tell him poor Dorothy will hardly recognise him if he isn't careful!'

Emily's mind raced as she filled in the gaps with assumptions and speculation.

'He asked me to give him a full report when I get back,' Annie concluded.

'I hope it will be favourable,' Henry teased.

'Of course!' Annie batted Henry's arm playfully. 'Oh, and before I forget, he sent on some paperwork for you, Henry. Remind me to fish it out of my bag later.'

Emily looked up. 'Paperwork?'

'Nothing important.' Henry got up to refill his glass.

'Stock investment reports, or something,' Annie said. 'I'll admit, I wasn't paying full attention when he explained. The blight of every new mother. Never able to fully concentrate! I can't remember the last time I had an uninterrupted conversation, or meal. If you're not careful you'll never get rid of me!'

Emily couldn't fully relax, conscious of Annie watching her as she went about her chores, following her around as if she were a rare species to be documented. She asked silly questions, bemused by all the quaint little habits and routines, by the fact that the toilet was outside, and that water had to be fetched from the pump to wash the dishes.

'It's all such a lot of hard work,' she said as she finished rinsing the last dish. She'd insisted on helping, even though Emily could have done the job in half the time. 'Don't you ever wish you could run the faucet, or flush the toilet, or pick up a bottle of milk from the store instead of extracting it from the cow? When do you ever get a minute to yourself?'

Emily invited her to sit on the porch. '*This* is when I have a minute to myself. My favourite time of the day,' she said. 'When the sun hangs low in the sky and the worst of the heat has passed and all the chores are done. I often sit here, just me and my thoughts, and sometimes the fiddle.'

As Annie swung the seat back and forth, Emily was reminded of the games they'd played as children.

'It's certainly peaceful,' Annie said. 'But don't you feel isolated? Cut off from the world? All that empty space makes me nervous. Aren't there wolves on the prairie?'

'Yes, and venomous snakes and spiders, so be careful when you need to use the outhouse.' Now it was Emily's turn to tease and taunt. 'I love it here, Annie. It was the city where I felt uncomfortable and hemmed in. Here, I can breathe. There's something about all this space that forces you to look inward, to figure out who you really are.'

'Well, that sounds truly awful.' Annie flicked a fly away from her face. 'You still think you made the right decision? No regrets? No secret longing to come back to Chicago with me?'

Emily smiled. 'No regrets. We're happy here. Very happy.'

Annie turned to her. 'But is it enough, Em? Really? Is it everything you wanted it to be?'

Emily laughed lightly. 'Of course! It's wonderful!'

They sat in silence for a while, the rhythmic creak of the seat like a clock pendulum ticking time away, like sand slipping through Annie's hourglass.

'Are you going to show me those photographs of Dorothy, then?' Emily said eventually.

'Oh yes! Let me grab them.'

Emily took a deep breath as Annie stepped inside to fetch the photographs. She would say all the right things. Avoid any awkwardness.

'Here we are.' Annie took her seat beside Emily. 'I'm sure there are far too many. Tell me when you get bored.'

She had a small album of photographs, each picture carefully dated and annotated. *Dorothy at the park. First trip to the lake. Dorothy and mommy. Family day out. Dorothy sleeping. Favourite teddy/Lion.* Emily was touched to see that Dorothy still had the toy lion she'd left for her.

Emily became lost in the images, absorbed by the sweet little girl who she hardly knew at all, and yet knew instantly. She was glad to still feel the pull of affection. If anything, it had grown even stronger in the months since she'd last seen her.

'How is motherhood?' she asked as they reached the end of the album.

'Exhausting! It's messy and worrying – and completely wonderful!'

'You must be missing her.'

'I missed her the moment I got in the taxicab to take me to the train station. She has my heart absolutely wrapped around her tiny little fingers. I honestly can't remember what I ever did before she was born, or before I was a mother. It's the most amazing thing, the bond you feel for this tiny helpless little thing . . .' She trailed off as she reached for Emily's hand. 'I'm sorry, Em. I didn't mean to go on. I forget, sometimes, what happened.'

'Lucky you. I think about it all the time.'

Annie reached for her hand. 'How did Henry take it?'

Emily stalled, suddenly wary of confiding in her sister.

'Em? You did tell him, didn't you?'

Emily stared at a beetle on the ground. 'I couldn't.'

'Why ever not?'

'I didn't want to bring such sadness to our new start here. And then time passed, and I guess it felt like something that belonged in the past, not here in the present. Besides, telling him wouldn't change anything, would it?'

'I suppose not.' Annie took a long sip of her iced tea. 'Sometimes ignorance is kinder than the truth.'

Emily felt the hint of an invitation, the crack of a door opening. Did Annie want her to ask? In the months since she'd left Chicago, she'd doubted herself, wondering if she'd imagined what she'd heard outside the bedroom door the morning of Dorothy's birth. Maybe she had things entirely wrong and there was no mystery or secret at all. The only way to know for sure was to ask Annie outright, but that felt too raw, too accusatory. Too dangerous.

'How is John taking to fatherhood?' she asked. 'I don't see any resemblance of him in the photographs of Dorothy.' She couldn't stop herself from poking at the truth.

'John is away a lot with work. But when he's home, he's very sweet with her. He adores her.'

'She'll be a daddy's girl, perhaps. Like you were.'

'I'd like that. I'd like that very much.'

There was a trace of wistfulness in Annie's voice. Emily definitely wasn't imagining it.

'And you? How is life as Mrs John Gale? Is he still as extravagant and romantic as ever?'

'It's a little harder when there's a baby to absorb all your time and attention, but we manage.' Annie stood up suddenly and pulled Emily to her feet. 'Now, how about we forget all about husbands and babies and put a record on that Victrola of yours and dance, for old times' sake. I mean, what does a girl have to do to get a drink around here?'

She still had it – the disarming ability to deflect and charm, just as she had when they were children, and as single young women navigating their way in a world full of promise. This was the Annie that Emily remembered. Full of life and fun. Unpredictable and exciting.

Who could blame her if she had rekindled the flames of romance with her beloved aerialist as Emily suspected. John had wanted a wife he could control, a pretty museum piece to display and admire. Annie was always too wild for him. She was a prairie fire that wouldn't be contained, and although it was illicit and wrong, part of Emily was glad to see that the passion Annie had tried to douse by marrying John Gale still burned within her.

And Emily felt the lick of its flame as Annie grabbed her hands and pulled her to her feet to dance the Charleston until the years peeled away and it was just the two of them again, chasing impossible dreams and wild adventures.

*

The storm broke just after nightfall.

Emily had never seen lightning or heard thunder like it. It was so powerful that even after it had passed, she felt something of its raw crackling energy settle within her as she turned Annie's words over and over. *'But is it enough, Em? Really? Is it everything you wanted it to be?'*

18

Annie stayed for a week. Like one of Emily's samplers, the prairie showed her a little of everything – sunshine, storms, rain – while Emily taught her how to make corn cakes and clean out the pig pen and the horses' stalls and collect eggs from the hens. Through the steady focus of the chores, they found their way back to each other, sharing memories and stories, singing favourite songs each evening to the familiar tune of their father's fiddle. They placed a telephone call to Nell from the general store. She was so excited and surprised to hear their voices, and so sad that she wasn't with them, that she could barely talk through her sobbing. They struggled to hear her anyway because of bad static on the line. Henry took a photograph of them together with an old Kodak, which they promised to mail to her.

On Thursday, Henry drove them both to the weekly supper club where everyone was delighted to meet Annie, who easily charmed them all with her talk of city life, and her playful good humour.

'I feel like we already know you, Annie,' Laurie said as they settled to a game of cards. 'Emily talks about you all the time. Telling stories about the two of you, and your sister, Nell.'

'Nice stories, I hope!'

'Of course! Makes me a little envious, if I tell the truth. I never had a sister. Always felt I missed out.'

'We were lucky,' Annie said. 'We always got along well. Apart from a few squabbles.'

'You and your husband will be hoping for a sister or two for baby Dorothy, no doubt,' May added. 'Lots of little Gales whirling around the place!' She laughed at her joke.

Annie smiled. 'Not too many, I hope. Gales develop into cyclones, and we all know how destructive they can be! I have nothing but admiration for women who have an infant to deal with at the same time as a wilful toddler. One is quite enough to manage for now.'

Emily observed Annie closely as the conversation unfolded, watching for any clues or unusual reactions.

'It's a shame we hardly see one another anymore,' Annie continued. 'First, Nell moved to California, and now Emily is all the way out here in the middle of nowhere. I was hoping to find her miserable and begging me to take her back to Chicago. Unfortunately, she appears to have made an absolute success of it all.'

Emily was surprised by Annie's generous endorsement, and in front of all the women, too. She brushed the compliment aside.

'Well, your loss is our gain, Annie,' May said. 'Emily has been a breath of fresh air. She's a born natural prairie woman. Has the gift. Would be a crying shame for her to have wasted it on a life in the city.'

Emily was touched. She'd so often felt like the curious outsider, it was lovely to hear how much she now fitted in, and belonged.

'What is it you do, Annie?' Ingrid asked.

Emily's confidence was buoyed by the kind remarks that had come her way. 'My sister is a kept woman,' she teased. 'She left her position as a window trimmer at a reputable department store to concentrate on her new appointment as Mrs John Gale. You won't find any callouses on those perfectly manicured hands, let me tell you!'

'I'm not *employed* anywhere at the moment,' Annie corrected. 'But I've never worked harder since becoming a mother.'

The others emphatically agreed with her on this, discussing how physically demanding motherhood was, not to mention emotionally exhausting. Emily sat quietly, conscious that she had nothing to add to the conversation.

'I was sorry to leave Field's,' Annie continued. 'But I can't say I miss our awful supervisor breathing down my neck, making everyone's life a misery. There's always someone intent on spoiling all the fun, isn't there.'

'Sounds like Wilhelmina West,' May Lucas said. 'You'd be afraid to look at her the wrong way.'

Emily had thankfully avoided running into Wilhelmina West so far. The other sister never seemed to leave the house.

'I feel sorry for the West sisters,' Ingrid offered. 'I think they're misunderstood.'

Laurie Miller turned to Annie. 'They lost their parents when they were very young,' she explained. 'Their aunt and uncle took them in. It's just the uncle now – Ike – and I'm not sure he's long for this earth.'

'Not that they'll mind,' May added. 'Sitting on a tidy inheritance, apparently.'

'I didn't realise they were orphans,' Emily said. 'How sad.'

'A sorry business,' May said. 'The mother died in childbirth, delivering Wilhelmina. The father drank himself to an early grave. Rumour is that Wilhelmina blames herself for her mother's death and that's where her bitterness and bad temper come from. She can't bear to see happy families – mothers and children especially.'

Something of the explanation resonated within Emily. She understood that inclination to look away, to avoid other people's contentment.

'That's why she's so protective of her sister, too,' May continued. 'Hardly lets her out of her sight, or out of the house, for that matter.'

The close bonds between sisters was something that Emily definitely understood.

As the evening progressed, the conversation inevitably turned to the latest gripes and moans about the men. Emily could laugh along with them now, joining in as they each shared a story or anecdote about something ridiculous their husband had done.

'I'm not sure I'll ever get used to washing Henry's underwear, no matter how much I love him,' she said.

'Buckle up, child. That's not even the half of it.' May added. 'Wait until he starts to lose his faculties, *then* we'll talk!'

'Surely one of us has found the perfect man,' Laurie said. 'Annie? Your husband sounds like he is fully house-trained.'

'My sister has a housekeeper,' Emily said. 'I doubt she has to deal with John's underthings!'

'And she intends to keep it that way,' Annie said, earning a supportive 'Amen' from the others.

'We love them all the same though, don't we,' Laurie said fondly. 'You learn to forgive – or ignore, your ear attunes to their strange noises, you watch their hair thin and their skin sag where they once had muscles, and you love 'em anyway.'

'Speak for yourself,' May Lucas said. 'I'd put my Zeb on the next train out of town if I could afford to.'

'Ah now, May. He ain't all that bad.'

'You try being married to him for thirty-three years, then tell me what ain't bad!'

'You must have loved him once, though, May,' Emily said.

'You'd have thought so, wouldn't you? But I can honestly say I never felt an ounce of love for that man. Truth is, I should never have married him.'

'Why did you?' Annie asked. 'If you don't mind saying.'

'Because he asked before anyone else, and because my folks couldn't afford to keep me at home. I should have married Fred Isaacs. Loved him all my life, but it wasn't meant to be for us. I still think about him. Only time I ever think about Zeb is imagining him six feet under.'

Everyone howled laughing at that, but a trace of poignancy laced the air.

'May, that's so sad,' Emily offered when they'd all wiped the tears from their cheeks.

'Maybe, but that's how life goes sometimes. We make the best of what we've got. I knew a woman got herself pregnant only to discover, months later, that her husband didn't have the good seed and could never father a child. He knew she'd cheated on him the minute she told him she was expecting.'

Emily watched Annie's face closely, observing her reactions.

'What happened?' Annie asked.

'The poor man never said a word about it. Accepted the child as his own. All I'll say is, if you're lucky to find a partner you truly love, look after him. Give him whatever he wants – five children, eight meals a day, sex in the middle of the afternoon.'

'Sounds exhausting!' Emily said.

Just then, Henry appeared at the screen door, ready to take Emily and Annie home. The women all looked at him and burst out laughing again.

As they prepared to leave, Emily overheard Annie asking May about the woman who'd had another man's child.

'Did the marriage last?' she asked.

May smiled. 'They made it work for a couple of years, but they were both miserable. Eventually, she took the child and ran off with her lover. They had three more children and were together for fifty years.'

'That's so brave, and romantic! She sounds like an amazing woman.'

'She was. That woman is my mother. She got her happy ending after all.'

*

Emily and Annie sat on the porch together when they got back from town that night. The humid heat clung to their skin like fabric and the 'hoppers sang in the tall grass as the seat swung gently beneath them. There was a sense of departure in the air – Annie was due to return to Chicago the next day.

She'd been unusually reflective on the way home and remained quiet as they sat together.

'You must be excited to see Dorothy,' Emily prompted. 'And John. Can't wait to get home to them, no doubt.'

For a moment, Annie didn't reply. 'I envy you, Emily,' she said at last.

'Envy me? Why?'

'For what you have here, with Henry. I see how happy you are together, how good you are together. May's right. True love is a precious thing. It should be treasured, protected whatever the cost.' She took in a deep breath before letting out a sigh.

Emily's skin prickled. Was she finally going to tell her? Admit to what she'd done?

'Which is why I think you should tell Henry,' Annie continued.

'Tell him what?'

'About the baby you lost.'

For a moment, Emily couldn't speak. She'd been prepared for

Annie's confession. Instead, she felt as if she were being accused of a similar deception.

'Well, I disagree. We don't always do what we should, do we.' Emboldened by Laurie Miller's generous measures of corn whiskey, frustrated by Annie's remark, and galvanised by her impending departure, Emily couldn't keep quiet any longer. 'Maybe there are things you should tell John, too.'

'What do you mean?'

She took a deep breath. 'I heard you, Annie. I heard you talking to Dorothy the day she was born, whispering about her father.' Emily turned and looked Annie directly in the eye. 'I know it isn't John.' She'd said it. The words were out now and could never be taken back. A sense of relief and dread washed over her. 'You should tell him the truth, before he finds out.'

Annie looked visibly shocked, as if she'd seen some terrible thing.

'It is none of your business, Emily. You don't have the faintest idea what you are talking about.'

'It's Leo, isn't it? The aerialist. He came back.' She reached for Annie's hand, but she pulled away, as if jolted by an electric shock. 'You can tell me, Annie. *Talk* to me.'

Annie stood up abruptly, sending the seat swaying erratically as she stared at Emily. Her hands shook. She'd never looked so hurt, or angry, not even when she'd found out that Emily had married Henry behind her back. For a moment, Emily was almost afraid of her.

'I'm going to bed. And I never want to talk about this again, Emily. Do you understand? Never.'

'Annie, sit down. Please. I just—'

'Promise me you will *never* mention this again, Emily. To anyone. Not even Henry.'

'I promise. I won't—'

'I know what I'm doing. If John finds out, it could ruin everything.'

Annie made her way inside, the screen door banging shut behind her.

Emily took a deep breath and closed her eyes.

'I really hope you do know what you're doing, Annie,' she whispered. 'I really hope you do.'

*

Annie left the next morning, as planned.

They stepped around each other at breakfast, avoided eye contact, talked about anything and everything else. Henry sensed there was something wrong, but Emily brushed it off when he asked.

'She's just ready to go home,' she said. 'Can't wait to see Dorothy. Best not to say anything. It'll only upset her.'

As Henry loaded the trunk, Emily went to Annie to embrace her.

'I'm sorry you're leaving like this, Annie, but I'm glad you came. It meant the world to me to have you here, to see the home we've built.' She lowered her voice. 'I couldn't bear for you to go back without saying something. You can tell me anything, Annie. We've always shared our secrets with each other.'

Annie stepped into the car. She wouldn't even meet Emily's eye.

Emily refused to give in, refused to let Annie leave like this. She bent down to the open window. 'Promise you'll bring Dorothy next time? We would both love to see her.'

Annie turned her face to Emily's. There was such sorrow in her eyes, such pain. The sparkling emeralds now dull, unpolished stones.

'Goodbye, Emily.'

Her words carried a chilling air of finality.

Emily watched from the porch steps as Henry cranked the engine and the tyres turned over the earth until the car was enveloped in a cloud of dust. The classic disappearing act. A grand finale, without the applause.

She shivered, despite the warm day. She wrapped her arms around herself and stepped inside, where she stood for a moment, lost and alone, like a stranger in her own home.

On the table, propped beside the milk jug, was a photograph.

She picked it up and looked at the image of a sweet little girl, curls the colour of a New England fall, rosy apples in her cheeks. It felt as if she was holding her heart in her hands as the name fell from her lips.

'Dorothy.'

She turned the picture over then. On the back were three words. *For Auntie Em.*

Extract from *Wonderful – A Life on the Prairie* by Emily Gale

Kansas winds are different from anything I'd ever known, whipped into great swirling, twisting funnels with the strength to tear up centuries-old trees and knock down homes as if they were nothing more than a deck of playing cards stacked into a flimsy tower. Nature wields a different power here. You can either let it scare you, or you can stand up and face it. Courage means something different here, too.

I believed we would be rewarded for putting our trust and our hearts into this ancient land, but I was wrong to think the prairie might care about us the way we cared about it. It is a wild animal that won't be tamed, no matter how much you think you can trust it, or how many naive fools come here to try. It is unforgiving and cruel, and yet it can be beautiful and generous. It is a treacherous enemy, and yet a faithful friend.

On the prairie, everything is exaggerated. The winds blow stronger, the sun burns hotter, the hailstones are bigger, the losses are greater ...

19

Five years later

August, 1929

The years blew by, carried away on fickle prairie winds that brought good harvests, record-breaking yields, and grain prices holding steady at a dollar a bushel. More and more folk arrived, lured by the promise of the Great Plains, and millions more acres were ploughed up until the nation had more wheat than it could possibly consume.

Emily attuned to the cycle of the seasons, the hot summer months that melted away to benevolent, bountiful falls before the winters blew hard and cold and everyone longed for the arrival of spring and all its promise of renewal. But it was the fall that Emily looked forward to the most, the time of year when she took a moment to gather herself after the heat of summer and prepare for the challenging winter months that lay ahead. She felt restored by the drop in temperature and the mists that rolled across the prairie in the early morning, lending an otherworldliness to the land, as if it was letting out a long sigh. But summer wasn't quite done yet, and the lingering threat of tornado season lurked around every corner.

Emily had never worked harder. She stubbornly stuck with it, even when the prairie tested them. They'd overcome cruel summer hailstorms that had destroyed entire crops, nursed sick horses and buried the stillborn runts from a litter of piglets, struggled on when Henry's foot was crushed beneath falling logs, hunkered down in the cellar while tornadoes roared above, and navigated the treacherous months of smallpox that had taken Ingrid's dear husband, Eric, from her and left their two children without a father.

Time and again, they'd picked up the pieces, dusted themselves off, and carried on. Prosperity and ruin were as finely balanced as a circus performer on a high wire. Nobody was sure which way things would fall, but nobody could look away. That was what it took to survive here, not only to prosper when times were good but to endure when things were at their worst.

Emily's calloused hands and broken fingernails bore the evidence of her toil. They were farmer's hands now, hands to be proud of. The ghost of her wedding band, lost somewhere in the fields, was marked now only by a ring of paler skin on her sun-browned finger. Henry had offered to buy her a new ring, but she'd told him to keep the money.

'I don't need a ring on my finger to prove my commitment to you. You're stuck with me, remember. For better, or worse. Not that I can imagine anything ever being worse with you.'

The one constant through so much change was her dear Henry. They'd had their struggles and disagreements, but their early rule of never going to bed on an argument had stood by them and, in many ways, Emily felt closer to him than ever.

'Besides,' she said when he offered again to replace the wedding band, 'I'm as wedded to the land as I am to you. It's only fair that the earth now carries a token of my betrothal!'

It was true. She loved this ancient land with all her heart, and it had started to love her back. The bare fields she'd first arrived to were now lush with swaying crops of corn and wheat. Her vegetable patch was a thriving garden, providing enough produce to see them through all year round and the fruit trees had borne their first fruit two years earlier than Henry had predicted. She'd picked the first apple herself, carefully removing the peel in a single magical coil in honour of her mother and sisters as she remembered the old oak table, warm brown bread thick with butter, the memories as clear and bright as leaves in the fall.

For all that she loved her Kansas home, she thought often of Ireland. More, it seemed, as the years passed. She still kept the piece of Connemara marble in her pocket – it had looked after her so far. The larder was well stocked, and they had money in the bank to see them through a bad year or two. Everything was just as she'd hoped, and yet she felt the undeniable ache of something missing.

Although Nell had eventually managed to make the long journey from California, spending a happy month with Emily and Henry where old affections were bolstered and new memories made with three of her boisterous children, five years had passed without another visit from Annie, or any invitation to travel to Chicago. The traditional Christmas cards, occasional letters and brief phone calls they'd exchanged over Emily's first months on the prairie had dwindled in the years since. There were long spells now when Emily didn't even think about Annie, although it wasn't as easy to forget about Dorothy. She often thought about the featherlight weight of her in her arms, the powerful surge of emotion she'd felt and how profoundly it had affected her. The photograph Annie had left behind took pride of place on the kitchen dresser, but even that had eventually become a source of anguish, a painful reminder to Emily of the child she had briefly carried during the weeks before Dorothy's birth. She'd placed the photograph in a drawer, buried beneath the clutter of matches, pins, cotton reels and buttons.

Despite the doctor's assurances, there hadn't been other pregnancies since. Like clockwork, she bled. Month after month, she met the dull, familiar cramps with the same confusing sense of relief and regret. Even Henry didn't talk about children anymore, didn't ask if she was expecting. There was nothing to be said about it.

Desperate to share the complexity of her feelings with someone, she confided in Ingrid Anderssen. She'd grown even closer to Ingrid since the shock of Eric's death.

'Is it normal?' Emily asked. 'To be afraid of having a child, even when part of you hopes for them?'

'Of course! I've dreaded each of my children, and longed for them equally. Will I be a good mother? Will they be healthy? Can we afford another child? So many questions and doubts.'

'It doesn't make sense. Surely if you want something, there should only be sadness when you don't get it. Not relief.'

Ingrid assured her it made perfect sense. 'Even if we instinctively want something, we might not be ready for it,' she said. 'Be patient, Emily. Time will bring what you need.' She wiped a tear from her eyes. 'And, sometimes, it will take away the thing you cherish the most.'

Emily drank coffee on the porch that evening as she watched the sunset. She thought about Eric and Ingrid, and how quickly life can change. With the community so tightly knit, any tragedy affected them all. It made Emily even more grateful for all that she had, and reminded her that life was to be lived and embraced, even when it frightened you.

She inhaled the sweet prairie air in deep, satisfying breaths. The summer months were some of the prettiest, when the meadows were carpeted with wildflowers, their dainty blooms like a ballet corps pirouetting and bobbing in perfect synchronicity with the breeze. She wished she was an artist so that she could capture the scene in oils or watercolours and keep the meadows in the full flush of their summer bloom all year round. Instead, she captured it in words.

Her journal had become a deeply personal account of her triumphs and despair, and a detailed report of the prairie. Each year, she recorded the date of the first apple blossom and the first prairie fires of the season. She tabulated periods of rainfall, dry spells, full moons, water levels in the creek, the direction of the wind and the temperatures Henry recorded on the thermometer he stuck in the ground. *The sky boils beneath the rising summer temperatures*, she'd written. *Thunderheads keep rolling in from the east.*

She liked to look back sometimes, reading over her early entries to see how far they'd come. She still felt the excitement and optimism of those early months, but her tone was tempered now with something more grounded and practical and with a hint of concern. She documented the changing shape and colour of the landscape as more and more acres were ploughed up. She noted that she hadn't seen as many prairie chickens that year, nor heard the sage grouse, or meadowlark, their familiar sounds replaced by the steady rumble of Henry's machines, and those of the many other farmers who had followed his lead. She often thought of Ike West's ominous words during that first week when Henry had shown the men his machinery. Was Ike right? Were they doing more harm than good?

The greatest lesson the years had taught Emily was that the prairie would not be easily tamed. For all that she loved its wild beauty, she was still wary of the power it held over them all. No matter how hard they worked, or how lovingly she decorated their home with cushion covers and patchwork quilts, she knew that nature had the ultimate power to destroy it all.

She lay in bed that night, the warm, sticky air washing over her tired body, the light of a full moon illuminating the room. As Henry snored softly beside her, she thought about poor Ingrid, all alone. A lifetime of lonely nights stretching ahead of her. Nobody beside her. Nobody to reassure her. When Eric had been sick, Laurie had said you never felt more alone on the prairie than when someone was ill, or dying. 'That's when the loneliness presses in on you. When you feel the miles of land between you and any help.' Life certainly felt more fragile here, the margins between living and dying, between thriving and surviving, gossamer thin. Emily said a silent prayer of thanks that she and Henry had been spared the anguish of anything more serious than a fever or a broken bone.

She placed a hand on his arm to make sure he was really there, not a vision, conjured from her dreams. She couldn't imagine life without him. He *was* her life, her soulmate, her dearest, kindest friend.

She watched him for a long while, remembering their first conversation at Annie and John's dinner party. She was so lucky to have found him in a city as big as Chicago, or perhaps she had Annie to thank for that.

Annie . . .

Her thoughts turned to her sister for a moment, but she pushed them away before they took root.

Unable to sleep, she reached for her journal to write an entry for that day. First, she turned back over the previous weeks' pages, reading over her thoughts and, as she did, a pattern began to emerge. Extreme tiredness. Unusual nausea. Strange reactions to familiar smells. No note of her monthlies arriving.

She sat upright, heart racing.

She'd stopped looking for signs long ago. But there they were, stark and irrefutable.

She picked up her pen and, hand shaking, wrote the date. Beneath it, she added six words that carried the weight of so many more.

I think I might be pregnant.

20

August, 1929

The air was full of prairie dust the next morning. Emily blinked, her eyes gritty as she collected the eggs from the coop. A dry summer had seen a growing number of what folk were calling sandstorms, when the wind blew the parched topsoil. They'd heard of a moving cloud of dirt that had passed through the Texas panhandle, creating static electricity and rubbing like sandpaper on the skin. Nobody had ever witnessed anything like it. The weather bureau had chalked it down as a one-off. A freak storm. A curiosity of nature.

Tornado season was almost over, but old-timers in town kept talking about the weather acting strange, and Emily was on high alert. Some big winds had come through in the years since they'd made the prairie their home. The house stood where the north and south winds met, and Henry joked that where the winds met, at the centre of a tornado, the air was still. 'Tornadoes will pass right over us, Em. We won't hear a thing.' But she *had* heard them, more times than she wished to recall.

Her first experience of a tornado was seared onto her mind, the terrible wind screaming and roaring over the house like a thousand steam locomotives. She'd come to dread the telltale rumble of an approaching twister more than she dreaded the rattlers and copperheads that lurked in the woodpile. Every day, during tornado season, she studied the sky, always on alert, looking out for the emerald hue that indicated an approaching tornado. She dreaded the big one that everyone experienced at least once in their lifetime. Every season that passed without severe damage felt like a stay of execution.

The weathervane swung erratically on the barn roof. Emily's skin prickled as she hurried back to the house, where she found Henry already hunched over his ledgers, his brow furrowed into a deep frown.

'It's really picking up out there,' she said. 'I was planning to drive into town a little earlier than usual, but I'm not sure it's a good idea.' It was Thursday, and that meant supper club.

She'd decided not to tell Henry yet about her suspected pregnancy, although she knew how happy he would be. She wanted to be sure before she got his hopes up. She would visit the doctor first, make certain of it, and make sure everything was going along as it should. She was wary, and afraid. The memory of her miscarriage still haunted her, even after all these years.

Henry looked up from his accounts. 'How about we both go in early? I could use the time to go to the bank.'

Emily detected a hint of concern in his voice. 'Is everything OK?'

He stood up and kissed her cheek. 'Everything's fine.'

The one part of married life that Henry kept from Emily was money. He didn't like to discuss it with her, believing it to be man's business. It was John he'd turned to for financial advice when he was saving and planning his move to Kansas, and John's business success made it hard to argue against him. Emily still didn't care for the way John conducted his deals, and gut instinct still stopped her from fully trusting him. All she knew was that he'd written, a month ago, to tell Henry prices had taken a big hit on the stock exchange and that he should sell off whatever shares he had in steel and electricity and put his savings in the bank. She'd found the letter when she was tidying Henry's things. She hadn't mentioned it. Whatever she thought about John, she trusted Henry to do the right thing.

The wind had strengthened even further by the time she and Henry arrived in Liberal that afternoon. Henry made his way to the bank before it closed, too preoccupied by his own thoughts to ask Emily where she was going.

'I'll see you later,' he called. 'Pick you up at nine.'

'Make it eight,' she replied. 'Just in case.'

She waited until he was out of sight and then, head down against the wind, hurried to the doctor.

By the time she was done and had arrived at the general store, the sky was already darkening.

'Wasn't sure we'd see you tonight,' Laurie said as she ushered Emily inside.

'Neither was I. Henry's picking me up a little earlier than usual.'

'Good thing, too. I don't like the look of that sky one bit. Now, come on inside.'

The tentative friendships Emily had formed in her first year on the prairie had solidified into strong bonds with women she now admired greatly and cared for deeply. They had even added some actual singing to their weekly gatherings as Emily taught them her favourite Irish ballads, and Ingrid taught them songs from her Dutch heritage, and they all sang the blues.

While the women shared their hopes and fears over pie and music at the Millers' home attached to the general store, the men gathered at the saloon to discuss yields and wheat prices. The wheat surplus had expanded again after another strong summer harvest and grain elevators across the state were stuffed full, which meant prices would inevitably drop.

'I've never seen Hank so worried,' Laurie said as the women discussed their husbands. 'He can't sleep at night for turning over everything in his mind, and then he's as irritable as a horsefly bite the next day.'

'I don't understand why the government won't buy back the surplus,' Ingrid added as she told little Eric to stop bothering his older brother.

'And still more folk arriving on the trains every week, and more acres being ploughed up,' Emily added.

The lush, fertile fields that had greeted her when she'd first arrived were now a torn and tattered patchwork of ploughed sod. Once again, she recalled Ike West's warning when they'd first arrived. She felt ashamed by what they'd done to the land.

'Eric! *Leg dat neer.*' Ingrid scolded her son, turning to her Dutch language as she often did when she was tired or irritated.

Baby Eric, named for his father, reluctantly put down the wooden spoon he'd been using as a drumstick on his brother's legs and sat, scowling, at his mother's feet. He was a sweet little boy most of the time, but Ingrid's struggle to raise the two boys on her own was plain to see. Emily had hoped to find a quiet moment to confide in Ingrid following her appointment with the doctor, but decided it could wait. She hated to see how tired Ingrid looked. She rarely smiled these days.

She'd felt the optimism fade among them all lately. They were bringing in record harvests, but for what. Barely a profit to be made between them. She tried to lift everyone's spirits with a song on the fiddle, but a string broke in the second verse. 'A sign of bad luck,' her father used to say. 'A broken string warns of a broken heart.'

*

Henry was quiet in the car and went straight back to his ledgers when they arrived home rather than sit with Emily on the porch to debrief each other on their evenings, as he usually did.

Emily left him a while before gently encouraging him to join her. 'You look tired,' she said. 'Come and sit with me. Shake the day off.' She was eager to get his attention and try to lighten the mood.

Eventually, he relented. He closed his ledgers and pushed his pencil behind his ear.

'A problem shared?' she prompted as he sat beside her. 'Laurie was saying she's never seen Hank so worried. It might help to tell me what's troubling you, or do I have to rely on Laurie Miller to know my husband's state of mind?'

Henry offered a tired smile. 'Seems like you already know. City folk are being encouraged to eat wheat three times a week, but if the surplus continues, wheat prices will tumble, no doubt about it.' He ran his hands through his hair. 'I don't care for how things are looking, Em. I don't care for it at all.'

Emily offered reassurance, just as he had reassured her so often over the years. 'We'll be fine, Henry. We've savings in the bank. You followed John's advice and, although it nearly kills me to admit it, he's proven to be right so far.' She kissed the top of his head. After five years of marriage and even with all the irritating little habits and ways that those five years had slowly revealed, Emily still adored her husband. Whatever happened, and wherever life took them, they would share it together. They complemented each other, like sunshine and rain. It was a powerful combination. 'Henry, there's something . . .'

He reached for her hand as he yawned. 'Sorry, Em. I'm beat. I'm no company tonight. I think I'll turn in,' he said.

Emily kissed his hand. 'Get some rest. I'll close up the coops and check on the animals. That wind's really picking up.'

Her news would have to wait.

*

Emily woke to a low ominous wail.

She sat up. 'Henry!' She pushed his arm to wake him. 'Henry, wake up.'

Beside her, Henry stirred. 'What is it?'

'Listen. The wind.'

The timbers already creaked all around them. The iron hinges on the doors squeaked as they were pulled and stretched. The sound was distinct, different from any other wind. They both felt a dull headache from the change in air pressure.

'Tornado!' Henry jumped out of bed. 'Get to the cellar.' In a rush, he pulled on his boots and ran to the door. 'Go, Em! Now!'

She hurried to the centre of the room, rolled back the rug, and pulled up the hatch. Her heart lurched as she made her way down the ladder into the cold dark space. 'Hurry, Henry!'

He was with her a moment later. 'Looks like a big one, Em. A real big one.'

They clung to each other in the dark as the house shook violently above, the floorboards straining against the joists as they began to pull away. Emily heard a sharp snap, then another, then a cacophony, like gunfire going off as nails sprang loose and the house seemed to heave and sway above her. The noise was like nothing she'd ever heard – the impossible crescendo of ever-stronger gusts, the deafening, blood-curdling shriek and whine and roar of the wind.

And then the unimaginable happened. The floor started to separate from the foundations and the house began to lift from the ground, heaving and swaying above Emily's head, tethered only by a few stubborn struts. Blinking against the roaring wind and sharp grit that peppered her skin, she saw the green-black sky above.

'Henry! What's happening!'

He held her tight to his side. 'Hold on, Em. Hold tight. I've got you.'

She gripped him like a vice as the house twisted some forty-five degrees before being dragged several feet and smashing into the ground. The windows and timbers were crushed and twisted. Everything that had once been inside was now outside, caught up and hurled in every direction by the storm.

In the cellar, Emily shut her eyes and clung to Henry. They cowered against the furthest wall as rain and dirt hammered down on them until she was sure they would be buried alive.

She couldn't speak. Couldn't cry out. Couldn't breathe. The wind and dirt choked her. Smothered her.

She prayed desperately, pleading for it to end – the deafening noise, the murderous wind, the terrifying bangs and booms and crash and shatter of God knows what above.

Please stop! Please be over! Please spare us!

She buried her face in Henry's chest and retreated into herself, longing for it to stop as terror and panic set her heart racing and made her body shake as violently as the house above.

It seemed to last forever,
screaming and roaring,
endlessly raging,
forever,
on and,
on,
and
on.

And then it was done.
All that remained was silence.

21

For a while, she was too afraid to move, too afraid to open her eyes, too afraid to see what had happened. She couldn't stop shaking.

Eventually, she opened her eyes and turned to Henry.

His face was covered in dirt and full of fear as he placed his hands on her cheeks. 'We're still here, Em. Whatever's happened, we are still here.'

'What time is it?' She wasn't sure why she asked. She needed something simple to root herself back to reality.

Henry checked his watch. 'Nearly ten past.'

They'd gone to the shelter on the hour. Two a.m. It had lasted less than ten minutes.

They stayed where they were. Emily held tight to Henry, afraid to let go, afraid to face what was waiting for them above.

Henry stood up first. He reached for Emily's hand and helped her up.

Her teeth chattered. Her whole body convulsed violently as she slowly climbed the ladder.

At first, she couldn't orient herself, couldn't find a single thing she recognised as she clambered out of the hatch and saw a scene of utter devastation, lit by the moon.

Then she saw it.

The water pump.

The only solid undamaged thing left standing.

She crawled on her hands and knees toward it and clung to the handle like a life raft as she took in the scene around her. Their beautiful home, their crops, their dreams, lay scattered all around her, like toys thrown in temper by a petulant child.

Emily had felt pain and loss in her life, many times over. But this was different. This was visceral and shocking and completely overwhelming. She felt as torn apart as their beloved home. She was the scattered, broken ruins strewn across the prairie.

It was gone.

Everything.

She let out such a heart-rending wail that she frightened herself. She had never heard a sound so utterly devastating.

She turned then and vomited onto the ground, retching over and over as the last of herself was purged to join the scraps and shattered fragments of what remained.

Henry placed his arms under hers, supporting her as he hauled her to her feet.

'Stand up, Emily. You have to stand up.'

She gripped his hands. 'It's gone, Henry. All of it. *Everything.*'

'Don't you dare give up, Emily Gale! Remember who you are. Who *we* are.'

She looked at him and saw such fear in his eyes. She didn't know who they were anymore. Without their home, their farm, what was there? When it was all taken away, what was left?

Just as Annie had predicted, it had all been a terrible mistake. *'But is it enough, Em? Really? Is it everything you wanted it to be?'*

She felt like a lost little girl who had wandered far away from her home and her family and couldn't find her way back to them.

She broke down in tears, and through her raw wild anguish, there was only one thing she wanted.

'I want my mother, Henry,' she sobbed, clinging to his shirt. 'I miss her. I miss her so much.'

*

They spent the night in the Model T which had miraculously survived the tornado, directionless passengers with nowhere to go.

They didn't talk much.

Neither of them slept.

At first light, they wandered around in a daze, recovering what they could. Like a child picking up dropped candy, Emily stooped to gather anything she could find, no matter how small: a single spoon, a chipped milk jug, her rolling pin, pillows and cushions covered in dirt, several books with their covers torn and spines broken, one tattered red shoe, then the other some distance away, the straps snapped and the buckles missing. The larder had remained relatively intact, her carefully preserved jars miraculously unspoiled, the wildflowers on the wallpaper still in full bloom. Three steps led to an invisible porch. The swing seat lay on its side in three pieces. She found a pair of Henry's dungarees wrapped around a clump of Russian thistle, and his hat impaled on the end of a broken fence post. All that remained of the scarecrows were torn shreds of Henry's old clothes, their straw stuffing blown clean out of them. She felt just as lifeless and empty, flapping aimlessly in the breeze.

Hours passed.

The horses returned. The surviving sow snuffled tirelessly through a bank of earth. Three chickens scratched in the dirt.

By mid-morning, the blue skies and a golden sun seemed out

of place among the scene of violent destruction below. Hank and Laurie Miller arrived after hearing a tornado had touched down a few miles south of Liberal. Hank brought hammers and nails, Laurie brought corn cakes and coffee. It was the saddest breakfast Emily had ever eaten.

Henry tried to lighten the mood. 'I would say pull up a chair, but our chairs are probably in Oklahoma by now.'

Laurie burst into tears.

Emily comforted her. She was too exhausted to cry anymore.

The four of them continued their despondent search throughout the morning, rounding up broken bits of Emily and Henry's life as if they were a team of old ranchers driving the herd. Emily found a window frame, the glass shattered, the blue-and-white gingham curtains she'd made still attached to the broken pole. Laurie found an upturned dresser drawer, the photograph of Dorothy still inside it. Emily didn't have the energy to be embarrassed when Hank found items of her underwear. She already felt as broken and exposed as the remaining timbers of her home.

Talk of Gale Farm being upended by the tornado spread like a prairie fire across town. More folk came to offer help in any way they could: a tractor to move the dirt, a pie, a bottle of hooch, more coffee, another pie. As Emily looked around their busy little patch of torn-up land, her heart broke to see such gentle kindness after such violent destruction. These were good people. The best people. She could never thank them enough.

'We've seen this before,' Laurie said. 'And, no doubt, we'll see it plenty again. We help one another. That's what prairie folk do. We pray it doesn't happen, but we come through for one another when it does.'

Sometime in the afternoon, Emily found her prairie journal, safe in the drawer of her nightstand. It had been carried over what was left of the barn and thrown at the base of the windmill, which was, miraculously, still standing. The journal was more valuable to her than she'd realised, her hopes and dreams captured among the pages: precious memories now of what they'd built, and lost.

Henry placed his arm around her shoulder as she turned through the dirt-streaked pages she had filled with her thoughts and hopes, and the empty pages that remained.

'See, so many more pages to fill,' he said. 'So much more of our story to tell.'

She laid her head on his shoulder. 'But I loved the story I was writing, Henry. I didn't want it to end.'

He pulled her to her feet and brushed dirt from her cheek. 'End? What is this talk of endings?' He offered a hopeful smile through his despair. 'We're only just beginning, you and me. We knew this wouldn't be easy, or always go our way. We've had a good run, Em – a *great* run, so far. This is our test, and we're alive and we'll survive it. It's done now, the thing you feared the most. It's over.'

They salvaged what they could find, and what wasn't broken beyond repair, or could be put to other use. In one final miracle, just before dusk, Emily found her father's fiddle, propped against a fence post, as if he'd left it for her there as a gift.

As they rode back into Liberal to stay with the Millers for a while, Emily's hand strayed to her coat pocket. The lump of Connemara marble was still there. After all these years, through all this time and upheaval, this little piece of Ireland was still with her.

It was that, in the end, that broke her.

She should have planted her dreams elsewhere.

*

Folk rallied around, everyone lending what bit of something they could spare: timber and nails, pots and pans, fabric and linen and clothes. The men worked every day and late into the night, hauling timber, helping Henry build a temporary shelter that would see them through until they could build a permanent home again. Ingrid gave Emily the black mourning dress she'd worn when she'd buried Eric. Laurie gave her an old black coat.

'It has seen better days,' she said. 'But the lining will make a decent shirt for Henry. And there's a pair of old boots here that Hank will never miss.'

Emily was grateful for everyone's generosity, but the good intentions only seemed to emphasise their helplessness.

'This is what life has come to,' she whispered as they lay, stiff and brittle as rusted old nails in a made-up bed in the Millers' living room. 'Funeral dresses, and old coat linings for shirts, and hand-me-down boots.'

'For now, Em. Not forever.' Henry reached for her hand in the dark. 'We won't give up. We don't quit, remember.'

She remembered. She also remembered what he'd said at one of Annie and John's dinner parties. *'Nobody farms for an easy life. It's an addiction. A love affair . . . a commitment, like a marriage . . . It's a life that chooses the person, rather than the other way around.'*

She wondered why the prairie had chosen her, wondered if it *had* chosen her, or if she was just an accessory to Henry's plans. She wasn't sure anymore. Was this the life she really wanted, the thrilling adventure she'd imagined when she'd agreed to marry Henry and build a life with him in this desolate wilderness?

She didn't know what to do with her despair. She silently blamed Henry for building their home in the wrong place, for not making it strong enough, for telling her everything would work out when it hadn't. And she blamed Annie for selfishly asking her to stay behind while Henry went ahead without her. Perhaps the prairie had never recognised her, this stranger who'd arrived as an afterthought. Like the great piles of mouldering grain stored beside the elevators, she was surplus to requirements.

But then she remembered that she *was* needed, that this wasn't just about her and Henry anymore. In all the chaos and fear, she'd forgotten that there was someone else to consider now.

'There's something I need to tell you, Henry.'

He turned to look at her. His eyes were glazed and empty. 'Can it wait? I'm exhausted, Em.'

'I'm pregnant.'

The words were blunt and raw. A stated fact rather than the emotionally charged announcement she'd imagined. It was the worst possible time for it to have happened, the worst possible way to tell him. But it was the only time, and the only way.

She took a deep breath and repeated the words, testing them out, trying them on, feeling the shape and weight of them.

'I'm pregnant.'

22

October, 1929

They wore their losses like a heavy shroud, hunched and weary beneath the weight of their despair as the rusted hues of fall decorated the cooler days of October in golds and crimson and bronze. Back in August their once-welcome friend of *Lughnasadh* had seemed to only increase their yield of sorrow that year. With much of their crops destroyed, there was little else to harvest.

They struggled on, trying to fit into the new shape of life in the simple home Henry had built in the footprint of the old one. Emily felt like a stranger there. She took no joy in it. She could barely bring herself to hang a single picture on the bare timber walls or place a cushion on their one remaining rocking chair. She took no joy in her changing body either. The colder nights left her stiff and tense, so that her whole body ached. The tug of her swollen breasts and the developing of life deep in her belly felt alien and unfamiliar. This wasn't how it was supposed to be. This wasn't the home she'd imagined raising a child in, but it was the home fate had given her.

Henry found her reading the letter Nell had written in reply to Emily's news of the tornado.

'Still thinking about Nell's offer?' He worried about Emily, and about their child. 'It isn't the worst idea.'

Nell had encouraged Emily to go and stay with her until the baby arrived. *I know a thing or two about babies! Besides, I hate to think of you living in a shack, at the mercy of the weather. Winter will be unbearable. Please come, Emmie. I worry about you. You'll be safe here.*

She'd thought about it, considered it seriously, but for all that she would be well looked after by Nell, it felt wrong to abandon Henry and the prairie at the first sign of difficulty. She would be running away – quitting – and she wasn't a quitter. Besides, it was what Annie had expected her to do all along, and she was too stubborn to prove her right.

She reached for Henry's hand. 'I can't go running to my sisters at the first sign of trouble.' She caught herself at the use of the word 'sisters'. There was no such invitation from Annie. She'd sent a short note offering her sympathies along with a bank draft from John to help with their repairs. 'I'll be fine, Henry. *We'll* be fine.'

Henry looked at her and shook his head, affection in his eyes. 'You're as stubborn as an ink stain, Emily Gale.'

In the evenings, she played the fiddle, choosing songs that reminded her of *Samhain*, the witching season. A favourite tune of her father's, 'She Moved Through the Fair', filled the house with its haunting melody. Henry listened quietly, spellbound by the music and Emily's voice. He loved to hear her play and sing, encouraging her to pick up the fiddle even when she wasn't in the mood. Music was a comfort during the nights when the wind howled at the eaves and the warm glow of spring and summer were a distant memory.

Henry kept busy, chopping wood in preparation for winter fires, fixing and improving anything on his machinery that had become damaged or broken, or which was perfectly fine, but which he tinkered with anyway. Emily had become accustomed to his 'fall fidgets' as she called them. She knew he wouldn't fully relax again until the spring thaws came and he could watch the fields for the first green shoots. Until then, the only thing they could harvest was hope, and love. And that, they had plenty of.

Emily's pregnancy, and the destruction of their home, had brought her and Henry closer than ever. It was the worst possible timing after the devastating tornado, but it gave them a reason to start over and look ahead. The thought of becoming a father had given Henry a new sense of purpose when it seemed that they had lost everything.

Emily tracked her progress in her journal, capturing her thoughts and feelings on the page as she found the words to express her ever-shifting moods, as unpredictable and turbulent as the sky. *Can't sleep for thinking about what's ahead. Twelve weeks now according to my calculations . . . Henry talks about little else. He is making a crib, although I told him it is too soon and bad luck. There's still a long way to go . . .* She was mindful of her mammy's *piseogs* – portents of bad luck – and found herself following old superstitions: avoiding graveyards, cats and rabbits, and not eating green potatoes.

As the nights turned colder, they burned surplus corn from that year's harvest as fuel for the fire.

'Smells good enough to eat,' Henry said as he came in from the fields. 'Who'd have ever thought we would see the day when there was so much corn we would happily throw it on the fire instead of selling it?' He let out a long sigh.

'I was just thinking how it reminds me of the circus,' Emily said. 'Of the popcorn and cotton candy we used to get as a treat.'

Henry sat beside her and took her hand. 'And it reminds you of your sisters?'

He knew her well.

Emily nodded and stared wistfully into the flames.

'You never really explained what happened with you and Annie,' Henry said as he sat beside her. 'What it was that caused such a rift between you?'

Emily sighed. She sometimes wasn't sure herself.

'We'd already drifted apart in Chicago, and she never forgave me for not telling her we were getting married,' Emily said. 'I guess it all came to a head when she visited that time and our differences became more apparent than ever. Life has pulled us in different directions ever since.' At first, it had felt that life was putting obstacles in the way of any chance of reconciliation: a broken ankle, bad weather, outbreaks of smallpox. After the tornado, Emily had stopped inviting Annie to visit. She hadn't even asked Nell to come. She didn't want them to see how she lived now, or how tired and broken she looked. Whatever desire she'd once had for Annie to admire what they'd built in Kansas had been smothered by the struggle of survival. The ache of Annie's withdrawal from Emily's life had dissipated over the years, the memories and regrets a distant echo now, but still heard and never fully forgotten. 'I hope she's happy,' she said. 'That's all I wish for her.'

'With John? Highly unlikely.'

Emily smiled. 'Henry. Don't joke.'

'Well, it's the truth. I never understood why she married him when she could have had any man in Chicago.'

'Perhaps not *any* man.' Emily longed to tell Henry what she knew about Dorothy's father, but she'd made a promise to Annie to never speak of it again. Not even to Henry. 'She'd had her taste of true love, and lost it. John was always second best.'

'She loves him, though, doesn't she?'

'I think so. But in a different way. John was a safe bet. She settled for him and the security he could offer her, but what she really wanted was something more thrilling and intoxicating. Someone mysterious.'

She threw another couple of corn cobs onto the fire, setting off a great popping sound.

'You mean that circus performer she fell in love with? The balloonist?'

'Aerialist.'

'Balloonist. Aerialist. It's all the same, isn't it? Magicians. Illusionists. Acrobats. Whatever you call them. What was his name anyway? You never told me.'

Emily hesitated. After protecting Annie's secret so carefully, she was afraid to even hear his name spoken aloud. 'His name doesn't matter. For years, part of me wished they would find each other again.'

'Which part? The hopeless romantic? Or the sister who cares deeply, even though she pretends not to.'

'The romantic,' Emily said, smiling as she reached for Henry's face. 'The part of me that loves you madly.'

Henry kissed her cheek and placed his hand on her stomach. 'I love you, too. Both of you.' He stood up and returned to his ledgers. 'Be careful what you wish for, Em. We wished for a good harvest and high yields, and look where that got us.'

A sombre mood had settled amongst the once optimistic farmers. Wheat prices were plummeting. There was now so much grain being produced across the millions of farmed acres of the Great Plains that it was costing farmers more to grow and harvest than they could earn by selling it.

'Only thing we can do is plough up more prairie grass to increase our yields next year and make up for the low prices,' he continued. 'Sow more seed – wheat, corn, and cotton. A few good harvests and we'll make back what we've lost.'

The farmers had discussed their options for months now. Henry was certain it was the right thing to do – the only thing to do – but Emily hated the relentless battle to make something from nothing.

'It's like a dog chasing its tail, Henry. Surely the cycle just keeps going? More grain, more surplus, lower prices – on and on. When does it end? *How* does it end?'

'It ends when we give up. So we plough up and keep trying, because I'm not one for giving up. I didn't think you were either.'

His words were unusually sharp, a challenge held within them.

'I was reading the newspaper earlier,' Emily said, eager to change the subject. 'Things seem pretty bad on the stock market. Folk are saying there might be a crash. I wonder if John and his investments will be affected?'

'I wouldn't worry about John Gale. He'll find a way to dodge whatever's coming. Some folk are lucky like that.'

'And us? We'd be all right, wouldn't we? We have money saved?'

'Of course.'

Emily stared into the flames a moment longer, watching them flicker and dance.

'And you should know me better, Henry Gale. I never give up.'

*

News of the stock market collapse hit the wires at noon a week later. Reporters called it Black Tuesday, the worst day in the history of the stock exchange.

Henry was ashen-faced as he crouched beside the Millers' wireless radio in the general store and listened to the latest bulletin.

'Fourteen billion of stock value lost,' he said as Hank joined him. 'Investors have lost everything.'

'Good job we ain't one of 'em,' Hank said. 'The bank is the only safe place for our money. Or a box under the bed, if you've a loaded gun to protect it with.'

Emily had heard enough. She placed a hand on Henry's arm.

'There's no point listening to it all day, Henry. Let's go home. Check on the animals.'

He hardly spoke as he drove back from Liberal, his brooding silence accompanying them until he turned the Model T through the farm gate and turned off the engine.

For a moment, neither of them moved.

'It's all gone, Em. Everything.'

Emily reached for his hand as she stared at the simple one-room dwelling that now stood where their lovely home once had. It still broke her heart to think of all they'd lost. 'We'll rebuild properly in the spring, Henry. We just need to get through the winter.'

Henry turned to her, his eyes hollow, shattered. 'I don't mean the house. I mean *everything*. Every damn cent. We're wiped clean. We have nothing to rebuild with.'

Emily froze. 'What do you mean?'

'John assured me the shares and investments would come good. That in five years we wouldn't have a debt to our name. I stretched us as far as I could, Em. Took a loan to buy the best machinery.'

'What about the bank? There must be money in the bank?'

'What money there is, I already owe to them.'

'But John advised you to sell the shares! I saw the letter when I was tidying your things. You did sell them, didn't you? Henry?'

There was such a haunted look in Henry's eyes. It frightened Emily to see it.

He shook his head. 'The bank advised me to leave them. I've let you down, Em. Ruined everything.'

'I'll write to Annie. Ask John to help.'

Henry shook his head. 'I've never taken charity from anyone and I don't plan on starting now.'

'It's not charity when it's family. And it would just be until we are back on our feet.'

'I'm not asking John Gale for help. We make our own way, deal with our own problems. Besides, John is probably in a worse situation than we are.'

He grabbed his hat and stepped out of the car, not even bothering to close the door behind him.

Emily's stomach lurched as she watched him walk away. If Henry was too proud to ask John for help, then she would. There was the child to think about now. If it meant going against Henry's wishes to secure their future, then that was what she would do, even though it made her heartsick to think that it had ever come to this. She would go to Annie and John, cap in hand, if she must.

She waited inside a while before she pulled on her shawl and made her way out to the fields, where she found Henry checking the corn beneath a beautiful pink sky. It seemed impossible that such beauty dared to show its face when such worry and despair was scattered among the furrowed fields.

'We'll manage, Henry. We'll start again.'

'With what?' Hope and fear and love warred in Henry's eyes as he looked at her.

'With the same passion and determination that first brought us here. Nobody can take that away from us.'

She shivered suddenly as a Cooper's hawk circled and wheeled above, its shrill cry the only sound beyond the soft rustle and sway of the corn. She instinctively placed her hand on her stomach. By next spring, they would have someone else to consider, another mouth to feed. Her heart ached at the thought. Her whole body ached. The thought of raising a child was daunting enough. The thought of raising a child in the circumstances they now found themselves in was terrifying, but they needed to be brave.

'I don't feel too good, Henry. I'll go back to the house, fix some supper.'

'I won't be long,' he said. 'Just need a bit of time.'

'Take as long as you need.'

She'd barely made it to the barn before the first sharp pain took her breath away. She leaned against the fence to steady herself, drawing deep breaths, in and out, before hurrying on to the house.

She would lie down for a while. She just needed to lie down.

To rest.

Sleep.

But as she reached the house, the pains came in fast excruciating waves.

It was all over before Henry had returned from the fields.

23

Emily walked, alone, to the creek at the edge of their claim and washed herself beneath the rose-violet light of sunset. She couldn't bear to draw water from the pump and fill the copper bath, couldn't bear to connect such an everyday, domestic chore to something so private and painful. She didn't even want Henry.

She needed to be on her own.

The creek summoned her. She stripped naked and walked into the frigid water with a gasp. The intense sting of cold was shocking and sharp, but the sensation soon passed to become invigorating and soothing. She sank down, spreading her knees wide, not caring for the sharp stones and gritty silt that dug into her skin. Pain was nothing to her now.

Silently, reverentially, she let the creek wash away the last traces of what, for several hopeful months, had been her child. She didn't weep and wail, didn't thrash about with anger or despair. She felt safe in the creek, cocooned in its silence.

A sense of peace surrounded her as her body was soothed by

the water, a moment of restorative calm after the visceral distress of what had happened.

And then she heard it, amid the ache of her loss: relief.

The lightest of whispers.

She ignored it, turned away from it, too ashamed to even acknowledge it. But it came again, carried in the soft rush of the water. The unmistakeable persistent whisper of relief.

They couldn't raise a child.

Not here.

Not now.

She stood up suddenly, disturbing the silence with the suck and splash of water as she scooped up noisy handfuls to wash herself clean, the russet hue of her blood returning to the muddy sediment beneath.

After, she dressed and walked back to the house. She scraped out a small hole in a patch of dry ground behind the barn and placed two of her pressed summer wildflowers inside, one for each of the children she would never see in full bloom. Tiny hopeful buds were all they would ever be. A promise of something more. Beginnings, ended too soon.

'For you are dust,' she whispered, reciting the lines from the Bible. 'And to dust you shall return.'

She sat for a while, alone with her thoughts, the small patch of earth darkened by her tears, as if she might water these two lost souls and bring them back to life.

As darkness fell, she fed the animals, taking a moment to rest her head against the warm muzzle of the horses. She drew water from the pump then and put it on the stove for coffee. There was comfort and simplicity in these mundane routines: the squeak of the pump handle, the tinny rhythmic thrum as the water hit the pail, the song of the kettle on the stove, Henry's boots by the door, the scrape of the butterknife over toasted bread, the cry of an eagle overhead. These were the sights and sounds of her life. This was what she knew.

Dust.
Dirt.
Life.
Death.

On and on the cycle went, turning with the seasons. She understood the prairie now, understood what was required to survive here.

Like a scattered seed taking root, she would begin again.

Rise from the dirt, once again.

Part Three

Chicago and Kansas, 1932

'I think you are wrong to want a heart. It makes most people unhappy.'
– L. Frank Baum, *The Wonderful Wizard of Oz*

24

Chicago, 1932

Emily stepped from the taxicab outside Union Station, and reached for Dorothy's hand. The morning was shrouded by granite skies and dim light, the dull palette of greys in the city's downtown skyscrapers reflecting Emily's pensive mood as she prepared herself for the long journey back to Kansas.

Union Station was as beautiful as Emily remembered when it had first opened, the beautiful domed skylight in the Great Hall flooding the space below with light. But the benches where passengers had once waited for connections were now occupied by homeless men, asleep on newspaper bedsheets, the excited buzz of arrivals and departures replaced by the sobering pause of economic disaster.

Emily hurried past, leading Dorothy toward the platforms as she pointed out the Night and Day statues on the east wall as they passed beneath.

'Look, Dorothy. One holds an owl, the other a rooster, to mark the coming and going of passengers at all hours of the day and night. We have a rooster on the farm. You won't believe the noise he makes to wake us all up.'

She kept the tone of conversation light, desperate to distract the child so that she wouldn't dwell on what was actually happening. She couldn't bear a scene if Dorothy refused to board the train or decided she didn't want to go to Kansas after all. In the short time they'd spent together, Emily had seen what a pleasant, well-mannered child Dorothy was, admirably self-assured and forthright for someone so young, and yet she was acutely aware of how easily she could become upset.

Thankfully, the Golden State train was on time. With the trunk loaded into the luggage car, Emily and Dorothy took their seats in the second-class carriage. Dorothy pressed her toy lion and tin man to the window so that they could see out. Emily sat stiffly beside her. She still wasn't sure the child fully understood that she was leaving Chicago forever. The months and years ahead seemed to spool at Emily's feet like a thousand unravelled cotton reels.

She stiffened her shoulders as the last of the carriage doors were slammed shut. A wave of grief and trepidation washed over her, and something else, something shameful: an undeniable pang of resentment.

What had been asked of her wasn't unusual or unconventional. All across America, families were taking in their relatives' children when they became too poor or ill or incapable of looking after them, but this had all happened so suddenly and shockingly that it somehow made it harder to accept. And despite the attorney's presumption that it was most likely due to the additional family connection between John and Henry, Emily still didn't fully understand why Annie had named her and Henry as Dorothy's guardian. Nell was the obvious choice, having raised several children of her own, and in much better financial circumstances. Was it Annie's way of atoning for Emily's fall that winter of

Dorothy's birth? Was it a last act to somehow punish Emily for her outburst about Dorothy's father, or was it simply an oversight that Annie had never changed her will after their falling-out? Whatever the reason, she had to get on with it now, no matter how much she was dreading the days and weeks ahead.

The shrill blast of the whistle signalled their departure, and the locomotive strained to pull away from the station, making the carriage jolt. Emily's stomach lurched with it as Dorothy sat quietly beside her, engrossed in a book about Amelia Earhart's Atlantic flight. The book was called *20 Hrs. 40 Min.*, the title being the exact duration of Earhart's groundbreaking flight.

'She's very brave, isn't she,' Emily offered. 'I'm not sure I like the idea of being up in the sky.'

Dorothy turned the pages, admiring the pictures of Miss Earhart. 'I think it would be wonderful to fly. Mommy liked the aviators, too. She said she would take me up in a plane, one day.'

The pain of all Annie's unfulfilled plans, and all Dorothy's lost adventures with her mother, settled in Emily's heart. She thought about the long journey ahead for Dorothy, and how oblivious she was to the fact that the life she might have known was slipping away behind her while an uncertain future stretched out along the tracks ahead.

Emily's hand strayed to her coat pocket, where her fingers found the small lump of rock she still kept there. She remembered the feel of it in her pinafore pocket as she'd travelled toward a new life as a child, the tug and pull of its weight as their immigration cards were stamped. That little rock tied her back to Ireland, to her granny and her mother, whose steady guidance and wisdom she longed for more than ever as the train picked up speed.

'Hold out your hand, Dorothy.'

'What is it?' Dorothy asked, inspecting the green stone Emily placed in her palm.

'Lift it up to the sunlight. See how it sparkles?'

Dorothy gasped. 'Is it a diamond?'

'It's Connemara marble. Irish Green, they call it back in Ireland. Those are crystals, millions of years old.'

'Is it really all the way from Ireland?'

'Yes, and every piece is unique,' Emily explained. 'Each one different from the next. There's no other piece like this anywhere in the world.' It was as precious to Emily as any of Annie's glittering jewels.

Dorothy turned the rock over in her hands. 'The only one in the world,' she whispered.

Like you, Emily thought as she looked at the child, her hair tied into bunches with powder blue ribbons. She was so like Annie it was as if she was hewn from her, like the piece of Connemara marble pulled from Ireland's ancient earth.

She curled Dorothy's fingers around the little rock. 'Keep it. A piece of Ireland, to take with you to Kansas.'

Dorothy showed the little emerald stone to her lion and tin man. 'We're on the way to Kansas now,' she said, her voice small and quiet. 'To our new home.'

Home.

Before her life in Kansas, Emily had always thought of home as a temporary thing: a place she stayed in for a while but would inevitably leave. She'd never allowed herself to get attached, didn't quite know *how* to get attached to a place. Her mammy always said it was people who mattered, not places or things. 'It's family that makes a home. The rest is just bricks and mortar, a plot of land, a pin in the map.'

The only place she'd ever felt she truly belonged was Kansas, with Henry, and she couldn't wait to get back to them both.

So why, as the locomotive picked up speed, did she have such a terrible sense of foreboding?

25

Dorothy slept at Emily's side, lulled by the steady motion of Hank Miller's motorcar, her head lolling and nodding until it found a resting place against Emily's arm. She looked so peaceful that Emily hardly dared move as she looked at the child's face: curls at her temples, a rosy flush in pale cheeks that had never felt the heat of a prairie summer.

Emily's mind raced – Dorothy would need a hat to keep the sun off her face, plenty of loose cotton dresses, a decent pair of boots for the winter. There was so much to organise. Too much to think about. Her chest tightened as a sense of panic rose within her.

The miles passed beneath bone-dry earth, the tyres kicking up great clouds of dry dirt as Emily scanned the landscape, noting the familiar landmarks guiding her home – the broken fence, the abandoned claim, the lightning tree – until Gale Farm emerged through the dust.

Emily's heart stirred at the sight of it. Such a forlorn little place, but so brave and resilient. For all that it was, and all that it wasn't, it was home. It was like seeing an old friend across a crowded room full of strangers.

Gently, she woke the child. 'We're nearly there, Dorothy.'

Dorothy stirred, rubbed her eyes, and knelt up on the seat, her head turning this way and that as she took in the vast expanse of land all around.

Emily leaned forward. 'There it is. Do you see?'

The white picket fence beckoned in the distance, a beacon amid the vast landscape of ploughed, dusty acres that would soon bear the first green shoots of that season's crops.

Dorothy peered into the distance. 'That one? Right over there?'

'Yes. That's it.'

'But it looks so sad, and alone.'

Emily had always thought of their home as a sanctuary, a respite from the clatter and chaos of the city she'd left behind. The distance from their farm to their friends in Liberal had seemed to shrink over the years so that she rarely felt alone, apart from in the depths of winter when the snow drifted as high as the roof and cut them off from everyone for weeks. But as she looked at the house through Dorothy's eyes now, Emily felt its isolation. What she saw wasn't sanctuary but solitude, a great distance from anyone who might help them, should they need it.

'Oh, but it isn't alone at all,' she said, forcing herself to be cheerful. 'Our neighbours are antelope and jackrabbits, the sun and the moon, hawks and meadowlarks and wild mustang thundering across the prairie grass.'

Dorothy pressed her nose to the glass and peered out further. 'I can't see any wild horses. Why is it all so grey?' she asked. 'Where are all the trees, and the pretty wildflowers?'

Emily felt like a fraud as she heard the disappointment in the child's voice. She wished she could have given her a different welcome, like the once she remembered so vividly, as if she'd walked into the pages of the pamphlet her mother had carried with her from Ireland. *Golden stalks of wheat . . . rivers of grain . . . a land of sunshine and rain . . . a shimmering mirage of emerald and gold . . .* She could still feel Henry's hand in hers, the prickle of excitement at the back of her neck, the burst of colour that had welcomed her. Now the wheels of Hank's Model T turned apologetically over the scarred parched land.

'We haven't had rain in a while,' she said. 'But when it comes, and when the wheat grows and sways like great waves on a green ocean, oh my, what a feast for the eyes. It will bloom again, in time.'

Time was what they all needed now. Time for the crops and wildflowers to grow, time for their fortunes to turn and the rains to return, time to adjust to a new rhythm of life amid the unpredictable whims of this ancient land, time to accept the awful truth that Annie was dead, and the daughter she'd loved with all her heart was left to seek out any scraps of colour or hope in this strange new place.

Emily's heart heaved with the lurch of the motorcar as it lumbered on over the rutted uneven tracks until, at last, Hank pulled into the front yard and came to a stop. He took the few items of luggage from the trunk and wished Emily good luck as he pressed his hands to hers.

'I'll leave you to it. Let little Dorothy get settled. You know where we are, if you need anything.'

Part of Emily wished she could drive back to Liberal with Hank. Part of her wished she could go all the way back to Kansas City, take her seat on the Golden State train and head west, to California, to Nell. They would ride horses together through lush fields and talk about the old days beside the fire, just the two of them. She'd turned down Nell's offer of a safe home, choosing instead to ride out their struggles in Kansas, to follow a road that had led her to this moment. She'd made her choice. Now she had to find the courage to see it through.

She had rarely felt more lost and unsure as she watched Hank drive away. She placed a hand to her head to secure her hat from a strengthening breeze, and the other to her heart to steady her rising sense of apprehension.

Dorothy looked at the little clapboard house in front of her. 'It's very small.'

Emily searched for the words to respond. Should she berate the child for being rude? Correct her, punish her, or reassure her?

'It's plenty big enough,' she said defiantly, suddenly protective of this place that had kept them safe through winter storms and scorching summers. When everything else was lost, this humble little home had become their castle.

The screen door opened with a familiar creak as Henry appeared, a wide smile on his face, the wind ever present in his rusted cheeks.

'Well, if it isn't the one and only Dorothy Gale, blown all the way to Kansas from Chicago!'

Dorothy looked at Emily for reassurance.

She placed a hand on the child's shoulder, and smiled. 'That's your uncle Henry, dear.'

Emily looked at Henry as if seeing him properly for the first time in years. She was shocked by his appearance – his long beard, the dark hollows around his eyes where time and worry had drawn cracks and fissures like a dry creek bed, the limp from his old ankle injury more pronounced than she recalled. He looked old and tired, bent by the worry he'd lugged around in the years since the tornado, and the financial ruin that had followed the stock market crash and the collapse of the National Bank that had taken the last of their savings with it.

He strode forward and held out a hand. 'Very pleased to meet you, Miss Dorothy!'

Dorothy took Henry's hand with a shy smile.

'But wait a minute! What's this?' He reached behind Dorothy's ear and produced a silver nickel, and then another, with a great flourish.

Emily had watched him perform the trick dozens of times at the county fair. He was never less than 100 per cent committed to the act, and the children all loved him.

Dorothy gasped as he placed the silver coins in her hand.

'Can I keep them?' she asked.

'Of course! Seems they were yours anyway! Now, why don't you come on inside and then I'll show you around the farm. I made corn cakes. Do you like corn cakes?'

'I don't think I've ever had corn cake. Is it like chocolate cake?'

Henry laughed. Emily hadn't heard him laugh for such a long time that the sound came as a surprise.

'It isn't a bit like chocolate cake, I'm afraid,' he said. 'And now I'm hankering for a slice. Is chocolate cake your favourite?'

'Yes.'

He placed his hands on his hips in mock surprise. 'You don't say! It's mine too!'

Emily's heart surged with love for him. He was a good man. She'd been so wrapped up in her own grief and worry that she hadn't much considered Henry's part in all this. Dorothy's arrival would be as much of a disruption to his life as to hers, and yet here he was, acting like the child had always lived there.

Emily walked to him and pressed her cheek to his, savouring the familiar earthy scent of him. 'Thank you.'

'What for? Making corn cakes? You haven't tasted them yet.' He smiled as he placed an arm around her waist. 'Everything OK?' he asked, his voice low as he tipped his head in Dorothy's direction.

There was so much Emily wanted to say, but it was impossible to talk with the child listening to every word – something else they would have to get used to.

'We'll talk later,' she said.

'She's a sweet little thing,' Henry remarked as Dorothy walked up the porch steps ahead of them. 'I see plenty of Annie in her. Nothing of John, fortunately for her! She's definitely got your Irish Kelly genes. Not so much of the Midwest Gales.'

Emily's stomach tumbled. 'Does that bother you?'

'Not really. Though I guess it would have been neat to see something of our side of the family in her.'

Emily could almost hear the unspoken words in Henry's head. *'Especially since I don't have a child of my own.'*

The old weathervane creaked on the barn roof as it swung around to the west.

The wind had already changed.

26

Henry had worked hard to make the place look welcoming – a pretty rose-patterned oilcloth had been set over the table, a jug of peach tea waiting for the thirsty travellers. He'd swept and tidied and set up a makeshift bedroom for Dorothy where there used to be a closet. A few timber posts and an old curtain had done a reasonable job.

'Go ahead, Dorothy. Take a look around,' Emily said, although there really wasn't much to look at.

The temporary shelter Henry had rebuilt after the tornado had become their permanent home. They'd added to it over the years, but it was still not much more than a single room with carefully positioned items of furniture to create areas they called the kitchen, living room, and bedroom. The bed even folded against the wall during the day to make better use of the space. Emily still grieved for the house they'd lost, but she'd grown fond of this new home in the way someone might love a careworn old dress or a favourite childhood toy. She knew every knot in every board, every shadow cast by the moonlight, every crack and creak as the timber flexed when the temperature soared and dipped. It was part of her story now, inseparable from the person she'd become.

And yet it was suddenly different.

Smaller.

Apologetic, almost.

Dorothy walked around, carefully inspecting her new surroundings. She opened the doors on the old cooking stove, lifted teacups and plates from the dresser that stood against the south wall. She reached onto her tiptoes to look out of the windows. She took a turn in each of the rocking chairs that Henry had fixed and remade after the tornado, and which, once again, stood either side of a small fireplace on the west wall.

Emily watched as small footsteps passed over the concealed tornado cellar and traversed the path of rag rugs that covered the linoleum floor. She found herself mesmerised as inquisitive little fingers pointed at the framed samplers and family photographs that hung from nails on the walls. 'Who's that?' 'And who's that?' 'What's that for?' 'Where's the bathroom?' Question after question. It was strange to hear a child's voice in this childless home. Unsettling.

'And this is where you'll sleep,' Henry said as he pulled back the curtain to Dorothy's makeshift bedroom. A little doll made of straw had been placed on her pillow.

'That's for you, Dorothy,' Henry said. 'Made it with my own hands.'

Dorothy picked up the little doll and admired her. 'What is she made of?'

'Straw. She's known as a Brigid doll. Something your aunt Emily taught me, an old custom from Ireland. We make the dolls from the last sheaf from the harvest and burn them the following spring to bring good luck to the new season's crops.'

'Burn them?' Dorothy clutched the doll tight to her chest.

Emily stared at Henry. 'Uncle Henry won't burn *your* doll, Dorothy. Will you?'

Henry shook his head. 'Gosh! Of course not!' He glanced at Emily and mouthed a 'sorry'.

Their first mistake.

Dorothy introduced the straw doll to her toy lion and tin man and stood them all up on the windowsill, so that they were facing out. 'That's Kansas,' she whispered. 'This is our home now.'

When Dorothy was hungry, they sat at the hand-carved pine chairs at the small table and ate corn cakes and drank peach tea. Three chairs. Three plates. Three glasses. For someone so small, Dorothy seemed to take up the room of ten men.

Emily could hardly eat, her stomach a tangle of knots. She ate quietly while Henry told Dorothy all about the county fair she could look forward to that summer, and the carnival stalls and sideshow performers who would arrive with their incredible illusions and magic. He captured her imagination with stories about the barnstormers who performed daring shows over the farmers' fields and offered dollar rides in their planes.

'Like Miss Earhart?' Dorothy asked, her wide-eyed excitement hard to resist.

'A bit like Miss Earhart, yes!'

Henry carried none of the awkward hesitancy Emily had felt in Chicago. She observed him carefully, hoping to absorb some of his easy manner with the child.

When they'd eaten, Henry asked Dorothy if she would like to meet the animals.

'Lions first, or bears?'

Dorothy's mouth fell open. 'Lions and bears?'

'Henry!' Emily scolded him for teasing. 'There aren't any lions *or* bears, Dorothy. Your uncle Henry is being silly.'

Henry winked at Dorothy. 'We'll start with the tigers, then.'

Dorothy laughed. She was beginning to understand her uncle's sense of humour. 'You're funny, Uncle Henry.'

Emily stiffened at the sound of the child's laughter. It felt so out of tune with this place of quiet struggle and serious conversation. She'd thought the hard part would be leaving Chicago, extracting Dorothy from the life she'd known. But now that they were back in Kansas, she understood that leaving had been the easy bit. This was where the hard work started, every unfamiliar moment a stark reminder of how different life would now be.

She watched from the window as Henry and Dorothy walked to the barn together. A little while later, the sound came again: a loud shriek of laughter.

Emily felt dizzy. She placed one hand to her chest and gripped the edge of the sink as she leaned over, retching until her body purged itself of the grief and guilt and regret she'd held in since learning of Annie's accident. She wiped her mouth with her sleeve and leaned against the sink to steady her breathing as the screen door squeaked and Dorothy wandered inside, arms full of apples.

'Uncle Henry said I could help you make a pie.'

Emily shook off her thoughts. 'Of course. That's a nice idea.'

She peeled and cored the apples, working methodically, but her mind was elsewhere as she passed the apples to Dorothy to cut into chunks for the pie.

'Will you show me the blossom, Auntie Em?'

'Hmm?' Emily was miles away.

'The blossom inside the apples. You showed me how to remove the peel all in one piece, and the shape of apple blossom inside.'

She had paid attention after all.

Emily's heart raced as she cut a thin slice of apple. 'There it is, see. A perfect apple blossom in every slice.'

Dorothy walked to the window and held the translucent slice of apple up to the light, but Emily didn't see Dorothy there. She saw Annie beside the old oak table, the wind rattling the windows, turf smoke in the air, a broadside ballad on her mammy's lips, and now on hers as she picked up the refrain and the haunting melody filled the little prairie house just as it had once filled the stone cottage in Connemara. She closed her eyes a moment and prayed. *Show me how to do this, Mammy. Please help me.*

'What's next?' Dorothy asked as she returned to the table. 'What do we do next for the pie, Auntie Em?'

Emily reached for the child's hand. What *did* they do next? How would she ever bear this? She felt the long hours and days stretching ahead, the months and years full of questions and uncertainty.

'We roll out the pastry,' she said, anchoring herself back to the practical tasks that she knew and trusted. 'Quick firm movements. We don't want to overwork the pastry or it will become tough.' She took Dorothy's hands and showed her. 'Roll and turn. Roll and turn. See, look how the circle starts to come.'

This was how she would bear it, with the help of the prairie and all that it demanded of anyone who lived there. They would sweep the floors and wash the windows. Lift the rugs and beat and air them. They would pump water from the well, strip the beds and hang the washed sheets on the line. They would make the bread, collect the eggs, tend to the vegetable garden, ride the tractor, turn the plough, reap the rewards of another harvest.

One task after another.

One faltering step at a time.

Courage when everything seemed hopeless.

That evening, when Dorothy was asleep, Emily opened the journal she'd written in since she'd first arrived in Kansas eight years earlier. She read the inscription inside: *To my dear Emily, Mammy used to say there is no place like your own home. I hope you will always be happy in yours. Annie x* Emily turned the pages then, reliving the memories of her life here, captured in her private thoughts and reflections.

April 5th, 1924. First day in Kansas. What an extraordinary place! Every colour is more vibrant, every sound clearer, every flower more beautiful and fragrant. Heaven, if you believe in such a thing . . .

July 18th, 1924. Bumper harvest. The grain is pouring from the threshers. Henry can hardly keep up as he records the yields in his ledger . . .

December 3rd, 1925. Snow! I might love the prairie even more in the wintertime. There's a peacefulness here when the winds don't howl. We are as cosy as hibernating bears . . .

January 1st, 1926. I stitched new curtains for the windows, blue-and-white gingham with a lace trim.

August 25th, 1929. I think I am pregnant.

Her heart ached as she recalled the joy and optimism she'd once known. She felt so entirely removed from that version of herself now. She didn't read the entries that had come after the tornado and the crash, afraid to acknowledge how suddenly everything had changed. Henry believed they'd had their run of bad luck now – the tornado, losing the baby, losing their life savings – but Emily couldn't shake the feeling that there was worse yet to come.

She added the date, and started a new entry.

February 8th, 1932. Home again. Her pen paused over the page. She didn't know what else to add, what to say about everything that had happened since her last entry, the night before she'd received the telegram about Annie's accident. Eventually, she wrote just three more words which seemed to hold the weight of the world within them.

Dorothy is here.

*

She snatched restless scraps of sleep until she was awoken by a piercing scream. For a moment, she thought a coyote had got inside. She lay in the pitch dark, heart pounding. The scream came again.

Dorothy!

She rushed to the child, gently shaking her shoulder to pull her out of her nightmare as Cora had shown her to.

'It's Auntie Em, dear. Wake up. It was just a dream. Just a bad dream.'

'*A black wind*,' Cora had said. '*Such a curious child.*'

Dorothy opened her eyes, her breaths coming quick and shallow, her face silvered by the moon that hung over the prairie. 'Where am I? Where's Mommy?'

'You're in Kansas, dear. With Auntie Em and Uncle Henry. Remember? You're safe here. It was just a dream.'

Dorothy sat up. Her cheeks were flushed and warm to the touch. She was desperately thirsty. 'Water. I need water.'

Emily fetched a glass of water and sat with the child as she drank in big, thirsty gulps. Gradually her breathing slowed and she calmed down.

'Will you tell me a story? Mommy always told me a story after a bad dream.'

A dull ache settled on Emily's forehead and her bones ached from the tension she'd carried around for the last week. She just wanted to sleep, but what *she* wanted was no longer a priority.

'Would you like the story of *Tír na nÓg*?' she asked.

Dorothy nodded her head.

Emily straightened the bedspread and tucked it around the child's narrow form. 'Now, close your eyes and think nice thoughts and I'll tell you all about the story of Oisín and Niamh and the *Tuatha Dé Danann*. The Little People.'

Eventually, Dorothy slept. It was hard to believe that someone so small and peaceful could hold such power over them.

As Emily watched this borrowed child who'd arrived like a changeling left by the fairies, she allowed her thoughts to roam through the darkness, recalling the nights through her last pregnancy when she'd imagined sitting at her own child's bedside, watching the rise and fall of the bedspread as they slept. She thought, then, of the stories she might have read to them, and the imagined conversations with toy lions and tin men that she might have heard from across the room if life had taken her in a different direction. 'Perhaps that's not our road to travel, Em,' Henry had said. 'Perhaps there's something else we're meant to do.' They would care for Dorothy, protect her and love her as if she were their own, but the trace of the illusion would always be there.

Emily returned to her bed, but she couldn't sleep, conscious of the child behind the curtain and distracted by the thoughts circling her mind. Henry's earlier remark about Dorothy's lack of resemblance to John sat like a stone in her stomach. She wondered how much Leonardo Stregone might know about Dorothy. Had he ever met the child? Did he know about Annie and John's accident and, if so, would he try to look for Dorothy now? Could he be the one to force her to share the truth with Henry – and Dorothy – and what then for them all? She thought back to all the forms she'd signed at the attorneys'. She and Henry were Dorothy's legal guardians, but would that matter if Leonardo could prove he was her father? Could he drag Dorothy off to live a life of a travelling circus performer, forever moving from town to town? And then there were Annie's letters to Dorothy. Had she revealed the truth about Dorothy's father in the sixteenth birthday letter?

Quietly, Emily crept from the bed and took the shoebox from the wardrobe. She pulled out the bundle of letters and lifted one toward the light cast by the moon. *Dorothy – Sixteen*. Emily's fingers traced the familiar loops and swirls of Annie's neat, cursive writing before she turned the envelope over to trace the outline of the sealed edges. The temptation to open it was overwhelming; the power it held, undeniable.

Behind her, Henry stirred. She returned the letters to the box, placed the box in the wardrobe, and crept back into bed.

Whatever secrets the letters held were not hers to know.

Yet.

27

The next day, Emily took Dorothy into Liberal. The child needed a sturdy pair of boots – she had nothing suitable for farm life, only city life. Emily hoped the thrift store would have something she could make do with.

Dorothy was pleased to sit up front in the motorcar where she could better see the colonial-style buildings and clapboard houses, the town library and drugstore, the saloons and diners. But what she saw was a town that was almost unrecognisable from the vibrant place Emily had once known: a place of Saturday dances and carefree laughter, the thump of the double bass carried on a warm summer breeze before a downpour sent them all dancing in the street to cool down. Now, those once-ambitious prosperous folk sat around on stoops and leaned against doorways, looking lost and tired. What they wouldn't give for one of those precious downpours now.

Emily pulled the motorcar to a stop outside the general store and led Dorothy inside, the bell above the door chiming its familiar greeting.

Laurie Miller looked up from her stocktaking. She smiled warmly when she saw who it was.

'Emily, dear! You're back!' She stepped out from behind the counter to embrace her friend. 'How was everything?' she asked, keeping her voice low. 'We've all been so worried.'

Emily clung to her friend and let out a long breath. It took all her strength not to crumble at Laurie's feet. She was so exhausted by the emotion and worry of it all. 'It was so hard, Laurie. And I expect it's only going to get worse before it gets better.'

Laurie tightened her embrace. 'We'll talk later.' She bent down to Dorothy then and held out her hand. 'And this must be Dorothy! Hello, dear. Welcome to Kansas!'

Emily placed an encouraging hand on Dorothy's back. 'Say hello to Mrs Miller, Dorothy.'

Dorothy clung to Emily's skirt and muttered a shy hello.

Laurie offered a warm smile. 'It's very nice to meet you, Dorothy. Would y'all like to choose something from the candy counter while I talk to your aunt a moment? You can pick anything you like.'

Dorothy's face brightened a little. 'Anything?'

Laurie nodded. 'Anything at all!'

'Not too much, mind,' Emily cautioned, feeling that it was the sensible thing to say.

With gentle encouragement, Dorothy let go of Emily's skirt and walked to the candy counter.

'She's adorable, Em. Those big eyes. And look at those precious red shoes. How's she coping?'

'She's up and down. Being incredibly brave about it all.'

'And you? What a dreadful tragedy for you all.'

'Honestly? I'm terrified, Laurie. I don't know how we'll ever afford—'

Laurie reached for Emily's hand. 'Henry told us about the financial situation. Good Lord. Did you have any idea?'

Emily shook her head. 'Nor did Annie, by all accounts.'

'We pulled together a few bits to welcome Dorothy.' Laurie reached for a box beneath the counter. 'A few toys, and a couple of books from the library. And I thought these old boots might come in handy. A bit big, but she'll grow into them. I don't imagine she needed anything quite so sturdy in Chicago.'

'That's so kind, Laurie. Thank you.'

'Least we could do.'

Emily took a copy of *Anne of Green Gables* from the box. It was a story she'd loved as a child, tucked up in bed between her sisters, Nell reading the story out loud, Annie pleading for one more page.

'I thought Dorothy might find something of a friend in Anne Shirley,' Laurie said. They both looked at Dorothy, teetering on scarlet tiptoes, straining to see what was available at the candy counter. 'The poor dear. Such a sweet little thing.'

'I just hope we can make Kansas feel like home. It's so different from the city.'

'She'll be settled in by the first harvest, you see if she isn't.'

Time here was measured not by clocks but by nature, everything counted by the seasonal changes. *'It'll be done by the first thaw.' 'She's due at the end of the wheat harvest.' 'It'll be ready by the fall.'* There was something reassuring about measuring time this way, the only clocks the moon and the sun, the movement of the stars, the coming and going of birds and flowers. Emily thought about Annie's hourglass in the box she'd brought from Chicago. She was reluctant to unpack it, afraid, almost, of the pieces of Annie's life that held such powerful memories. The hourglass and her silver shoes, especially.

'You'd best put that back, child, unless your mother has the money to pay for it.'

Emily stiffened at the brusque voice behind her. She turned to see Wilhelmina West, nosing around as usual with her haughty superiority. She'd only spoken to the woman a handful of times in the years since arriving in Liberal, and that was plenty enough.

Dorothy quickly put a liquorice whip and a chocolate bar back onto the counter and rushed to the safety of Emily's skirts.

Emily glared at Wilhelmina defiantly. 'You can pick those back up, Dorothy. It's quite all right.'

'She's with you?' Wilhelmina frowned at the girl.

'Yes. She's with me.'

'Your sister's child. Of course. My sympathies to you both.' Wilhelmina studied Dorothy for a moment, as if weighing up her next move. 'She's a pretty thing. Didn't mean to startle her.'

Emily stood her ground. 'Then maybe you shouldn't go around throwing accusations at innocent children.'

Wilhelmina huffed. 'Most of them deserve it. Nothing but trouble.' She left the money on the counter for a can of castor oil and left the store with a swish of her skirt.

The three of them watched as she jumped onto her bicycle and set off, ringing her bell harshly at a group of boys playing hopscotch in the street.

'That woman!' Laurie said under her breath. 'Lord forgive me, but I wouldn't be sorry if her and that bicycle found themselves at the bottom of a very deep ditch!'

Laurie took a scoop of lemon drops from a jar and added them to a paper bag along with the other candy. 'You make sure to enjoy them, Dorothy. We're all looking forward to seeing you in the schoolroom Monday.'

Emily hadn't even thought about Dorothy's schooling. Once again, she was grateful for Laurie's steady pragmatism.

'Who was that mean lady?' Dorothy asked as they left the store. 'She looked like a witch.'

'Goodness, Dorothy! We mustn't say unkind things about people, even if they're not very kind to us.' For all of Wilhelmina's unpleasantness, Emily couldn't help feeling a little sorry for her.

'But she did look like a witch,' Dorothy continued. 'Do you think she *is* one?'

'There's no such thing as witches. They're made-up people who live in stories.' Emily's mind filled with a memory of her Granny Mary telling stories about *An Chailleach*, the queen of winter, and the festival of *Samhain* that signalled the beginning of winter and the witching season. She could almost smell the musty turnip lanterns they'd carved and left at the windows to ward off evil spirits. 'Besides,' she continued as they walked to the haberdashery, 'even if there was such a thing, all the witches would have left Kansas years ago.'

'Why?' Dorothy asked.

'Because of all the scarecrows in the fields. Didn't you know? Witches are afraid of scarecrows.'

Emily was pleased to see the curve of a smile at Dorothy's lips.

She allowed herself a rare moment of satisfaction as she recalled Cora's words of advice. *'You don't have to become Dorothy's mother, Mrs Gale. You only need to remember what it is to be a child.'*

*

The hourglass kept turning, and the first disruptive weeks of Dorothy's arrival leaned into more settled months as they lurched through the last breaths of February's winter, stumbled through an unusually warm March, and struggled into a dry, dusty April. And still the rain didn't come. The parched earth had turned the once-colourful oasis of purple verbena and verdant buffalo grass into a dull palette of sepia, the landscape altered beyond all recognition.

Life was just as different for Emily, Henry and Dorothy, everything taking on a new shape as they stretched and bent around one another like the rods of iron the blacksmith hammered to make the horseshoes. Some days, Dorothy was compliant and yielding. Other times she was stiff and brittle, refusing to conform to her aunt and uncle's will. Her arrival had disrupted the familiar melody of Emily and Henry's life, and everything sounded off-key.

Emily tried her best to remain patient and make allowances for the child, but the flux of emotions she provoked in Emily were unsettling. She felt lacking when Dorothy became upset, too stern when she had reason to chastise her, and she still couldn't bear to hear the child's laughter without hearing the echo of her own lost children within it. What sort of a person was she to resent the child's fleeting moments of happiness? Was she becoming as bitter and resentful as Wilhelmina West?

The weather that year was as unpredictable as the child, refusing to bring the rains they all desperately needed after the unusually dry winter and spring. Emily watched the sky every day, searching for a sign of rain clouds, praying for sundogs – the telltale halo that formed around the sun and a sure sign that the rains were coming – but still the rain didn't come as the sun rose ever higher and the temperatures soared with the arrival of summer and the first day of May – *Bealtaine*. This was the time of year when the veil between worlds was at its thinnest, when magic and folklore laced the air. Emily and Dorothy picked the few wildflowers they could find and laid them on the porch steps to protect their home over the coming year. It was a tradition Emily had observed since she was a child, but she paid particular attention that year as she placed her posy of yellow cinquefoil on the steps.

'Are the Little People real?' Dorothy asked as she carefully placed her bunch of flowers on the step. She was fascinated by the ancient Irish traditions and the stories Emily told her.

Emily wasn't sure if she should fill the child's head with notions of faery folk, but she remembered something of being a young girl and believing in something magical. 'Of course they're real. But only very lucky people ever see them.'

Emily and Henry talked about little else now. What Dorothy

was thinking, doing, feeling consumed every thought and conversation. They often disagreed on the best course of action, at odds with each other in a way they had never been before. Emily hated it when they argued. Henry blamed the high temperatures for their short tempers. The heavy heat of the day lingered long after sundown, leaving the air inside the house still and stagnant.

'Everyone is hot and irritable,' he said. 'A good downpour will bring us to our senses. Heard talk of a rainmaker over in Dalhart last week. Maybe he'll make his way to us soon.'

Emily tutted. 'Rainmakers! Never heard such nonsense. They're no better than carnival showmen with their tricks and illusions.' She'd heard of these men launching sticks of dynamite into the sky tied to balloons, peddling their dubious science to susceptible crowds. 'Desperate folk will believe anything,' she said. 'There's only one man with the power to make it rain, Henry. And He seems to have forgotten us.'

Yet despite her scepticism, she understood the allure of the rainmakers and the willingness of farmers to believe in their promises. Without rain, the crops wouldn't grow. Without rain, the parched topsoil blew.

And that meant dust.

All across the Great Plains, folk were reporting more and more of the awful dusters and black blizzards, great clouds of earth that rolled across the prairie, spewing dust and dirt over farms and towns, choking people half to death. Even on days when the dusters didn't roll, there was no escaping it. When Emily ran her hands through her hair she felt the grit with her fingertips, like sandpaper against her scalp. Sometimes she thought she would go mad, but no amount of washing or bathing got rid of it. When she swept the floor, a fine gritty film settled again within an hour. If she cleaned a plate and set it on the table, it was speckled with dust by the time dinner was out of the stove. Dust crept through the wet rags and newspapers they stuffed against the windows and doors. It seeped into the damp cloths they held to their mouths and noses. Sometimes she felt she would suffocate beneath it. Even when Emily picked up her father's fiddle, she couldn't catch a clear note, the bow scratching horribly over the strings. She blamed the dust. She blamed the dust for everything lately.

But even worse than the dust Emily could see, was the dust she couldn't.

Animals were falling sick and dying from dust fever, and prairie folk were dying from dust pneumonia caused by a layer of dust settling deep in their lungs. The prairie was slowly choking them, killing them from the inside. And still the rain didn't come, and tempers remained as frayed as an unstitched hem on a feed-sack dress. As Emily watched Dorothy playing with her few toys, she worried that she'd brought her to the worst place on earth.

That evening, as she got ready for Thursday supper club, Emily stared at her reflection in the hand mirror. She hardly recognised the stern, world-weary person looking back. There was no colour there, no joy. The vibrant, determined woman who'd thrived here in their first few summers had faded away.

She'd known that life here would be tough, but she could never have imagined just how hard it would be. Nobody had ever known it this bad. Not even the old-timers. It was a test for them all. Almost like a physical pain, she yearned for the life she'd known before the drought and dust and – if she dared to admit it – before the added responsibility and worry about Dorothy.

She longed for something to change, for rain and colour to return to the prairie, for a sense of joy to return to her life.

Desperate and afraid, she looked to the sky and prayed for help, for guidance.

'Show me,' she whispered. 'Give me a sign that everything will be all right.'

*

Although she was weary, she was glad to spend time with the other women at their weekly supper club. It was a relief to leave Dorothy with Henry for a few hours and she already felt a little lighter as she drove the Model T into Liberal.

They spent the evening talking about the approaching county fair and the barnstormers Hank had seen practising over Ike West's farm.

'Couldn't have picked a worse place in all of Kansas,' May Lucas joked. 'Mina West will have them arrested for trespassing.'

'I'm not sure you can trespass in the sky!' Emily said.

May rolled her eyes. 'I'm quite sure Mina West thinks she owns the damn sky, as well as most of the town.'

Emily laughed. 'They're such an odd pair, aren't they. The other sister never seems to leave the house. What does she do all day?'

'Who cares?' Laurie said. 'They only cause trouble when they're around.'

'I do feel a bit sorry for them, rattling around that big old farmhouse. Do you think we should invite them to join us one evening?'

Everyone stared at Emily, a look of shock on their faces.

'I'll take that as a no,' she said.

As the women talked, they kept their hands busy, making dresses from empty flour or feed sacks. The Gingham Girl flour sacks were the most popular. All the girls liked those dresses the best. Others wore dresses made from sacks patterned with cornflowers, primroses, or checks. Emily had learned quickly that nothing was wasted on the prairie, and that even for the child of the poorest family, a pretty sack dress could bring a much-needed smile. Dorothy had asked Emily to make her a sack dress, even though she had several perfectly good cotton dresses. She said she wanted to be like the other girls at school. As Emily sewed the stiff fabric, she thought about the expensive silk her mother used to work with as a dressmaker for Marshall Field's. There was something admirable about these simple homemade thrift dresses, with many hours of care, sacrifice and love sewn into them.

'Well, ladies,' Laurie said eventually, 'let's say another prayer for rain before we finish up. Surely the Heavens will answer soon.'

'Henry was telling me about another of those rainmakers, out Dalhart way, performing his tricks,' Emily said.

'Hank was talking about it, too. Reckons he's going to raise a collection to pay for one to come here,' Laurie said.

'You don't believe in it, do you?' Emily asked. 'Secret ingredients to conjure moisture? TNT and nitroglycerine exploding to create rain? I'm sure it's just swindlers taking advantage of desperate folk, telling them what they want to believe.'

Laurie let out a heavy sigh. 'I don't know what to believe anymore, but if it takes a stick of dynamite to bring the rain and stop those damn dusters rolling through, I'll believe anything they tell me.'

The women held their hands in prayer and asked the Lord for rain and a good harvest and higher prices, and to keep them all safe from dusters and tornadoes.

On the way home, Emily looked to the cloudless skies and the ripe summer sun sinking low on the horizon, and prayed again for a miracle, for the sky to give them something – anything – other than this relentless, suffocating heat and dust. Surely the rain would come soon.

As she turned onto the track toward the house, Dorothy came running to meet her.

'Auntie Em! Auntie Em! Come and see!'

Emily pulled the motorcar to a stop and jumped out, her heart racing. 'Is it Henry? What's happened? Why aren't you in bed?'

'There's a lady! And a real airplane! In the barn! She says I can go up in it!'

Emily told the child to stop talking nonsense.

'It's true! I saw her fall right out of the sky. Come and see!'

Dorothy grabbed Emily by the arm and practically dragged her toward the barn.

'Goodness, child, slow down!'

As Emily reached the barn door, she could hardly believe what she saw. Dorothy wasn't talking nonsense. There *was* a plane. And a woman, standing beside it.

Emily cleared her throat. Dorothy stood at her side, jumping up and down with excitement.

The woman turned, put down an oil can and stepped forward. A warm smile spread across crimson lips as her eyes met Emily's.

'You must be Auntie Em!' She thrust out a hand. 'Adelaide Watson. Real pleased to meet you, Mrs Gale! This little firecracker here has told me all about you!'

28

Adelaide Watson was the most beautiful woman Emily had ever seen, a dazzling vision in khaki green, hair that fell in perfect golden waves to her shoulders, scarlet lips that formed a playful smile. Emily felt like a sack of flour beside her.

'Well, this is all quite the surprise!' she said, looking to Henry for an explanation as her arm was pumped energetically up and down like a piston.

Henry shrugged, a bemused look on his face.

'Sorry to land on you folks like this,' Adelaide said. 'Took a bit of engine trouble in a duster and had to pitch her down real quick. Turns out your field was the one to catch us.'

'I watched Miss Adelaide fall out of the sky, Auntie Em! I told Uncle Henry right away!'

Dorothy's excitement was contagious. Emily had never seen her so animated.

'Seems I chose just the right place to come down, too, Mrs. Gale. Dorothy has been such a dear. And your husband has been very helpful.'

Henry was clearly as enchanted by Adelaide as Dorothy was. 'I'm sure he has,' Emily said with a wry smile. 'And please, call me Emily.' She walked toward the aircraft. 'I'm glad you made it down safely. What sort of plane is it?'

'This here's a Jenny.' Adelaide affectionately ran her hand over the paintwork of the fuselage. 'One of the best – or, at least, she was, in her heyday. She's a bit beat up now, the old dear.'

'Aren't we all,' Emily added wryly.

Adelaide laughed. 'Sure feels like it sometimes!'

'Isn't she pretty!' Dorothy grabbed Emily's hand.

For a moment, Emily thought the child was referring to their visitor, before she realised she was talking about the plane.

'What does the number 99 mean, Miss Adelaide?' Dorothy continued.

'I'm part of a group called the Ninety-Nines, a special club set up for female pilots and aviators. Our president is a wonderful lady called Amelia Earhart. You might have heard of her.'

Dorothy gasped. 'You know Amelia Earhart?'

'Sure do! You like her?'

Dorothy nodded enthusiastically. 'My mommy kept a scrapbook about her. She even had a travelling case with Miss Earhart's name on it. I have a book about her!'

'Is that so! Then you know she's from Kansas, right?'

Dorothy's eyes widened. 'She's from Kansas, Auntie Em!'

Emily smiled. 'Isn't that something!'

'And a fine Kansas woman, too,' Adelaide added. 'Raced against her in the Powder Puff Derby of '29. Best female flyer I ever met, or likely ever will. She's planning a solo transatlantic flight in a few weeks. Has me thinking about trying it myself one day.'

Dorothy asked question after question: Was it hard to fly a plane? Was it scary to be up so high? How did the plane stay in the sky?

'Say, would you like to sit in the cockpit, Dorothy?'

Emily stepped forward. 'Oh, I'm not sure that's a—'

Dorothy was already halfway inside before Emily could finish her sentence.

Adelaide took Dorothy's hand to help her up. 'That's it. Climb up those steps there and just slide yourself right in.'

'I'm sure Miss Watson has plenty to be getting along with, Dorothy,' Emily said. 'We don't want to get in her way.'

Adelaide reassured them she didn't have much to be getting on with at all. 'Not until this old lady is fixed up. That's the beauty of a life like mine. No schedule to follow. No appointments to keep, or miss. I make my own rules.'

'Well then, mind you don't touch anything, or break anything, Dorothy,' Emily added as she stepped beneath the nose to admire the propellers.

'Touch away!' Adelaide countered. 'No fun sitting up front if you can't try out a few pedals and switches. Only way to learn how to fly is to have a go, right?'

Emily heard the contrast of her careful caution and worry compared to Miss Watson's have-a-go enthusiasm. She and her Jenny seemed to have stepped right out of a page of Dorothy's book about Amelia Earhart, or one of the photographs she'd seen in the newspapers when Charles Lindbergh had flown the Spirit of St. Louis across the Atlantic. She had followed the daring exploits of the aviators with a passing interest over the years, reading accounts of their latest achievements in the newspaper and listening to wireless reports, but it was something entirely different to come face-to-face with one in your barn. A woman, especially.

There was something about the female aviators' bravery and glamour that Emily admired, not to mention their determination to match whatever the boys could do – beat them, even. For someone whose life was so rooted to the earth, it was fascinating to read about these daring women in their flying machines. Miss Watson encapsulated the sense of freedom and adventure Emily had once dreamed of with Annie when they were shopgirls at Field's, and only seemed to exaggerate her flagging sense of direction, and self-worth.

'Have you been flying long, Miss Watson?' she asked.

'Since I was Dorothy's age. My grandpa took me up one day and I was hooked! I'm one of the last of the barnstormers, scratching out a living from carnivals and county fairs, riding the coattails of the circus sideshows.'

Emily recalled the excitement the barnstormers had caused when they visited the prairie during the flying circus heydays of the twenties. 'We used to see plenty of you loop-the-looping over the fields, didn't we, Henry.'

'Sure did. We'd get dizzy, craning our necks to watch the show! We've hardly seen any barnstormers in recent years.'

'Since the federal government's restrictions came in, we can't perform as often as we did back then. I take my chances where I can. The circus is due to arrive in town next week and I'm hoping to run a bit of a sideshow if I can get this old dear fixed up.'

Dorothy's excitement increased. 'The circus! Can we go, Auntie Em? See the circus and Miss Adelaide's show?'

Emily was reminded of Dorothy chasing the old circus pamphlet down the sidewalk in Chicago, and how she'd promised her there would be other chances to go.

She'd seen the Ringling's circus posters in town earlier, and had tried to ignore them. For so long now, she'd put Annie's aerialist to the back of her mind, but seeing the posters and hearing Dorothy's excitement brought it all rushing back. It was silly to think that Leonardo might still be performing his Amazing Ascensions – after all, who cared about someone dangling from a balloon when people were performing stunts on the wings of airplanes? – and it was even more absurd to think that he somehow knew he had a daughter living in Kansas, yet an irrational worry nagged and nagged at Emily. For years, Leo had lurked like a shadow in her conscience, never quite real, but always there. He was, after all, the reason she and Annie had fallen out and grown apart. He was a dark secret she kept from Henry, even now, after Annie and John's accident.

The task of raising Dorothy worried Emily terribly, but her greatest fear was that they would learn to love the child beyond all measure, and have to, one day, let her go. Henry had longed for a child so dearly. If Leonardo appeared now to try and take Dorothy away, or even if he arrived and exposed the secrets Emily had kept from Henry . . . there was too much at stake, too much of their life that was already precariously balanced. She couldn't bear to think about anything upsetting Henry so deeply. He was hanging on by a thread as it was.

She pushed the thoughts from her head as Dorothy tugged on her arm.

'Please, Auntie Em! Can we go?'

She didn't want to appear boring in front of Adelaide. 'Very well. But you must do all your chores first.'

Dorothy promised she would. 'I'll do extra chores. I'll even clean out the pigs!'

She'd taken a dislike to the pigs after falling into their sty – even after she'd been specifically told *not* to walk around the top of the fence – so this offer was testament to just how eager she was.

'Don't suppose I could interest you folk in a free ride in exchange for a barn to sleep in for a few nights, and a landing strip in your field?' Adelaide asked, her face hopeful. 'But only if I'm not imposing.'

Henry popped his head up from beneath the wheels. 'I'm sure we can manage that, although you should know that we've had a couple of vagrants show up lately. Homeless folk headed west and looking for a place to rest the night. Mostly harmless, but you've to keep your wits about you. Desperate folk can be unpredictable.'

'I'll sleep with one eye open! I'm saving up for a solo transatlantic attempt. Have to take folks' generosity and hospitality where I can.'

'A solo flight?' Emily said. 'That's very brave.'

'Brave, or foolish? My mother can't understand why I would want to do such a thing. Know what I say to her in reply? Why not?'

The words reminded Emily of something she might have said years ago, when she'd been a fearless optimistic like Adelaide. Now, her life was one of hard facts and careful calculations. She could neither emotionally or financially afford to ask such an open-ended question as 'why not?'.

'Don't have to worry about anyone else when you're flying solo,' Adelaide continued. 'Although I'm hoping to team up with one of those rainmakers for a while first. Travel across the prairie towns. Take a share of the profits,' she explained. 'The closer you get to the clouds, the better those explosives must work, right? We'd be a match made in heaven. Quite literally!'

Henry was interested. 'I heard of a rainmaker out Dalhart way. Might be a good place to start looking, although from what I've heard they seem to move around quickly, so he might already be someplace else.'

Adelaide was grateful for the tip-off. 'I'll head out that way when I have this old girl fixed up. See if I can track him down.'

'And if you do find this sorcerer, bring him back, will you? We sure could do with some rain.' Henry's light humour hid the despair Emily knew he held in his heart. 'In the meantime, you are very welcome to stay, isn't she, Em?'

Emily smiled graciously, although she didn't know how they would ever manage to feed the woman. She was slender, at least.

Perhaps she didn't eat much. And despite her reservations, and the dizzying sense that her life was spinning wildly out of control, she heard herself saying, 'Of course. I'll set an extra place for dinner.'

'Sounds like a deal! Thank you. And please, let me provide dinner.' Adelaide reached into the back seat of the Jenny and lifted out a dead jackrabbit. 'Knocked him clean out when I landed.'

Emily couldn't help but smile. It seemed that Adelaide Watson had an answer for everything.

After they'd all eaten and Adelaide had taken herself off to the barn to sleep, Emily sat for a while on the porch, watching the stars as she turned the events of the day over in her mind. It had all happened so quickly that she'd barely had time to process everything. Not only was Dorothy living with them, but they now had a stranger staying in their barn.

'Quite a day, huh,' Henry said as he joined her.

'It certainly was.' Emily suddenly worried they'd all been bewitched by Adelaide's vivacious manner and beauty and had made a mistake in inviting her to stay so readily. 'Do you think she's legit? She's not going to rob us in the night and fly away, is she?'

Henry laughed lightly. 'Yes, I do think she's legit. And no, I don't think she's going to rob us in the night. For a start, what do we have that's worth robbing?'

He made a good point.

'Besides, it's heartwarming to see Dorothy so excited.' He shook his head. 'Isn't life strange. It's almost like we wished for Miss Watson, and she appeared, like a genie from a lamp.'

'Perhaps we did wish for her,' Emily said, remembering how she'd prayed for a sign that better times were coming. 'Maybe she's the change we've all been hoping for.'

There was certainly a different feeling to the house that night, a lightness Emily hadn't felt for a long time. For a few precious hours, as they'd listened to Adelaide's stories, and laughter had filled the house, she'd forgotten about dust storms and grain yields and drought.

While the sky hadn't brought the rain she'd prayed for, maybe it had delivered something just as valuable. Adelaide Watson was a burst of colour in their faded, dusty world. She was a glimpse of the dreams they'd once held, a vibrant reminder of the sense of wonder they'd lost along the way.

29

Within a week, the Jenny was patched up and Liberal was all talk of *The Flying Watsons* as Adelaide swooped over town, dropping leaflets to promote her afternoon show and the dollar rides she would offer as a sideshow attraction to the circus that had pitched up overnight. The weather was perfect for flying. No wind meant it was unbearably hot, but at least the dust didn't blow. It was dust that had caused Adelaide's engine trouble. It was dust that caused all their troubles lately, it seemed.

Emily was apprehensive as they drove to town. She couldn't fully relax until she was sure Leonardo wasn't there. After all, circus folk moved around. In many ways, there was more chance of him showing up in Kansas than there was of him staying in Chicago.

'You haven't said a word since we left the house,' Henry said as they arrived at the fairground. 'Something bothering you?'

'Nothing especially. I'm just quiet today.'

Quiet. Watchful. Her senses on high alert.

'Hurry up, Auntie Em!' Dorothy jumped out of the car. 'We don't want to miss anything!'

Dorothy's excitement reminded Emily of herself, Nell and Annie when the circus came to town: restless feet hurrying to get there as soon as possible, eager hands dragging their parents along, wide-eyes staring in wonder at the brightly painted stalls and the majestic big top in the middle of the show grounds.

It was the same now, the sights and smells exactly as Emily remembered as she walked among the colourful stalls and past signs promoting the mysterious sideshow attractions. Even the spectacle of the circus tent held the same tantalising air of mystery as she stepped through the heavy velvet curtain. It was like opening a door to another world, transporting her back through the years until it was Nell's hand pulling her eagerly along and Annie's voice that came in a stream of excited chatter as she pointed out jugglers on unicycles, a clown towering above her on stilts, and a strongman swallowing batons alight with flames.

'Look, Uncle Henry!' Dorothy shrieked. 'Real lions!'

'And tigers!' he added. 'And a dancing bear!'

Dorothy stared wide-eyed at the wagons containing the wild beasts that would perform in the ring for their tamers. Several wagons had open sides to allow a glimpse of the snarling animals pacing back and forth behind the iron bars. She said she wished they could be set free, and hurried off to watch acrobats in sequinned costumes as they tumbled and performed to the delight of the gathered crowds.

But it was at the entrance to a fortune-teller's tent that Dorothy stopped.

'Can I have my fortune read, Auntie Em?'

Emily had been fascinated by the fortune-tellers when she was a young girl, but her mother would never let her go inside, declaring it a waste of a nickel. Frances Kelly had no time for such nonsense.

'Can I, Aunt Em? Please?'

Emily relented. 'Very well. But you're not to believe anything she says. It's just a bit of fun.'

The interior of the tent was dark, lit only by the light of a flickering candle. It took a moment for Emily's eyes to adjust. On a small table, a crystal ball sat on a wooden ring, elevating it slightly above a crimson velvet cloth. A woman sat at the table. A veil concealed most of her face, leaving only heavily kohled eyes visible.

She beckoned Emily forward. 'Come closer, dear. And your daughter. Let us look into the crystal.'

'Oh, this isn't my daughter. She's my niece.' Emily turned to Dorothy. 'Go ahead, Dorothy. Sit down.'

Dorothy slid into the chair opposite the veiled lady and passed a nickel across the table.

Emily stood to one side as the fortune-teller swirled her hands around the crystal orb, never quite touching it as she muttered a sort of incantation.

'Yes, here we are. I can see a pretty lady, and a man. He has his arm around her. She has a child in her arms. A baby girl.'

Dorothy leaned forward, peering into the crystal. 'That will be my mother and father. They d . . .'

'Died. Yes, dear. A terrible tragedy. And I can see that a great sadness is upon you, and your dear aunt. Your mother's . . .'

'Sister!'

'Yes. Her sister. She misses her terribly. Regrets things that were left unsaid.' She glanced at Emily briefly.

Emily let out a frustrated breath, realising she'd given the woman too much information by saying Dorothy was her niece.

The fortune-teller returned her gaze to the crystal. 'I can hear laughter in a happy home. But not here. In a city, far away.'

Dorothy's eyes widened. 'That must be Chicago. I used to live there.'

'Yes. With your parents. But now you live in Kansas, with your aunt and uncle. And a little dog?'

Dorothy looked puzzled. 'We don't have a dog. We have horses and cows, though.'

'Then perhaps the dog will come later, dear.'

Dorothy turned to Emily. 'A dog, Auntie Em! I promise I'll look after him!'

Emily looked on with a cynical eye as the well-rehearsed charade continued.

'And now, what is this I see? A picket fence, a farm, and—' The woman leaned back suddenly, as if the crystal had given her a shock.

'What is it?' Dorothy asked. 'What do you see?'

'I see a dark cloud approaching . . . such darkness . . . a black, swirling wind . . .'

Emily had heard enough. She grabbed Dorothy's hand. 'Come along, Dorothy. We don't want to miss the start of Adelaide's show.'

The fortune-teller covered the crystal with the velvet cloth. 'Does the child have dreams?'

Emily hesitated. 'Of course. All children have dreams. And you're nothing but an impostor, filling her head with nonsense for a dime.'

Emily pulled Dorothy out of the tent. 'Come along now. Hurry, or we'll miss the start of the show.'

Dorothy ran to Henry. 'We're getting a dog, Uncle Henry! The fortune-teller said so.'

He looked at Emily, puzzled. 'Is that so?'

Emily shook her head. They were *not* getting a dog.

The three of them set out to the field to join the potluck picnic where they met Ingrid and her children, the Millers, and Zeb and May Lucas. Dorothy and Pieter couldn't sit still with excitement. Adelaide's show didn't disappoint.

The plane looped in ever higher circles, twisting and turning as it fell in a steep dive back toward the field, pulling up just in time as everyone gasped and shrieked with delight. Dorothy was especially enthralled.

'Says she's planning to take a rainmaker up with her,' Henry said to the other men. 'If he lets off his dynamite sticks that high up, the rain might come after all.'

Hank thought that was a great idea. 'Does she know someone?'

'She's headed to Dalhart to find that man everyone's been talking about. Promised she'd bring him back if she finds him. It'll cost some, though.'

'Do you think we could raise the money?' Hank asked.

Henry shrugged. 'Folk are struggling bad. I don't know that we could. Doesn't mean we shouldn't try, though.'

Toward the end of the show, Adelaide did a loop-the-loop high over the fields, a plume of smoke billowing from the tail as letters appeared magically in the sky.

Dorothy shrieked with excitement. 'Look, Pieter! It's spelling out a word!'

Emily tipped her head back, shielding her eyes from the dazzling sun as the trail of smoke formed the words, T H E   E N D!

Everyone on the ground burst into applause as a banner trailed behind the plane declaring THE FLYING WATSONS WILL BE BACK SOON! and Adelaide guided the Jenny back to the makeshift landing strip in the parched field.

Wilhelmina West tutted. 'Maybe everyone will get back to work now, instead of standing around staring at the sky like prairie dogs on watch.'

Laurie turned to her. 'You came to see what all the fuss was about though, didn't you.'

'I came to spread the word about a more sensible life.' Wilhelmina pressed a Kansas Woman's Christian Temperance Union pamphlet into Laurie's hands. 'Always room for more to help our cause.'

The West sisters were proud supporters of the Temperance Union and had recently started lobbying for movie censorship.

They wore their white ribbons with pride as they marched around with their banners and high morals. The gathering for Adelaide's show had offered an opportunity to press their message into lots of people's hands. Emily had no time for them and their strict moral code. She'd seen enough prohibition marches in Chicago to last a lifetime.

Laurie returned the pamphlet. 'Oh, you don't want the likes of me showing up, Mina. I'm as morally bankrupt as I am financially bankrupt.'

Emily, Ingrid and May stifled a laugh and turned to look the other way.

Pieter stood up suddenly, bumping Dorothy's elbow just as she was taking a drink from a bottle of soda. Dorothy dropped the bottle, sending the brown sticky liquid all over Wilhelmina's shoes.

'Look what you've done!' she shrieked. 'Brand-new shoes, ruined!'

Dorothy apologised. 'I'm sorry, Miss West. It was an accident. I didn't mean to do it.'

Wilhelmina dabbed dramatically at her shoes with a handkerchief, making a great fuss about it before she stood up and jabbed a finger at Dorothy. 'You should pay more attention, foolish silly girl!'

Emily had heard enough. 'It was an accident. The child has apologised.'

'The child's a nuisance.'

'And you're a mean bully, Wilhelmina West!' Emily countered. 'Why don't you take your pamphlets and your precious shoes and go home. Nobody wants you here.' Emily was surprised by the anger in her voice but was glad of it all the same. 'Come along, Dorothy. Pieter. Let's see about getting you a ride in Miss Adelaide's plane.'

As they walked away, Henry laughed. 'Well said, Em. She needs bringing down a peg or two.'

Emily's heart raced. 'I didn't mean to lose my temper but the woman is insufferable. I'd happily see an entire house dropped on her new shoes, never mind a bottle of soda.'

They watched from a safe distance as Adelaide brought the plane safely down, the wheels bouncing over the hard-baked fields until she came to a stop and jumped down from the cockpit. She signed autographs and posed for photographs for the local newspapers, and gave a peck on the cheek to the men who dared to ask and shook the hands of women who expressed their admiration for her in a more respectful way than their silly schoolboy husbands.

An eager line of those who could afford a dollar ride waited patiently for their turn to be taken up in the Jenny over the fields.

Pieter grabbed Ingrid's hand. 'Can I have a ride, Mama? Please!'

Ingrid shook her head. 'I don't have a dollar to spare. Maybe next time.'

The boy's face fell. He couldn't hide his disappointment.

Henry leaned toward Pieter. 'Wait a minute. What's this you're hiding?' He pretended to pull something from behind Pieter's ear and produced the two tickets Adelaide had offered in return for board and lodging. 'Go along, you two. See what all the fuss is about.'

Emily bit her tongue as Dorothy and Pieter ran off. She'd always been considered the brave one among her sisters when they were little. Even during the war, when she'd volunteered with the Red Cross, she'd put her own fears aside and done what was best, what was right. But caution and experience had crept up on her with age, and her mind seemed to always turn to the worst possible outcome, especially when it came to Dorothy. Where she'd once seen adventure, she now saw danger. Slow down. Be careful. Don't go any further. Don't go any higher.

'I hope it's safe,' she said, her hand at her chest as the plane took off and climbed higher and higher. 'Adelaide said the Jenny was a bit beaten up.'

Henry put his arm around Emily's shoulder. 'Not everything is dangerous, Em. Sometimes it's fun. You should ask Adelaide to take you up.'

'Up there? I'd rather join Wilhelmina West's Temperance League.'

But as Emily watched the Jenny looping effortlessly through the sky, part of her longed to leave this decaying land, to soar above the dusty fields where the air was clean. Up there, maybe all her troubles would melt away, if only for a little while.

For now, she tried to relax and enjoy the spectacle. After all, she'd seen no posters for a balloon aerialist, no sign of Leonardo anywhere. She'd been silly to even entertain the idea. There was nothing for her to worry about. No need to give Leonardo Stregone another thought.

30

That evening, when Dorothy had recounted her ride in the Jenny for the twelfth time and had eventually fallen asleep, exhausted by all the excitement, Emily invited Adelaide to sit with her a while on the porch as they had every evening since Adelaide's arrival. It was a perfectly still night. Hardly a breeze. The heavy heat of the day lingered in the sticky evening air so that Emily's dress clung to her skin and a light dew of perspiration settled at the back of her neck. She could hardly remember what it felt like to be cold.

'It's so quiet here,' Adelaide said as she sipped a glass of Henry's corn whiskey. 'I'm not sure I could get used to it! Makes a person think too much. All that sprawling emptiness.'

Emily smiled. 'You adjust to the silence, *and* the thinking. Strange, isn't it, how somewhere so vast can make a person feel so small. But you do get used to it. Learn to adapt. Besides, where *you* hear silence, I hear the prairie. The howls of wolves and coyotes, and how close they are. The difference between approaching thunderheads and a herd of wild mustang. The soft cry of a golden eagle and the *kac-kac-kac* of a Cooper's hawk. The rattlers, the 'hoppers, the scratch of mice and centipedes in the walls. It's not so quiet when you know what you're listening for.'

Adelaide studied her as she spoke. 'You're really connected to this place, aren't you.'

'I am now. It took a long time to figure it out, to feel like I belonged.'

'What brought you to Kansas?' Adelaide asked. 'And don't you dare say it was Henry! What brought *you* here?'

Emily had grown accustomed to Adelaide's directness during the week she'd spent with her. She saw a lot of Annie in her – the same confidence and devil-may-care attitude and three different shades of lipstick in her purse – and they'd struck up an easy friendship. She talked about things with Adelaide that she wouldn't have discussed with the other women in Liberal. Laurie Miller had become a dear friend over the years, but she was older than Emily by some twenty years – more like a mother figure. Ingrid was an intensely private woman and although Emily had occasionally opened up to her, the connection she felt with Adelaide was different. May was just May, great fun but not someone to confide in unless you wanted half of Kansas to know your business. Perhaps it was Adelaide's impermanence that made it easier for Emily to tell her things she didn't feel comfortable telling anyone else. Adelaide would take her confidences and secrets with her.

'A sense of adventure brought me here, I guess. A dream. A longing to do something different besides fold women's lingerie.'

Adelaide laughed. 'Sounds like you made a good decision if that was the alternative.'

Emily let out a long sigh. 'It was a good decision, but I've doubted it these past months. We hoped for so much when we first came here, and it all seems to have crumbled around us. Sometimes I'm not sure we should be here at all.'

'Really? Would you consider leaving?'

It was a question Emily had circled around again and again since the dusters had started to blow. 'If things don't improve soon, maybe we won't have a choice.'

'We always have a choice, Emily. It's what we do with it that matters. Anyway, it sounds to me like I'd better go and find that Okie rainmaker and bring him back for you folks!'

Emily smiled thinly. She wished she had the same faith in this rain man that Henry and the others had. 'When will you leave?'

'First light. Catch the sunrise. Best time of day to fly. You and Henry have been kind enough already.'

'Dorothy will miss you terribly,' Emily said. 'She's really brightened since you arrived.' They all had.

Over the last week, Dorothy had taken imaginary journeys in the Jenny, sitting at the controls in the cockpit as Adelaide told her which levers to pull as they pretended to take off. Adelaide educated the child through entertaining her. Emily's approach was more like her mammy's: stern instruction, pragmatism, common sense. She'd observed Adelaide's easy connection with Dorothy with a pang of envy. Adelaide was the aunt that Emily wished she could be: fun and carefree, beautiful and a little mysterious.

'She's a cute kid,' Adelaide said as she leaned back in the rocking chair. 'Must admit, I've grown awful fond of her. And don't worry. Dorothy will be fine. I explained that I would only be here a few days – that some friends are just passengers you travel with for a short while.' She took a sip of her corn whiskey. 'You're good people, you and Henry. It must have been tough, taking her in.'

'Anyone would do the same. Lots of folk have. You do what you have to, and hope for the best.'

'Well, as far as I can see, you're doing a great job. She's lucky to have you both. Family is important. Makes me miss mine when I see you all together.'

Emily had been surprised to learn that Adelaide had been born in Australia and brought to Nebraska by her mother when she was a baby, after her father died in the war.

'Have you ever been back?' Emily asked.

'To Aus? Nah. Too far away.'

Emily thought for a moment. 'The banner you flew from the plane at the end of the show said "The Flying Watsons". But there's only one of you.'

Adelaide took a moment before she replied. 'Used to fly with my brother, but that's in the past now. Maybe it's time to get a new banner.' She stood up suddenly and stretched out her arms.

'Do you want to talk about him?' Emily offered.

'Not especially.' Adelaide's eyes softened into a smile. 'Anyway, I'm beat. Think I'll turn in. I've a good day's flying ahead of me tomorrow.' She thought for a moment. 'Say, how about I take you up for a spin before I go? Try those big beautiful Kansas skies on for size.'

'In the plane?'

'Yes, in the plane! Unless you've a pair of wings you're hiding beneath that dress?'

Emily felt a leap in her heart. 'I couldn't, Adelaide.'

'Why not?'

There it was again: Why not?

'Well, for a start I've never been in a plane before. And I'm not good with heights.'

'Afraid?'

Emily nodded.

'Me too. Every time.'

'Really?'

'Yes!' Adelaide grabbed Emily's hand. 'That's what makes it exciting – the fear, the uncertainty. But you know what scares me even more? Forgetting how to live. Not taking the risk. Never saying yes. *That* scares the heck out of me.' She looked at Emily, her eyes dancing with adventure. 'Fear is a temporary thing, Em. Face it, and it doesn't exist anymore. Turn away from it and it'll haunt you forever.'

Emily didn't know what to say.

Adelaide took her silence as an acceptance. 'I'll see you at first light. And dress warm. It's pretty cold up there.'

'I didn't say I was coming.'

Adelaide laughed as she walked down the porch steps. 'You'll come!'

*

Emily crept outside just before dawn, careful not to wake Henry or Dorothy.

Adelaide was already at the plane, ready to go. 'See! I knew you'd come! What changed your mind?'

'*You* did. What you said last night, about forgetting how to live.'

'Well then, no better time to start remembering. It's a beautiful morning for flying!' She threw Emily a pair of goggles and a flying jacket. 'You'll need these.'

As Emily put them on, Adelaide fired up the propeller and climbed into the cockpit. 'Come on up!'

Emily felt like a giddy schoolgirl as she clambered up into the seat behind Adelaide. Her heart hammered in her chest and her skin prickled as Adelaide guided the Jenny out to the landing strip they'd cleared during the week.

'You won't do any of those loops, will you?' Emily shouted as Adelaide pulled back on the throttle and they began to race down the strip, the plane bumping and juddering over the baked earth beneath them.

Adelaide turned to Emily. 'What? Can't hear you!' She pulled back on a lever and Emily felt her stomach turn cartwheels. 'Off we go!'

With a rush of air and a sickening heave, the Jenny lifted from the ground. Emily screamed. Adelaide said something but Emily couldn't hear her beneath the thrum of the propeller and the roar of the wind in her ears. She clung tight to the iron struts in front of her and closed her eyes as the ground seemed to give way beneath them and they sank and rose in terrifying lurching gulps.

Eventually, the plane straightened out.

Emily allowed herself to open one eye, then another.

It was astonishing. Terrifying. Exhilarating.

They were surrounded by beautiful peach-coloured skies as far as she could see. Below, the prairie stretched impossibly far, a patchwork of flat, dry land, punctuated here and there by a white homestead, a distant railroad, a meandering riverbed, devoid of any water. From up here, the effects of the drought and dust were even more stark.

'Beautiful up here, isn't it!' Adelaide called.

'It's incredible!'

There was something so freeing about being untethered from life in every sense. Emily instantly understood the addiction of the aerialists and barnstormers, the seductive appeal of this life in the sky. She thought about how Annie would have loved it up here. So often during these past months, Emily had looked up to the sky, imagining Annie there, looking back at her. She imagined her now, her bright smile and infectious laughter. She tentatively reached out a hand, grasping at the air as if she might touch her.

Tears streamed from her face, summoned from the wind or from her heart, she didn't know. Whatever it was, she knew this was a safe place to come undone. She would give herself this moment, these dipping soaring minutes, to let go of everything she'd held inside for so long. Slowly, she released her grip on the struts and held her arms out at her sides as she closed her eyes and felt as if she was floating. She was alive in a way she'd never been before.

As she adjusted to the sensation, she began to let go of her fear and embrace the moment, because suddenly the most terrifying feeling of all wasn't the sudden pitch and roll of the Jenny, but the heave in her heart as she thought about going back down and having to confront everything she'd temporarily left behind.

'You doing OK back there?'

'Yes!' she gasped, the wind snatching her breath and her words away. 'Yes!'

Adelaide pointed up and pushed the plane into another steep climb.

Emily screamed, but it was a release of pure exhilaration, not fear. 'Keep going!' she shouted. 'Climb higher! Go faster!'

She'd forgotten what it felt like to let go, to be wild and reckless.

She wanted to keep flying. She wanted to chase the sunrise forever.

Excerpt from *Wonderful – A Life on the Prairie* by Emily Gale

It took me a long time to understand that the prairie gives folk what they need, not always what they want. When Adelaide Watson fell from the sky like a wish, she gave us both. She changed me – changed us all in some way – restoring our sense of wonder. When she left, we all hoped she would return with the rain, but I also sensed that Adelaide's purpose was about more than that. After only a week in her company, I somehow knew she would always be part of our lives. The how and the why would become clear, in time. Patience is another virtue that prairie folk learn. Nothing happens in a hurry here, except when a twister comes roaring through, or when a duster blows.

Before that summer of dust, I used to look up at the big prairie skies in awe, but I learned to use it to read the signs: the crackle of static electricity fizzing in the air, the car shorting, the thick rolling cloud of dirt. We didn't understand it, even though we had caused it.

Some 250 million bushels of wheat were harvested in the year before the rains stopped. Some thirty million acres tilled in the southern plains alone. A record harvest, met with plummeting prices and untold damage to the ancient prairie. Unsold grain toasted beneath the scorching sun. The smell of dreams left to rot beside the railroad. Foreclosure notices and Russian thistle were the only things that grew on the Great Plains that summer when Adelaide Watson blew into our lives.

We watched the sky, waiting for her to return.

And still the rain didn't come, and still the dusters rolled – the dreadful black blizzards, when day turned to night and dust covered every surface. Dust in our hair, in our eyes, at the back of our throats – a dark stain of dirt in Dorothy's cotton handkerchief when she coughed or blew her nose . . .

31

Only Henry knew that Emily had been up in the Jenny. Only he noticed her restlessness, the way she gazed at the sky with a faraway look in her eyes in the days and weeks that followed. He saw her excitement when she brought home the newspaper to show Dorothy the triumphant news that Amelia Earhart had succeeded in her attempt to fly solo across the Atlantic. Kansas was rightly proud of its girl.

'The first woman to do it!' she said as she spread the newspaper on the table. 'And the fastest transatlantic crossing, too. Lindbergh will be furious! Look, Dorothy. She'd intended on flying to Paris, but she landed in a field in Derry, in Ireland. Surprised the heck out of the locals!'

The news of Miss Earhart's success only reminded Emily of her flight with Adelaide.

'Still up there, aren't you?' Henry said later that week as they fed and brushed the horses. 'Still chasing the sunrise.'

Emily leaned her cheek against the old mare's flank. 'It was unforgettable, Henry. I wish you'd been there.'

'No, you don't.' He looked at her fondly. 'But I'm glad you came back. When I heard the plane taking off, I thought I'd lost you.'

'Of course I came back, Henry. I was always coming back.'

But she could just as easily have urged Adelaide to keep flying.

What she'd felt up there had frightened her, but not in the way she'd expected. The scale of devastation she'd seen from above had shocked her, and the thought – even momentarily – that she didn't want to go back down and face reality had scared her. She'd tried to brush it off, forget it, but the nagging doubt remained that the thrilling adventure she'd chased by coming to Kansas had eluded her. With the added responsibility for Dorothy, and the constant struggle to salvage something from their withering crops and finances, she was now as stuck and restless in Kansas as she'd once been when she'd clocked in and out at Field's. Annie's words taunted her. *You don't know the first thing about farming. What if the crops fail, or a prairie fire rips through, or a tornado tears your home apart? What if it all goes wrong? What if you hate it?'*

What if Annie was right?

As she combed the mare's mane, Emily felt ashamed to see how thin the animal had become, and how dull her once-gleaming coat was now. These hard years had taken their toll on them all. She rubbed the mare's velvet-soft muzzle and thought about the happy years when she was a new wife here, madly in love, longing for the intimate press of Henry's body against hers. Despite the hard work, life had seemed so simple then, their determination and dreams untouchable, but like the parched earth, their hopes and affections had cracked and hardened. Now, too tired to make love, too concerned with the coming and going of crops and rain, too preoccupied with storms and dust, they'd neglected the most important thing of all: each other. Dorothy's arrival had only emphasised the distance between them.

She'd been with them just four short months, but it already felt much longer. Like the plague of 'hoppers that had devoured their winter wheat four summers ago, the child was an unstoppable force, whirling around their fragile little home like a tornado, disturbing the careful order of things.

Emily became increasingly exasperated by the child's forgetfulness as she found another window left open, or a trail of breadcrumbs not swept up: flies, ants and mice the willing benefactors of the child's absentmindedness. Time and again, Emily reminded Dorothy. Time and again, Dorothy forgot.

'She's only eight years old, Em,' Henry said as Emily reminded him about the latest mishap with the pigpen gate being left open. 'Don't be so hard on her.' He'd adapted more easily than Emily. He was able to forgive the child her mistakes and overlook her small acts of disobedience.

'Someone needs to be hard on her, Henry. The last thing we need is the animals wandering off, or a cottonmouth getting inside. She needs to pay attention, never mind wandering around with her head in a book or talking to imaginary friends.'

She hated to argue with Henry, but she was tired and couldn't let the issue rest. Everyone was irritable lately, exhausted by the heat and tormented by the physical effects of the dust: the cracked skin, itchy eyes, sore throats.

Henry wouldn't budge on the matter. 'She's just a child, Em. She'll learn, in time.'

'And it looks like I'll have to be the one to teach her, since you're afraid to ever say no to her.'

Henry put down the pail of animal feed and ran his hands through his hair. 'She doesn't need a teacher, Emily. What she needs is a family, a mother and father.'

'But we're *not* her mother and father, Henry. We will *never* be her mother and father.'

'Perhaps not on paper, but you could be more like a mother to her – love her like a mother – if you would only let yourself.'

His words cut through Emily like an axe through wood. Not quickly or cleanly, but in blunt, heavy blows.

The wounds allowed her emotions to seep to the surface.

'I wish she'd never come here, Henry! We've had nothing but bad luck and cross words since. I wish things could go back to how they were before Dorothy Gale ever set foot in Kansas!' The words flew out of her in a temper. She'd thought them privately, in her darkest moments, but had never intended to voice them out loud.

Henry was visibly shocked, his eyes wide, his face furrowed with concern. 'You don't mean that, Em.'

'Don't I?'

She couldn't even look at him. She walked out of the barn and kept walking, Henry's apology smothered by the clouds of dust she left in her wake.

She walked to the creek at the edge of their claim and screamed her frustration and despair at the cloudless sky. The once-cold, restorative waters were barely a trickle now as she sat on the hard earth and scraped at the surface of the creek bed with her nails, clawing her way in or out, she wasn't sure. She picked up a handful of the dust-dry earth and wondered which part of it had once been her child. She held it to her heart and cried a river of her own.

It was dusk when she returned to the house.

Dorothy was playing hopscotch in the yard, such a lonely little thing, always on her own.

Henry was waiting on the porch. Relief crossed his face when he saw her. 'I'm sorry, Em. I didn't mean it. You're doing a wonderful job. Of everything.'

She was too tired to fight anymore. 'I'm sorry, too. I didn't mean what I said.'

They accepted each other's apology. What else could they do?

The prairie was too lonely a place to bear a grudge. Besides, they needed each other. Now more than ever, they needed to find a way to work together, and a way for Dorothy to fit into the misshapen scraps of the life they had built here.

*

Nobody slept well, tossing and turning in the oppressive stagnant heat as the last days of May slipped into June. Whenever she did sleep, Emily was often woken by the child's fretful whimpers. Not screams, but quiet panic, as if she was trapped in some place she couldn't escape from. By morning, the dream that had gripped her so thoroughly had dissolved to nothing other than a patchy memory about things falling from the sky and a black wind.

Always the black wind.

'It was just a dream, Dorothy. Nothing is falling from the sky.' But a sense of brooding disquiet took root in Emily's mind as she recalled the fortune-teller's words at Ringling's circus.

Nonsense she told herself. *A clever performance.*

But more troubling even than the dreams was when Dorothy started to walk in her sleep. The first time, she got no further than the screen door before Emily woke with a start and guided her back to bed. The second time, she got as far as the barn before the horses' whinnying woke Henry. Dorothy remembered nothing of it the next day.

'What if she walks further, Henry? What if she falls down the well, or meets a coyote, or worse?'

'We can't very well chain her to the bed, Em. We can lock and bolt the door, I guess.'

'And live like prisoners? Besides, she might find the key. We'll have to think of something else.'

'Like what? Get a dog to guard the door?' Henry looked at Emily, his eyes crinkling into a smile. 'Actually, that's not a bad idea.'

'It's a terrible idea, Henry.'

'You're right. Forget I ever mentioned it.'

*

The puppy arrived the following week.

Emily watched through the window as Henry carried it from the car. She met him at the door with her hands on her hips.

'I hope that isn't what I think it is, Henry Gale.'

He put the writhing creature into her hands. 'It's a dog, dear. Walks on four legs. Wags a tail. Occasionally barks.'

Emily held the puppy at arm's length. It was a raggedy little thing, no bigger than a two-pound bag of sugar, its stiff little tail beating like a clock pendulum as it looked at her. 'Yes, I can see it's a dog. What I'd like to know is what is it doing *here*?'

Henry pushed his hair from his eyes. 'It's a surprise. For Dorothy.'

'It's a surprise all right. I thought we'd agreed a dog was a bad idea.'

'Did we? I don't remember.'

Emily raised an eyebrow.

'Look at it, though.' Henry took the dog back into his arms. 'Poor helpless little orphan.'

'And I presume this poor helpless little orphan is the fierce guard dog that will stop Dorothy from wandering at night. *This creature is going to protect us all?*'

Henry shrugged. 'I guess.'

The dog licked Emily's hand as she stroked it. 'Wherever did you get it anyway?'

'A farmer out Kismet way. The mother was hit by a car in a dust storm. Left four puppies behind. It'll do Dorothy good to have something to care for. Don't you think?'

Emily let out a weary sigh. 'I don't know what to think anymore, Henry.'

'Then why don't we let Dorothy decide? In fact, here she is now.'

Dorothy squealed. 'A puppy! For me?' She scooped the dog into her arms and buried her face in its fur. 'Oh, thank you, Auntie Em! Uncle Henry! I love him more than anything in the world!'

Henry looked at Emily and shrugged. 'Looks like it's staying then.'

Emily turned away to hide the smile on her face.

That evening, Henry made the dog a bed from an old tomato crate lined with newspaper. Emily said the poor creature looked uncomfortable and stitched together a rough patchwork blanket from scraps of fabric in her sewing box.

'I thought you didn't want a dog?' Henry teased as she set the blanket into the crate.

'I don't. But if we must have one, it should at least be comfortable.'

It really was impossibly sweet, and despite worrying about feeding and caring for it, Emily couldn't help being fond of the little thing.

'Have you thought of a name, Dorothy?' Henry asked.

She thought for a moment. 'Toto.'

'*Toto*? What on earth does that mean?'

'That's what his bed says. Look!'

Emily looked at the old tomato crate. The dog's head was covering the middle *m* and *a*, leaving the word *To to*. She laughed. 'Toto it is then! I think it quite suits her.'

'Him,' Dorothy corrected. 'Toto's a boy.'

She was so certain that Emily didn't have the heart to correct her, nor the energy to explain why.

Henry took Toto's paw and shook it. 'Welcome to your new home, Toto.'

Emily watched as the child played with the little dog for hours, laughing as he hopped in and out of the basket. The sound of Dorothy's laughter no longer sent a chill down her back. It was a sound she had come to cherish.

She sat back on her heels and took in the simple scene. A husband and wife. A child and her dog. They were an unconventional rag-tag collection of strays and orphans and down-on-their-luck farmers, but somehow Toto had balanced them out and turned their odd little trio into something complete.

For a moment, she thought about the fortune-teller's words to Dorothy – *But now you live in Kansas, with your aunt and uncle. And a little dog?* – before quickly dismissing the notion that she had somehow known. A lucky guess was all.

The little house that had felt so small and empty for so long was full of love. As Emily looked around, she realised that what they didn't have was more than made up for by what they did.

Emily stroked the dog's head. 'Welcome to the family, little Toto.'

The word hung in the air before settling around them.

Family.

32

The heat was unbearable, and still the rain didn't come. Nobody could remember a summer like it. Day after day, record temperatures were marked by the thermometer Henry pushed into the earth and noted in his ledgers. There was no relief, not even at night when temperatures remained so uncomfortably high that it felt like midday at midnight.

Emily felt she was going mad. Her cotton dresses stuck to her skin, the starched cuffs and collars scratching and irritating. Even the flowers on the faded scraps of wallpaper in the pantry seemed to wilt in the heat. And still the dusters rolled, dumping their filthy cargo over the farms and towns, and a fine layer of dust settled over every physical thing until Emily didn't know where she ended and the prairie began.

Life became a continual battle against the dust. They smeared Vaseline around their mouths and noses and wore respiratory masks distributed by the Red Cross. Several times a day, when the dusters rolled, Emily covered the doors with wet sheets, and stuffed damp rags and newspapers around the windows to seal them. Nobody shook hands in the street, or touched metal handles, fearful of a shock from the static that crackled in the air. Chains dragged behind cars to ground them against the electricity. The dust had even found its way into hospital operating theatres, and the flour mills had to stop production. When Emily stripped the pillow slips to wash them, the imprint of their heads was marked by the dust that had settled over them while they'd slept. Even the paint on the outside of the house was flaking away because of the endless onslaught of dust.

Every night, and at church on Sunday, she prayed for rain, for a miracle, for Adelaide to return with the magic man who could conjure moisture from the sky. She didn't care what it took to raise the money, didn't care if some carnival huckster was to profit from their desperation. If he really could bring the rain, she would give him everything she had in return.

During the stifling afternoons and the long days when she wasn't at school, Dorothy was given jobs to help Emily and Henry, just like all the local farm children who were expected to pull their weight and help their families. Dorothy did as she was asked, but she worked sullenly, not willingly. It was clear that the child had been spoiled by her mother and had never been asked to help with household chores.

Emily bit her tongue as she taught Dorothy the little tricks she'd learned over the years: how to look for the wrinkle when setting jam, how to stick the handle of a wooden spoon into bread dough to test if it has proved, how to scald plucked chickens to kill bacteria, how to put pork fat against a flame to burn off the hairs. But the child had no patience for such things. She sulked when Henry went off to the fields without her, and grumbled when Emily asked her to help with the cooking and laundry. She longed to be outside in the fields, or in the barn with the animals.

'It's not fair, Auntie Em. Why do the boys get to do all the fun things? Pieter Anderssen doesn't have to darn socks or sweep the floors.'

'Is that so? Well, you're not Pieter Anderssen, so let's get this wheat ground up and then we'll see about helping Uncle Henry.'

Just as she refused to waste the surplus corn, Emily found a way to use the excess wheat they couldn't sell, incorporating it in some way with every meal. They ground it into a cereal for breakfast, sifted it to make flour for bread, and added it to the juices of a rabbit meat stew to make grits to accompany their supper. It was hard to digest and left them all with a stomach ache, but she couldn't bear to see it wasted.

When they were finished, Emily told Dorothy she could help Uncle Henry for the rest of the day. 'But you're not to get under his feet, and you're to pay attention, especially around the machinery, do you hear?'

Dorothy promised she would do exactly as Uncle Henry told her.

She didn't mind getting her hands dirty, or her knees muddied, or her dresses torn, and Henry indulged her. He let her ride on the tractor and taught her how to change a tyre and how to check the oil on the Model T. He showed her how to plough a straight furrow, how to clean the dirt from the mare's hooves, how to oil the saddle with linseed, how to rub the cow's udders with axle grease to reduce the painful friction from the dust. He proudly told Emily the child was becoming quite the little farmer. He'd grown so fond of her.

'And I'll still need the eggs collected,' Emily called as Dorothy hurried outside, but the child was already gone, skipping down the road toward the fields, a wicker basket full of corn cakes and coffee swinging in her hand, Toto at her heels. She was a four-foot-high menace, yet Emily's heart squeezed as she watched her disappear.

She took the photograph of Dorothy from the dresser drawer

and turned it over. *For Auntie Em.* The term had never meant much to her. It was a label she'd adopted by merely being Annie's sister, but she felt the weight of the words now – the connection and responsibility they carried – and for the first time since Dorothy had arrived in Kansas, Emily felt the child's absence in the silence that descended on the little house that afternoon.

She went about her chores as usual, but found herself pausing by the door, watching at the window, keeping one eye on the fields until she heard the child's distinctive piping voice in the distance.

Life with Dorothy was a conundrum. When she was in the house, getting under Emily's feet and disrupting the careful order of things, Emily wished she was elsewhere. When she was elsewhere, the house was oddly silent and Emily missed her.

Only when Dorothy was safely home did Emily's heart truly settle.

*

Slowly, gradually, they fell into a rhythm. In the evenings, while Henry puzzled over his accounts and grumbled about government mandates to list the fields as part of Hoover's wind erosion programme, Emily patched up old clothes or played the fiddle, and Toto dozed on Dorothy's lap as she studied the atlas she'd borrowed from the library. She liked to make up stories about a little girl who travelled the world and went on daring adventures.

Emily listened patiently as Dorothy recited her work, but she worried that the tone was too dark, the story full of frightening things and wicked witches.

'Do you like it?' Dorothy asked as she finished reading.

Emily tried to be encouraging. 'I do, dear. Very much. But isn't it a bit sad? The little girl in your story is all alone and afraid. Maybe you could give her some friends to meet along the way, like how you met Pieter, and Miss Adelaide, and Toto. It's more fun to have adventures with friends, don't you think?'

Dorothy thought for a moment. 'A friend who is brave. And one who is clever. And one who has a kind heart.'

Emily smiled. 'Yes. Something like that. And maybe fewer witches.'

*

At supper club that Thursday, Emily mentioned Dorothy's stories to Laurie Miller.

'She's so like her mother,' Emily said. 'Annie used to make up stories when we were little girls. Her "Wonderfuls" she called them. Magical lands and talking animals and all sorts of silly ideas. At least her stories were pleasant. Dorothy's are terrifying. Do you think I should be worried?'

'No such thing as a silly idea,' Laurie said. 'A child's imagination is a precious thing. Encourage it!'

Ingrid agreed. 'It might do Dorothy good to express her fears and worries through a story. Maybe if it isn't all in her head, she won't have so many bad dreams. Pieter had vivid dreams about his father in the months after he died.'

It wasn't the worst idea. Emily wrote in her journal every day, capturing her changing thoughts and feelings. She still struggled to accept that their lives had changed so dramatically, but she was beginning to let go of the things she couldn't control. It had helped to write things down, to put shape and structure around such fluid intangible things as feelings.

'As y'all know, I'm more of a talker than a writer,' Laurie continued, 'but I always feel better getting things out in the open rather than keeping them in. Why don't you look through some of Annie's things with Dorothy. Encourage her to talk about her mother. Maybe she'll write her into one of her stories.'

Emily thought about the box of Annie's possessions from Chicago still hidden away in the cyclone cellar. Maybe it was time to bring them out and make peace with the memories they stirred.

'That's a good idea, Laurie. I will. Thank you.'

The conversation turned then – as it always did – to the dusters, and the growing numbers of foreclosure notices, and their mutual longing for rain. They all felt so helpless, and were increasingly worried about their men, who were being pushed to the limit and were on the brink of revolt.

'Millions of farmers across the Great Plains are on their knees,' May said, her voice rising as she voiced her frustration. 'Directionless, aimless, hopeless. Zeb found a hobo in the pantry last week, helping himself to our supplies as if he lived there. Half-starved, the poor man.'

'Henry found another homeless man sleeping in our barn,' Emily said. 'Begged him for food, or work. Had to see him off with the rifle. I'm not afraid of them myself, but I worry about Dorothy coming across someone. You hear such awful stories of drunk drifters and thieves.'

'Hank was telling me about a planned protest march on Washington to demonstrate against Hoover's disastrous federal aid policies,' Laurie said.

May nodded. 'We heard the same. And who'd blame them? Mandatory listing of fields, wheat burns, cattle slaughtered at sixteen dollars apiece – none of it has stopped the dusters. None of it has made any damn difference at all.'

Emily shared her worries about Henry, how he frowned over his ledgers, gazing at the empty columns where he should have recorded yields and earnings. Their bank account lay as parched and empty as the fields. Mandatory listing, when the government paid a fee to farmers who left the land fallow as another measure to prevent the dust blowing, had done its own damage. More acres ploughed in desperation had added even more dust to the great smothering clouds that had blown prairie dirt as far as Chicago and New York.

Laurie reminded everyone that back in the spring of '30, Hoover had stated that the worst effects of the crash would be over within a few months. 'And yet, here we are, two years later, and it's only getting worse. Wheat selling for nineteen cents a bushel, corn prices at less than nothing. Even if we *could* grow a decent crop, it ain't worth it. No wonder folk are rioting over food shortages when mountains of grain sit idle at train stations.'

'Look at us,' May said with a heavy sigh. 'Grouching and whining. We're all 'bout as flat and lifeless as the damn prairie.'

'It's looking more than likely Hoover will be gone after the election this fall,' Emily added. 'FDR is making ground. Maybe he'll come good on his promise to remember the forgotten man at the bottom of the economic pyramid.'

She thought about their first harvest, when the same acreage of wheat that sat fallow now had brought in four thousand dollars. Nobody needed to be a mathematician or an economist to see how impossible it was. And it wasn't just on the prairie where folk were struggling. The entire country was on its knees. In New York, nearly half a million people were on city relief – just eight dollars a month to get by. Emily remembered the flop houses and soup kitchens she'd seen in Chicago, the homeless men sleeping on benches in the Great Hall at Union Station, their bedsheets made from yesterday's newspapers.

'I've never seen Henry so desolate,' Emily said. 'When I try to talk to him about it, he shuts me out, bottles it all up until he meets the other men.'

'They're too proud to talk to us about it,' Laurie said. 'It near breaks Hank's heart to list the land, to see fields sit fallow as he sits idle himself. He needs to be busy. It's the helplessness that's killing him. Eats him up from the inside.'

Foreclosure sales were humiliating and increasingly common.

The farmers had all agreed to never bid more than a dime for anything: not for a combine, or a horse, or a hoe. It was the only way they could beat the bankers. Strength in numbers. Unity. The ten-cent sales had become a vital lifeline.

'Let's just pray Miss Watson comes good and finds that Okie rainmaker,' Ingrid added. 'Seems like she might be our last hope.'

'She will,' Emily said. 'I'm sure she will. Adelaide didn't seem like the sort of person to make a promise she couldn't keep.'

Laurie sighed. 'Never thought I'd see the day when we were harvesting promises to make a living, but here we are, ladies. Here we are.'

Emily didn't play the fiddle that night. Nobody asked, and she didn't have the energy to offer.

As she arrived home, she drove past the Western Union telegraph boy, cycling back along their track. A sense of dread washed over her. Telegrams usually meant bad news.

At the house, she found Henry and Dorothy making paper planes, seeing whose could fly the furthest. They seemed to be in good spirits.

'Telegram just arrived,' Henry said.

'Yes, I just passed the telegraph boy. 'Is it . . .?'

'It's on the dresser.'

Emily picked up the piece of paper, almost afraid to know what it said. But a tired smile spread to her lips as she read the typed message.

> Tracked down that Okie rainmaker. Italian-American from the Midwest.
> Calls himself the Rain Man. Will come as soon as we can. Adelaide.

33

Everyone's spirits were lifted by news of the telegram from Adelaide and the prospect of the rainmaker coming to help them. Finally, they had a shred of hope to cling to where there'd almost been none. Folk scrounged up whatever money they could, ready to pay the man when he arrived.

The following day, when all the chores were done and she had a few moments alone, Emily fetched the shoebox of Annie's things from the cyclone cellar. The birthday letters Annie had written for Dorothy were still inside, and the sixteenth birthday letter the attorney had given to Emily. They hummed and twitched like living things, alive with Annie's words to her daughter, but they were not Emily's letters to read. The letter she'd written for Dorothy's eighth birthday, just weeks after she'd brought her to Kansas, was the only one Emily knew the contents of. She'd added it to the box, for Dorothy to open on her sixteenth birthday along with the others. She'd kept the sentiments short and simple. There was, after all, no cause for celebration that year, but Emily hoped there would be happier things to write about in the years to come.

She pushed the letters and circus paraphernalia aside and picked up the hourglass. There was still something mesmerising about watching the sand slip through the pinch in the glass. Minutes became years as she allowed her thoughts to look backwards.

Finally, with a deep breath, she lifted the silver shoes from the box. What power they held over her still. Such visceral memories.

She held them behind her back and went to find Dorothy. She'd been waiting for the right moment to give the shoes to her, and this felt like as good a time as any.

'Dorothy, there's something that belonged to your mother that I thought you might like. Close your eyes and hold out your hands.'

Dorothy squeezed her eyes shut, but it was Annie who Emily saw in front of her, arms stretched out in eager anticipation on a cold Christmas morning. *No peeking!*

'No peeking, Dorothy!'

Emily rested the toes of the shoes on Dorothy's upturned palms, just as she'd done with Annie. *Open your eyes!*

'Open your eyes, Dorothy.'

'Mommy's dancing shoes!' Dorothy immediately put on one shoe, then the other, her feet easily slipping inside without unfastening the buckles. The shoes sparkled as she tottered around the room. She wobbled on the heels.

Emily placed a hand to her chest. It was Annie, prancing around in the shoes on Christmas morning.

'How do they feel?' she asked. 'They're a bit big now, but you'll grow into them.'

Dorothy wobbled again. She sat down and started to take the shoes off.

'Don't you like them?' Emily asked.

'They remind me of Mommy. I miss her.'

Emily's stomach sank. It was too soon. Too much. 'Oh, Dorothy, dear. I'm sorry. I didn't mean—'

'Well now. Have you ever seen such a fancy pair of shoes?'

Henry appeared through the screen door. 'Wherever did you get them, Dorothy? I wish I had a pair of magic silver shoes.'

'Magic?' Dorothy's ears pricked up.

Henry winked at Emily. He must have been listening to their conversation. He pretended to look bored and disinterested. 'Yes, but who cares about magic shoes anyway.'

Dorothy slipped her feet back into the shoes. 'What makes them magic?'

At this, Henry stalled. He glanced at Emily.

She looked at the shoes, at Dorothy, and she saw Annie, so clearly, in the boarding house room on Kildare Street, flapping her hands and swivelling her feet in a terrible Charleston dance. *'You look like you're having a seizure, Annie! You're doing it all wrong! Try it this way. Click your heels together, then step to the front with one foot. Click your heels, step behind with the other foot, click your heels, step in front, click, step behind.'* Suddenly, Emily knew what to do.

'Why, didn't you know, Dorothy? All silver shoes are magic. If you're ever in a pickle and you have a pair of silver shoes, you just tap the heels together and make a wish.' Emily clicked the heels of her own shoes together three times. 'Just like that, although there's no magic in my shoes. Why don't you give yours a try. Make a wish.'

Dorothy looked a little uncertain, but curiosity got the better of her. She closed her eyes, scrunched up her nose in deep concentration and clicked the heels of the silver shoes together three times.

Emily looked at Henry.

He smiled and nodded.

They were a good team. They barely spent more than a few hours apart every day, but in that moment, Emily realised she missed him terribly.

'How about a reel on that fiddle of yours?' Henry said. 'Dancing shoes need music.'

He often encouraged Emily to play the fiddle. She'd lost interest in it lately, finding that she had no energy to play, and that the dust affected the sound when she did.

'Just a little burst of something,' he urged.

Emily recalled the promise she'd made to her mother in the days before she'd died, as if she'd sensed her death approaching. *'Talk about Ireland sometimes, will you, Emmie? Sing the old songs. Play the tin whistle and the bodhrán and the fiddle, and when I'm dead and buried, keep telling the myths and legends and sing the ballads and reels. Will you promise me that?'* She missed her mother so much. Her death had been sudden and unexpected, yet peaceful: a silent departure while she'd slept, without fuss or fanfare, as was always her way, never one for prolonged goodbyes or gushing sentiment. Her broken heart had simply stopped beating.

Emily took up the fiddle and played the music of her childhood and her homeland, in honour of her mammy and daddy. Dorothy liked the jigs and reels, the faster songs that she could dance to. She watched Emily closely as she played.

'How does it make all the different sounds?'

'Would you like to try?' Emily passed her the instrument.

Dorothy made a few awful scratching noises, her brow furrowed in concentration, and then in frustration. 'How do you make it sound nice?'

Emily smiled to herself as she remembered being frustrated that her father could make it sound so lovely while she could only make it sound like cats fighting. *'I could show you how to play a note or two, if you'd like,'* he'd said. She hadn't cared so much about playing the fiddle but loved the time it gave her with him, just the two of them. Playing a note or two, and then a chord, and then a chorus and verse and eventually a full song was the outcome, but the real gift had been spending that precious time together.

'I could teach you, if you'd like,' she said now.

Dorothy's eyes lit up. 'Would you? Really?'

Henry caught Emily's eye from across the room.

She was a patient teacher and Dorothy was a fast learner. She soon had the bow playing individual notes, and then an almost harmonious chord.

'I'm playing, Auntie Em! Listen, Uncle Henry. I'm playing the fiddle!'

Emily listened to the few faltering notes and the enthusiastic praise from Henry, and for all that the fields lay bare and so much of their lives was lacking and empty, her heart was full.

*

That evening, Emily reached for Henry's hand as he sat in the rocking chair beside her.

He looked up from a book he was reading about wind erosion. 'What did I forget now?'

Emily smiled at him. 'Nothing, Henry. Nothing at all.' She kissed his cheek. 'It's me who has been forgetful.' She glanced toward Dorothy's little bed behind the curtain. The child was fast asleep, Toto curled up at her feet. 'Come on,' Emily whispered as she pulled Henry to his feet. 'Come with me.'

She led him to the creek. In the cool ribbon-thin strands of the last remaining water, they found each other, searching and remembering, forgetting about everyone and everything else other than the touch of their bodies against the other's. She gave herself fully to the sensations and movements of her body, responding to the thrill of Henry's touch as she clawed at the earth with her fingertips and drew him closer. She had never felt stronger or more beautiful, the riverbed at her back, years of dust and hard work buried deep in the cracks and wrinkles on her skin as they moved together in an exchange of affirmation and affection and love.

Afterwards, she lay in Henry's arms and felt a surge of power within her, as if charged with the electricity that crackled in the air before a duster. She was more than dust and dirt. She had a purpose. A future to believe in. She closed her eyes and absorbed the simplicity of the moment, letting go of all that had come before, or what might lie ahead. All that mattered was that she was with Henry, the love of her life; immense prairie skies soaring above, the earth reaching far below. For a precious fleeting moment, she was happy to be where she was. To be *who* she was.

'We should go back,' she whispered.

But what she wouldn't have given to stay.

Back at the house, she picked up the fiddle again, singing *as Gaeilge,* as the familiar melody summoned memories and she felt her parents and Annie beside her, filling her heart with love.

Dorothy was awake when Emily went to tuck in her covers.

'My wish came true, Auntie Em!'

'It did?'

'Yes! I wished that I could hear Mommy's voice again.'

Emily's heart cracked at the earnest little voice as she reached for Dorothy's hand. The child had such a vivid imagination that Emily was no longer surprised by anything she claimed to hear or see.

'I heard her, playing the fiddle and singing a song from Ireland,' Dorothy continued. 'I closed my eyes, and she was right there, on the other side of the curtain.'

*

Toto was yapping and barking.

Emily stirred. 'Toto! Stop that.' She nudged Henry. 'Henry. The dog.'

Henry woke. 'What on earth's got into him.' He called to the dog, but Toto wouldn't stop barking. 'Another damn hobo, no doubt.' He sat up. 'Stay there. I'll deal with it.'

Emily's eyes took a moment to adjust to the darkness before she saw that the door was open.

Her stomach filled with dread.

'Dorothy!' She rushed to the child's bed.

It was empty.

'Henry! Dorothy isn't in her bed.'

Within seconds, Henry had pulled on his boots and a flannel shirt. 'I'll go. Wait here in case she wanders back.'

'Hurry, Henry. Take Toto.'

Henry called to the dog as he hurried outside. 'Where is she, Toto? Where's Dorothy?'

Emily stood barefoot on the porch, peering into the darkness, desperately looking for any sign of Dorothy's white nightdress. She could hear Henry calling out and Toto yapping.

A moment later, she heard Henry call out again. 'I have her, Em! She's fine.'

Emily clasped her hand to her heart. 'Thank you, Lord. Thank you.'

Toto got back first, Henry just behind him. Dorothy was still asleep in his arms, oblivious to the worry she'd caused.

'Where was she?' Emily asked as she closed the door and bolted it.

'With the old mare. She was just standing there, rubbing her hands over her neck. Calm as anything.'

They settled the child back into her bed and made a great fuss of Toto.

'Good boy,' Emily said as she found a bit of bacon rind for him. 'You're a very good boy for telling us.'

Toto wagged his tail and tilted his head to one side, as if he understood that was the reason he'd been brought here. To protect the child. To help her whenever she was in danger.

'Auntie Em!'

Dorothy had woken.

'What is it, Dorothy? Did you have a dream?'

'I dreamed that I was riding the old mare with you. We were going ever so fast. And Toto was there, too,' Dorothy said.

Emily smiled. 'That sounds nice. I like riding the horses.'

Dorothy looked a little shy as she pulled Toto into her arms. 'I liked riding the horse with you most of all.'

A knot of emotion tightened in Emily's throat. 'You did?'

Dorothy nodded. 'Could we really ride the mare together sometime?'

'Of course, dear.' Emily leaned forward and pulled the covers up to Dorothy's chin. Without thinking about it, she bent down and kissed her on the forehead. 'Goodnight, Dorothy.'

'Goodnight, Auntie Em.'

Emily lay awake for a long time, a cyclone of emotions swirling in her heart as she turned over the events of the days and weeks and months that had come before. So much of her life had changed, and while the road ahead was unpredictable and uncertain, she remembered to be grateful for all that she had. She'd come here as a young woman in love, eager to embrace the thrill of excitement and adventure that a life on the prairie offered. What she needed now was security and stability as those delicate first blooms of naivety and enthusiasm settled into firmer roots of practicality and resilience.

In the bed beside her, Henry snored. Across the room, Dorothy muttered a few words of nonsense as Toto turned a circle at the foot of her bed before they both settled and fell silent.

Outside, the wind began to dance as the remnants of a summer storm crackled in the distance. Emily listened as the wind tugged at the windows and rattled the timbers in the roof. It would once have kept her awake. Now she was lulled by it. As she drifted into a deep sleep, she dreamed that she became the wind, lifting the house and carrying them all to some distant land where the rain fell in great curtains and the fields bloomed in every shade of green, and the deep distant rumbles of thunder that crept into her subconscious became the exhilarating pounding of hooves as she rode across the prairie, outrunning the storms, a little girl up front on the saddle urging her to go faster and faster, further than she'd ever gone before.

Extract from *Wonderful –
A Life on the Prairie* by Emily Gale

This land had become my heart; my soul. I grieved as I watched it die.

It was only when I returned from Chicago that I saw how desolate it had become. Bone-dry and lifeless, the lush swaying grass just a memory to those of us who'd known the good times. Perhaps nobody will believe that there ever were good times here. Perhaps we will become nothing more than a story someone once heard, a cautionary tale of the Last Chancers and suitcase farmers lured to the prairie by the prospect of turning wheat into gold. We will become a fable, a fading legend of dreams turned to dust.

Even as I lived among the dust and drought, I didn't understand what we had done. We blamed everything and everyone else: the weather, the government, bad luck. But it was all us. We had destroyed the land we claimed to love. We had farmed the land too aggressively, destroyed the ancient prairie grass that held the topsoil in place. Without it, and without the rain, the earth *had nothing to hold onto. We had done exactly what the Native Americans who'd first settled on the land said we would. Folk talked about the warnings and prophecies, the prairie having its revenge. If it couldn't chase us off the land, like white men had chased the native tribes and buffalo away, then the prairie would bury us here.*

They said we had a choice to stay or leave, but it wasn't really a choice at all. There is no real choice when both alternatives break your heart.

Good choices were as rare as raindrops in those years, and decisions were as hard as the baked earth. We made our mistakes, but we learned from them.

The prairie taught me that that life never goes as planned. It is the hardest lesson of all, to accept that we are nothing but tumbleweed, blown by the whims of fortune and destiny. We try to set our course and follow our path, struggle and fight to cling to the life we've imagined with every ounce of our being, but I now know that the bravest thing to do is to let go, give up the life we wanted to make room for the life we need.

There is a peacefulness then, a comfort in knowing you will always be on the right path, following the road you were meant to take, even if it leads you in a new and frightening direction . . .

34

July fourth burned white hot from sun-up. There wasn't a single cloud in the sky and barely a breath of wind. Emily fanned her face with the end of her apron as she swept centipedes and spiders from the walls, but the flapping only disturbed the dust and made her eyes gritty. She draped a wet towel over her neck and shoulders and pressed a damp cloth to her face. It was the only way she could cool down.

The animals were particularly lethargic too, conserving what little energy they had as they lay in any patch of shade they could find. The rivers and creeks were as dry as the cracked skin on Emily's hands. The ground was baked iron-hard beneath the Model T as Henry drove into town that afternoon. Emily held an apple pie in her lap. Dorothy held Toto in hers. They all held a silent longing for some respite from the relentless heat.

Despite the temperature, Emily was glad of the excuse to get out of the house. Closing the windows and doors was a necessity to keep out the bugs and insects that were thriving in the hot dry conditions, but it made the place feel like a furnace.

'Will Pieter be there today?' Dorothy asked. 'Will there be a carnival?'

Emily said she was sure Pieter would be there, yes. The two of them were inseparable. 'I don't know about a carnival, but I'm sure there'll be plenty to keep you busy.'

'I wish Miss Adelaide was here,' Dorothy said as she peered out of the window. 'I'd like to go up in the Jenny with her again. It was such fun.'

Emily followed Dorothy's gaze skyward and let out a wistful sigh. She wished she could go up there again, too, but real life had rooted her in the prairie dirt.

'I'm sure Adelaide will be back soon,' she said, and wished she could be more specific. Every day since the telegram had felt like a month, and still, she didn't return. 'Although she'll be very busy helping the rainmaker, so you're not to be pestering her for a ride.'

Dorothy promised she wouldn't.

Emily didn't believe her for a second.

Hank and Henry and the other farmers had already raised a decent collection to pay the man whenever he showed up, and they hoped to raise even more during the day's celebrations.

'What does the rainmaker do?' Dorothy asked. 'Can he really make it rain?'

Henry glanced at Emily. 'Sure hope so, kid.'

Emily wasn't entirely sure how the rainmakers operated. 'He has special machinery, and rockets, and fireworks that explode in the sky to bring the rain.' It was quite the spectacle by all accounts, although she remained sceptical until she saw it for herself.

'He sounds very clever,' Dorothy said.

Emily hoped they weren't building this rainmaker up only to be let down. He'd become something almost mythical. Their last chance.

'Shall we talk about something else?' she said. 'How about we sing a song?'

But it was too hot for songs.

They travelled the rest of the way in silence, glad of the light breeze that was stirred by the motion of the car.

*

The town was modestly decorated with patriotic displays of flags and bunting in red, white and blue. The Women's Club and Beautification League had done their best, but it was a far cry from the impressive exhibits Emily remembered from her first years here. Still, the place looked pretty with the added bursts of colour.

Despite the heat, folk came out of their farms and homes, grabbing any patch of shade they could find. With so little to celebrate in these testing times, they all welcomed the opportunity to shrug off their worries and talk to friends and neighbours for a few hours.

Music and song carried from the shaded porch of the town hall, but only a few children and younger adults had the energy to dance, and although tables had been brought outside for the food, and plates were passed around, the heat stole everyone's appetites.

'Just as well,' May Lucas said as she looked at the meagre display. 'There ain't that much to go around.'

Folk had done their best with canned vegetables, dried beans and salt pork pulled from their personal stores, but the excesses of past years that had seen the tables piled high with pies and salads, corn breads and biscuits and hams, were a distant memory. It was hard to believe there had ever been such extravagance and abundance here.

Even Wilhelmina West was too hot to care what anyone else was doing, her usual need to interfere and chastise melting away in the heat. She barely reacted when Toto bared his teeth at her, shooing him away with a weary flick of her hands.

Dorothy scooped the dog up. 'Toto! That isn't very nice.'

Emily offered an apologetic smile. 'He's usually so good with people.'

'Dogs don't care for me,' Wilhelmina said. 'Nor children,' she added as Dorothy set her face into a scowl. 'Don't care for them much myself either.'

Emily tried a different approach. 'How is your sister? I heard she wasn't well.'

Wilhelmina seemed surprised that Emily had asked, or that anyone cared. 'The dust has taken to her lungs. The doctors are doing what they can.'

'I'm sure she'll be home soon. I have sisters. Well, just the one now. I know what a worry they can be.'

Wilhelmina looked at Emily, as if seeing her properly for the first time. 'I was sorry to hear your sister died. I can't imagine life without mine.'

Dorothy pulled on Emily's arm. 'Auntie Em! Come on. There's a ring toss.'

Emily turned to leave. 'Enjoy the day, Wilhelmina.'

She nodded. 'I'll tolerate it.'

Dorothy and Pieter went around the stalls, inseparable as usual, Toto trotting along at Dorothy's heels whenever he wasn't bundled into her arms. She was utterly devoted to him, constantly patting and squeezing him close. Not that the dog seemed to mind. Toto needed Dorothy as much as she needed him.

Ingrid noticed a rash on Pieter's neck as they waited for a turn at the ring toss. 'Come here, Pieter. Let me see.' She looked at the rash and asked Laurie for her opinion. 'Is it a heat rash?'

'Looks more like measles to me. See how he is in an hour or so. Plenty of fluids and rest if it is.'

Ingrid turned to Emily. 'Has Dorothy had the measles? If not, she's likely to get it. She's been practically attached to Pieter all day.'

Emily wasn't sure. Yet again, the void in her relationship with the child stretched between them. 'Dorothy? Do you know if you've ever had the measles?'

'I don't think so. I had chicken spots once.'

Emily smiled. 'Chicken*pox*, perhaps? I'll keep an eye on you. If you start to feel itchy or poorly, you're to tell me right away.'

Emily tried to enjoy herself, but the heat wilted her enthusiasm and her thoughts were elsewhere. She exchanged small talk with her friends and played a few games at the carnival stalls, but her heart wasn't in it. While Dorothy played with Pieter and Toto, and Henry sat with the men in a huddle of serious conversation, Emily quietly stole away to the restorative solitude of the church.

It was cool and dark inside, a welcome break from the day's searing heat. She lit a candle and prayed for her parents and her sisters and baby Joseph, for Dorothy and Henry, for rain, and for the little souls she'd carried for such a short time. Tears filled her eyes as the ache of the losses washed over her.

She'd had good reason to doubt her faith over recent years, but she took comfort from the practices and beliefs instilled in her by her parents. She would be forever grateful for their careful instruction and firm discipline, for their kindnesses and guidance. Like the fragile soil that blew loose from the tattered prairie, their deaths had left her uprooted and untethered. It was part of the reason she'd come to Kansas. The prairie had offered a fresh start, a chance to build a different life with Henry, but the most difficult parts of her past had followed her, nevertheless. Part of her was still a child grieving her parents, an orphan who longed for their steady encouragement and advice and love. Perhaps she had more in common with Dorothy than she realised.

She felt for the piece of Connemara marble in her skirt pocket, but it wasn't there. She panicked, afraid she'd lost it, until she remembered she'd given it to Dorothy. She missed the familiar weight of it, but she hoped it would give the child the same comfort and assurance it had given her over the years. She closed her eyes and said a final prayer to echo that hope.

She took a deep breath and readied herself to leave the quiet sanctuary and return to the scorching day, where nobody knew of the heavy ache in her heart. Like a circus illusionist, she revealed only what she wanted people to see. The rest was all a charade.

The sky had darkened and the wind had picked up while she was in the church. Hats were pulled from heads and blown down the street like tumbleweeds. Traffic lights swung back and forth on their wires. The air was gritty, blowing dust into Emily's eyes and scratching sharply against her skin like sandpaper. There was a heaviness in the air. Emily felt the onset of a headache. She was glad when the celebrations – such as they were – came to an abrupt end as everyone felt the unmistakeable static prickle of a duster and hurried to their homes and cars.

Emily called for Dorothy while Henry cranked the motor.

In the distance, a great cloud of dirt was gathering.

*

Henry navigated by counting telegraph poles, the dimming light and the lingering drifts from previous dusters obscuring other landmarks.

He reckoned they were almost halfway home when the duster hit.

The car came to a sudden stop, the engine shorting out from the surge of static electricity. The hairs on Emily's arms stood up.

High above, the heaving cloud marched on. It moved in a peculiar way that Emily had come to recognise. Not twisting like a tornado or blowing hard like an approaching hailstorm, but an unstoppable rolling motion.

They were in the middle of nowhere. Exposed, with no shelter as the duster drew closer, dense and brooding. The bright afternoon sun faded behind the black mass, leaving an eerie twilight.

Toto fussed and whined in Dorothy's arms as she reached for Emily's hand. 'Is it a twister, Auntie Em?'

'A duster, Dorothy. Quickly. Help me seal up the windows.'

They had learned to go nowhere now without rags and newspaper to stuff against the car windows, and cloths to put over their faces.

Emily pulled the child close to her, remembering the times Annie had held her during a thunderstorm. 'Keep the cloth to your face and keep your eyes closed. Do you understand?'

Dorothy nodded and clung tight to Toto.

Within minutes, coarse grit flew against the car windows, rattling against the glass like gunfire. The finer particles of prairie dust crept easily inside the car through the smallest gaps, peppering their skin like needles. They coughed and sneezed, their noses and throats irritated by the abrasive dust, their eyes sore and streaming from the fine grit as the duster rolled overhead, and day became night, and the windows rattled so hard Emily was certain they would shatter.

Toto whined and barked. Dorothy tried to reassure him.

For a minute that felt like an hour, the sky rumbled and the dust rolled. Then the noise fell away, and daylight began to return.

Emily said a prayer of thanks.

'Good job it wasn't the big one they keep talking about,' Henry said as he cranked the engine. The motor started up again as the sun reappeared. 'Even that was plenty big enough.'

Emily released her grip on the child. 'It's all right now, Dorothy. It's over. Look, even Toto is wagging his tail.'

But when Emily looked at Dorothy, she saw fear in her eyes.

'It was like my dream, Auntie Em. A terrible blackness.'

'And now it's over, dear. Like your dream, it has gone away.'

But the dust never truly went away. It settled wherever it had been, leaving its mark on everything and everyone.

Dorothy coughed all the way home. When she sneezed that evening, black dirt discoloured her handkerchief.

A terrible blackness.

Emily put the handkerchief into the copper to wash.

The dust storm was a warning and a reminder all at once. She'd heard of more and more people getting sick with the dust. Many families across the Great Plains were sending children away to stay with relatives in states and cities where the dust didn't blow. For months now, Emily had watched the dusters roll through and heard Dorothy coughing at night, and she couldn't help thinking that she'd brought the child to the worst place imaginable. Not for the first time, she found herself lacking when it came to her ability to keep Dorothy safe, and no matter how much she wished she could turn away from the reality facing her and Henry, it was clear that Annie had placed her trust – her daughter – in the hands of the wrong sister. The facts were clear: Dorothy would be much safer with Nell and Bill in California.

Never quite able to find the words or the courage to broach the subject with Henry, she'd put it off. Until now.

'I was thinking I would write to Nell,' she said that evening.

'That would be nice. You haven't heard from her in a while.' Henry was distracted by a nagging pain in his stomach and wasn't really listening.

Emily took a deep breath. 'I think it would be safer for Dorothy to go and stay with Nell. Just for a while. Until the dust stops blowing.'

Henry looked up from his books. 'Send her to California? Are you serious?'

Emily nodded. 'I don't think Kansas is safe for her anymore. She'd be better off in California with Nell.' She drew in a long breath and let out a sigh. 'Maybe we'd *all* be safer there.'

At this, Henry sat up. 'You want to leave?'

'No, Henry. I don't want to leave. But I don't know how to stay either. I don't know how to make this work. Not with Dorothy. I'm afraid she'll get sick with the dust pneumonia. The hospital is overrun with folk struggling to breathe. Plenty of children, too.'

Henry was silent for a long time. The facts were hard to argue against. 'You really think we should send her away?'

'I do.'

He ran his hands through his hair. 'I'd miss her, Em. I'd miss her something terrible. But if you think it's for the best, then I guess that's what we must do.'

Emily turned at the creak of a board behind her.

Dorothy was standing inside the screen door, Toto in her arms, tears falling down her cheeks.

'Please don't send Toto away, Auntie Em! Please, Uncle Henry!'

Emily ran to the child. 'Oh, Dorothy, dear.' She pulled her into her arms. 'We're not sending Toto away.'

'But I heard you talking about sending him away to California, to Aunt Nell. Please don't! I promise I'll look after him.'

Emily looked at Henry, guilt etched across both their faces.

Henry stood up. 'We're not sending anyone away, Dorothy. Now, how about you and Toto go to bed.'

Emily took Dorothy's hand. 'Come along. Time for bed, both of you.'

But as she tucked a curl behind Dorothy's ear and Toto settled at the child's feet, Emily felt the stab of dishonesty pierce her heart.

No matter how distressing it would be for the child – for them all – sending her to California was the only sensible and safe thing to do. The prairie had already taken so much from them. Emily refused to let it take Dorothy, too.

She would write to Nell in the morning.

She would beg her to take Dorothy if she must.

Extract from *Wonderful – A Life on the Prairie* by Emily Gale

We couldn't bear to leave, and yet how could we survive if we stayed? We were stuck, stranded in a desert of dust that had once been an ocean of prosperity. But every day we somehow moved forward, kept going: one step, then another. Without ever leaving our patch of land, it was the hardest journey we would ever take.

We were short of everything – water, food, money, hope – but the one thing we had in abundance was love. No matter how many times the dusters blew, or how hard it was to put food on the table, our days were bookended with gratitude, and the trace of a smile found our sunburned cheeks.

I did a lot of thinking during those hot, dusty days and sleepless nights. The prairie makes you look at yourself – not from the outside but from the inside. It forces you to figure out who you are, what you want, what you believe. There's nowhere to hide, no easy way to avoid bumping into yourself. I fought against it for a *long time, turned away, busied myself with chores that didn't need doing, working until I was too exhausted to think. But the prairie is patient. It was in no hurry.*

Who are you, Emily? it asked. What is it that you want?

Turns out, what I wanted had been there all along.

35

Within a matter of days, Dorothy was running a high temperature and her nose streamed. The telltale rash had developed by the end of the week.

'Measles,' Emily confirmed.

'The same as Pieter?' Dorothy seemed almost pleased. 'Will I have to go to the hospital?'

'Yes, the same as Pieter. And no, you don't need to go to the hospital. Plenty of bed rest for you, my girl. You'll be back on your feet in no time.'

Dorothy was confined to bed with her *Anne of Green Gables* books and Toto, and although Emily slipped easily back into her role of nurse, she couldn't help worrying.

All children got the measles, and while most only had a mild case, for some, it could be more serious. Emily kept a careful vigil, making sure Dorothy had plenty to drink, pressing a cool, damp cloth to her head, encouraging her to take small sips of bone broth. While she still felt clumsy and inadequate with so much of the business of being Dorothy's aunt, caring for the child when she was sick came naturally to her. She checked on her throughout the day, feeling the now-familiar tug of tenderness as she watched the child sleep or pressed a hand to her forehead. She longed for her to get better, yet she partly dreaded it, too. As soon as she was better, there would be no further reason to delay their plans to send her to Nell.

'How's the patient?' Henry asked when he came back from another foreclosure sale.

'She's bored and too hot and wishes she could go outside, but doing fine on the whole.' She reached for Henry's hand. 'And how are you?'

'Me? Nothing wrong with me.'

They both heard the lie. Everything was wrong. He hadn't been anything like himself for weeks now. He was worried, tired, drained by the heat, and his temper was unusually short. He also complained intermittently of an ache in his gut. Emily had heard of plenty of men getting an ulcer, or putting a strain on their heart with all their worrying. She was increasingly concerned.

'I wish you would talk to me, Henry. It isn't good to stew on things alone. You don't discuss things with me the way you used to.'

'There's nothing to discuss, Em. That's the problem. There's nothing we can do.' He tapped his yield book with his finger. 'The facts speak for themselves.'

Henry liked life to follow a pattern. He worked in neat, ordered columns and the detailed records he kept in his journals and farm accounts. He knew when to plant winter wheat, when to harvest, when to prune the fruit trees. He worked to the predictable rhythm of the seasons, clear dates, known facts. This period of uncertainty, without pattern or precedent, had left him rattled.

Emily hated to see him so helpless. 'This isn't a private battle between you and the prairie. It's *our* battle. I'm your wife, Henry. Don't shut me out. Let me help. Please.'

He shook his head as he let go of her hand. 'Help how? There's nothing you can do, Em. There's nothing any of us can do.'

He picked up his hat and went outside. He didn't say where he was going. Emily didn't ask.

She watched Dorothy and made bread, desperate to do something practical, kneading her worry into the pliant dough.

He still hadn't come back by sundown.

Checking that Dorothy was asleep, Emily went to look for him.

She found him behind the barn, knelt on the ground in front of a small mound of earth.

'Henry?'

He turned to her. His face was streaked with tears.

'Had to dig it out,' he said as he lifted up a small wooden cross. 'Damned dust isn't content with choking the living half to death. It's burying everything that's already dead, too.'

Emily walked over and knelt beside him.

She'd thought it was her own private sorrow to heft around, forgetting that while she'd been denied the chance to be a mother, Henry had also been deprived of the chance to be a father. The losses were his, too.

He'd insisted on driving her to the doctor that awful October day after she'd returned from washing herself at the creek. He'd wanted to do something to help, pleaded with her not to shut him out. The doctor had said there was no reason for what had happened. 'There'll be others,' he'd said. 'My best advice to you is to keep trying, Mrs Gale. They come along eventually.' He'd spoken without an ounce of compassion. He might as well have been talking about a lost crop after a bad hailstorm.

There hadn't been others. Not a hint of a new life ever since.

'Why didn't you tell me you were coming out here?' she asked.

Henry shook his head. 'I don't always know what to say to you, Em, but I think about it, often. More so lately.'

Emily reached for his hand. 'Because of Dorothy?'

He nodded as he let out a long sigh. 'All this talk of her leaving has me torn apart, Em. Seems like the kid only just got here, and yet it's as if she was never anywhere else.'

*

Emily was woken by a low, distant moan. She opened her eyes to see Henry doubled over in agony. The bedsheets were soaked with sweat.

She sat up. 'Henry? Henry, whatever's the matter?'

He could hardly breathe the pain was so bad. 'My stomach.'

The pain made him vomit. His face was clammy. His pulse was way too high. Emily applied pressure to various places on his stomach. His reactions indicated possible appendicitis and there wasn't a thing she could do to help him if it was. If the appendix burst, it could be fatal.

'You need to go to the hospital,' she said.

The low moan came again, but this time, it wasn't Henry.

Emily rushed to the window. A familiar ominous green hue coloured the sky. A sure sign of a twister forming.

'Let's go,' Henry gasped. 'Now, Em.'

'What about Dorothy?' Emily was frantic, but tried to stay calm and think clearly. They couldn't drag the child out in the middle of the night, not when she was sick in bed with the measles and running a temperature.

Henry could barely talk he was in so much pain. 'We have to leave her.' He'd barely got the words out before he groaned again in agony.

Emily didn't have time to think. She rushed to Dorothy and shook her arm until she woke. Toto started yapping from his tomato crate bed.

'I have to take Uncle Henry to the hospital, Dorothy. He has a pain in his stomach. You're to stay right here, with Toto.

And if the wind picks up, you're to go to the cellar. Do you understand?'

Dorothy was still half-asleep. 'Where are you going?'

'To the hospital . . .' Henry let out a great wail. 'I'll be back soon. Stay right here with Toto. And if you need to go to the cellar, wait there until I get back.'

Dorothy scooped Toto up into her arms. 'I'm scared, Auntie Em!'

There was no time to debate or explain further. Emily pulled the child into an embrace. 'Toto will look after you. Be a good brave girl. I won't be long.'

It was absolute torment to leave her, but there was no time to second-guess herself.

Emily helped Henry out to the car, turned the crank, and willed the engine to start. After a few attempts, it caught. She jumped into the driver's seat and pressed down on the accelerator. The vehicle lurched forward, but all that she could think about as she drove away from the farm was the little girl she had left behind.

The night was ink black, the moon hidden by clouds that rushed across the sky, blown by the strengthening wind. Twice, she nearly turned the car around, but twice Henry cried out in pain. She carried on, going as fast as she dared, navigating by the dim beam of the headlights and the telegraph poles.

'Hold on, Henry. We're nearly there. I told you it was a good idea for me to learn how to drive this thing.'

Henry groaned and begged her to hurry. He vomited again. His groans and moans terrified her.

After what seemed like an age, she reached the turn for Liberal and the road widened a little. She pressed her foot flat to the floor and willed the motorcar to go faster. Henry cried out with every bump and pothole she drove over.

Finally, the hospital emerged in the distance.

'We're here, Henry! I can see it. Just a few minutes more.'

At the hospital, everything moved quickly. The doctor confirmed appendicitis.

'We've given him something for the pain and will operate as soon as we can. Don't worry. Henry will be fine. You should go home, Mrs Gale. Looks like that storm's changed direction and headed our way. If you set off now, you might just make it home in time.'

Emily didn't hesitate. Henry was in the best place now, and poor Dorothy was all alone and now the storm was coming.

As she reached the motorcar, she kicked out at the tyres in frustration and let out a muffled cry of despair. Why was this all happening now? What had they done to deserve such bad luck?

As she made the turn out of town, hailstones began hammering on the roof. She thought about Dorothy alone at the house, and how afraid she would be. If the wind was bad in town, she knew it would be far worse out on the exposed prairie.

She put her foot on the gas and drove as fast as she could.

She had to get home.

She had to get back to Dorothy.

The wind nearly blew the car off the road several times. Emily gripped the steering wheel and leaned forward, peering out through the murk. The headlamps lit up swirling clouds of dust kicked up from the parched road, the wipers making no headway against the disorienting soup of hail and dirt that smeared the windshield. She could barely see a few feet in front of her, but she drove on.

*

The gusts blew stronger and stronger. Tumbleweeds flew against the windows, blinding Emily's view. She hit a pothole hard, and too fast. The tyre burst, sending the motorcar veering wildly across the road until she came to a stop in a narrow ditch. The rim of the wheel was wedged tight. She was stuck.

Abandoning the car, she continued on foot, head bent against the painful hail that pummelled her skin and the gritty dust that irritated her eyes. She ran as fast as she could, her breath snatched from her by the gusting wind.

The last stretch of track to the house was blocked by the gate which had been pulled from its hinges and lay at an awkward angle. Emily tried to pull it to one side, but it was too heavy. She kicked at it until it gave way.

'Dorothy! Dorothy! I'm here!' She cried out again and again as she ran to the house, desperate not to leave the child alone a second longer than necessary. 'Dorothy! It's Auntie Em!'

As she rushed inside, she glanced at the child's bed and saw that it was empty. There was no sign of Dorothy, or Toto. They must have gone down to the cellar.

Emily grabbed the latch of the trap door and pulled it open. 'Dorothy! It's Aunt Em. I'm coming down. Don't be afraid.'

The cellar was pitch-black. She could hardly see where she was putting her feet, and almost fell as she missed a rung on the ladder. Steadying herself, she continued down into the dark.

'Dorothy? Are you in here?'

She grabbed the flashlight from the shelf and swung the beam from left to right, but the cellar was empty.

Dorothy wasn't there.

36

Emily's heart thundered in her chest.

'Dorothy?' She hurried back up the ladder, calling for the child over and over. 'Dorothy! Dorothy! Where are you?'

Panic stole all sense of logic as she rushed around the house, opening cupboard doors and peering beneath tables and beds, and all the time the wind roared at the windows.

She ran back outside, calling the child's name, fear snatching her words as she ran to the barn. It was the only place she could be.

'Dorothy, are you in here? It's Auntie Em.'

A bark came from the back of the barn, behind the tractor.

'Toto! Oh, Toto. There you are? Where's Dorothy? Where is she?'

The dog yapped and yapped as Emily ran toward him and there, huddled in the corner, her knees to her chest, her arms over her head, was Dorothy.

'Oh, thank goodness! There you are.' Emily rushed to her. 'It's OK. I'm here now. Are you hurt?'

Dorothy slowly lifted her head. The look of fear and vulnerability in the child's face turned Emily's heart inside out.

'You left me, Auntie Em. You left me.'

The words cut through Emily like a hundred knives. 'I'm so sorry, Dorothy dear. I hated to leave you, but I had to go to the hospital with Uncle Henry and . . .' Her words tailed off. It didn't matter. However she tried to justify it, there was nothing she could say or do to make the child understand. She had left her all alone, in the middle of the night, in a storm. There was no explanation that would ever make that all right. She reached out a tentative hand and placed it on Dorothy's. 'I promise I will never leave you again.'

And she meant it. It had frightened her to be away from Dorothy, just as much as it had frightened Dorothy to be left alone.

The child looked up at Emily, her eyes full of fear. 'Promise?'

Emily squeezed Dorothy's hands. 'I promise, with all my heart. Now, come along. Let's hurry to the cellar.'

'Can't we stay here, Auntie Em? Please! I don't want to go into the cellar. Please!'

Emily faltered a moment. The child was so terrified, and the storm was abating a little. It seemed to have switched direction again at the last minute.

She pulled Dorothy into her lap and wrapped her arms tight around her. 'We'll stay right here, together. You're safe now.'

Emily's dress was sodden from the hail, her shoes covered in dust and dirt, her face burned with the sting of the wind, but Dorothy was safe, and that was all that mattered.

Toto curled up at their feet as they clung to each other while the storm rattled the barn roof. They played counting games and guessing games to pass the time. Emily sang an Irish ballad her mother used to sing when the wind whipped across the Atlantic and rattled the eaves of their Connemara cottage.

'Why didn't you go to the cellar?' Emily asked eventually when Dorothy had calmed down a little.

'I tried to, but Toto was afraid. He wouldn't go down. Would you, Toto?' The dog licked Dorothy's hand. 'He got a fright and ran outside.'

Emily was so afraid of what could have happened if Toto had run off further, if the storm had been worse, if something had fallen and hit Dorothy on the head. And while she was so grateful that Dorothy was safe, she was still desperately worried about Henry as images from the night flashed across her mind and the echo of his agonised cries tormented her. On the prairie, the margins between life and death were dangerously thin.

Eventually, the storm passed and everything fell silent apart from the drumming in Emily's heart as she thought about Henry in the hospital and prayed she'd got him there in time.

*

Emily watched the first lavender light of the new day settle over the prairie. She hadn't slept a wink. In her arms, Dorothy slept soundly.

She stood up carefully so as not to wake the child and carried her back to the house, quietly calling for Toto to follow.

Outside, the air was so still it was hard to believe such wild winds had roared just a few hours earlier, the only sound now the familiar hum of the 'hoppers. The prairie was such a riddle. Furious one moment, peaceful the next, lurching from one mood to another like a petulant child. Which was why she didn't fully trust this peaceful truce.

She recalled a conversation with Adelaide. *'You adjust to the silence, and the thinking. Strange, isn't it, how somewhere so vast can make a person feel so small. But you do get used to it. Learn to adapt.'*

Had she got used to it? Really? As it had so often since she'd come here, Emily felt the prairie, once again, asking questions of her. Was she brave enough to stay when it turned against her?

Could she do any of this without Henry – manage the farm alone if anything happened to him, like Ingrid after Eric's death? And the hardest question of all: What is it you really want, Emily?

As she looked at the sleeping child in her arms, she remembered the featherlight feel of Dorothy as a newborn, the almond-sweet scent of her, the way the infant had looked at her with such innocence and love, the ache of letting go. What she'd felt that day, and so many times since, had frightened her, but no more. Finally, she understood that what she'd felt was nothing dark or sinister. What she'd felt was love. A great and powerful love.

It settled now in the map of her heart as the answer to the hardest question came to her. What she wanted wasn't important. It was what she needed that mattered, and she had everything, right here. There was no feeling – no place – like it.

Inside the house, Emily laid Dorothy on her bed and pulled up the bedspread she'd made with her own hands through the long winter nights in her first years on the prairie. As she bent down to kiss Dorothy's cheek, the child's hand reached for hers.

Emily had promised she would never leave her again, and she meant it. No matter how hard things might become, she couldn't bear to send Dorothy away, not to Nell, not to anyone. Wherever Dorothy went, she went, too. They were connected now. Two ends of an hourglass, forever turning together.

She lay down beside Dorothy and closed her eyes.

She was just drifting off to sleep when she heard it. Distant at first, and then louder.

The pitch and whine of an engine.

Getting closer.

She stood up and walked to the door, opened it a crack, and then wider as the roar of an engine filled the air and dust blew in whirlwinds on the porch.

Adelaide!

Adelaide had returned.

Part Four

Kansas, 1932

'No matter how dreary and gray our homes are, we people of flesh and blood would rather live there than in any other country, be it ever so beautiful. There's no place like home.'
— L. Frank Baum, *The Wonderful Wizard of Oz*

Extract from *Wonderful – A Life on the Prairie* by Emily Gale

During the winters, we burned unsold corn on the fire for fuel. We threw the cobs onto the flames, and waited for them to start popping, like gunfire. That sound, and the smell of fairground popcorn, became the background to our little home as the nights closed in around us. It filled my head with memories of cotton candy and circus sideshows. It reminded me of my sisters. It reminded me of happier times.

When you have next to nothing, you look back often. We clutched at the straws of our productive past and prayed that the present would reward our patience and resilience.

But summer hailstorms and wicked tornadoes care nothing for such things. And when the rain doesn't fall and the sun-scorched earth rises up in great clouds of choking dust, what becomes of a person's patience and resilience then? And what of all their hopes and dreams and love?

That is when the prairie asks the question of all who come here: Do you have the will to go on, and if not, do you have the courage to leave? To answer that question is to understand who you truly are; to discover what it is that you need, and not what you want.

Hope returned with the arrival of the rainmaker, but fear remained.

And they say hope makes fools of desperate men . . .

37

Emily could hardly believe it. Adelaide Watson, back in their house, as striking and flamboyant as ever. Not a hair out of place, ruby lips curving into a playful smile, laughter on the tip of her tongue as she rubbed Toto's belly and told Dorothy a tall tale about being chased by an enormous duster in Oklahoma.

'Biggest you ever saw. At least a hundred feet high and twice as wide. Thought I was done for, but the Jenny flew faster and we landed safely.'

Dorothy sat wide-eyed as she hung on Adelaide's every word, her trio of little toys – Lion, Twig, and Straw Brigid – clasped tight in her hands. She was almost over the measles now. Her temperature had come right down and the worst of her rash was subsiding. It was almost as if she'd willed herself better because Adelaide was here.

Emily looked at Dorothy and smiled to herself. The child was just as enchanted by their guest as she had been the first time she'd landed in their lives. The long, anxious weeks waiting for her to return were quickly erased so that it felt as if she'd never left at all. And while Emily couldn't express her delight quite as openly as Dorothy, she was surprised at how glad she was to have Adelaide back, especially since she hadn't returned alone.

Just as she'd promised, Adelaide had found the rainmaker and persuaded him to bring his magic to the skies above Liberal. The tension in Emily's shoulders eased as she reflected on their brief spell of good fortune: Henry had come through his operation and was making a good recovery, Dorothy was almost better, and the news of Adelaide's return with the Okie rainmaker had lifted everyone's spirits. The anxious days of waiting and watching the skies eased, and hope returned. Maybe all was not lost after all.

'How did you find him?' Emily asked as Adelaide took a ride into town with her, Dorothy and Toto happy passengers in the back seat. The motorcar had been repaired thanks to Hank Miller who'd retrieved it from the ditch where Emily had abandoned it on the night of her dramatic trip to the hospital.

'Finding him was the easy part! He's hard to miss with his thunder-mugs and lightning-mugs and Lord knows what other weird and wonderful contraptions. And he's a very persuasive showman. Loves to draw a crowd.'

'Then what took you so long? We thought you'd forgotten about us.'

'Convincing him to team up with me was a little harder. He likes to do things his own way. Doesn't like the thought of anyone else to answer to or worry about. Says he's always done things his own way. Thinks a bit too much of himself if you ask me. The adulation has gone to his head!'

'What changed his mind? Couldn't resist those red lips of yours?'

Adelaide laughed lightly. 'You mean, did I have to turn on my charms and convince him *that* way?'

Emily was embarrassed. 'Gosh, no. I just meant... Well, anyway. How *did* you convince him?'

'Took him up for a spin in the Jenny. Explained that I could take him up much higher to detonate his dynamite, and that he would be doing something no other rainmaker has. Something unique. That got his attention. But it was when I mentioned Kansas that he really seemed to change his mind. Told him I'd promised a bunch of decent Liberal folk that I would bring them a rainmaker. We went to some other towns first. Word spreads quickly when folk are desperate, and he needs the money.'

'I hope he's paying you a decent cut.'

'Enough. I might attempt that solo transatlantic flight yet.'

'Well, whatever it took to get him here, we're very grateful. Folk have been talking about little else: When will the rainmaker come? Will his tricks and explosives work? Henry and Hank and the men have raised a reasonable pot of money. Everyone's all in. Boom or bust.' She paused for a moment. 'Do you think he's genuine, Adelaide? Has he actually made it rain anywhere?'

'We moved on before his chemical compounds had time to take full effect. He says it can take up to five days to work, and he's in such demand he can't afford to wait around to see the results for himself. He certainly seems to know what he's doing, though, and it has to be worth a try, right? Doing *something* has to be better than doing nothing.'

Emily sighed as she pulled up outside the hospital. 'You're right. Things are bad, Adelaide. Really bad.'

'It sure seems that way.' Adelaide stepped out of the car and covered her face with her scarf. 'Things are bad out Dalhart way, too. Seems there isn't a prairie farmer across the Great Plains who isn't suffering.' She looked toward the hospital. 'You sure I can't come with you? Do anything to help?'

'No, thank you. I've got this. There'll be no chance of keeping Henry in the hospital if he sees you! He keeps pestering the nurses to let him go home, but I keep telling them to keep him here. He'll only try to do too much and burst his stitches.'

'Bet you can't wait to have him home all the same. Oh, I nearly forgot!' Adelaide pulled a leaflet from the pocket of her pants. 'Show Henry this. My new business partner. Might make him feel a bit better.'

Emily took the leaflet and read the print.

THE REMARKABLE RAIN MAN!
*The world's best in precipitation conjuration.
The leading moisture scientist in concussion
theory and aerial agitators.*

'Whatever all that means,' she said.

'Sounds impressive, though, doesn't it.'

Emily studied the leaflet again. 'When do we get to meet this mysterious Rain Man anyway?'

'Tomorrow. He's making his way in his truck with all his equipment. I said he could catch some sleep in your barn. Hope that's all right?'

Emily nodded. She didn't much mind where the man slept as long as he did what he promised.

'He's planning to do a demonstration in town first,' Adelaide continued. 'Get folk fired up, if you'll pardon the pun!'

'We're already fired up. It feels like this is our last hope. The last roll of the dice.' Emily looked at the leaflet again. 'I just hope this Remarkable Rain Man lives up to his name.'

38

Henry was discharged later that day and had never been happier to return home.

Once again, the little house that had often felt small for two, stretched its arms wide and made room for more as Henry returned, and Adelaide joined them once again, and life fell into a new rhythm, moving to the beat of four hopeful hearts and Toto's exuberant tail.

The women of Liberal were also pleased to have Adelaide back with her cheerful personality, but they couldn't summon the same enthusiasm as the first time she'd arrived. Everyone was jaded, fretful, distracted. The Thursday supper club had dwindled as people left town and, for those who remained, there was no energy for the gossip and stories they'd once exchanged. The story was always the same now: drought, dust, despair.

Dorothy's enthusiasm hadn't dwindled at all. 'I'm so pleased Miss Adelaide is here again, Auntie Em. She's terrific fun!' She was feeling much better and was eager to read Adelaide the stories she'd written, and to show her the silver dance shoes.

'They're magic shoes,' she said proudly as she clopped around in them.

'Is that so?' Adelaide glanced at Emily, who nodded firmly. 'They're very beautiful. You'd best take good care of them.'

'Oh, I will. They were Mommy's dancing shoes. Auntie Em says I'll grow into them.'

Adelaide leapt up from the chair and grabbed Dorothy's hands. 'Dancing shoes, you say? Then let's dance!'

Emily looked on as the pair danced and twirled around the little room, the silver shoes sparkling in the light. It reminded her of how she and Annie used to dance with such joy and carefree abandon. She'd forgotten the simple pleasures of music and dancing and laughter, too worn out and hardened by the everyday struggles she and Henry faced to indulge in such things. Once again, Adelaide had shown her how easy it was to bring a smile to Dorothy's face. Adelaide was the aunt that Emily wished she could be: entertaining, exciting, a little wild and reckless.

'You're a terrific dancer,' Adelaide said when they were both out of breath and had to stop. 'You clearly have your mom's dancing feet! Or maybe your father was a good dancer, too?'

Emily stiffened.

Dorothy thought for a moment as she put the shoes away. 'I don't remember seeing Daddy dance.'

'I don't think John – your daddy – was much of a dancer,' Emily added. She was keen to draw a line under the conversation and change the subject.

'Mommy had a special friend who liked to dance,' Dorothy added. 'He could do real magic tricks, too.'

For a moment, Emily couldn't catch her breath. She felt lightheaded as she stood up, brushed her hands briskly against her apron, and announced that she'd forgotten to check on the pigs.

Outside, she hurried to the barn, glad to step into its dim light and hide in its shady corners. She needed to calm down, to think, to process what Dorothy had just said.

Mommy had a special friend . . . He could do real magic tricks, too.

It could only be one person and, if it was, the implications were enormous. After all these years, had Annie still been in touch with Leonardo? Perhaps seen him regularly, even? Suddenly, Annie's distance and withdrawal made sense: She'd been protecting herself from further interrogation or judgement from Emily. And what of Dorothy? How well did she know this special friend? And – the bigger question – how well did he know her? Well enough to come looking for her in Kansas?

Emily's stomach churned. If only she'd told Henry she could confide in him about it. But she'd locked him out, and now it was her heavy burden to bear, alone.

*

'The kid seems much happier,' Adelaide said as she and Emily watched Dorothy play a game of hopscotch in the yard that evening. Henry had laid out sticks to make the numbered squares, but Toto kept running off with them, so he'd marked out the grid with stones instead.

'The dog has made a huge difference,' Emily said. 'She still has strange dreams now and again, and her imagination is as active and vivid as ever, but she's stopped sleepwalking. She's much more settled.'

'And you?'

'Me?'

'Yes! You! How are *you*?'

'I'm fine.'

'Are you? Really? Looks to me you folks are going through hell. You seem afraid, Emily. Like you're constantly looking over your shoulder.'

Emily had missed Adelaide's straight-talking, no-nonsense approach to life. She let out a long sigh. 'There's plenty to be afraid of,' she said. 'This place teaches you to be wary.'

'I guess so.'

There were many things Emily feared: dust storms and tornadoes, cottonmouths and rattlers in the woodpile. But it was the fear of failure that haunted her the most: the fear of not fulfilling the trust Annie had placed in her, the fear of admitting that the prairie had defeated them, the fear of uprooting Dorothy all over again. She had awful dreams of the child being lifted up and carried away, but she could never tell if it was a dust storm, a twister, or some other thing – or person – that took her. Like a circus performer on a high wire, the life they were building together was precariously balanced. One wrong move and it could all come crashing down. She thought of the desperate letter she'd written to Nell. If the rainmaker could summon the rain, maybe they wouldn't have to send Dorothy away after all.

'And you, Adelaide?' she asked. 'What are you afraid of?'

Adelaide seemed surprised that Emily had turned the question back on her. 'Me?'

'Everyone is afraid of something, Adelaide. Some of us just hide it better than others.'

'Maybe so.'

Emily wished Adelaide would talk to her about her brother, tell her what had happened to stop them from flying together, but she decided not to press. She knew how hard it was to talk about some parts of your past.

'Dorothy seems very fond of Henry,' Adelaide continued. 'I get the feeling she wasn't especially close to her father. She doesn't talk about him much.'

Again, Emily felt herself tense at the turn of the conversation. 'John was away a lot. With business. He was a good bit older than Annie, too.'

'I see. And Annie's special friend? Was he closer to her in age?'

A shiver ran across Emily's skin. 'What do you mean?'

Adelaide looked at her. 'It's none of my business, but I wasn't born yesterday.'

'You're right. It's none of your business. You have no idea what you're talking about.' Emily's tone was unusually curt. She sounded just like Annie, her reaction the same as Annie's had been when she'd broached the subject of Leonardo with her. The spectre of Leonardo Stregone had intensified as Emily and Henry's bond with Dorothy had grown closer. Learning that Dorothy knew him, as Emily now suspected, and that he knew her, only complicated things even further.

Adelaide could tell she'd hit a nerve. 'I'm sorry, Em. I didn't mean to pry.'

'I'm sorry, too. I didn't mean to be rude.' Emily stood up and called to Dorothy and Toto. 'Come along, you two. Time for bed.'

'I guess I'll turn in, too.' Adelaide placed a hand on Emily's shoulder. 'I'm a good listener, if you ever want to talk.'

Emily did want to talk, desperately, but this was too big a secret for idle conversation.

At bedtime, Dorothy asked if she could look through her mother's collection of circus memorabilia instead of having a story. Emily had started to talk about Annie more with Dorothy, conscious of her duty to keep Annie's memory alive through photographs and stories about their time as young children. But it was these colourful treasures that most fascinated the child, while Emily tried to ignore the heavy secret carried among the brightly coloured posters with their bold declarations of *Daring Feats!* and *All Manner of Wonders and Marvels!* They reminded her of the pamphlet promoting the rainmaker, which Henry had left on the table. '*THE REMARKABLE RAIN MAN. The world's best in precipitation conjuration. The leading moisture scientist in concussion theory and aerial agitators.* More trickery and false promises, no doubt.

'Which was Mommy's favourite act?' Dorothy asked. 'Was it the Aerial Lorraines?'

Emily winced at the question. 'Yes, dear. She liked that one the best.' Lord forgive me, she added silently to herself.

It all felt like such a long time ago, yet as Dorothy leafed through the tickets and posters and idly turned the hourglass, Emily saw time turn the other way, leading her back to those magical evenings at the circus, and her sister as a young woman in love.

'You still think about him, don't you, Annie.'

'Every day. Every minute. Every hour... You only get one true love of your life, Em. When you find yours, hold tight and never let him go.'

It would seem that Annie hadn't let her dear aerialist go after all. Emily wished she could be glad for her, but it felt wrong and dangerous. Worst of all, it might have put Dorothy in a very difficult situation, now that Annie was gone.

Emily had tried to find the right moment or words to gently ask Dorothy about Annie's special friend, but she was afraid of what she might discover if she did. She'd decided it was best left alone.

'Is it bad that I don't think about Daddy as much as I think about Mommy?' Dorothy asked as Emily tidied the things away.

Emily stalled for a moment. It was a difficult question to answer. 'Well, I know you loved your mommy very much. Sometimes we don't have room in our hearts to love everyone the same way. And that's OK.'

The child was happy enough with the response, but Emily felt the hollow echo of Annie's secret in her words.

'You have my eyes, and your granny's nose, and I just know you have your father's brave heart and adventurous spirit ... Maybe you'll meet him one day ... Maybe we can be together after all.'

Emily put everything back into the box, glad to replace the lid and return it to the cupboard.

*

The next day was to be the rainmaker's demonstration, organised by the men who'd raised the money, to impress the townsfolk and show them that their precious dollars were being well spent. Henry had gone ahead into town to help organise things. Adelaide had taken herself off for a quick test run in the Jenny.

Emily was restless and anxious, not least because a reply had arrived from Nell.

She opened the envelope and unfolded a single page of writing paper.

Dearest Emily,
I'm so sorry to hear how bad things are there. We hear reports on the wireless about the awful dust storms. It must be terrible for you all.

Dorothy will be well looked after here with us, and far safer by the sound of it. She can return to you when things improve.

Maybe you and Henry will reconsider and come with her? I hate to think of you suffering and struggling.

Let me know, and we can make the necessary arrangements.
Your dear sister,
Nell

'Is it time to go yet?'

Emily jumped, startled by Dorothy's sudden appearance. The child couldn't wait to see the rainmaker's explosives.

She pushed the letter into her pocket. 'Not yet, dear. Uncle Henry will come back when everything is arranged. Why don't you take the wildflowers from the flower press. Try and draw them.'

With the child occupied, she put Nell's letter into the dresser drawer and went out to the barn to feed the animals.

So much seemed to hinge on the outcome of the next few days and whether the rainmaker would succeed. As Emily looked out at the great expanse of decaying prairie, she confronted the question that she and Henry had been steadfastly avoiding. Not whether they had the courage to stay and see this through, but – if things didn't go the way they hoped – did they have the courage to leave? All she knew for certain was that she couldn't bear to send Dorothy away. Not to Nell. Not to anyone.

As she turned to pick up the spade, she noticed a scruffy pair of boots sticking out from behind the tractor, striped socks tucked into the bottom of each pant leg.

She held her breath, heart thumping.

They'd had plenty of hobos passing through since the stock market crash, and more in recent months as farms foreclosed and exhausted broken men looked for somewhere to shelter for the night as they headed west. She'd heard of farms being ransacked and wasn't prepared to take any chances.

She crept out of the barn and hurried back to the house, where she took Henry's rifle from the wall.

Dorothy looked up from her sketching. 'Oh, please don't shoot the old mare, Auntie Em! Uncle Henry said she won't be long for this earth and he might need to put her out of her misery.'

'I'm not shooting the mare, Dorothy. Just saw a snake, is all. You stay inside with Toto. Don't come out until I say.'

Could she shoot a horse to put it out of its misery, let alone shoot a man to protect herself and her home? She'd only ever shot a cow they'd found, half-dead with the dust fever. But a man was an entirely different proposition.

Arms shaking, she approached the barn. Aside from the rifle, surprise was her best weapon. Her heart thumped in her chest as she stepped through the barn door.

She waited a moment for her eyes to adjust to the dim light, then crept past the horses, praying they wouldn't whinny at her.

She inched forward, making her way towards the back of the barn until she could just make out the shape of a man lying in the straw, a broad-brimmed hat pulled over his face.

She cocked the rifle and pointed it at him. 'What do you want here?' She kept her voice low and steady, masking the fear that sent her heart racing.

He sat up, arms raised in surrender. 'Don't shoot. I only sleep. I bring no danger.'

Emily faltered a second. His accent was strange. Was he drunk? 'Why are you in my barn?' She held the rifle dead straight, not entirely sure which part of him she was aiming at. It was hard to see in the dim light. 'My husband will be back from the fields any moment.'

The man began to get to his feet. 'I am sorry for the trouble. I—'

'Stay where you are, or I'll shoot you!' Emily kept her rifle trained on him.

Behind her, the barn door opened. Daylight flooded inside, illuminating the interior.

Emily didn't move, didn't take her eyes off him for a second as Toto ran forward, growling and snarling as he made a grab for the man's ankles.

She glanced over her shoulder. 'Go back to the house, Dorothy. There's no need to worry. I'll be right there.'

Emily called Toto to her as the man stood up.

'Please. I do not hurt you,' he said. 'You misunderstand. I am the rainmaker. I come to bring the rain. Miss Watson tells me I can rest here until she returns.'

'Miss Watson? But—' Of course! Adelaide had mentioned that the rainmaker would come to their barn.

Emily lowered the rifle and applied the safety as the man stepped out of the shadows behind the tractor. He was now clearly visible.

Emily's heart thundered. Her mind raced. Her breath was knocked clean from her lungs, as if she'd been winded. Courage leached from her as she stared at the face looking back at her, and the years tumbled and turned as her past collided with her present, and the moment she'd so often feared in her imagination became a terrible reality.

The man looking back at her was The Amazing Aerialist.

The love of Annie's life.

Dorothy's father.

He reached out a hand as a familiar smile curved at his lips. '*Buongiorno*, Miss Emily. It has been a very long time.'

Emily squared her shoulders, took a deep breath, and tried to keep her voice steady. 'I think we should go inside.'

As she spoke, Dorothy appeared at her side.

The child's face filled with surprise. 'Mr Stregone! Whatever are you doing here?'

39

Emily passed him a glass of water and wished she could throw it over him – a whole bucket of water, preferably. She was angry, confused, and afraid, all at the same time. The rainmaker she had so fervently hoped for was the very man she'd feared ever seeing or hearing from again. She couldn't comprehend that they were the same person, couldn't yet make sense of what it might mean for them all.

The years had not been kind to him. The striking olive-skinned face she remembered was now thin and lined and weathered. Shadows traced his eyes, the mischievous sparkle they used to hold now lost. Grey flecked his once jet-black hair. There was some relief, at least, in seeing no resemblance to him in Dorothy.

Emily observed him carefully, assessing his character and temperament, watching for any clues as to his real intentions. There was still the slightest chance that this was all a coincidence, that there was nothing suspicious about him being in Kansas, yet she distrusted him, doubted every motivation he had for being there. On the other hand, he was Annie's great love, Dorothy's father, and the town's last hope. She felt dizzy with emotions, her mind spinning with questions. She needed to act quickly, establish the facts before Henry returned.

She kept the conversation brief and functional. Dorothy had been briskly dispatched to collect the eggs and brush the old mare.

'I believe you've made a long journey to be here,' Emily said as she kneaded the bread dough. She had to keep busy, had to do something to stay calm.

'Yes! And this is why I fall asleep in your barn!' Again, the disarming smile. 'I am sorry again for the trouble, Miss Emily. I did not mean to alarm you. Miss Adelaide told me I would find her here, and to rest until she comes.'

'You're lucky I didn't mistake you for a hobo. I'd have shot you if it had been necessary.'

'Then I am glad it was not.'

For a moment, they studied each other. A stand-off? A truce? Neither of them was sure who should make the first move.

There was a momentary pause as Dorothy returned with the eggs, Toto at her heels. She placed the basket on the table and smiled, a little shyly, at their guest. Emily's heart ached to know the truth behind the smile he offered in return.

'Can you really make it rain, Mr Stregone?' Dorothy asked. 'Miss Adelaide said you have magical potions. And rockets. Where are they?'

He glanced at Emily before answering Dorothy's questions. 'Some of the magic is chemistry. Elements and compounds. Explosives do the rest. All my equipment is in my truck, behind the barn.'

'But what else?' Dorothy pressed. 'You said *some* of the magic. Where does the rest come from?'

At this, he laughed. 'You ask the right question! The other magic, dear child, is belief. That is where the real magic happens.'

Emily couldn't bear to listen to another word. 'Did you brush the horse, Dorothy?' Her tone was brusque. Her shoulders were tense, her hands clasped tight in front of her, her entire body stiff and brittle.

'I forgot. I'll do it now. Come along, Toto!' Dorothy ran outside again.

Emily looked at Leonardo. For a moment, neither of them spoke. 'She is a very sweet child,' he said eventually. 'You raise her well.'

Emily couldn't stand it any longer. She leaned against the sink, hands gripping the edge as she kept a close eye on Dorothy through the window. 'You know, don't you.'

For a moment, silence.

Emily waited; breath held.

'That Dorothy is my daughter? Yes, I know.'

The words settled on Emily like pinpricks. She took a deep breath as the impact of his words settled around her. There was no going back now. She must confront it, whatever the outcome.

'How long have you known?' She kept her back to him, determined to maintain her composure.

'Since she was the baby. Annie told me.'

'How did you find her? Us? After all this time.'

'You have many questions!'

Yet the only question that mattered, she couldn't bring herself to ask: Why? Why had he really come here, and what did he want?

She thought about the official forms she'd signed at the attorneys', and the copies that Henry kept in his desk drawer. She could use them to warn him off, if necessary. He couldn't take Dorothy away from them. Surely?

'It is a shock, I know,' he continued. 'The great surprise for you. I understand . . .'

At this, she turned to face him. 'No, Mr Stregone. You *don't* understand. You can never understand.'

The sound of a motorcar approaching caught Emily's attention. Henry.

She told Leonardo to stay where he was as she hurried outside, desperate to tell Henry something – she wasn't entirely sure what – before he entered the house.

'Henry! Thank goodness you're back. There's something I need to tell you—'

He gripped her arms, a broad smile on his face. 'I already know! He's here, isn't he. The rainmaker. I saw Hank in town. Told me he'd called in at the general store, asking which was Gale Farm. Is he inside?'

Emily hurried after him, her mind whirling as he strode purposefully toward the house. She hadn't seen him this enthusiastic in an age. 'Henry! Wait! There's something else!'

But he wouldn't be stopped. He was already inside.

'Well, if it isn't the Remarkable Rain Man himself, sitting at my table!'

Leonardo stood up as Henry shook his hand. 'Leonardo Stregone, at your service!'

'Henry Gale. And am I glad to see you! If there ever was a good omen, I reckon it's a man who can bring the rain, sitting in your home!'

Emily stood in the doorway, her heart in her mouth.

She'd imagined – feared – this moment so often, that to see Leonardo now, shaking Henry's hand, was almost unbelievable. He was a good few inches shorter than Henry, reminding her of the scrappy young boy who'd climbed to the top of the human pyramid formed by his uncles and brothers. But what he lacked in stature he more than made up for in personality. He oozed confidence and carried the same air of charismatic charm she remembered from his circus days. It wasn't hard to see why Annie had fallen for him, or why Henry absorbed his every word now, or why Dorothy – charmed by her mother's special friend – returned from the barn as soon as she'd done her chores, eager to see more of this magical rain man for herself.

Worried that the child would say something in front of Henry, Emily bustled her outside again to fetch the washing from the line.

'There are so many chores today,' Dorothy said, a small frown on her face.

'Yes, there are. Now, off you go before another duster rolls in and dirties everything all up again.'

Emily busied herself as the two men settled into conversation. Henry asked Leo about his methods and techniques, fascinated by the science behind it all. Leo asked Henry about the farm and the drought and the dusters. They talked about silver iodide and salt powder and nitroglycerine, then about combustion engines and irrigation.

'I follow the principles of concussion theory,' Leo explained. 'I learn it from the war. The noise and chemicals released in explosions disturb the weather patterns. Always, after a military battle, comes the rain. My aerial bombing – the same! And finally, a little magic and good fortune helps.'

'Magic?' Henry looked a little puzzled. 'I was hoping there would be more science than magic!'

'Mr Stregone used to perform in the circus,' Emily added, desperately trying to keep one step ahead in case Leo said something that would reveal his connection to Annie, or worse, to Dorothy. If Henry knew Leonardo was the man Annie had loved, maybe everything else could remain a secret. 'In fact, he is The Amazing Aerialist I've told you about,' she said, forcing a smile. 'Can you believe it!'

Henry looked at her. '*Annie's* aerialist?'

Emily's heart thumped in her chest. It was a risk, but she had to say something to disarm Leonardo, to lead him to believe that Henry knew as much as she did. 'Yes! Isn't that something?'

Henry looked at Mr Stregone and back at Emily, his face full of surprise. 'Is that so! Well, I'll be darned. Of all the farms across the Great Plains, and this is where you land. It is a small world indeed!'

Emily breathed a sigh of relief. Henry was too enthused about the rainmaking experiment to dwell on the past. The risk had paid off.

'Circus performer turned rainmaker. Is there anything you can't do, Mr Stregone?' Henry continued.

Leonardo glanced toward Emily.

She stared back at him. 'Well, Mr Stregone? There must be something?'

Leonardo at least had the decency to look contrite. 'There is plenty I cannot do, Mr Gale, but I learn to adapt. The circus is not what it was. People cannot afford a ticket, and we cannot afford to feed the animals. We are all scattering now, like the seeds.' His Italian accent had been softened by the years, but it was still there. 'When Miss Adelaide said she can take me up in her Jenny, and I detonate the dynamite to bring the rain, we make even more the rain, and even more the money!'

'It must be a hard life, moving from town to town, sleeping where you can, no home of your own,' Henry said.

'My home is here, and here.' Leo tapped his head and his chest. 'I do not like to settle. Like the tumbleweed, I turn and turn until I stop somewhere.'

Henry laughed. 'The free life of a man without a wife and children! You'd better not say any more, Mr Stregone. You will make me envy you!' He planted a kiss on Emily's cheek to assure her he was only teasing.

She turned to the basin to wash her hands, unable to prevent the huff of breath that escaped her. 'A life without responsibility, or consequence? Wouldn't we all envy that.'

'I think I have offended your wife, Mr Gale!' Leo looked at Emily, his eyes searching hers. 'I am still a child. I do not grow up, even as a man. I am like the Peter Pan. Forever a boy.'

As he spoke, Dorothy returned, catching the end of the conversation. 'I like Peter Pan! It's one of my favourite stories.'

Leo smiled. 'Second star to the right . . .'

Dorothy's face lit up. 'And straight on 'til morning!'

Emily closed her eyes to steady herself, rattled by this shared moment between the two of them.

'You are most welcome to sleep in our barn, Mr Stregone,' Henry said. 'While you're here, performing your experiments.'

Emily turned and wiped her hands on her apron. 'But Adelaide is in the barn, Henry. I'm afraid you will have to find somewhere else to stay, Mr Stregone.'

Henry was taken aback. 'Emily! Are we forgetting our manners? I'm sure Miss Watson won't mind. They are business partners now, after all. And not forgetting that Mr Stregone is an old friend of your sister's. We would be delighted to have you, Leo.'

Emily stalled. There was nothing else she could say.

Leonardo seized the offer gladly. 'You are very generous. I will repay you with the rain.'

Henry put his hands on his hips. 'You'll do it for free?'

Leo laughed. 'We are both men of business, Mr Gale! A discount, perhaps, in return for your kindness.'

Henry looked at Emily. 'What do you say, Em?'

Dorothy jumped up from the chair. 'Please, Auntie Em! Please say yes!'

Emily couldn't think straight. Annie's secret, and the secret she had kept from Henry, had finally caught up with her. She had reached the inevitable, unavoidable fork in the road, uncertainty and worry in both directions. If she told Henry now, she might put everything at risk. If she didn't, would he ever forgive her?

As hopeful expectant eyes looked back at her, her gaze settled on a photograph of Annie on the dresser.

'Very well,' she said, ignoring the nagging sense of dread that whirled in her heart.

'Then it is agreed!' Leo stood up, dipped his fingers into his glass of water, and flicked drops into the air before bowing with a theatrical flourish. 'Ladies and gentlemen! The Remarkable Rain Man, at your service.'

At that moment, Adelaide opened the door and stepped inside. 'Leo! You made it!'

40

News of the rainmaker's arrival spread fast and far. Liberal folk turned out in great numbers to watch the demonstration that afternoon.

Everyone was desperate for this man to live up to their expectations, for his equipment to work and bring the rain. From prayers and dances to old farming superstitions, they'd tried everything since nature had abandoned them. The sight of snakes, killed and hung belly-up on barbed wire fences turned Emily's stomach inside out. She was as eager as the next person to see what Leonardo could do.

The level of excitement and anticipation climbed, until the gathered crowd were on the cusp of impatience, when a voice appeared, as if from nowhere.

'Good people of Kansas!'

A gasp rippled through the crowd as everyone turned to see where the booming voice was coming from. The makeshift stage in front remained empty.

'You have suffered long enough!' the voice continued. 'Together, we will bring the rain back to your farms!'

Henry glanced at Emily, a tired smile on his face. Dorothy gripped Emily's hand, a little afraid of the booming voice.

Behind Emily, Hank Miller couldn't hide his delight. 'Should see the equipment he has, Henry. Sure looks like a man who knows what he's doing.'

Emily looped her arm through Henry's. 'You really think he can make it rain?'

'I guess nobody can know for sure, but I believe God loves a trier, Em. And, Lord knows, we've tried. Let's see what he has to offer in those canisters and contraptions of his.'

Cheers and applause mingled with the chatter of anticipation and expectation until a bright flash of light and a fizzing crackle drew everyone's attention to the stage. Leonardo had appeared, his arms spread wide in grateful acceptance of the enthusiastic applause.

The scruffy clothes he'd worn earlier had been replaced by a smart pair of green serge pants and a matching waistcoat worn over a crisp white shirt. His hair had been brushed and slicked back. He'd even shaved. All that remained of the homeless wanderer Emily had found in the barn earlier were the scruffy boots and striped socks. This was the bombastic showman she remembered, the great orator and performer she'd watched so many times and whom Annie had been enchanted by.

He addressed the crowd, thanking them for the warm welcome and assuring them he was the best precipitation conjugator across the Great Plains. He turned to his left, then, and held out his hand.

'And now, meet the Daring Darling of the Skies! The Antipodean Earhart! The Wonderful Woman from Aus. Miss Adelaide Watson!'

Adelaide jumped onto the stage beside him, beaming in an elegant two-piece aviation suit of loose slacks and a zip top with

99s stitched onto the breast pocket. She looked every inch of Amelia Earhart or Amy Johnson.

Dorothy squealed. 'Look, Auntie Em! It's Miss Adelaide!'

'Yes, dear. It is.' Emily tugged self-consciously at a loose thread on the cuff of her old prairie dress and ran a hand over the straggly hairs that had fallen loose from the bun at the nape of her neck. The practical style aged her, but it was too hot to let her hair hang loose.

'With my sophisticated techniques and equipment,' Leo continued, 'and ably assisted by the wonderful Miss Watson here, we will blast the clouds apart and bring rain by the bucketful!'

Emily looked on, partly fascinated but still highly sceptical as Leonardo performed an impressive demonstration of his chemical concoctions, sending coloured smoke into the air as glass tubes and jars full of liquids fizzed and sputtered.

'When this same chemical reaction is absorbed by the atmosphere, the rain will come,' he announced with absolute certainty.

He was certainly persuasive. Everyone was enraptured. Emily was sure they would have believed him if he'd said his concoctions could make an elephant appear.

'And now, the pièce de résistance!' For the final part of his demonstration, he sent a balloon skyward, a small, timed explosive device attached to it. When it reached a certain altitude, he detonated it, sending a mighty crack and boom rippling across the sky above. Everyone gasped and clapped.

'If you're really a magic man, make yourself disappear!' Pieter Anderssen called out, earning himself a sharp reprimand from his mother.

Dorothy giggled and held her hand to her mouth.

Leo wasn't concerned. 'The young boy demands that I disappear!' he said. 'How can I bear to disappoint him?'

The crowd responded with oohs and aahs.

As if rehearsed, Adelaide sprang into action, passing Leo several items – matches, a thermos of hot water, a canister. Emily stretched onto her tiptoes to see better. After a moment or two, Adelaide set off firecrackers that fizzed and flashed. Emily squinted against the bright lights, shielding her eyes as a great cloud of smoke formed and then cleared, and all that was left on the stage was a pair of scruffy boots and striped socks.

Pieter jumped up and down and clapped his hands. 'He did it! He really did disappear!'

It was quite the display. Mr Stregone had impressed them all.

Bar one.

While the smoke had obscured the crowd's view, Emily had seen him scurrying beneath the cloth that covered the stage. He was nothing but a fraud, a well-rehearsed circus showman, hiding beneath old tomato crates.

*

Emily had presumed Leonardo would get on with his *precipitation conjugation* right away, but he said it was important to wait until conditions were optimal to launch his chemical explosions. She hoped it wouldn't be much longer. Every day that Leo remained with them, the greater the chance of something being said that would place her in a difficult situation. And the longer they waited for the rain, the worse the dusters seemed to become. More and more rolled in every day, sending them all scurrying inside with damp cloths over their noses and mouths while newspapers and rags were stuffed uselessly against the windows and doors. It was relentless. Unbearable.

Emily hardly let Leo out of her sight as he helped Henry with tasks around the farm. It was good to see Henry take an interest in things again as he talked about the record harvests of their early years and what they'd hoped the future would bring. He showed Leo his ledgers where he'd carefully recorded the yields they'd once brought in and the high prices they'd secured. He told him about the tornado that had destroyed their first home, and the financial crash that had followed, and the influx of farmers that had seen millions of acres of prairie torn up and sent prices spiralling because of record grain yields. Emily didn't like Henry being so open about everything, but she left him to it while quietly watching and listening.

'You've had the bad luck,' Leo said. 'You didn't have family to help?'

'I'm too stubborn and proud,' Henry said with a sorry shake of his head. 'Not that there would have been anything to help us with. Turns out our family were no better off than we were.'

Leo seemed surprised. 'The crash spread far,' he said, but his attention seemed to have wandered.

While Emily watched Henry and Leo carefully, it was Leo's interactions with Dorothy that she observed most closely.

He was pleasant with the child, patient and encouraging as he taught her how to juggle two apples, then three at a time. Emily felt the sting of envy as she watched the easy way between the two of them, remembering her own faltering attempts to connect with Dorothy over an apple.

'He has her mesmerised with his clever tricks and potions,' Henry said as the two of them watched the eager pupil and her enigmatic teacher.

With Toto as an audience, Dorothy practised the tricks until she got them right, earning an enthusiastic '*Brava, bella* Dorothy! *Brava!*' from Leo.

'That man could charm a snake,' Emily said. 'And Dorothy should be doing chores, never mind learning silly tricks.'

'You don't like him much, do you?' Henry placed an arm around her shoulder. 'Ever the protective sister.'

The feel of Henry's touch was fortifying, even though the

reference to Annie pained her. She'd been so anxious since Leo's arrival, doubtful of his true motives and always on edge in case he or Dorothy said something that revealed more than she'd already shared with Henry.

'I just wish he would get on with what he came here to do,' she said. 'That's all.'

'I'm not especially keen on him myself, to be honest. Bit too showy for my liking. You can tell he used to be a circus performer. But he's charming, that's for sure.'

Their attention was diverted by Dorothy calling to them.

'Look, Uncle Henry! Auntie Em! This one's my favourite trick,' she cried, before turning back to Leonardo. 'I always asked you to perform this one, didn't I, Mr Stregone!'

Henry glanced at Emily. 'Always? Whatever does she mean?'

Emily stiffened. For a moment, she couldn't find the words to respond. She looked on silently as Leonardo made a ball appear to float along the edge of a silk handkerchief.

'I presume Annie took Dorothy to the circus,' she said, eventually. 'She must have seen him perform the trick there. Either that or she's imagining things again.'

Henry seemed placated. 'Most probably! Anyway, like the man or not, if he can do what he says he can, I'm sure we can tolerate him a little while longer.' He pulled Emily closer to him. 'This won't last forever, Em. Hang in there.'

She knew he was talking about the drought, but her thoughts were elsewhere.

She couldn't deny the lift that Leonardo's arrival had given to Henry, and the rest of the town, but while everyone else longed only for the rain, she also longed for a release from the secret she carried. She wrestled with her conscience, remembering her solemn promise to Annie, but regretting her decision to hide the truth from Henry. Since Annie and John's accident, she'd come close to confiding in him. After all, he was Dorothy's guardian now. But she'd stalled and stalled, afraid of how he would react to knowing she'd kept the truth from him all these years, and reluctant to rob him of his own Gale family connection to Dorothy. How might Henry react if he discovered that Leonardo and Annie had deceived his cousin? She couldn't risk ruining everything, not now that they were so close to Leo bringing the rain, and with Henry finally feeling hopeful again. He had a spring in his step. A purpose. Now wasn't the time to unearth old secrets.

But the possibility of losing Dorothy to this charismatic magic man continued to grow from the first nagging seeds of worry to a deeply-rooted sense of anxiety. As Emily walked, alone, among the failed crops and dry dusty tracks, she couldn't help wondering if a transient life with an enigmatic showman would be preferable to whatever she and Henry could offer. Leonardo could take Dorothy away from all the dust, somewhere where the air was clear, where she could breathe properly. Questions and doubt tumbled and turned through her mind as a Cooper's hawk wheeled above. Would Annie want her daughter to be with her father? Should Dorothy perhaps be the one to decide?

She sat alone for a long time, watching the hungry hawks that circled above. As she listened to their peeping cries, she closed her eyes and returned to the shores of Lough Inagh, her hands in her sisters', her mother telling them to always remember this place: their home.

She said a silent prayer, asking her mother and Annie for help, for a sign, for something to guide her in the right direction.

*

The sun began to set on another rainless day. It had always been Emily's favourite time, that perfect in-between hour when everything was bathed in a rosy glow and something of an enchantment settled over the land as it shifted from day to night. But there was nothing of enchantment or magic that day.

Emily couldn't be sure how much longer Leonardo would stay. She needed to know his intentions, even though it frightened her.

She invited him to sit with her while everyone else was occupied. 'I would like to ask you about my sister,' she said.

Leo sat down and took his hat from his head. 'Then I will answer my best.'

'How did you find her again?' she asked. 'After the war?'

He explained how he'd been conscripted into the Royal Italian Army, and how terrible it had been in the cold winters, fighting on the northern borders in the Alps. 'I couldn't stand it,' he said. 'After the Battle of Caporetto, I leave.'

'You deserted?' Of course he had.

'*Sì*. Yes, I run away. You think I am the coward?'

Emily didn't answer.

'I was to be executed, but the war ended and amnesty was granted. I look for Annie when I return to America many years later. But everywhere I look, she is vanished. And then I find her. In the newspaper.'

'The newspaper?' Emily didn't remember Annie being in the newspaper.

'A picture. Of her wedding day.'

Of course. The announcement in the formal notifications.

'The day I find her is the day I lose her,' Leo continued. 'My Annie was married. I was too late. But I couldn't put her from my mind. I look for John Gale. He was easy to find – known by half of Chicago – and I follow him home from his office, and I see her. She is so beautiful – and, I think, a little sad.'

'How did she find out you were back?' she asked.

'I write to her. She write back. At first, she is very confused. We agree not to meet, that it is too late for us.' He took a deep breath. 'But you cannot deny the things you are meant to have. We meet when Mr Gale is away. And then I must leave with the circus. But when I return the next year . . .'

'She'd had the baby.'

He nodded. 'She tell me the child is mine. That she is certain. And she is afraid that John will know the truth, so she ask if I will take her and Dorothy with me.'

Emily couldn't believe it. Had Annie really been prepared to leave John, to give up her comfortable life for a life on the road, with Leonardo and the circus? 'But you didn't take them,' she said. 'You left them.'

Leo shook his head, unable to meet Emily's eye. 'I was afraid to be a father. As I tell you, I am forever a boy. I want the pleasure of your sister, not the responsibility of a child.'

Emily's fear and worry was quickly replaced by anger. 'We are all afraid of responsibility, Mr Stregone – the responsibility for a child, especially – but some of us are brave enough to take it on anyway.'

'I tell Annie to forget me, that John should raise the child as his own. That it was for the best to be this way.'

Emily's mind spun wildly as the missing pieces of the puzzle fell into place. Her heart broke for Annie as she thought back to her desperate pleas for her to stay until the baby arrived, and how reluctantly – resentfully – she'd agreed. All that time, Annie had carried her secret, afraid of John finding out, and unable to tell Leo that she was carrying his child. And then she'd been abandoned by the man she truly loved. Might Annie still be alive if Leo had taken her and Dorothy with him, as she'd wanted?

Emily felt sick to her stomach. 'You told her you would marry her one day. She turned that hourglass thousands of times while she waited for you to come back. You left her when she needed you the most.'

He hung his head as he took a photograph from his pocket. 'She give me this photograph of Dorotea. Named for my mama.'

Emily looked at the picture of Annie with baby Dorothy in her arms. The photograph that *she* had taken. Annie looked so young and beautiful. Emily turned the photograph over. On the back, Annie had written: *Dorothy/Dorotea.*

'When I am travelling with the circus and I look at the photograph, I know I have been the fool. I go back the next time I am in Chicago. I see Dorothy when I visit Annie.'

Emily's mind reeled. 'How often? How well do you know Dorothy?'

'I see her only once a year. I bring her a toy animal, for her birthday. A monkey, elephant, tiger, bear. Circus animals.'

Emily thought about the toys Dorothy had left behind in Chicago.

'When did you last see Annie?' she asked.

At this, Leo looked a little guilty. 'Two years ago. After the money crash we need to work harder, more towns, more shows, to make the money. It is very hard to return to Annie. When I read about the accident, my heart is breaking. I go to the house. The lady tells me Dorothy is gone, taken by her aunt and uncle to Kansas. A town called Liberal. I write it down. Liberal, Kansas.'

'You must have seen Cora,' Emily said. 'The housekeeper.'

Cora had remembered what Emily had told her. '. . . *promise you'll visit sometime. Head to Liberal and ask for Mrs Miller at the general store. She'll point you in our direction.*' She wished she'd never uttered the words.

'I look for Dorothy,' he continued. 'And then I meet Miss Watson and she is looking for *me*, to bring me to Liberal to summon the rain. And here is Dorotea. It is almost the miracle.'

Emily flinched at his words. 'Her name is Dorothy! Besides, I still don't understand why you came looking for her.'

At this, Leo looked her straight in the eye. 'Why? Because she is my daughter, Mrs Gale.'

The words landed on Emily in heavy blunt blows. Dorothy

wasn't his daughter. Not in any true emotional sense. If she was anyone's daughter, she was hers, and Henry's. Leo had been a bit-part character in Dorothy's and Annie's lives. Nothing more. Yet had she been any better? She'd hardly known the child at the start of the year. Now she couldn't bear to think of being without her.

'So, what happens next?' she asked, bracing herself for his reply. 'Do you plan on telling Dorothy?'

The words hung in the dry dusty air around her as life seemed to pause, waiting to know in which direction it should turn, but before he could answer, Adelaide returned from the barn where she and Henry had been working on the Jenny.

'She's all set,' Adelaide said. 'Folk are getting restless, Leo. They want to know why it's taking so long and asking when the conditions will be right.'

Leo looked at Emily for a moment before turning his eyes to the sky. 'Tomorrow, is the answer. Tomorrow we will answer all of the questions.'

41

By midday, everyone had gathered at the edge of the field beside the barn where Leo had set up his equipment: large earthenware crocks filled with his chemicals, pipes to emit the fumes, balloons loaded with nitroglycerine and ready with timed detonators which Adelaide would release into the clouds.

A hush descended as he started to activate the contraptions, and noxious fumes began to spew from the pipes, drifting skyward in a great black cloud. Next, Adelaide took off in the Jenny with the balloon bombs. Everyone craned their necks to watch, eyes shielded against the glare of the sun as they were detonated at different altitudes. The thunderous sound of the explosions was impressive, the pyrotechnic lightshow of sparks even more so. It reminded Emily of herself and Annie and Nell, necks craned as they'd watched The Amazing Aerialist tumble and turn on the trapeze suspended beneath his balloon high above their heads, the crowd spellbound by the performance. Now, as then, there was something magical, something undeniably powerful in how he brought a community together, uniting them in purpose and wonder and hope.

The children gasped in awe, their eyes trained skyward, enraptured by the spectacle. They'd never seen anything like it.

Dorothy couldn't look away. 'It's so pretty, isn't it?'

Emily smiled. 'It is, dear. Very pretty.' But among the dazzling spectacle, she also saw their hard-earned dollar bills being blown to pieces and prayed that it would all prove to be worthwhile.

Impressed and encouraged by what they'd seen, the men agreed on a price with Leo to do another round. After sundown, the show continued. The bright lights, the crackle and fizz from calcium flares, the booming rumble and roar of more explosions filled the air for a second time.

Eventually, Leo ran out of dynamite, and the crowd ran out of enthusiasm, and he declared that he had done all he could.

'And now, ladies and gentlemen, we wait. If rain comes within the next five days, the experiment will be deemed a great success! If not, then I am afraid there was something wrong with the atmospheric conditions.'

'Another fraud,' Wilhelmina West said as Emily wished her a good night. 'Style over substance, no doubt.'

Emily paused. 'Let's wait and see, shall we.' But she agreed with Wilhelmina, and spoke only for the benefit of Dorothy beside her.

As Wilhelmina hopped onto the seat of her bicycle, she trod on Toto's tail.

The dog yelped and made a retaliatory lunge at her ankles before Dorothy quickly scooped him up.

'That dog's a liability!' Wilhelmina snapped. 'If you can't keep him under control, I'll have him taken away.'

Dorothy stood her ground and held Toto tight in her arms. 'You can't do that! You're just a mean old woman.'

Emily chastised the child. 'Dorothy! That's quite enough. Apologise to Miss West.'

Dorothy refused.

'The girl is as badly behaved as her dog,' Wilhelmina said. 'Maybe I'll have them *both* taken away.'

Dorothy looked at Emily, aghast. 'She can't send us away, Auntie Em? Can she?'

Emily was furious. 'No, dear. She can't.' She gave Wilhelmina a piece of her mind before grabbing Dorothy's hand and hurrying them away. 'She can't send anyone away. Now, let's find Uncle Henry before he sends out a search party.'

Dorothy was still upset by Wilhelmina's threats. 'What's a search party?'

'It's when friends and neighbours go looking for someone when they're lost.'

'Would you send a search party if me and Toto were lost?'

Emily stopped walking and bent down so that her eyes were level with Dorothy's. 'Oh, Dorothy dear, I would never stop looking until I found you!' The words were out before she realised how much she meant them. 'Now, let's forget all about it. Nobody is being taken away, or getting lost.'

But Dorothy was unusually quiet that evening and didn't want to eat her supper. She even went to bed before being asked and wouldn't let Toto out of her sight.

'Honestly, Henry. That Wilhelmina West is insufferable,' Emily said as they sat together that evening. 'She's the most unpleasant woman I've ever met. I wouldn't wonder if Dorothy was right all along.'

'About what?'

'About her being a witch.'

Henry laughed lightly. 'Witches in town. Wizards summoning the rain. And there I was, thinking we'd come to Kansas for a quiet life.'

Emily couldn't stop a small smile reaching her lips. 'I don't deserve you, Henry Gale.'

He squeezed her hand affectionately. 'Oh, you do. You deserve the best of everything, Mrs Gale!'

The hours passed.

The rain didn't come.

Still, the dust blew.

*

Once again, they waited.

The sound of Dorothy clicking the heels of her silver shoes together became the background accompaniment to the little prairie home.

Click, click, click.

Nobody needed to guess what she was wishing for. They all wished for the same.

'Be patient, *bella*,' Leo said as he tousled Dorothy's hair. 'Give it another day or two. Why don't you check the rain catcher down by the creek. You might find a few drops of moisture in there. And then we'll know the experiment worked, hey, kid?'

Emily had noticed he was restless and keeping a low profile. People in town had already started to turn against him, calling him a rain faker. Some were demanding their money back. Even Henry had become doubtful that the experiment had worked.

'Where will you go next, Leo?' he asked. 'You and Adelaide headed off to bring rain across the Midwest, I presume?'

'Yes. We should already leave, but the dust is causing the problems with the engine.'

Emily feigned surprise. 'Do you not intend to stay, to see the result of your experiments? Share the town's joy?'

'A watched pot never cooks, Mrs Gale. I must move on, find another town to help.'

Emily watched him as carefully as she watched the skies.

Another day passed. Still, the rain didn't come.

Adelaide insisted on doing her share of chores around the house and farm, and did odd jobs to fix bits of farm machinery for folk around town. The money she earned she added to Emily's account at the general store to put towards her keep. Emily gratefully accepted it. They needed every cent they could get. Henry occupied himself by working on the rusted plough that hadn't sown a decent crop in months. Leonardo tried everything to fix his truck, but the dust was winning so far, much to Emily's despair. She wanted him gone from their lives before he caused any lasting damage. And she didn't like the way he turned every conversation with Henry back to their financial situation, or the interest he took in John's businesses back in Chicago.

'You shouldn't tell him so much, Henry,' she cautioned.

Henry thought she was being over-dramatic. 'There's not much to tell him, Em. We're broke. John was financially ruined. I'm not exactly spilling state secrets.'

Emily had heard Leo that morning, filling Dorothy's head with more nonsense about concussive precipitation and reminding her to check the rain catcher. 'It is very important, Dorothy. Moisture might be there, even if we don't see it fall from the sky.' He'd given her a packet of lemon drops from the general store, as if a bag of candy could make up for her disappointment.

With so much of their farming life on hold, Emily clung to small, manageable tasks she could control: sewing flour-sack dresses, keeping the fiddle clear of dust, hauling pails of water from the well to the orchard in a desperate attempt to keep the fruit trees alive. She collected the eggs, wrote in her journal, sketched the wildflowers she'd picked from the last blooming summer meadows and placed in her flower press. A reminder of better times.

Dorothy inspected the flowers carefully as Emily lifted them from the press, as if she was admiring a rare treasure in a museum.

'I can hardly believe anything so pretty and colourful ever grew here,' Dorothy said.

It broke Emily's heart that the child had never seen the prairie in full bloom. The only pretty thing that had grown through those months of drought and dust was Dorothy. The girl seemed to stretch in her sleep, the notches they'd marked each month on the timber post a marker of the time passing. The year had brought such turbulent change, but they had somehow settled into this strange new life together; like a blown tumbleweed that eventually finds shelter against a doorway or some other nook, they'd settled into the folds of one another.

'What's this one, Auntie Em?' Dorothy asked as they continued to organise the pressed flowers.

'That's a prairie violet,' Emily said. 'Pretty, isn't it.'

Dorothy wrote the name of the flower beside each one Emily had pressed onto the pages through the years since she and Henry had arrived: dandelion, verbena, groundsel, poppy. Almost a decade of flowers.

'Why did you keep them all?' Dorothy asked.

'To remember the spring and summer. To have flowers all the year round – it's nice to look at them through the winter. Look, these are the ones I picked and pressed the year before you came to live here.'

She removed a few more layers from the press, lifted up the delicate, paper-thin flowers and placed them in Dorothy's palm.

'It's a nice way to look at the flowers, to notice all the little details. The shape of the petals, how many petals there are, the patterns and lines on the leaves.'

'They're like paper,' Dorothy said, turning them over carefully and then lifting one up to the light at the window. 'I can see right through it! Like glass!'

Emily was pleased to see how fascinated Dorothy was by them, just as she had been as a little girl when she'd pressed flowers between the pages of her mother's Bible. The translucent petals reminded her of a slice of apple, held up to the light. ' . . . *you'll always remember this little cottage in Connemara on the edge of Ireland, and that the three of ye ate slices of apple while the autumn sun turned Annie's hair to flames, and Nell got a fit of the giggles when your da took to snoring, and Emily was after playing the fiddle like a banshee.*' She heard the echo of her mother's words, remembered standing on the banks of Lough Inagh, turf smoke in the air, the sound of uilleann pipes in the distance, her sisters' hands in hers. She drew strength from the memory of these women who had raised her, comforted her, guided her. They had all faced difficult decisions and endured hard times, just as she must now.

As Dorothy looked at the flowers, Emily consulted a floriography book she'd found in the town library about the language of flowers, reading out the symbolic meaning of each: Violets for love. Verbena for healing. Dandelion for hope. Poppy for remembrance.

Dorothy added the last pressed flower to the page. 'What's this one, Auntie Em?'

Emily smiled. 'That's my favourite. Yellow cinquefoil.'

'What does it mean?'

Emily checked the floriography book and faltered for a moment.

'Auntie Em? What does it mean?'

She looked at Dorothy and placed a hand against the child's cheek. 'It means, "beloved daughter".'

42

Emily watched Leonardo like a hawk. He was taking far too much interest in John's business affairs and Henry's farm accounts for her liking.

Adelaide asked if she could speak to Emily in private, in the barn.

'I don't want to speak out of turn,' she said. 'But I took a quick look at Leonardo's truck while he was out with Henry earlier. There's nothing wrong with it. It's working perfectly well.'

Emily wasn't entirely surprised. 'Is that so.'

'Why would he pretend it wasn't working? Why would he want to stick around when folk are calling him a fraud? I don't like lies and deception, Emily. Makes me mistrust the man.'

Adelaide's words settled on Emily, leaving her horribly conscious of her own lies and deception. And while she had her suspicions about Leo's motives for delaying his departure, she couldn't reveal them to Adelaide without also revealing the truth about him. 'I'll talk to him,' she said. 'Thank you for telling me.'

As she returned to the house, something caught her eye as she passed the window. Leo was inside, standing beside Henry's desk.

She ducked down, keeping out of sight as she watched him open the desk drawer and pull out some of Henry's papers. He leafed through them quickly, keeping half an eye on the door. What was he up to? She was about to march inside and ask him what on earth he was doing when Dorothy appeared from the pantry, Toto at her heels.

'Mr Stregone!' she gasped. 'Those are Uncle Henry's things!'

Leo startled at the sound of her voice. 'Oh! *Buongiorno*, Dorothy. You give me the fright!' He pushed the papers roughly back into the drawer and forced a smile. 'Shall we try some more tricks?'

Dorothy frowned. 'We're not allowed to pry into Uncle Henry's private papers. He told me so.'

'I – I look for something for him.' Leo kept his hands behind his back. 'But I cannot find it.'

Emily looked on. Part of her wanted to run inside. Part of her wanted to see how this played out, hoping that Leonardo would reveal himself to Dorothy for who he really was.

As Leonardo turned to look again through the drawer, Toto barked and made a lunge for his ankles. Leonardo jumped to get away, dropping something from his hands as he did. It fell to the floor with a clatter.

Dorothy ran forward. 'Mommy's ring!' She picked up the ring and looked at Leonardo, eyes wide as she realised what had happened. 'It is very wicked to steal, Mr Stregone! I'll tell Uncle Henry.' She crossed her arms defiantly.

'I wasn't stealing! I was just looking. It is a beautiful emerald. Let me see it again?'

Dorothy snatched her hand back as he reached for it. 'Why, you're nothing but a coward, and a thief! Stealing from people who have been so kind to you.'

Emily's heart swelled with love for the child. She was so proud to see Dorothy stand up to him, and yet she hated to see her let down, hated that he had shown his true colours, hated that she had to learn the tough lesson that sometimes what you believe to be true is just an illusion.

Emily had seen and heard quite enough. She marched inside and pulled the child protectively into her side.

'I'll talk to Mr Stregone now, Dorothy.' She held out her hand. Dorothy placed the emerald ring in her palm. 'Why don't you go and help Adelaide brush the horses? I won't be long.'

Dorothy took another look at Leonardo, scowled at him, and called for Toto to follow her.

Emily waited until she'd gone. 'So, this was your intention all along. You're not here for Dorothy at all, are you? You're here for nothing more than opportunistic greed. You've used your time here, stalling and prevaricating, to snoop around and talk to Henry and see what we – what *Dorothy* – might have that could be of value to you.'

For a moment she thought Leonardo was going to defend himself and claim otherwise, but he simply slumped into the chair and put his head in his hands, defeated. This once seemingly powerful man was reduced to nothing but a crumpled pile of tattered old clothes.

'There is no inheritance,' Emily continued, sensing that she had the upper hand. 'John went to his death financially ruined. There is nothing of financial value left for the child. All that she has now is whatever Henry and I can offer her.' As she spoke, a knot of emotion squeezed her heart in a moment of realisation. Their means were few and humble, but Dorothy didn't need material things. What she needed was love, and people she could depend on. As Emily looked at Leo, hunched and submissive, she summoned a strength from the knowledge that she and Henry could give Dorothy those things in abundance.

Leo looked up. He wiped a solitary tear from his eyes before slowly holding up his hands.

A surrender.

'You are right,' he said, shaking his head. 'I think about the money, and Dorothy's inheritance. I fall on hard times, Mrs Gale. Become desperate.'

'Desperate! Don't tell me about desperate. You're not desperate. You're just a boy who is afraid to grow up. You turned your back on my sister when she needed you – when she believed in you, and loved you. She thought you loved her too, but it was just another trick, wasn't it. Another con.'

As she spoke, she felt a sense of power rise within her. She had no reason to fear him anymore. After all these years holding Annie and herself under his spell, he had revealed himself for who he really was: a coward who was afraid to face the realities of life. He didn't deserve Annie. He would, no doubt, have broken her heart in the end. And he most certainly didn't deserve Dorothy.

He refused to look at her. 'Please, forgive me, Mrs Gale. I am the fool. A clown.'

'And a fraudster, hiding behind your illusions and explosions,' Emily continued. 'You take advantage of good people who give you their hard-earned money and believe everything you tell them.'

He finally met her gaze. 'I bring hope, and wonder,' he said, a last gasp to try and redeem himself. 'Is there a price too high for that?'

Emily thought of the hopeful faces that had watched his experiments: Henry and Dorothy, Laurie and Hank, Ingrid and Pieter, May and Zeb. Even Wilhelmina West. Emily had gone along with the charade, keeping her doubts to herself. She'd thought they needed to believe that Leo could bring the rain more than they needed the truth, but she now realised that the truth was all that mattered.

'You bring nothing but false promises,' she said. 'Tricks and lies, disguised as hope.'

For a moment, he didn't speak. He stared at the floor, his hands clasped tightly together, as if in prayer. 'I only wish to remain a friend to Dorothy,' he said eventually, his voice small and quiet. 'Even if I cannot be her father.'

Emily refused to pity him. This show of remorse was, no doubt, just another act. 'Dorothy has plenty of friends, Mr Stregone. What she needs is a family. Stability, and security, and a loving home. Henry and I will give her that.'

Henry was twice the man, twice the father, Leonardo Stregone could ever be. Henry would love Dorothy as if she was his own child. They would both love her with every ounce of their being. Dorothy was where she belonged. Emily understood this now; embraced it, without doubt.

She drew strength from her certainty as she released her grip on the back of the chair and stood up straight. 'When will you leave?' she asked, eager to bring things to a conclusion. 'I believe the truck is fixed.'

Leonardo let out a long breath, resigned to the inevitable conclusion. 'I will leave tonight,' he said, picking up his hat. 'While everyone sleeps.'

Emily crossed her arms and huffed out a derisory breath. 'A magic man after all. The classic disappearing act.'

As Leonardo stood up, a small vial dropped to the floor and rolled toward Emily.

She stooped to pick it up and turned it over to read the label. *Glycerine. Fake Tears.* Of course.

Leonardo walked to the door, where he turned to face Emily, a wry smile at his lips.

'The show is over, Mrs Gale. The curtain has fallen.' He bent into a low bow, arms spread wide before standing upright again. 'I did love your sister, and I will keep her and Dorothy in my heart. But, as P.T. Barnum once said, "I am a showman by profession . . . and all the gilding shall make nothing else of me."'

*

That night, Emily watched the stars and the moon, turning her gaze away from the earth that had let her down. So often, her eyes had turned to the prairie skies, watching for signs of rain or snow, dusters and thunderheads and tornadoes. It was the sky that held all their fates now; where their greatest hopes lay, and where the greatest dangers lurked. One devastating dust storm or tornado was all it would take for them to be erased from the prairie, wipe them away as easily as their machines had stripped away the ancient grass. Yet one prolonged spell of rain could turn their fortunes the other way.

In the end, it would be the unstoppable power of nature – not a man with a rainmaking machine – that would have the final say.

43

True to his word, Mr Stregone had disappeared by the next morning. Emily felt that she could breathe properly again for the first time in a week.

Nobody was sorry to see him go. They had all accepted that the experiment had not only failed, but had never been likely to succeed.

Dorothy was especially disappointed. 'My silver shoes didn't work, Auntie Em. My wishes for rain didn't come true. Maybe they're broken, and now none of my wishes will come true.'

Emily encouraged her not to lose heart, but she felt the lingering sense of disappointment herself.

The air was unusually crisp and clear that day. No dust, no wind, not a cloud to be seen. It was a rare calm day, and Emily didn't trust it. Prairie folk knew well that the calm always came before a storm, that when the air stilled and the bedsheets hung as lifeless as a hanged man on the line, that was the time to prepare.

A sense of sorry resignation clung to her as she looked out at the drab, lifeless prairie. It was no longer the dream – the home –

it had once been. They'd watched countless others pack up and head west, and even as it broke her heart to admit it, she knew it was the right thing for them to do, too. There were no medals given out to those who stubbornly refused to leave, no accolades awarded for foolish determination. Besides, the decision to stay or leave was no longer about her and Henry. It was about Dorothy: what was best for her. Where was safest for her. Kansas, with its cruel choking dust, was no place to raise a child. It was no place for any sensible person to call home.

*

By mid-afternoon, the air was still curiously calm. The house, even more so. Taking advantage of the clear day, Adelaide had taken the motorcar into Liberal to fetch supplies for her next trip. She was planning to head east, where she could better prepare for her transatlantic flight.

Dorothy was still terribly upset about Miss West's threats to send Toto away and wouldn't let the dog out of her sight. The two of them had gone off to the creek, as they had every day recently, to check the rain catcher. Emily knew the child would only come back disappointed and disillusioned again and had encouraged her to stay and help with the chores instead, but Dorothy had her mind set.

'Mr Stregone said I should check it every day, just in case.'

Emily swept her frustration into the unrelenting dust, corralling it into restless piles, each one an ever-shifting hourglass to measure the months without rain. She no longer knew where the parched earth stopped and she began.

Suddenly the broom stilled in her hands. The dust piles at her feet had started to blow, swirling and shifting. A prickle of static electricity stirred the sun-bleached hairs on her arms – a sure sign of a duster approaching.

Dread settled in her stomach as she looked to the west.

A huge black cloud towered hundreds of feet above the prairie, as wide as it was tall. It had arrived without warning, devouring the gentle day in furious gulps as it rolled toward them with the ominous rumble of a hundred steam locomotives.

The wind picked up, blowing faster and stronger by the second until Emily felt herself rocked by it. She grasped the broom handle to steady herself.

'Em! Emily! Get inside!'

Henry's cries from the direction of the barn whipped around the eaves of the house as her neat piles of dust became whirling cyclones at her feet. She drew in a sharp, shocked breath as the first fine particles of grit peppered her skin like pinpricks.

The broom fell to the ground with a clatter. The sun guttered like a candle flame, the light fading fast as Emily rushed to meet Henry, unable to tear her eyes away from the terrifying mountain of earth rolling towards them as the wind blew harder still, gathering the strength of a tornado.

Fear flared in her chest.

'Henry! My God, it's a monster!'

'Go back to the house, Em! You know what to do.' Henry's words were snatched in gasping breaths and smothered by the screeching wind. 'I'll see to the animals.'

As he spoke, a bird dropped like a stone beside them. Emily recalled the *piseogs* her mammy used to speak of, old Irish folklore about dead birds and bad luck.

'Hurry!' Henry urged. 'And find Dorothy.'

His eyes carried a wildness Emily hadn't seen before. Dorothy and Toto hadn't returned from their trip to the creek.

She hurried back to the house, shouting for the child. 'Dorothy! Dorothy!'

Fear pressed down on her as the sky boiled above, the dense black cloud expanding as it gorged on the parched land. Emily could taste the dust now, gritty against her teeth. She imagined it spreading inside her, filling her lungs until it choked her. Panic rose in her chest as she turned in every direction, eyes narrowed against the unrelenting dust and the snarling wind as she searched, desperately, for any sign of the child.

'Dorothy! Dorothy, come home!'

Inside the house, she worked quickly to seal the windows and doors, pushing wet rags into every possible crack and crevice to stop the dust from coming inside. It was a futile exercise. Even as she worked, dust covered the sink and smothered the table. She called for the child, again and again, her cries increasingly urgent, but still Dorothy didn't answer, still she didn't come running through the fields with Toto at her heels.

Please, Dorothy! Please come home!

Her mind raced. For a moment, she was back in the fortune-teller's tent. *'I see a dark cloud approaching . . . such darkness . . . a black, swirling wind . . .'*

A terrible blackness.

Within minutes, the temperature had plummeted. The sky was now pitch-black, swollen and heavy with the earth it had inhaled. The storm was almost upon them.

'Is she here?' Henry's face was black with dirt, his eyes narrowed against the painful grit as he stumbled inside.

'No! She must still be down at the creek.' Emily ran to the child's bed. It made no sense to expect to find her there, but she had to do something.

Henry glanced at the door, then back at Emily as the house began to rattle. 'I'm going to look for her.'

'Henry, no!' Emily was desperate – terrified for the child, terrified of losing Henry. 'It's too dangerous.' She ran to the door again, disoriented by the deafening noise, the dirt, the choking dust. She couldn't breathe, couldn't see. 'Dorothy! Dorothy!' Her strangled cries were snatched away by the wind.

Henry grabbed her arm. 'It's too late, Em. We have to go down.' He opened the hatch to the cyclone cellar and almost pushed her inside. 'Now, Em! Hurry!'

Frantic with fear, Emily climbed down the ladder into the small space, slipping and stumbling in the dark. Henry was right behind her. They put wet cloths to their faces and clung to each other as the mournful rumbling intensified and the house shook violently. Above them, glass shattered. Earth rained down, slamming against the house as the dust blew hard, sifting down onto them in endless waves until Emily was certain they would be buried alive. And all the while the terrible noise continued: scraping and banging, creaking and roaring. On and on and on.

And Dorothy was still out there.

Again and again, Emily desperately cried out for her, until her voice was hoarse and she couldn't bear it any longer.

She turned to go back up the ladder. 'We can't leave her, Henry! She'll be killed out there.'

In the dark, Henry grabbed her hand. 'It's madness to try and look for her in this, Em. I'll go out when it's over. She'll have found somewhere to shelter. She knows what to do.'

But this dust storm felt different. Nobody was prepared for anything this big.

Emily was suffocated by fear. They had left it too late, waited too long to leave Kansas, and now the child was in grave danger.

'This is all his fault,' she said. 'He should never have come here!'

'Who?'

'Leonardo. Dorothy wouldn't have gone to the creek if it wasn't for his silly rain catcher. He should have stayed away.'

Henry disagreed. 'It's my fault for bringing him here in the first place.'

Emily gripped his hand tight. She couldn't bear for him to take the blame when she knew the truth. 'It isn't your fault, Henry. None of this is your fault.'

As the wind roared and the dirt blew and great drifts of dust smothered everything and everyone in its path, the awful words Emily had once spoken in temper swirled around her. *'I wish she'd never come here, Henry. We've had nothing but bad luck and cross words since. I wish things could go back to how they were before Dorothy Gale ever set foot in Kansas!'* She would do anything to take those words back now, undo such wicked thoughts, but some things, once shared, became a storm of their own.

Then, the last scraps of light were extinguished.

Pitch-black.

It was worse than any twister they'd known, worse than any hailstorm, worse than all the other dust storms combined.

This was a monster, the most appalling, terrifying thing Emily had ever experienced.

She clung to Henry in the dark. There was nothing they could do but wait.

*

For too long, the dust heaved and the wind rampaged above.

And then, silence.

It was over.

Coughing violently, Emily clambered out of the cellar. A thick layer of dirt and dust had settled over everything inside. She kicked open the front door, pushing against a drift of dirt that had settled against it. The devastation that greeted her took her breath away. It was barely recognisable from the scene she'd looked out on not thirty minutes earlier.

Huge mounds of dirt and dust lay everywhere. The fence posts that lined their farm track only stuck out a few inches above the earth. Some drifts were as tall as a child: as tall as Dorothy.

Emily sank to her knees and retched into the dirt as fear and filth purged from her in pulsing waves and the child's name fell from her lips in a strangled whisper.

'Oh, Dorothy! My dear, darling Dorothy, I'm so sorry.'

Henry appeared beside her. 'I'm going to look for her.'

'How, Henry? How can you get further than the end of the lane? Look at it. You'll have to dig your way through.'

'Then that's what I'll do. Stay here in case she comes back.' He grabbed Emily's hands and looked into her eyes. 'I'll bring her home, Em. I promise I'll bring her home.'

He waded through the dust toward the barn, dug out his shovel with his bare hands and set off toward the creek.

*

It was several agonising hours until he returned.

Emily hadn't moved.

She stood up when she saw him stumbling through the dirt, almost unrecognisable he was so covered in dust, and there, lifeless in his arms, was Dorothy, and Toto peering out of a knapsack at Henry's side.

'I found her,' he said as he collapsed at the porch. 'She needs to go straight to the hospital.'

In that moment Emily cared nothing for failed crops, or drought, or any hardship they'd ever endured. She would keep it all, every awful part of it, if only Dorothy could be safe.

Dorothy was all that mattered now.

44

Henry had found her sheltering in an old dugout from an abandoned claim, drawn to her by the sound of Toto's frantic barks. It was a miracle.

But although Dorothy had survived the duster, it had filled her lungs with the filthy earth and left her desperately sick.

Emily's worst fears had come true.

She had waited too long.

It was unbearable to see the child in the hospital bed, her body weak, her face flushed hot with a fever. The doors and windows were covered with wet blankets to keep out the worst of the dust that still blew, but too much had already crept into Dorothy's lungs over the dry months. The wards were full of children suffering from dust pneumonia, struggling to draw breath. The room smelled of the kerosene and turpentine salve that had been applied to Dorothy's chest to try and ease her breathing.

Emily sat at her bedside, utterly distraught.

The poor child coughed so hard Emily was sure she would choke. She patiently wiped the filthy black dirt from her mouth and washed away the ruby flecks of blood that settled on her skin.

Days and nights passed, and still the child lay desperately ill, consumed with a fever. Emily refused to leave her side. She remembered the promise she'd made, and she wasn't going to break it.

'Come home, Em. Get some rest,' Henry urged.

Home.

Emily had wrestled with the sentiment all these months, yet as she looked at Dorothy now, she understood that she'd been holding onto the wrong meaning of the word. Home wasn't their little prairie house, or Liberal, or Kansas for that matter. Home was wherever she wanted to be the most – and right now, that was here, in the hospital, beside her dear Dorothy.

From her bedside vigil, she read to Dorothy from her prairie journal, travelling back through the early months and years when there wasn't any dust at all and the prairie had danced in all the colours of the rainbow. She told her the stories of old Ireland, of the Little People and magical lands. She told her all about Annie, her mother, and her Aunt Nell, and sang the songs of their childhood.

Adelaide kept Emily company. In the aftermath of the dust storm, she'd dug her way through the drifts of dust to make her way back to the farm in the motorcar, where she'd found Henry carrying the sick child. Thanks to Adelaide, they'd got Dorothy to the hospital hours before Henry could ever have managed on foot, saving vital hours that could make all the difference.

'What will you do now, Emily?' Adelaide asked. 'Will you stick it out in Kansas or leave?'

Emily had asked the same question a thousand times. She'd shied away from it, tried to ignore it, but she'd finally made a quiet peace with the unavoidable truth: They could no longer stay. And so, they must leave.

'I wish I was free-spirited, like you, Adelaide. Not tethered to one place.'

'Be careful what you wish for. There's worry and fear in freedom, too. The restless quest for happiness isn't always an enjoyable road to follow. Just around the next corner, a bit further, tomorrow, next year . . . Always the lure of something else, something better, something more. What if? Where next? It's a trap all of its own. And, for what it's worth, I envy what you have.'

Emily thought of the barren, dust-smothered patch of prairie they called home. 'Well, there's not much to envy.'

'I don't mean material things. I mean, what you have with Henry and Dorothy. A family. Love.' She paused for a moment. 'After Cooper died, I didn't want to be responsible for anyone else. I was afraid to let anyone in, afraid to let anyone trust me.'

'Cooper is your brother?'

Adelaide nodded. 'Named after Cooper Creek in Australia. He was such a great kid. God damn, I miss him.'

'I'm so sorry. You never told me what happened.'

'Mechanical failure on the plane. They said it could have happened any time during the performance, but it was me who insisted we push for one more trick. I wanted to prove something to all the men who think women don't make decent pilots. Turns out all I proved was that I'm a reckless fool.' She took a moment. 'I always go too far, Emily. Never know when to stop or pull back. It's my fault he's not here. My fault we crashed.'

Emily offered her condolences. There wasn't much else she could say. She recognised the ache of loss, the guilt and regret that followed in grief's silent wake.

Adelaide drew in a long breath. 'Truth is, I lost part of myself the day I lost him. That's why I fly solo. Take my own risks. Enjoy my own successes and only have myself to blame for my failures. I keep flying, keep moving on, too afraid of what might happen if I stay still for too long.'

'You once told me fear is a temporary thing,' Emily said. '"*Face it, and it doesn't exist anymore. Turn away from it and it'll haunt you forever.*"'

'I said that? Huh. Maybe I should listen to my own advice.'

Emily tore her eyes from Dorothy and looked at Adelaide. 'Maybe you should. I've thought about your words often. Maybe it's time for you to team up with someone again – in the cockpit, and in life.'

'Marriage, you mean? Scares the heck out of me.'

'Scares the heck out of me, too.'

Adelaide smiled. 'You know, seeing you and Henry has made me think about things differently. I always thought marriage had to be perfect, but it seems to me you're still figuring it out. But you do it together, as a team. I miss that – the partnership, the fun. Someone to share the highs and lows with along the way.'

Emily reached for Adelaide's hand. 'Then maybe it's time for us both to face the thing we fear the most. Confront the monster in our fairytale.'

During her visits, Adelaide also brought news of the others in town. Everyone had suffered terribly, but Emily was relieved to hear they'd all survived. All, except Wilhelmina West's sister.

'The barn she was sheltering in collapsed under the weight of the dirt,' Adelaide explained. 'It was Wilhelmina who found her.'

Emily was genuinely sorry to hear it. 'That's terrible. The poor woman.'

'She's distraught. And furious. Taking it out on the weather bureau for not issuing a warning. It's like a madness has taken over her.'

Emily couldn't blame her. Nobody had ever seen a duster like it. The dirt had blown as far as the White House, and had turned day to night as far away as Chicago and New York. Maybe, finally, somebody would take the farmers' concerns seriously and do something to help them.

'Folk are saying it was the rainmaker's explosions that disturbed more earth and caused the black blizzard,' Adelaide continued. 'Do you think it might be true?'

Emily shrugged. 'I guess we'll never know. Just like nobody can ever be sure if the rain would come anyway, with or without the rainmakers' gadgets. That's the con, isn't it? Dealer always wins.'

'Rainmaking! Can't believe I ever fell for it.'

'We all fell for it, Adelaide. Men like Leonardo Stregone can be very convincing.'

In the chaos of the duster and the aftermath of Dorothy's sickness, Emily had thought about Leonardo often. She'd blamed him for Dorothy being at the creek, blamed him for hurting Annie, blamed him for trying to steal from them and take advantage of them. It was easier to blame someone else, but as the dust settled, she accepted that she only had herself to blame for the danger she'd exposed Dorothy to.

'Did Leo say anything to you before he left?' she asked.

Adelaide shrugged. 'Not much. Just that it was time to move on.'

'Did he say where he was going?'

'Said he didn't know. That he would follow the road. And good riddance to him, I say. Turns out the man who claimed to have all the power was the weakest of us all.'

*

Through the long, anxious nights at Dorothy's bedside, Emily thought about the give and take of life. She'd always believed that one thing was gained at the sacrifice of another. The prospect of a new life in America came with the agonising decision to leave family and friends in Ireland. The price of freedom to farm your own land was a life full of uncertainty. What would be taken in exchange for Dorothy's survival? She would give it all away – every last thing, relinquish her dreams for this little girl's precious life.

In her fevered delirium, Dorothy spoke of her mother, of Toto, of a man made of tin and another made of straw, and over and over she whispered a refrain. *No place like home. No place like home.*

Emily wiped the child's brow and told her to rest. 'Come back to us, Dorothy, dear. Wherever you are, please come back to us. Please come home.'

Part Five

Kansas, 1932

"'My darling child!' she cried, folding the little girl in her arms and covering her face with kisses; 'where in the world did you come from?'"
– L. Frank Baum, *The Wonderful Wizard of Oz*

Extract from Wonderful – A Life on the Prairie by Emily Gale

The men insisted on sowing more wheat in the hope that the rain would come and they would have a harvest again next year. Everyone believed things had to improve soon. Like gamblers at the poker table, they went all in. One last throw of the dice, man versus nature, winner takes all. There would be many more anxious months and years before they would know if the gamble had paid off.

We prayed that the dusters would settle, that we would be spared from the relentless onslaught. Surely there was no more dust left to blow, no acre of land left that hadn't already been scooped up and thrown back down again?

What little scraps of faith we had left were tested to the limit. It was too long since the rivers and creeks had been full and the crops had grown abundantly. Those years of good weather and bumper yields were a fading memory. Future generations would never believe we'd harvested so much grain that we left *it to rot in the sun and burned cobs of corn on the fire in the winter.*

Fact became legend as folk gave up and sold up and headed west, taking their dreams and their stories with them. Only the most resilient or foolhardy remained, determined to stick it out, certain that next year their fortunes would change.

Next year, they said.
Next year things would be better.
On and on.
Year after year.

45

At last, the fever broke and Dorothy returned.

'Auntie Em! Auntie Em? Where am I?'

Emily stirred. For a moment she didn't know if she was awake or dreaming as she raised her head from the end of the bed.

'Dorothy! You're awake!' She rushed to her, stroking her face and smoothing the hair from her forehead. 'Oh, Dorothy, dear, we've been so worried. You're in the hospital.'

'Am I hurt?'

'You've been very sick. After the dust storm – do you remember? We were so afraid. How do you feel?'

Dorothy rubbed her head. 'A little strange. I had such a curious dream, and you were all there. You, and Uncle Henry, and Toto and—'

Emily shushed and soothed her. 'That's right, dear. We were all there. Keeping you safe. But you need to rest now, get your strength up.'

'Where's Toto?' Dorothy tried to sit up. 'Oh, Auntie Em. Did Miss West take him away?'

'Toto is fine, dear. He's with Uncle Henry. Toto stayed with you at the creek until Uncle Henry found you both.'

At this, Dorothy relaxed a little. 'Is Miss Adelaide still here? She was in my dream too, except, she wasn't Miss Adelaide, she was a good witch. And Lion was there, and my tin man, and one of the scarecrows from the fields. And Mommy's silver shoes really were magical . . .'

Emily smiled and brushed a curl from Dorothy's cheek, so pleased to hear her tell her little stories again. 'Gosh! What an adventure you had! And, yes, dear. Adelaide is still here. She will be so happy to see you!'

'And Mr Stregone?'

Emily shook her head. 'He had to leave. Remember?'

Dorothy thought for a moment. 'My, people come and go so fast around here.' A frown formed across her brow as she looked at Emily. 'I'm not sure he was a magic man at all, Auntie Em.'

'Why do you say that?'

'I saw him hiding under the stage that day when Pieter asked him to disappear. He didn't really disappear at all, did he?'

Emily put her arm around Dorothy's shoulder. 'You know, I think the idea of magic is sometimes more important than the magic itself.' She reached into her purse. 'He left something for you. Adelaide found it in the cockpit of the Jenny after the dust storm.'

Dorothy took the package of brown paper and untied the string. Inside was a carnival token, and a note.

'What does it say?' Emily asked, intrigued and a little anxious to know what he'd written.

Dorothy read the words. '*Magic is everywhere. Coraggio, Dorothy. Courage, always.*' The coin was imprinted with the words *Good Luck Will Accompany the Bearer*. 'What do you think it means?' Dorothy asked as she studied the coin.

'I think it means exactly what it says. That it's a lucky coin,' Emily said.

'Then I'll keep it very safe.' Dorothy leaned back against her pillow, suddenly tired again.

'You rest now,' Emily said as she tucked the blankets around her. 'We'll go home as soon as you're feeling stronger.'

'In my dream, I wasn't in Kansas anymore,' she said. 'But all the time I was away, I was trying to find my way back home.'

'To Kansas?'

Dorothy looked at Emily. 'Yes. All I wanted was to get back to you and Uncle Henry, so we would all be together again. But I don't think it matters where that is.'

46

A week passed before Dorothy was well enough to return to the little prairie house she had briefly called home. Adelaide sat with Emily that evening as they watched the sun slip below the horizon, the ambered light turning everything to gold.

'It was the prettiest place on earth when the wheat was ripe and swaying like a great golden ocean,' Emily said. 'We hoped for so much when we first came here. Now it's like we were never here at all.'

Adelaide turned to her. 'But you tried, Emily. And for a while, you succeeded. I admire you for that. Besides, this place doesn't define you and Henry. You'll build a new life together, someplace else. Succeed again.'

For so long, Emily *had* felt defined by what they'd planned to build here, as if this was the only place they could ever be happy.

'I hope you're right, Adelaide.'

'I *know* I'm right.'

They watched the broad strokes of light that fanned out from the sun, an invitation, a golden path urging them on.

'I reckon it's time for me to move on,' Adelaide said. 'I'll start growing roots if my feet stay on the ground much longer.'

'Where will you go?'

'I'll catch up with Ringling's circus troupe and perform with them for a while. Then make my solo attempt across the ocean. See if I can't earn myself a bit of Earhart's fame and fortune. And I've been thinking about teaming up with someone after all. Two women breaking men's records. Now that would give them something to fill their column inches!'

Emily smiled. 'I like the sound of that. When will you leave?'

'First light.' Adelaide turned to Emily. 'You fancy coming along for the ride? Watson and Gale has a nice ring to it!'

Emily let out a small sigh. 'I'll be up there with you in spirit. And Dorothy will miss you terribly. You've been like a fairy godmother to her. I think she saw something of her mother in you.'

'I'll miss the kid, too. I've promised I'll write. Send a postcard from wherever the wind blows me.' Adelaide stood up and raised her glass. 'To you, Emily. I'm glad to have travelled some of my road with you good people, and I'm glad to have shared one last Kansas sunset with you. A reminder that there is beauty in endings, as well as beginnings.'

Emily smiled and knocked her glass against Adelaide's. 'Amen to that.'

*

She heard the plane at first light.

She crept to the door and watched as Adelaide steered the Jenny out to the landing strip in the field, pushed the throttle and accelerated across the dusty ground before lifting the nose and sending the plane airborne. Emily placed her hands to her chest and mouthed a silent 'thank you' as she watched the plane turn to the east.

She sat alone for a while then, listening to the sounds of the prairie. It was strange to feel such stillness after everything, and everyone.

She made grits and fed the animals, taking a moment to rest her head against the warm muzzle of the old mare. She drew water from the pump and took eggs from the hens, working her way around her familiar routines, saying a goodbye of her own.

When Dorothy woke that morning, she found a notebook on the foot of her bed. Inside was a short message.

To my dear Dorothy,
I hope you have the most wonderful adventures among these pages. Keep telling your stories. People come and go in life, but stories last forever.

Thank you for being part of my adventure. I will see you again, when the wind blows me in the right direction. Think of me when you look up at the sky and I'll be thinking of you. Maybe one day, you'll see me flying right back.

Your dear friend,
Adelaide Watson

There was a note for Emily too, beside Annie's hourglass.

To dear Emily,
You can know some people your whole life and never really know them at all. I've known you for a fleeting moment, and it's like you were always there.

Thank you for reminding me that it's OK to stop and look around every once in a while. I hope, in return, you will remember to let go, and leap.

Here's to flying high, and to those who pick us up when we fall.

Your friend, always,
Adelaide

47

A prickle of anticipation tiptoed around the small home, as if it knew they were leaving.

Emily took a moment alone on their final day, glad to have the prairie to herself one last time before anyone else woke. She prepared herself for their departure, packed away any lingering regrets and sorrow.

When Henry joined her, they shared the silence together for a while.

'And so, we have reached the end of the road,' he said eventually. 'We must leave.'

Emily reached for his hand. 'The end of one road, yes. But the start of another.'

'Would you still choose it?' he asked. 'This life? These hard years? Would you have come with me, agreed to marry me if you'd known what we would face?'

For the briefest moment, she paused, checking her response before she turned to him with absolute certainty.

'In a heartbeat. I would take it all on again tomorrow to be here with you, right now. We wouldn't have had the wonderful if we'd never had the wicked. It's all part of the same story, Henry. All connected.'

Now that they had said their goodbyes to the few friends who remained, the final farewell was the hardest.

Behind the barn, Henry reached for Emily's hand as he recited the Lord's Prayer and they each scooped up a handful of dirt and added it to the little mound in front of them. It was there, in their hands, that they carried the story of their successes and struggles. The powder-fine dirt was so deeply burrowed into the cracks and lines on their weathered skin that no amount of scrubbing could shift it. Like their grief, the prairie was part of them now. Part of them that would always be rooted here.

'I once asked my mother how she'd felt to leave Ireland with baby Joseph buried there,' Emily said. 'I asked her how she could bear it.'

Henry looked at her. 'What did she say?'

'She said there are some things you can't take with you on life's journey. No matter how much they mean, or how precious they are, or how painful the parting.' She reached for Henry's hand and placed it against his chest. 'And she said that she was never a day without him, that a heart is the very best home of all.'

He offered a tired smile. 'You'd have been a wonderful mother.'

'And you, a wonderful father. And we will be the best aunt and uncle we can be, for Dorothy.'

For now, there was no room for looking back, only forward. Whatever lay ahead, they would face it together.

'Oh, I forgot to tell you.' Henry pulled a packet of dollar bills from his pocket. 'Seems that Mr Stregone has a decent bone in his body after all. He left this, the extra bit of money we raised for his second round of aerial bombing. He left a note to say Dorothy might like to save it for a rainy day. He left this for her, too.' He pulled a crumpled envelope from his shirt pocket, Dorothy's name scribbled on the front. 'He said you would know when it was the right time to give it to her.'

Emily considered it for a moment before she pressed it back into Henry's hands. 'Keep it somewhere safe,' she said. 'Remind me about it every now and then.'

*

Dorothy packed the few possessions she'd brought from Chicago, and the other things she'd collected during her short time in Kansas. Her toy lion, her tin man, the Brigid doll made of straw, the notebook from Adelaide, the carnival coin from Leonardo, Annie's silver shoes and emerald ring and circus memorabilia, and of course, Toto, along with his tomato crate bed and the blanket Emily had made for him. But she didn't pack the piece of Connemara marble Emily had given her when they'd left Chicago.

Emily noticed it on the table. 'Don't forget the Irish Green, Dorothy. For good luck.'

'Can we leave it here? If we bury it in the ground, it might help to turn the prairie green again. Emerald, like Ireland.'

Dorothy believed in such goodness and wonder. If that little piece of Ireland carried any trace of her kind heart, Emily was hopeful that colour would return to this lifeless land.

As they dug a hole in the hard ground to bury it, Emily spotted a single grain of wheat. She picked it up and put it in Dorothy's pocket.

'For luck, *a grá*,' she said with a smile.

'Is California nice?' Dorothy asked as they walked back to the house. 'And Aunt Nell? Will I like her?'

'I don't know about California, dear. I've never been, so I guess we'll find out, together. As for your Aunt Nell, she's one of the kindest, cleverest people I've ever known. You'll love her, that's for sure.'

As Emily packed up the last of her things, she took the bundle of letters from the old shoebox. One for each of Dorothy's eight birthdays so far. But it was the sixteenth birthday letter that still held a strange power as Emily tucked it into her purse. Whatever secrets it held would be revealed in time. And Emily would make sure Dorothy was ready to hear them.

That evening, as she wished Dorothy goodnight for the last time in their Kansas home, Dorothy said there was something she wanted to ask. It was a habit of hers to wait until bedtime to ask some of life's most puzzling questions, a ruse to stay awake. Emily and Henry had become wise to it.

Emily sat on the edge of the bed. 'Well, what is it tonight?'

'It isn't something to ask, really, more something I wanted to say.'

'Goodness, child, spit it out! It'll be Christmas soon!'

'I wanted to say that you can call me Dot sometimes. If you like.'

Emily's hands stilled as she pulled up the covers. 'Dot . . . That's the name your mommy used to call you.'

Dorothy nodded, her inquisitive green eyes searching Emily's.

Emily fought back her emotions. 'I would like that, Dorothy, dear. I would like that very much.' She pulled the bedcovers taut and kissed Dorothy's forehead, astonished by the love she felt for her, as wild and strong as any storm that had ever rushed over the prairie.

As Emily brushed her hair that night, letting it hang loose around her shoulders, she looked at her reflection in the hand mirror and saw the face of a woman she knew. The face of a woman who had struggled and survived.

The face of a daughter. A sister. A wife.

The face of a mother.

*

The winds were picking up, blowing hot from the south as Kansas slipped away behind them.

Emily held her father's fiddle on her lap as she looked to the west and heard her mother's voice, urging her on.

'*Dá fhada an lá tagann an tráthnóna. No matter how long the day, the evening comes. Courage, Emily. Courage, a grá.*'

She held her head high and pushed back her shoulders as she remembered a slice of apple, held up to the light. '*The same way the apple remembers the blossom it grew from, and the way the peel remembers the shape of the fruit it was attached to, you'll always remember this little cottage in Connemara on the edge of Ireland . . .*'

She remembered. She remembered it all.

Home was in the tracks behind her, and in the unknown roads ahead. It was a familiar memory, and the prickle of uncertainty at the back of her neck.

She looked back, just once, as she recalled Annie's words. '*But is it enough, Em? Really? Is it everything you wanted it to be?*'

It had been more than enough. For a while, it had been her world.

Extract from *Wonderful – A Life on the Prairie* by Emily Gale

Hugson Ranch, California, 1937

*I*n the worst of times, we became the best of ourselves.

I had clung to the dream of Kansas for so long that I was afraid to let go. It is only now, looking back, that I understand that our failures and struggles were all part of that dream. It was all connected: the ups and downs, the good and the bad. The prairie tested us in every way possible and changed us in ways I could never have believed, but it filled our lives with more hope and love than I could ever have imagined.

Life before Dorothy was an adventure. Life after, was a whirlwind. And what joy she blew into our hearts. I still struggle to comprehend the depth of my love for this wild, restless girl with the wind in her heart. She has taught me far more than I could ever hope to teach her.

I watch her as I write these words. She is busy and determined, as always, Toto at her heels as she tends to the animals, her wicker basket on her arm as she heads off to where the wildflowers grow beyond the cotton fields. She likes to pick specimens to add to the flower press, a gift for the winter months, for her dear Auntie Nell. They have become quite inseparable, the two of them. Peas from the same pod. There is so much of Annie in Dorothy too, and more than a little of her father's sense of magic and performance. What tales she conjures in the adventures she imagines! One day, she will know the truth about Leonardo Stregone. What happens next will be her story to write.

I finish her thirteenth-birthday letter, using the words with which I have closed each letter I have written to her: 'Be brave, Dorothy. Trust your mind, listen to your heart, and always be willing to follow the fork in the road. Who knows what wonderful things are waiting for you.' *I find it easier, each year, to allow my true feelings to embroider themselves among my words.*

Of course, we all miss Kansas – the life we built there, the friends we made. The rain has still not returned and the dusters still smother and suffocate. We hear that those who stayed behind are suffering beyond all comprehension. My heart breaks for them, and for the land I loved.

The journal I wrote in through my Kansas years has become my touchstone to that time and place. I look back through it often, to the inscription at the front, especially. To my dear Emily, Mammy used to say there is no place like your own home. I hope you will always be happy in yours. Annie x

But what is home? I have asked the question many times, searching for an answer in the walls that surround me. I have called many places home, each of them different. One is the home of my heart. One filled my mind with hope and possibility. One put fear in my path. Who are you, Emily Gale? *it asked.* Do you have the courage – the fortitude – to go on?

To answer that question, I had to let go, start again, with nothing but hope in my heart and a single grain of wheat in my pocket. That was when I began to understand who I really was. Henry once asked me if I would still have gone with him to Kansas if I'd known what was waiting for us there. I answered without hesitation.

Home, I now know, isn't a place at all. Mountains or ocean, city or prairie – that's just landscape, the view from the window when you wake. The most desolate place imaginable can feel safer than the prettiest place on earth, as long as those you love are with you.

Finally, I found the answer.

My home is wherever Dorothy is. And Henry. And Toto.

Home is, quite simply, wherever there is love.

Epilogue

Many years later...

Seven years passed before the rain returned to Kansas and the prairie bloomed, once again, in all the colours of the rainbow. It would be many more years before I returned to finally see for myself the golden stalks of wheat dancing in the gentle morning breeze, to hear the song of the meadowlark and watch an ocean of wildflowers stretch as far as the horizon. But that's another story, for another time.

This is Auntie Em's story. Hers and my dear mother's. It is also the story of all the women and men who endured those hard years of dust and drought, and who somehow found a reason to hope, to wonder, to dream once again. Auntie Em always believed in the magic of this place. Most of all, she believed in me.

She taught me a sense of wonder, to see not just the apple but the beauty of the blossom inside. She taught me to stop for a moment and look at the sunset, to marvel in its splendour. She taught me to see rain and hail and snowstorms and sun, not just as the day's weather but as part of a greater cycle of connected things: strings on a fiddle, notes that only make sense when played together. But perhaps the most important thing she taught me is that home can be anywhere, as long as you are with those you love, and who love you in return.

She gave me the package of letters on my sixteenth birthday. A letter to mark the occasion of each of my birthdays. Some from my mother. Some from Auntie Em. There was such love stitched among the words.

Plenty of secrets, too.

It was difficult to read my mother's words in the final letter, to feel her anguish in telling me that the man I had known as her friend was, in fact, my father. She wrote of him with such affection. Leonardo Stregone. The man she had loved for most of her life, even though most of her life had been spent without him. *I hope you can forgive me for keeping him a secret. I hope that you will know him, in time.* I have often wondered what she would have thought of his rainmaking claims, and of the man he had become.

I eventually learned that Auntie Em had told Uncle Henry everything she knew about Mr Stregone not long after the big dust storm. After a while, he accepted her reasons for keeping the truth from him. He understood that it had come from a place of love, not deceit; that she had wanted to protect him and couldn't bear to take away the joy and hope that my arrival and our relationship had given him. He wished she'd shared her secret with him all the same. He hated to think of her worrying on her own. 'We are a team,' he said. 'Always.' There were other secrets she told him in the aftermath of the storm, too. They hid nothing from each other ever since.

Despite the passing years, dear Uncle Henry still pulls coins from behind my ear. And the silver shoes finally fit me. When I wear them, I think of my mother. I feel her at my shoulder, gently guiding me in the pursuit of my wishes. Sometimes I flip my carnival coin and think of my father. He writes occasionally, just a line or two, but it is enough. He didn't succeed in bringing the rain to Kansas with his marvellous machines, but I remember the hope and wonder he brought for a few precious days as Adelaide flew the Jenny and he sent his balloons into the sky. Not a magician after all, but the possibility was magic enough.

Auntie Nell finally encouraged Auntie Em to turn her prairie journal into a book about those hard years. She says nobody will ever read it, that nobody will be interested in hearing the story of an ordinary farmer's wife, but I think she will be surprised. She is the beating heart of so many lives, a great and powerful woman who taught me that an inquisitive mind, a kind heart, and a brave soul can take you anywhere. In any event, she was glad to have written it all down. She wanted people to understand what happened here, to make sure that it will never happen again.

On quiet mornings, when the wheat dances in shades of green and gold, and I have the prairie to myself for a few precious moments, I think of her, thank her, whisper her name to the wind.

My dear Auntie Em. My sun. My moon. My north star.

My home.

Historical Note

Although this is a work of fiction, history formed the roots of this book, underpinning everything in the imagined lives and experiences of my characters.

The stock market crash of October 1929 was the start of the financial crisis we know as the Great Depression. Over the following weeks, months, and years, millions of Americans would lose their income, homes, and dignity as the ripple effect of the crash spread across the United States with devastating consequences.

For some, this was just the start of their troubles. At the same time, an environmental disaster was unfolding across the Great Plains, expanding from southern Texas, to New Mexico, through Oklahoma, Colorado, and Kansas and as far as Nebraska. For years, farmers had flocked to the fertile prairies, enticed by government incentives and persuasive railroad salesmen to work the land and bring life to the new prairie towns. Throughout the 1920s, farmers had enjoyed high crop yields and buoyant prices, which, in turn, brought more and more people to the area to try their luck for themselves. With the help of new machinery, which could do the labour-intensive manual work in a fraction of the time taken to work by hand, prairie farmers were producing more grain than the nation could use. Unsold grain was left to rot, and prices plummeted. It would soon cost a farmer more to plant and harvest his crops than he could earn by selling it. What the farmers didn't realise was that the ancient prairie grass they had ripped up with their efficient combustion machinery had held the topsoil in place. They had done irreparable damage to the fragile prairie ecosystem.

Drought added to the crisis as the dry exposed topsoil began to blow in dirty great clouds. These 'dusters' were misunderstood at first, the early dust storms explained as sandstorms. Over the following nine years of drought, the situation would worsen drastically. Some dust storms even blew the dirt as far as New York and Chicago, blocking out the sunlight for days at a time. By 1935, farmers experienced dozens of dust storms every month. Unable to grow anything, financially ruined, and suffering from bad health due to the persistent dust and dirt, countless men, women, children, and animals fell sick or succumbed to the dreaded dust pneumonia. Farms foreclosed and people packed up what few belongings they still had and headed west.

While we are all familiar with the twister in the Oz book and movie, it was these devastating dust storms that I wanted to explore as a destructive force. (Although Liberal, Kansas, was hit with a devastating tornado in 1933. When it was reported in the *Kansas City Star*, one girl claimed to have 'flown through the air' – a real-life Dorothy, perhaps?) The most devastating dust storm hit the region on 14 April 1935, a day that would become known as Black Sunday. It is estimated that as much as three million tons of topsoil blew from the Great Plains that day. We have images of the immense black dust cloud thanks to Arthur Rothstein, who had set out to document the ecological crisis. Robert E. Geiger and Harry G. Eisenhard, a reporter and a photographer from the

Associated Press, respectively, also recorded images of the Black Sunday storm. Geiger's report for the *Lubbock Evening Journal* the following day used the term 'dust bowl' for the first time. Dorothea Lange also photographed iconic images associated with the Depression and the Dust Bowl.

Through the Depression and Dust Bowl years, women looked for thrifty ways to clothe their families. Flour and feed sack dresses became a popular choice, with the cotton sacks sewn together to make dresses and other items of clothing. As the producers realised what was happening, they started to print patterns onto their sacks. As early as 1925, *Women's Wear* reported that the George P. Plant Milling Co., in St. Louis, had introduced 'flour packed in pink and blue gingham bags.' This became known as the Gingham Girl line. 'The printing on the bags is of such a nature that it can be washed out easily, leaving a large piece of gingham which may be used for an apron or dress.' The gingham pattern became a firm favourite across the prairies and was the perfect inspiration for me as the source of Dorothy's iconic gingham dress.

For inspiration for my wizard, I turned to the prairie rainmakers – travelling showmen like Charles M. Hatfield and Tex Thornton who operated across the Great Plains during the Dust Bowl. With their impressive equipment and an array of chemicals and explosives for aerial bombing, they claimed to be able to bring rain to desperate communities – for a price. Of course, this was a con, a confidence trick used on the most vulnerable and desperate.

Barnstormers and travelling carnivals were popular across America during the 1920s and into the 1930s. For many, the annual county and state fairs, and the magic and fun of the travelling carnivals and circus acts, offered a short spell of relief from the years of hardship and suffering. This fleeting glimpse into an almost otherworldly place of magic and mystery must have brought a much-needed lift to the men, women, and children of the region, and served as inspiration for my high-flying Adelaide

Watson, as well as providing the background story to the character of Leonardo Stregone.

If you would like to know more about this period of history, or the Dust Bowl, please see the recommended resources list that follows.

Historical research sources:
The Plow That Broke the Plains, 1936 documentary film produced by Pare Lorentz
The Worst Hard Time, Timothy Egan
Black Sunday, poems by Benjamin Myers
Prairie Fires: The American Dreams of Laura Ingalls Wilder, Caroline Fraser
The Grapes of Wrath, John Steinbeck
Dust Bowl Ballads, Woody Guthrie
Harpsong, Rilla Askew
Kansas State Historical Society

The Wizard of Oz resources:
L. Frank Baum, *The Wonderful Wizard of Oz*
Victor Fleming, *The Wizard of Oz*, MGM pictures
The Wizard of Oz, an essay by Salman Rushdie for BFI Film Classics
The Annotated Wizard of Oz: Centennial Edition, Michael Patrick Hearn
Finding Dorothy, Elizabeth Letts
Wicked, Gregory Maguire

Author Note

L. Frank Baum's *The Wonderful Wizard of Oz* is one of the most beloved tales of all time. The book, which Baum described as 'a modernised fairytale,' was first published in 1900 and has remained in print ever since, but most of us probably met these characters in Victor Fleming's classic 1939 MGM movie starring Judy Garland. That was how I first stepped into this wonderful world.

The Wizard of Oz was a Christmas Day TV staple throughout my childhood. I was terrified of the Wicked Witch of the West, and yet I couldn't look away and have never forgotten those characters and songs. I desperately wanted to audition for the part of Dorothy in our school musical in 1987, but as I was in an exam year, I wasn't allowed to participate (I would get my turn as Eliza Doolittle in the 1988 production of *My Fair Lady*, but that's another story, and which also inspired another of my books!)

Since those early Christmas Day memories of Oz, Baum's characters have been threaded throughout my life. I read Gregory Maguire's *Wicked* on the way back from my honeymoon in 2004, saw the *Wicked* show in London's West End in 2008 (and again in Dublin in 2024), and first had the idea to write a contemporary Oz spin-off novel back in 2009 when I was an unpublished writer. The thirty thousand or so words and rough pages of that idea have languished in a drawer ever since. I finally found the Oz story I wanted to tell when Auntie Em whispered in my ear many years later, in September 2022. But who exactly was she?

The rather stern woman we meet in the MGM adaptation fits a certain narrative, but there are clues in the original text that suggest a different character. Auntie Em is mentioned only a handful of times in Baum's book, firstly in the opening sentence, but it is the second time she is mentioned that sparked my interest. *When Aunt Em came to live there, she was a young pretty wife. The sun and wind had changed her, too. They had taken the sparkle from her eyes and left them a sober gray; they had taken the red from her lips, and they were gray also. She was thin and gaunt, and never smiled, now.* What had happened to change her so drastically? What had her life looked like before she married Henry, and when they first moved to Kansas? And, perhaps, the biggest question of all, never answered by the author or the movie: How did Dorothy come to live with Emily and Henry Gale? What a wonderful puzzle to explore, and what a joy it was to meet Emily Gale as if for the first time: to discover who she was, who she might have been, and who she became. And although there is no specified era in which the book and movie are based, it made sense to me to set Emily's story amid the backdrop of one of the most turbulent economic and environmental periods in American history: the Great Depression and the Dust Bowl of the 1930s.

There is a certain trepidation in sending your imagination to roam among such a well-worn road as that we have all walked with Dorothy in her adventures in Oz. From the outset, I wanted to write a story grounded in the harsh reality of the farmers who lived through the devastating years of the Dust Bowl, a story of strong courageous women, a story of the choices and sacrifices we make and of the connections and secrets within families that we can all relate to.

All the best stories are timeless, and as we reach the 125th anniversary year of Baum's *The Wonderful Wizard of Oz*, it could be argued that this classic fairy tale is among the most timeless tales of all. While my book leaves Oz where it rightly belongs, it was such a joy to imagine the lives of Emily, Henry, Dorothy – and Toto – before Dorothy ever stepped onto the Yellow Brick Road. Whether you came to these pages with or without *The Wizard of Oz* in your life, I hope you have enjoyed the journey. I certainly had the most wonderful time writing it.

Hazel

x

P.S. For those wondering, the silver shoes Dorothy inherits from her mother are a direct reference to the silver shoes in Baum's original story. *There, indeed, just under the corner of the great beam the house rested on, two feet were sticking out, shod in silver shoes with pointed toes.* The shoes were changed to the iconic ruby slippers in the MGM movie, as they stood out better against the Yellow Brick Road, and why not show off the film in all its Technicolor glory!

Acknowledgements

Over the years of writing acknowledgements, I've learned that there are far too many people to thank in writing, and that the best way to do this is in person, preferably with an Aviation cocktail (which Adelaide Watson would fully approve of)! But before the cocktails are shaken, the following brilliant individuals deserve a very special mention.

Before Dorothy is the story of the woman who raised a beloved heroine, and I am blessed to work with a team of incredible women who have raised me as a writer. Thank you to Michelle Brower, Anna Carmichael, Amanda Bergeron, Lynne Drew, Randi Kramer, and Belinda Toor for motivating, inspiring, and challenging me. Together we have shaped this book into something I am incredibly proud of. Thank you also to Theresa Tran and Olivia Robertshaw for calmly keeping me on track through all the stages of production, and to Tara O'Connor, Susanna Peden and Kathleen Carter for bringing such enthusiasm and expertise to the project. I'm thrilled to work together again! Thank you to the cover designers Eileen Carey and Ellie Game for making magic happen, and thank you to Kate Westbury, who donated to my

Book Aid for Ukraine fundraiser back in 2022, and, as the highest bidder, donated her name to a character in the book.

Of course, no cocktail party would be complete without Helen Plaskitt, Catherine Ryan Howard, Carmel Harrington, Heather Webb, Tanya Flanagan and Ciara Morgan – my fairy godmothers, who I talk to most days and would be thoroughly lost without.

As always, my love and thanks to Damien, Max and Sam. We've made another two years of memories together since I wrote the first words, and while I've spent many long hours among these pages with my characters, my favourite story is always the one we are writing together.

Finally, I'd like to thank all my readers for sharing this journey with me, L. Frank Baum for giving us these unforgettable characters, and Auntie Em for whispering in my ear one quiet September morning. It was wonderful to meet you.

Discussion Questions

1. *Before Dorothy* imagines the character of Emily Gale as a young woman embarking on a new life on the Kansas prairies. How did you respond to her, and what surprised you the most about the challenges she and Henry face as they establish their new life in Kansas?

2. Emily's mother keeps the pamphlet about Kansas with a dream of going there one day, and Emily shares her almost instinctive sense of destiny to move there. Where do you most long to visit, or move to? Is there a place your north star pulls you toward?

3. Adelaide Watson arrives as a fairy godmother character in Emily's and Dorothy's lives, renewing their sense of hope and purpose when they feel lost. What were your thoughts on Adelaide and her impact on the other characters' lives? Do you have a similar person in your own life?

4. How did you react to the character of Leonardo Stregone, and in what ways did you see parallels between him and the wizard in the original *Wizard of Oz* book and movie? What

are your thoughts on the rainmakers who travelled across the Great Plains during the Dust Bowl?

5. Nature and our connection with the natural world play a central role in the book, both in how Emily responds to the environment around her and in the destructive forces of the tornadoes, drought, and dust storms. Which scenes and events captured the sense of the prairie the most vividly for you?

6. What is your own connection or response to the natural world? What more could you do to change how you interact with and respond to nature?

7. What are your thoughts on the traditional homesteading life we see among Emily and the other women of Kansas? Do you still follow any of these traditional ways of living (making or repairing clothes, cooking your own jams and preserves), or are there any aspects of that life you would like to adopt? If not, why?

8. Annie and Emily's close relationship deteriorates throughout the book as they are pulled in different directions. How did you respond to the breakdown of their connection? Why do you think Annie still chose Emily as Dorothy's guardian?

9. The roles of women as sisters, friends, daughters, wives, aunts, and mothers – and how they are perceived to have succeeded or failed in those roles – is explored throughout the book. What was your emotional response to the development of the relationship between Emily and Dorothy? Which other relationships in the book particularly resonated with you.

10. *Before Dorothy* is set during the Depression and Dust Bowl of the 1930s. Why do you think the author chose that period in American history, and in what ways do you think the economic and ecological events of that time reflect the references to power that we see in *The Wizard of Oz*?

11. The devastating drought and Dust Bowl drove many families to leave their homes across the Great Plains and head west. What was your response to Emily and Henry's decision to leave Kansas? What would you like to see happen to Dorothy, Emily, and Henry next?

12. In writing *Before Dorothy*, the author enjoyed weaving in a number of 'Easter eggs' as references to *The Wizard of Oz*. Which did you spot?

13. What are your favourite lines or quotes from the book? Share them with your reading group and discuss why they especially resonate with you.